secrets
after
dark

Sadie Matthews is the author of six novels of contemporary women's fiction published under other names. In her own work, she has described decadent worlds of heady escapism and high drama. FIRE AFTER DARK was her first novel to explore a more intimate and intense side of life and relationships. SECRETS AFTER DARK is the next exciting novel in the series, and the final novel in the trilogy will be available in early 2013. She is married and lives in London.

Find Sadie Matthews on Twitter at www.twitter.com/sadie_matthews

Also by Sadie Matthews

Fire After Dark

secrets
after
dark

SADIE MATTHEWS

HODDER

First published in Great Britain in 2012 by Hodder & Stoughton
An Hachette UK Company

1

Copyright © Sadie Matthews 2012

The right of Sadie Matthews to be identified as the Author
of the Work has been asserted by her in accordance with
the Copyright, Designs and Patents Act 1988.

A CIP catalogue record for this title is available from the British Library.

ISBN 978 1 444 76670 7

Typeset by Hewer Text UK Ltd, Edinburgh
Printed and bound by Clays Ltd, St Ives plc

Hodder & Stoughton policy is to use papers that are natural, renewable
and recyclable products and made from wood grown in sustainable
forests. The logging and manufacturing processes are expected to
conform to the environmental regulations of the country of origin.

Hodder & Stoughton Ltd
338 Euston Road
London NW1 3BH

www.hodder.co.uk

To

H. B.

PROLOGUE

Every day I wake with the same word going through my mind. One word.

Dominic.

The strange thing is that sometimes it's just a statement, like a reaffirmation or a mantra, an expression of faith. Sometimes it's a question – *Dominic?* As though I'm hoping that his voice will echo in answer through my mind and reassure me that he is still thinking of me, still mine. That we are still connected. And at others, it's like a shout, a desperate call through the darkness of the night, just as day breaks.

But no matter how hard I listen, I never hear any reply.

Sometimes it's hard to keep the faith, to believe that he'll come back to me. But I know he will.

I just don't know when.

CHAPTER ONE

I'm glaring at the man opposite. Using all my strength, my fists clenched, my jaw set with effort, I set my standing leg like steel and pull the other up, ready to put all my force behind it. I pivot slightly on my heel, feel my knee against my chest, then:

POW!

I strike out with a kick, powering it through with everything I can muster. My foot slams into the pad my trainer is holding up, and I note with satisfaction that he wobbles a little under my blow.

'Good,' he says. 'Very good.'

Back on both feet, I stand, panting. 'I'm ready for another,' I say breathlessly.

Sid laughs. 'I think that's enough for today. I'm beginning to wonder if you slipped some speed into your coffee by mistake. Where are you getting your energy?'

I take off my helmet and shake out my hair, which falls in damp, clammy tendrils round my neck. 'Oh, you know . . . I just need to release some tension.'

Which is true. But what kind of tension? Half the time I'm trying to work my unslaked desire for Dominic out of my system. The other half, I'm pretending it's his boss's face I'm pounding, the man whose business has kept Dominic out of London all this time. Not that I know what his boss looks like, but that doesn't matter. By the time I've finished my imaginary pummelling, you can't make out his face anyway.

'Okay, well done, Beth,' Sid says, taking off the pads. 'I'll see you again next week.'

'Wow, I've managed to work up a real sweat.' Laura pulls a damp band from her dark hair and shakes it out, wriggling her nose and laughing. She gives me a sideways look. 'You look like you've had a healthy workout yourself.'

'I'm wiped out.' I can't see myself but I know my cheeks are glowing and I can feel the prickle of sweat in my hair and over my brow. 'But I feel good on it.'

'Me too.'

It was Laura's idea to start the kick-boxing classes. I knew she was feeling itchy with suppressed energy now that she's started her new job. After three years of being a student, and then months of freedom as she backpacked around the world, she has been finding the restrictions of working life a strain.

'I have to be in the office so early!' she complained one night, slumping on the sofa in the comfy old tracksuit she changed into after a hard day. She sighed. 'And all day long I'm supposed to be at my desk, late into the night if I want to show the boss I'm taking it seriously. With only three weeks' holiday a year! I don't know how I'm going to cope.' She gazed at me enviously. 'You're so lucky having such an interesting job.'

I shot her a look. 'But I don't get a trainee management consultant's salary, remember?'

She made a disgruntled face. 'Well, we'll have to see if it's worth it, that's all.'

Her pent-up energy was obviously causing her real problems because when she saw that there were kickboxing classes at the gym around the corner from our flat, she signed both of us up without so much as asking me if it was okay. Actually, it was. I needed some release myself, but maybe not quite in the same way that Laura did. I surprised myself by taking to it almost immediately and really enjoying it; the sense of the power flowing through my body gives me a rush that's addictive. I always come home feeling strong and confident, thanks to the rush of endorphins and the proper tiredness that comes from actually doing something energetic, rather than the weariness of work and commuting.

As we let ourselves into our flat, Laura says wonderingly, 'I still can't believe that we're here. Just think – you and me, living together in London, with proper jobs and everything! It feels like only yesterday that we were a couple of scruffy students spending our evenings in the bar making our drinks last as long as we could. Now look at us. It's kind of glamorous, don't you think?'

I laugh but don't say anything as I follow her inside. Laura knows very little of how I spent my summer, or of the incredible things that happened when I met Dominic. If she thinks our slightly down-at-heel place in East London is glamorous, it's because she never saw the Mayfair apartment from where I first glimpsed Dominic in the flat opposite; or, for that matter, the tiny but luxurious boudoir that he arranged for us on the top floor of the apartment block.

The boudoir. It's still there, waiting for me. I picture the key, sitting in my jewellery box in a black pouch. *But I can't bring myself to go there. Not without Dominic.*

'I guess a lot has changed since then,' I say as we go to the kitchen to get some cold water.

Laura fixes me with a knowing look. 'You certainly have. Sometimes I wonder exactly what happened to you while I was in South America. When I left, you were dead set on settling down with Adam back home. And now . . . well, I came back to a glamour puss with an incredible job in the art world and the old boyfriend ancient history. All of which is absolutely brilliant but . . .'

'But?' I take a couple of glasses from the cupboard and a jug of cold water from the fridge.

'Beth, the truth is . . . I'm worried about you.'

'Worried?' I echo, watching the water splash into the glasses. I've been trying to act as normally as possible. Maybe I haven't succeeded.

Laura takes the glass I hold out to her and gives me another of her X-ray stares. With her ability to read people and situations, I'm sure she's going to be an excellent management consultant, but it can make life a little uncomfortable when I'm trying to keep a secret.

'You haven't told me much about the man in your life, this Dominic guy,' she begins in the kind of gentle voice that means something important is coming. 'But I do know that you're completely mad about him and that he hasn't been in touch with you for weeks.'

Six weeks, four days and three hours. Approximately.

I make a kind of non-committal 'uh' sound.

'So I can tell it's making you unhappy,' she goes on, still in that gentle tone. 'You're trying to hide it but I'm your friend and I know you. So why don't you just send him a text or an email? Or phone him? Find out what on earth is going on?'

I use the long drink I'm taking as an excuse not to answer for a moment or two, then say, 'Because he said he was going to contact me. And that's what I'm waiting for.'

'I'm all for playing a waiting game,' Laura says quickly. 'I mean, not being too eager and too obvious. But from what you said, you guys went far beyond a few dates. You were really serious about each other, weren't you?'

I note the past tense, and feel a horrible twist of pain. I've been trying to convince myself it's not really over, but Laura's casual assessment of the situation is like a bucket of cold water landing on all my hopes.

'So,' she continues, oblivious, 'get in touch. Demand an explanation. Ask him when he's coming back and how he feels about you.'

'I can't,' I say gruffly. I wish I could tell her why it's not that simple but there are things about my relationship with Dominic I've never told anyone. I imagine what it would be like to explain to Laura about the things we did in the boudoir, or the events in the dungeon at the The Asylum, but even though she's my best friend and experienced enough in the ways of the world, I don't think she would understand. She'd be horrified. She'd tell me to dump him pronto, and find myself someone nice and normal.

Maybe I should.

But I know in my heart that I don't want someone nice and normal. I had that and I can never go back to it.

Laura is looking exasperated. 'I don't understand why you can't get in touch with him. It's obvious this is driving you crazy! You're unhappy, I can see it!'

'I'm not unhappy,' I reply.

'You're not?'

'Nope. I'm furious. That's what I am. Mad as hell. He can stay away for ever as far as I'm concerned.' My declaration rings false even as I'm saying it. I *am* furious, but I can't tell whether it's with Dominic for not contacting me, with myself for trusting him in the first place, or with his boss, for sending him out of the country just at the moment when we were sorting everything out.

Laura stares at me, and then says, 'Just call him, Beth. Get yourself out of this torment.'

I smile at her. 'You don't need to worry about me. Honestly. But I'm not going to call him. Or text. Or email. If he wants me, he knows where I am. Until then, I'm getting on with my life. Talking of which, whose turn is it to make dinner? I'm starving.'

It's only much later, when I'm in bed, that I'm able to let my strength ebb away. I lie on my back, hugging myself for comfort, sending out my question to the universe:

Where are you, Dominic?

'Beth, how are you?'

Mark Palliser, my boss, greets me in his usual friendly way as I come into his office. He calls it his office, but really it's such a beautiful room there should be some other kind of name for it, less personal than study but more appealing than office, with its over-tones of fluorescent strip-lighting, filing cabinets and photocopiers. This room couldn't be further from that. It's circular, with a glittering chandelier hanging from an ornate plaster rose, and egg-and-dart cornicing that skirts the ceiling. Its three large windows, framed by voluptuously draped curtains, overlook a garden and in the bay sits Mark's desk, a huge polished piece of Regency furniture inlaid with exquisite marquetry work. The floor is gleaming parquet covered with rich and elegantly faded Turkish rugs, and the room glows with the golden light cast by the lamps that sit on the desk and sideboards. Best of all, though, is the art that covers the walls: oils in intricately carved and gilded

9

frames, watercolours, pastels, charcoal sketches, prints and engravings. The subjects are wide and varied: a beautiful oil landscape of a Scottish loch sits happily beside a glorious Renaissance sepia pencil sketch of an angel. A portrait of a melting-eyed spaniel is next to a dark engraving of a scene of Regency debauchery. Every now and then, something disappears and a new treasure takes its place, because Mark has found a home for it with one of his many clients. I'm beginning to learn how it all works. Only last week, I arranged for a tiny Impressionist oil sketch of a girl bathing to be packed up in Mark's signature style: he has wooden frames to contain the works, protective sheets, specially designed boxing, pale green bubble wrap and acid free tissue paper, all stamped with his personal emblem, the letters MP in an oval frame. When the little picture was securely packed, I had it insured for a sum that made my mouth go dry when I read it, and then sent it to one of the most expensive addresses in the world.

All this is so far from the way I grew up, in a tiny Norfolk village, I can sometimes hardly believe that this is where I pass my days, and get paid for it too.

Mark is sitting behind his desk, as elegantly turned out as ever. He has thick dark hair sprouting from a low forehead, tiny but bright blue eyes, a long nose over a small mouth and a receding chin. He is not at all good-looking, and yet he carries himself with the air of someone who is distinguishedly handsome, and he is always so well dressed and perfectly presented that I can't help believing somehow that he is.

'Good morning, Mark,' I say in response to his greeting. 'I'm fine, thank you. Can I get you anything?'

'No, thank you. Gianna brought me some coffee earlier.' Mark smiles at me. 'Now. To business.'

I sit down, as usual, in the leather bucket chair opposite his desk and take out my turquoise ostrich-skin notebook – a present from James, my old boss, given to me when I started this job – to take down details of whatever Mark wants me to do today. The work is always varied and always interesting – I never know whether we'll be going off to Sotheby's, Bonhams or Christie's for an auction, or visiting a client in one of their extraordinary homes, whether we'll be travelling across the country to an estate sale or called to evaluate a new find. Mark is a respected and successful private art dealer – successful enough to have a Belgravia house, and some extremely valuable art in his own private collection.

I make quick notes, scrawling rapidly over the fine light paper of my notebook, as Mark runs through a few things he wants me to do. I've only been working for him for a few weeks but already I feel an important part of his team. There is also Jane, his secretary, who deals with a lot of the boring admin, which is lucky for me as Mark can barely type an email and prefers to write everything out longhand and have someone else transcribe it. She comes in twice a day, in the morning to collect work in the dark green leather wallets embossed with gold MPs, and in the afternoon to deliver it back, as she works from her

11

little Chelsea flat with her two King Charles spaniels for company.

'So.' Mark puts down his vintage Cartier fountain pen, and sits back in his chair. He fixes me with his bright blue beady look. 'I've got something to ask you. Your passport. Is it up to date?'

I visualise my passport sitting in my knicker drawer where I keep it. The burgundy cover is pristine, it's so unused, but it's certainly valid. 'Yes.'

'Good. How would you like to go on a little trip with me? Nowhere too exotic, I'm afraid. Just the South of France.'

I gape at him.

He looks back at me, obviously interpreting my silence as reluctance. 'I quite understand if you'd rather not, and I'm sure I can manage perfectly well on my own—'

'No, no,' I say hastily. 'I'd love to. Really. I've been to France, of course, but only family holidays to Normandy and a school trip to Paris. I'd love to visit the south.'

'It is very beautiful there.' Mark smiles. 'But I don't know how much sightseeing I can promise. We will be working and so we'll probably spend most of our time at the villa, but I'll see what I can do about arranging a chance to slip away.'

'The villa?'

'Yes. We're going to see perhaps my most prestigious client. Certainly the richest, if that's how one measures these things. Andrei Dubrovski is an extremely successful oligarch – have you heard of him?'

The name almost winds me as I hear it drop from Mark's mouth. *Dubrovski.* It's the name I've been muttering in my mind while aiming strong kicks at Sid's pads. *Take that, Dubrovski! And that!* It's been a part of my life from when Dominic first mentioned him: *Andrei Dubrovski. My boss.* Since then, the mysterious Russian tycoon has been a shadowy yet important part of my life. It was his mission that sent Dominic to Russia just when our relationship hit its crisis.

It seems so long ago now, that warm summer's night at a restaurant on the bank of the Thames, where the breeze blew fresh and briny across our faces. That was when Dominic and I agreed that he would initiate me into a world of excitement, pleasure and pain that I had only previously imagined. I was high with antici-pation and giddy with a sense that he and I were taking this journey together. I was utterly bewitched by him. And for a while, the adventure was a beautiful one, taking me to places of extreme physical pleasure I hadn't known existed. The joy lasted until the night in The Asylum, when he went too far and caused me real and desperate pain, both in my body and my heart. I forgave him, but he was devastated by what he'd done. He needed to sort himself out, he said. That was when Dubrovski summoned him to Russia on some project or other, and Dominic took the chance to put some space between us while he cleared his head. 'Wait for me,' he'd said. And I had.

For all the good it's done me.

I've always known that Mark and Dominic worked for the same man, and I knew one day Mark would have dealings with Dubrovski. If I'm honest, it's part of the reason I took the job as Mark's assistant. Now it's happened, and he wants to take me right to Dubrovski. I'll finally get a look at this mysterious person who's had such an influence on my life. Perhaps I'll even get to understand a little more about Dominic himself.

'Beth? Are you all right?' Mark is leaning forward, concerned. 'You look a little pale.'

'I . . . I'm fine,' I say, taking a deep breath. I'm feeling that odd mixture of pleasure and pain I've become so accustomed to since I first met Dominic. Just thinking of him gives me that delicious ripple of desire and excitement, but always accompanied by a bitter stab of unhappiness. *God, I miss you.* Then, sure as night follows day, I feel the bubbling anger. *How dare you leave me like this, after everything we went through together?* 'Yes, of course I've heard of Andrei Dubrovski. Who hasn't?'

'Then if you're sure you'd like to come . . .'

'Yes, I am.' I sound like myself again, I'm sure of that. And I'm also sure that I want to go to the South of France with Mark. For one thing, it's a connection with Dominic, and I can't resist that.

'Good.' Mark looks satisfied that I'm on side. 'When men like Dubrovski summon us, we go as quickly as possible. He keeps our bread well buttered after all. So we'll be leaving tomorrow, and we'll be gone a couple of days at least. Will that be all right?'

I nod. 'Fine. You know me. My schedule is very flexible.'

'Excellent. Don't forget that passport. Now, shall we think about heading over to Bond Street? Oliver tells me that a real treasure has just come in that I really ought to see.'

'Of course,' I say, getting up. 'I'll just get my things.'

CHAPTER TWO

I don't have time to think about my forthcoming trip to France during the morning, and it's only when Mark and his colleague Oliver decide to have a quick lunch together at Mark's club that I have some time to myself. I head for the café in Sotheby's, a place I've become quite familiar with in the weeks that I've been working for Mark. While I'm standing at the entrance, looking for a likely table, I hear a familiar voice.

'Beth, over here!'

Looking across the crowded room, I see James sitting at one of the tables, a newspaper on the table in front of him. I feel a rush of affection for him; he took a chance on me and gave me my first job in the art world. When he heard that Mark, an old business associate of his, was looking for an assistant, he recommended me for the position and Mark took me on just when I needed a job. I owe him a lot. He waves, a big smile on his face, beckoning me over. 'What brings you here, darling?' he asks, putting big kisses on my cheeks as I bend down to greet him.

'Mark came to see Oliver. Do you know him? He's head of nineteenth-century art here.' I sit down in the empty seat on the other side of the table. 'Now they've gone off for lunch. What about you?'

'I came in to inspect some bits and pieces that are coming up for sale soon.' James folds up his newspaper and looks at me over the top of his gold-rimmed spectacles in that certain way he has, as though he wants to examine me properly and understand what I'm really thinking. 'How is life?'

'Fine, fine . . .'

'Come on, Beth. You look nervous. What's up?' His expression softens. 'Any news from Dominic?'

James is one of the few people who know almost the whole story of what happened between Dominic and me. There is no one else I can imagine telling – not Laura, not my mother, not Celia, my wise old friend and my father's godmother. It's strange that the only person I can confide in about my relationship is my gay, gallery-owning ex-boss whom I've known for less than a year, but that's how it is. He's kind, broad-minded and not inexperienced in the sort of world I found myself in over the summer. And he cares about me in a platonic way that makes me feel safe and looked after.

'No, no news.'

'How long has it been now?'

I stare down at the tabletop. James's teacup sits there, half full of cooling tan-coloured liquid and I examine the reflections in its surface. 'I've heard nothing since the day he left me. He sent me a text that night but since then, zilch.'

'And have you contacted him?'

I shake my head slowly. 'He knows where I am. He said he'd be in touch.'

James sighs, as if he's saddened by my stubbornness and by Dominic's vanishing act. Then he frowns. 'But there's something else?'

I laugh despite myself. 'James, how do you know me so well?'

He smiles back, his thin face unexpectedly cheery-looking. 'Darling, you're an open book to me. You'll never be a woman of mystery as far as I'm concerned, no matter how veiled and impenetrable you are to everyone else. I can read it all over you – and you're practically trembling like a little aspen leaf. What's happened?'

I lean forward, my eyes sparkling. 'I'm going to the South of France with Mark,' I say excitedly, and tell him about the planned trip. Even as I speak, I can hardly believe it's actually going to happen. *Tomorrow. Oh my God.*

James doesn't seem particularly enthused. I'd assumed he'd clap his hands, and congratulate himself at getting me this job with Mark, the kind of job that means I can travel and see the world, and not exactly budget-style either. But he's looking more concerned than anything else.

'Aren't you pleased for me?' I ask.

He pauses before answering and then says slowly, 'I've heard a lot about this Dubrovski character and from what I can make out, he's not a particularly

18

pleasant man. Now I don't suppose that anyone rises from the slums of Moscow to unimaginable wealth as a commodities trader without having a bit of an edge to him. But nonetheless, he's not someone I would want to come into close contact with. I don't like the idea of you near him.'

I smile at James's protectiveness. 'I'm not going to have anything to do with him. He's Mark's client. I'll just be there to help Mark.'

James narrows his eyes. 'Then why are you in such a state?'

'You could have a very successful second career as a criminal psychologist,' I say, trying to sound jokey, 'with your ability to read minds.'

In that instant, he understands. Realisation fills his eyes and he looks at me with an expression of sympathy. 'Oh, honey. You think he might give you some clue to where Dominic is.'

My cheeks flush. It sounds ridiculous spoken aloud like that. 'Well . . .'

James evidently doesn't know what to say. He doesn't want to rain on my parade and destroy my dream, but I can tell he also doesn't want to get my hopes up in case of the all-too-likely disappointment. 'It might happen, I suppose. After all, he does work for Dubrovski – at least, as far as we know he still does. But don't pin too much on it, that's all I'm saying.'

'I won't,' I promise. 'I know it's not very likely. I'm not really thinking about it, to be honest.' But I know the truth is that ever since Mark broke the news about the trip this morning, the hope has been growing inside me that somehow I'll find out something about Dominic in France. Even Dubrovski just mentioning his name would make me feel closer to him. It's the first ray of sunshine I've had in weeks. Even if it proves a false dawn, at least I can enjoy this hopeful moment while it lasts.

'Let's order you some food. You must be starving.' James looks away to summon a passing waiter and I close my eyes for a moment to offer up a silent prayer that I might somehow make a connection with Dominic in France. I hardly dare admit to myself that in my very secret heart, I'm hoping that Dominic will actually be at the villa, even though I know it's just a ridiculous fantasy.

I'll be happy just to hear his name, I tell myself firmly. *That will be enough for me.*

'It sounds lovely, dear. I'm very envious. Fancy that, a villa! Your life has got very glamorous lately. But have you got everything you'll need for a trip to France? Will it be warm? What sort of state is your bathing suit in?'

That's my mother all over. Two seconds and she's worrying that I won't be properly kitted out. Laura screamed when she found out, and bounced around the room chanting, 'You lucky thing, you lucky thing, you lucky, lucky, *lucky* thing!' My mother is anxious I might embarrass myself in a holey swimsuit.

'I don't think I'm going to have much time for swimming, Mum.' While we're talking, I'm taking clothes from my drawers and wardrobe and putting them on the bed, wondering what exactly I'll need for a villa in the South of France. 'It isn't a holiday. I'm working.'

'Wear your warmest things on the plane, just in case it's cold,' advises my mother, not hearing me. 'That way you won't need to pack them. It's always tricky when you've only got a cabin bag. Put on two jumpers if you can. It is October, after all.'

I laugh again, as I imagine myself turning up dressed in half my wardrobe, a puffy Michelin man made up of sweaters, trousers and skirts. Just the thing to impress Mark, show him what a woman of the world I am. I don't have the heart to tell my mother that I won't be flying on a budget airline to Nice, but rather on a small private plane from a London airport. If I want to take a case full of jumpers, I probably can.

'How long will you be gone for?' my mother asks, trying to sound pleased for me rather than worried, which I'm sure she is. She was so relieved when I decided not to go backpacking with Laura; she wouldn't have slept the entire time I was away if I had.

'Just a few days,' I say comfortingly. 'And I'll be in touch – I'll let you know where I am.'

'That's good. You must remember to enjoy yourself. Don't work too hard.' My mother only has a vague idea of what I do, even though I've explained it several times. I'm not sure she really thinks of it as work at all. 'Now, would you like to speak to your father?'

21

While I'm chatting to my dad, I pull an old red bikini out of my drawer and, on impulse, add it to the pile on the bed. There's bound to be a pool, after all. I might get the chance to use it, who knows? I've just said goodbye and rung off when I see a flash of colour where the bikini used to be and look down into the drawer. I gaze down for a moment, then take out the smooth blue silicone column with a little outcrop at the base. It is one of the few things that I brought from the boudoir, although I haven't touched it since the night that Dominic used it with great effect. I remember how he ordered me to prepare it, oiling it gently until it shone slick and promising, and then, much later, how he let it come to life inside me, sending me into an orbit of starry pleasure as it drove me to an extraordinary climax. The memory makes me gasp involuntarily and feel a twitch of excitement. For the first time since that night, I wonder what it would be like to let that harmless-looking thing do the job it was designed for.

I try to damp down the tiny rush of bubbles that erupt inside me at the thought. I need to focus on getting ready, not being distracted by various erotic memories of Dominic. I've tried to close off that part of myself while I wait for him to return.

If he ever does, I think grimly.

I frown at myself. I can't lose faith. He will come back and if he doesn't, I'll just go and find him and damn well make him explain why.

And that's why this trip is giving me butterflies. Because there's a little voice in my head that whispers: *you might find out more. You might find out where he is.*

CHAPTER THREE

This is like no plane journey I've ever been on.

It's usually a long drawn-out process: travelling to the airport, checking in, getting through security, waiting for long hours in the giant duty-free shopping mall, then heading with the rest of the crowd to the gate for another wait, and then the scrum of boarding. That's all before we've actually gone anywhere.

This time a sleek dark car collects Mark and me from his Belgravia house, our luggage loaded into the back by the shaven-headed sunglasses-wearing driver, and then we fly through the London traffic as though we've got some kind of special dispensation to ignore the speed limit, the red lights and the bus lanes. It seems as though we're at the airport in only minutes. Mark takes my passport and at some point it's handed over to someone else through the car window, and then we are driving again. When we get out of the car, we are, to my astonishment, next to the actual plane. We've skipped the airport terminal altogether.

'Come on, Beth,' Mark says, smiling at my evident amazement, even though I'm trying to act smart, sophisticated and unflappable. 'Let's get on board.'

The plane's interior is immaculate and luxurious: the lighting is soft and welcoming, a thick pale carpet covers the floor and large butter-yellow leather seats face each other across walnut-inlaid tables. An elegant stewardess is waiting for us just inside the door and smilingly shows us to our seats. I'm loving every minute so far. *I could definitely get used to this.*

'We'll be taking off as soon as you're settled,' says the stewardess. 'I'll be back when we're airborne to check on you. Happy take-off.' Then she heads off to a door towards the rear.

The seat is incredibly soft, and I'm almost absorbed into the buttery leather seats. I relax into it and snap my seat belt shut.

Mark leans over to me, fiddling with his rose-gold cufflinks as he often does. He's smiling, his eyes twinkling with amusement. 'You can't say I don't show you some of the high life, eh, Beth? Literally, today.'

'You've done nothing but!' I reply, laughing. It's true. Ever since I started working for Mark, I've been allowed glimpses into a world I always vaguely knew was there, but not accessible to anyone from my way of life. Now, here I am, on a private plane. I shake my head. 'It's crazy.'

'Enjoy it.' Mark leans back in his seat, fastening his seat belt across his lap. 'The rich at play can be an excellent spectator sport. As long as you don't get tempted to join in.'

A few minutes later, the little plane taxis along to its runway, jolting slightly over the uneven ground.

Outside the October day is overcast and I can already sense the evening approaching even though it's only lunchtime. The plane pivots into position and, after a humming pause, it begins its take-off, the engine revving furiously as we gather speed. The nose tilts, we begin to lift and then we're airborne, powering upwards into the sky as the land retreats below us. A minute ago, I was safely on the ground. Now I'm so high in the sky that if anything were to go wrong, it would mean death. So little between safety and peril. The thought sends a strange kind of excitement shimmering through me. We're alive. We're in the sky. Tremors ripple in my stomach with something like arousal. How odd – a plane taking off has never done that to me before.

Perhaps it's an added bonus of private plane travel – a bit of extra excitement thrown in.

The beautiful stewardess appears, her make-up so perfect it looks as though it is part of her actual face and not painted on at all, and asks us in her soothing way what we would like to drink. Mark asks for champagne for both of us.

'I want you to have the full experience,' he says as the stewardess goes off to fetch it. 'I wouldn't usually advise drinking at work, but just this once . . .'

Before long, we have flutes of cold champagne, the bubbles popping quietly against the glass, and lunch is served: a delicious light autumnal meal of cold roast pheasant with a salad of chicory, squash and pear, and cubes of thyme-scented sautéed celeriac. A tiny apple charlotte with Sauterne custard follows, and then a plate of creamy ripe cheeses with fresh-baked oatcakes. Mark and I chat as we eat, and I could almost believe we were in a luxurious restaurant rather than flying at 35,000 feet over the Channel and across France.

As we approach Nice airport, I remember James's warning words about going into Dubrovski's orbit and wonder what exactly I've let myself in for. Am I going to be sitting down to dinner with the Russian mafia tonight? I imagine Dubrovski like a Russian Al Capone, big stomach straining behind a waistcoat, and a dinner table lined with men in dark suits, pistol handles bulging at their armpits, chewing gum and staring implacably from behind sunglasses, all on a hair trigger, ready to start a firestorm if someone coughs out of turn. Maybe I'd better practise a few of my kick-boxing moves when we land, just in case. I smile to myself. I already appear to think I'm in some kind of Bond movie . . . I'd better rein in my vivid imagination or I'll give myself nightmares.

And my mafia scenario is not the only thing I'm imagining. As we begin our descent, I tell myself sternly to get a grip. *All secret inner fantasies banned! Dominic won't be there and I probably won't even hear his name. In fact, it's bound to be tedious and I'll long to be home again. I've probably had the best bit with this flight.*

I yawn, just to show myself how very grounded and realistic I am.

*   *   *

Evidently, for Mark, all this is familiar. When we've landed and the pilot has brought us to a halt by the terminal, he calmly unbuckles his seat belt and tells me that our car will be waiting for us.

I don't know how the usual customs, security and passport control is bypassed so easily but once again, a black car with shaded windows is waiting for us on the tarmac, and within minutes we are gliding on to the French roads and away. Mark hands me back my passport. I never even saw it being returned to him.

'That's the way it works when money is involved,' he says, seeing my expression. I can't help thinking that it makes a bit of a mockery of the laws the rest of us have to abide by. I could have just smuggled anything I liked into the country, but I keep quiet. That's going to be my modus operandi on this trip.

The weather is hotter and brighter than it was in London. The October day here is a bright shining blue, the sun low and dazzling in the sky. The cashmere sweaters that I brought already seem redundant and my red bikini more enticing.

'How far away is the house?' I ask Mark.

'About an hour or so,' he says. 'It's in a very beautiful place. You'll love it.'

'How long have you worked for Dubrovski?' I ask, curious.

'About five years now. Ever since he began to make really serious money. It's impossible to have the kind of art habit that he has without it. He wants old masters and famous names. He wants to be like Francis I – with the *Mona Lisa* hanging in his bathroom. A Rembrandt in the hall; a Titian in the boot room. For him, it's the ultimate way of expressing his success. And that is where I help him: I'm always on the lookout for the kind of work he'll appreciate, and he calls on me for my expert opinion when he finds something he likes. It's a good arrangement, as I understand his taste and he trusts me completely. He pays me a handsome retainer so that I can be at his beck and call, and of course a healthy commission too, on everything I purchase for him.' Mark smiles happily. 'Like I say, a good arrangement.'

It sounds it. Is that something else about the world of the rich? I wonder. Vast sums of money changing hands for what seems like not much effort? Perhaps when you've got lots of it, money changes its character and value, and you start thinking that huge sums are really not much at all. That's why wealthy people start tipping waitresses in the hundreds, and paying for meals in the thousands.

'Do you like him?' I ask boldly.

'Of course,' Mark returns. 'Why wouldn't I?'

'I read somewhere that he's got a shady past.' That's what James hinted at least.

'I don't concern myself with that, and nor should you,' Mark says a little strictly. 'Our clients are accepted for themselves, and for their dealings with us. He's always been very fair to me.'

And to Dominic? I can't help asking silently. *What kind of a boss is he to him?* I never knew much, just that Dominic's employer is a very rich and powerful man. Mark isn't aware of my connection to Dominic, although he knows Dominic himself. James went to visit Mark on business the day that he saw Dominic in Mark's house. No doubt Dominic was sorting out something to do with Dubrovski's affairs with Mark, and James overheard him telling Mark he was leaving for Russia that evening. When James passed this information on to me, I knew I had little time to see Dominic again, and I summoned him to the boudoir that afternoon – it was the last time we saw one another.

For a moment, I'm back there. We are making love as tenderly and passionately as any couple could: the pain and misunderstandings are forgotten in the joy of his skin against mine, his body moving in me, our kisses and panting breaths and the climax of pleasure that engulfs us both. Then he's explaining why he has to leave.

But I've never really understood. I know he was appalled by his mistake, the night he really hurt me. But it was forgiven, and he'd changed. So why did he have to go?

It wasn't just because he needed some space. It was also because of this man. Dubrovski. He summoned Dominic away. And since then, I've heard nothing.

The car draws to a halt before a pair of large iron gates. A guard emerges from a hut behind the gates and comes out to speak to the driver, inspect us through the window and then let us in. So we're here, I think. And just for a second I get a marvellous rush of adrenalin at the thought that perhaps Dominic is waiting for me at the end of the driveway that curves away in front of us.

The drive takes us between elegantly manicured bushes and perfectly arranged flower beds, and then the house appears: a vast, white villa, with that particular French nineteenth-century squarish grey roof edged in curling wrought iron. It's beautiful but, somehow, unremarkable except for the fact it's so big. Late flowering roses climb up white trellising as if arranged by an artist, lavender bushes sit in perfect rows: it's all very pretty and perfect.

A butler comes out to open the car door and we emerge on to the gravelled driveway. I stay behind Mark as he converses with the butler in fluent French. From what I recall from school French lessons, he's asking if he is going to see Monsieur Dubrovski at once.

'*Oui*,' replies the butler. '*Immediatement. Suivez-moi, s'il vous plaît.*'

My stomach plummets and I realise that I'm nervous about meeting Dubrovski. It's all very well bravely kicking at Sid's training pad, but now the real thing is so close, some of my bravado is melting away. What will he look like? A squat, mean-faced gangster? Spoiled, selfish and haughty? He comes from a world I can hardly imagine, and I remember James's warning, that no one gets to where he is without being tough.

I follow Mark, who seems completely at ease, as we are led through the large hallway and along a corridor.

It's decorated in unobtrusive hues of peach and apricot, the furniture modern and comfortable. It's all done in very good taste, but there's nothing unusual about it. I suppose I've been a bit spoiled by being around Mark: everything he owns expresses character and charm, wit and intelligence. But now I see it's perfectly possible to have lots of money and like everything to be as bland as can be.

We have stopped in front of a pair of large white doors inlaid with gilt. The butler is knocking discreetly, then pressing down the golden handle and the door is opening. He is stepping inside, murmuring, '*Monsieur Palliser est arrivé, monsieur.*'

Then we are entering the room beyond. The first impression is of light. There are tall windows overlooking the garden through which the liquid sunshine spills in. I'm not accustomed to the brightness after the shady hall, and I blink. On the walls are blobs of colour, begging for attention. As my vision clears, I realise there are wonderful works of art on every wall, famous ones or else created by unmistakeable hands.

Isn't that a Renoir? And a Seurat? Oh my God . . .

I resist the impulse to go over to them, and the next moment my attention is drawn to the heart of the room where there is a core of energy that cannot be ignored. A man is standing there, one hand pressing a mobile phone to his ear, the other in the pocket of his loose linen trousers.

So that's him. Dominic's boss. Maybe that's Dominic on the other end of the line . . . The possibility makes

32

me feel trembly and loose-limbed. *But he's speaking Russian. I'm sure he'd talk to Dominic in English.*

Dubrovski waves at Mark and points towards the armchairs scattered around the room. He hasn't noticed me at all, it seems, so I'm able to take in what he looks like. He's taller than I imagined, not at all the short, stocky-looking mafia boss I'd painted in my imagination. Instead of a black suit and sunglasses, he's wearing a summery white linen shirt over the baggy trousers and a pair of shabby deck shoes. He's not dark but fair: hair once blond that's darkened to gold-specked brown, with shards of grey at the temples. Mark leads the way and sits down, and I take the chair next to him. Dubrovski is talking away in Russian, his voice absolutely compelling despite the fact I cannot understand a word. It's rough with a gravelly undertone, as though he's smoked a million cigarettes, or sung so loudly and often that he's cracked his voice into a permanent hoarseness. And it's loud and commanding, the kind of voice that's accustomed to being obeyed. He speaks, and people snap to it. No wonder he's made such a fortune.

His conversation comes to an end and he turns to face us full on for the first time. He has the most intense blue eyes I've ever seen: pale but fierce. I hardly notice the prominent nose, the broad expressive mouth and the jutting chin, I can't take my eyes off that powerful gaze. But it's so cold. There's nothing tender or even smiling in it.

'Mark!' He walks towards us, his hand outstretched, still unsmiling. Mark leaps up and takes it, and they shake hands vigorously. His English is only faintly accented and sounds more American than Russian. I'd been expecting the full Bond villain voice, and he sounds more like the hero. 'Great to see you. How are you?'

'Wonderful, Andrei, and delighted to be here.'

I've stood up too, mesmerised by the incredible energy that emanates from the man when he stands up close. He turns that brilliant blue gaze on me and I feel incredibly small and unimportant. A chill goes through me as I register how icy it is.

Doesn't he ever smile?

'My new assistant, Beth Villiers,' Mark says smoothly. 'She's my right-hand woman.'

He grunts but doesn't bother saying anything to me. He turns his attention immediately back to Mark and I'm relieved he's taken that intense stare off me.

'I'm glad you could come, Mark,' he says. He seems agitated. Perhaps that's normal for him. 'I've got some interesting news, very, very interesting, and I need your help on it. Immediately.'

'Yes?' Mark says, smooth as ever, his eyebrows raised. I get the feeling he knows exactly how to handle Dubrovski, and how to play his role of courtier in the presence of the all-powerful king.

Dubrovski sits down in one of the pale armchairs and immediately we sink back into our own. It really is like being in the presence of royalty. Stand when they do, sit when they do, wait to be spoken to. I'm not sure

I'm comfortable with all this subservience. What, apart from money, gives him the right, after all?

He says in that gravelly tone, 'I've heard of a very exciting find. My people were approached by a representative of a monastery in Croatia. They claim to have discovered a completely unknown Fra Angelico in their possession. It's unbelievable, of course, and yet they insist that it is completely genuine. They're prepared to sell it me without taking it to the open market.'

Mark puts his head on one side as if considering and says gravely, 'That is a little suspicious, if you don't mind my saying. And a previously unknown Fra Angelico is practically impossible. Since the missing panels of the San Marco chancel piece were located a few years ago, I believe everything is accounted for. What is it they claim to have?'

'It's the central panel of an altarpiece,' Dubrovski says impatiently. He's leaning forward, his elbows on his knees, staring intently at Mark. 'And let's say it is what they claim – it's an amazing opportunity. They want a fortune for it, of course, but only what I imagine they could hope to get on the world market.'

A look of uncertainty flits over Mark's face, but only for a second. I don't think Dubrovski has even noticed it. The Russian goes on without pausing.

'So we will go together and assess this painting, okay? I want you to see it right away.'

Mark is immediately the consummate art expert. 'Of course, Andrei. When shall we leave?'

'We'll go tomorrow first thing, stay overnight at the monastery, then return.' His gaze slides to me for a second. 'You come too.' Then he's focused on Mark again. 'That's my plan.'

'Excellent,' Mark replies. 'I'm looking forward to it immensely. If what they claim is true, it's extremely exciting.'

I stare at him. *A trip to Croatia? This is a surprise, to put it mildly.* Mark avoids my gaze for the moment.

Dubrovski's mobile phone rings again. He picks it up, looks at it and immediately rises to his feet, snapping something in Russian. He waves his hand at us and we're dismissed.

I follow Mark as he stands up and walks quietly out of the room, leaving Dubrovski to his telephone call. The butler is waiting for us in the hall and immediately steps forward, speaking English this time.

'Follow me, I will show you to your rooms.'

'How was that? What you expected?' Mark says under his breath as we're led back to the hall and up the curving staircase to the first floor.

'I don't know. Sort of.' I can't really explain how pale and unformed my imagined Dubrovski is next to the pulsating strength of the reality. But all that rippling power, that extraordinary focus, is compelling but not endearing. 'I certainly wasn't expecting an unscheduled trip to Croatia!'

Mark smiles. 'That's what it's like around Andrei; you never know what's going to happen. Once we're settled in our rooms, I want you to fire up your laptop and prepare me a full report on Fra Angelico – I'll need my memory refreshing before tomorrow. Goodness knows what we're going to find when we get there. He badly wants it to be genuine but it will be my neck if he buys it and then it's revealed to be a fake.'

I can't believe that no sooner have we got here, than we're leaving again. *Croatia? It doesn't sound quite as glamorous as the South of France.* And yet … my imagination is tickled by the idea of a monastery and a lost masterpiece. How incredible if I was among the first people to see this painting since its discovery – assuming it's the real deal, of course. I'm sure Mark will have the expertise to know.

The butler is opening a door, indicating that this is my room, and I step inside. It's like a plush, luxurious hotel room, everything perfectly nice but without character. My case is already in there; in fact, it's been unpacked and everything tidied away. I wonder if the kind soul who unpacked it will mind redoing it for me in the morning, seeing as we're off again first thing. A wash of relief passes over me when I think that I almost brought my vibrator with me in case the glamour of my surroundings awakened that kind of a mood.

Thank goodness I didn't! Imagine the embarrassment … I shudder inwardly. I don't have the insouciance to carry off that sort of thing very well.

'Why don't you stay here and have your supper in your room?' Mark suggests. 'I'll take on Dubrovski on my own over dinner. I think it would be tiring for you.'

'Good idea,' I say, gratefully. I've had enough excitement for one day. I don't know if I can take Dubrovski's fierce energy for a couple more hours, especially as we're heading off for more adventures tomorrow. Now that I'm here, my silly fantasy that Dominic might be waiting for me with open arms is revealed for what it is. *I need to get on with reality.* 'I'll start on that research for you and find out all I can about any lost Fra Anglicos.'

'Excellent. I'll see you in the morning. Set your alarm good and early. Dubrovski barely sleeps. He'll want to be on the road sharpish.' Mark smiles. 'Sleep well.'

'You too.' I close the door behind him. The butler is taking him to his suite nearby. I lean against the door and sigh. Then I say out loud, 'Dominic, I'm running out of patience. You'd better keep your promise soon, or I'm going to consider us over.' It sounds strange spoken out loud but the minute I do, I feel happier. It's the waiting that's been killing me. Well, how about if I just stop waiting?

Seems like a good idea to me. And I've got plenty of other things to be getting on with.

I unpack my laptop so I can get started.

CHAPTER FOUR

If I thought yesterday marked a high point in my life experiences, I'll have to rethink.

Oh my goodness. This is incredible.

We're in a helicopter, soaring out over Italy and onwards to Croatia. It's a beautiful craft, cherry red and as sweet and round as a bell pepper. I'm in the back, next to Mark, buckled firmly into my seat by an X-shaped belt and with a pair of headphones that block out some of the engine's roar yet still transmit the conversation between Dubrovski, Mark and, occasionally, the pilot. I have a mic attached to my headphones, but I don't expect to be using it. I'm too busy drinking in all the impressions I'm getting. This is my first helicopter ride, and it's amazing. It's not like being in a plane, where you look out on the outside world through those little oval windows, well insulated from the outside by the dense fuselage. I think this might be as close as it's possible to get to feeling as though I'm actually flying. The view curves from above our heads to below our feet and the world seems astoundingly close. The craft is so nimble and responsive as it dips and turns and noses up and down that it's almost as though we've been sprinkled with fairy dust so that we can fly like Peter Pan himself.

Mark, next to me, seems calm as usual. All this must be old hat to him. He's read the report I emailed him late last night, the one that said that actually there is a likelihood of unknown Fra Angelicos being discovered. Mark already knows that only a few years ago, a pair of lost panels was found; they'd been hanging on the wall of a modest Oxford house since the sixties, when medieval art, even Florentine Renaissance master-pieces, was deeply out of fashion. It's possible that there are other panels or copies of altarpieces in exist-ence. And with Croatia so near to Italy, its trading and religious links entwined over the centuries, it's not at all unlikely that something could turn up there. After all, it was ruled by the Venetian Republic for three hundred years.

I spent a few happy hours last night roaming through the catalogues of art collections around the world, getting my eye accustomed to the religious art of the fifteenth century, with one foot in the Gothic era, flat and gilt, and one in the early Renaissance, when perspective and naturalism began to appear. I soaked in the azure blues, vermilions, arsenic greens, carnation pinks and glittering golds of Fra Angelico's glorious creations. With that God-given talent to create such beautiful art no wonder he became known as the Angelic Brother. I'm looking forward to seeing whatever these monks have uncovered.

We're flying over blue crystal waters over the narrow channel of the Adriatic Sea. Islands sit green and grey in the bright water, and land stretches out before us, where Eastern Europe begins: Croatia before us, Serbia, Bosnia, Romania and Bulgaria beyond. Just names to me before but now approaching in massy reality – cities, hills, forests, mountains and roads.

'That's Split,' announces the pilot, his voice tinny through the headphones.

Below, a beautiful golden city sits on the edge of a harbour, stretching its long fingers into the sea.

'Nearly there.' Mark's voice comes into my ears.

'Yes.' It's Dubrovski's voice, even harsher through the microphone. I'm sitting directly behind him and can see the back of his head, the fine linen of the dark blue jacket he's wearing. He's ignored me totally since he first strode out over the lawn that morning to where the helicopter waited on its landing circle. Not that I'm complaining. He looks set and serious today, his expression bad-tempered. I can only imagine what it must be like when all that energy is turned to something vicious. 'The monastery is in the hills. We'll be there very soon.'

The light through the windscreen is dazzling and the city below glitters as the autumn sunshine is reflected off the pale stone. Mark points out at something ruined and grand below and says, 'Diocletian's Palace. The city of Split formed around it centuries ago.'

I'm breathless at the stunning view, and the beautiful ancient stones below. There's so much of the

41

world to see and know. As we sail above Split and beyond, I'm filled with determination to spread my wings and experience as much as I can. Life has thrown me this amazing opportunity and I want to make the most of it. Within a few minutes, we're approaching a craggy hilltop rising out of the dark green forest below. The peak is entirely covered by an impressive stone building, a cross between a church and castle, that looks as if it's formed organically as part of the rocky hill.

How on earth are we going to land? There isn't an inch of space beyond the walls.

We soar upwards, over the turrets and crenulations, and I can see that we're going to land on the top of one of the four towers that form the corners of the monastery. They have flat roofs and someone has painted a crude white cross on one – a landing pad – but I still find it hard to believe that our aircraft can fit in the narrow space between the battlements. I hold my breath as the pilot guides us in, hovering high above the roof and then slowly bringing us down, the nose tipping then straightening as we descend. Surely the blades will catch and jam against the stone, I think, already hearing the harsh squeal of them grinding on the walls, but they don't. It's been perfectly judged, and we're sitting safely on the landing square, the blades slowing down and the noise of the engine dying away.

Safely? We're on top of a monastery on top of a hill.

At the thought, I want to laugh wildly, it sounds so crazy. Being here is exhilarating and a little daunting at the same time. The others are unbuckling their belts and hanging up their headphones, so I do the same. From the corner of my eye, I see a man in a black robe emerge from a door in the tower. Dubrovski jumps out and goes to meet him. Now that we've got our headphones off and can talk privately, Mark turns to me with a smile. 'Are you okay? How was that?'

'Fantastic,' I say, smiling back.

'Good. Now the work begins.' A worried expression crosses his face. 'Dubrovski is in a very bad mood. I've no idea why. It's not going to make things any easier. Up here, there's nowhere for him to release it, except on his nearest companions. Still, if we stay calm and focused, we should be all right.'

'You make him sound really terrifying,' I say, worried myself by Mark's evident discomposure. 'Have you ever seen him lose it?'

Mark looks awkward and glances out to where Dubrovski is already shaking hands with the black-robed man, his hair ruffled by the strong wind. 'Come on,' he says without answering me, 'we'd better get a shift on.'

Outside, the wind buffets us. I can hardly hear what anyone is saying but follow Mark as we are led through the wooden door and into the tower. The instant quiet within is disconcerting after the hours of engine noise. It's dark inside, the cool stone interior lit by small electric lights tucked at intervals just beneath the ceiling, linked by loops of black wires, and our footsteps echo as we start to descend the spiral staircase.

It's atmospheric all right. I feel like I've just walked into a horror film. The chill prickles my skin despite the jacket I'm wearing. Ahead of me, the men are descending, talking in English but the booming echo means it's not easy to understand what they're saying. We go down, down and down, until at last the man at the front opens a door and we're stepping out into daylight. I'd almost forgotten it was still daytime outside, with the creepy nocturnal feel inside the tower. Now we're out, in a flagged corridor with white-painted plaster walls. It's lined with wooden doors with iron handles, and iron sconces holding candle-style electric bulbs tilt from the walls every few feet. But there's still something odd about the atmosphere. My skin is still tingling and my breath seems to be coming a little shorter.

Maybe the atmosphere is thinner up here. Goodness knows how high we are.

Mark lingers until we are walking side by side, and then bends down to mutter to me as we go. 'You see how that monk is wearing a black robe over the white? That's why they were known as Black Friars in England. They're Dominicans, named for the order founded by St Dominic.'

My heart plummets and I can't stop a gasp coming to my lips. The word echoes through my mind and, without meaning to, I say weakly, 'Dominic?'

'Yes. A man who believed in charity and self-denial, and . . .' Mark smiles a little '. . . mortification of the flesh. The spiritual benefits of physical discomfort of all kinds, including flagellation.'

A vivid picture flashes into my mind. It is Dominic stretched before me, his naked back open to me, his hands gripping the frame of the leather seat. I'm holding a flogger, a cat o' nine tails, its soft leather strings ready to bite into his flesh. Then, against every instinct, I'm drawing back my arm and driving forward with all my force, striking him over and over, making the skin on his back redden, weep and finally bleed. I don't want this. I long to run my hands over his body, caress him, kiss him and be tender with him, but he's telling me to go on, to go harder. I know it's because he needs the redemption my blows are giving him. They're cleansing him of the sin he couldn't escape – the sin of hurting me.

'Are you all right, Beth?' Mark looks at me closely, puzzled.

I can't speak. I'm feeling dizzy. I manage to nod, and Mark seems satisfied that I'm okay.

I have to get control. I can't fall apart here, not now. But the vivid vision of Dominic is both wonderful and agonising.

The monk in front opens another larger door. Dubrovski goes inside and Mark and I follow. We are in a huge refectory lined with trestle-tables.

'Oh good,' Mark says with satisfaction. 'Lunch.'

*   *   *

As it turns out, we don't eat in the refectory. It's obvious that we're being given very special treatment, no doubt to butter Dubrovski up nicely and prime him for viewing the painting. Perhaps they don't realise that he isn't a man who is used to being kept waiting. Glancing at Dubrovski discreetly as we are seated at a polished wooden table in a private room with the abbot at the head, I can tell that his impatience is growing. He's practically boiling with suppressed energy, and his blue eyes are glowering. Now that I've got the chance, I observe him properly without being noticed. I wonder how old he is – in his late thirties or early forties? He's good-looking, not smoothly handsome like Dominic, but in a battered, experienced way. His skin is tanned and he has deep lines running down beside his mouth and cross-hatching his forehead that make him look weather-beaten and tough. His mouth is broad and generally unsmiling, with a jutting lower lip that gives him an obstinate air. His nose is too large to be classically handsome but it suits him, as does his strong chin. It's an interesting face, I think, a face you could look at for a long time. Today he's wearing a white shirt and a dark jacket that his shoulders fill out with muscle and a kind of simmering strength. I get a mental image of a young Dubrovski setting about his business rivals, using his fists in a back alley to win ascendency in his world. The thought makes me shiver lightly.

The abbot is droning on as two black-robed monks glide around the table, laying out a meal. Dubrovski is twitching, obviously hardly listening to our host. Mark is watching him carefully, poised as if to follow in whatever he does. At last, plates of rice and a spiced meat stew are placed in front of us, but just as we are about to eat, the abbot clasps his hands, closes his eyes and begins to intone a long grace in a language I don't understand. I dip my gaze politely, and notice that Dubrovski hasn't waited. He's shovelling his stew into his mouth with almost indecent haste. The abbot looks startled as he opens his eyes and realises that his guest has started, but says only, 'Good appetite to you, sir.'

I take a few mouthfuls of the stew. It's delicious and I suddenly realise I'm ravenous. I eat hungrily. It must be the mountain air that's stimulating my appetite like this – and I also have a feeling we won't be getting long to eat.

I'm not at all surprised when a few moments later, Dubrovski pushes his half-empty plate away, stands up and announces, 'Right! Enough waiting. Now we see the painting.'

Even though no one else is close to finishing – the abbot has barely started – we obey, leaving our lunch and standing up.

When he says jump, we jump. Mark and I exchange glances. Our moment is almost here.

We're led by the monk who greeted us on our arrival, following him out of the private room and down another corridor. He opens yet another wooden door and takes us into a small chapel. It's beautiful, with frescos on every wall. I want to stop and examine them, but instead we approach the small bare altar where a board covered with a cloth awaits us. My breath is speeding up, butterflies fluttering anxiously in my stomach. I don't know whether to hope that we are about to see a lost masterpiece or not.

The monk is smiling, pleased and proud as he gestures to the hidden treasure. The abbot tucks his hands into his sleeves and looks on. We are all staring, tense with anticipation, but Dubrovski is the most on edge. I think he is actually holding his breath. This really matters to him. How amazing to have such passion and to be able to indulge it, I think. I realise that I'm looking at him instead of at the sight about to be revealed.

He really is magnetic.

Then he glances up and locks me in that powerful blue beam. A strong surge like an electric current passes through me: is it fear? Should I not look at him? For a moment I think he's going to shout at me, but then, to my astonishment, his gaze softens and a smile curves his broad mouth. The relief that drenches me is almost sweet and, without thinking, I smile back. For a second, it's as though we are in a tiny conspiracy of excitement about the painting. As though he's saying to me, *Let's pretend we don't care as much as we do.* Then he looks back at the altar and our connection is broken.

The monk takes hold of the cloth and says, 'Sir, I'm proud to reveal to you a lost masterpiece by the sainted brother of our order who was endowed by God with supreme talent.' He swipes the covering like a magician revealing his best conjuring trick.

The cloth ripples away. I gasp. A painted wooden panel is revealed, a gentle arched shape on which is a stunning depiction of the Madonna and Child, with a gathering of saints and Dominican monks around them. The Madonna, a pale, golden-haired beauty, her perfect face serene and lovely, sits on an ornate golden throne while the plump baby on her lap kicks and gazes skyward, lifting one hand in the air as if reaching up to his Heavenly Father. The throne is placed in a grove and surrounded by trees and flowers, with an Italian city rising gently in the landscape behind. The colours are vibrant and gorgeous, but wonderfully subtle too, and the details are exquisite, from the folds of the Madonna's cloak to the roses and lilies that flower around her.

We all stare, speechless. Even if it is not by Fra Angelico, it is a beautiful thing, but something in the mastery of it indicates that it is genuine.

Dubrovski glances at Mark and says roughly, 'Well?'

'A sacred conversation,' I murmur without really realising I've spoken out loud.

'What?' Dubrovski's stare is focused on me again, but without any hint of a smile this time. 'What did you say?'

'A sacred conversation,' I say more firmly. Mark is looking at me, a smile in his eyes though his expression is serious. 'That's what's going on between the monks and the saints. Do you see? They seem to be talking among themselves about what they're witnessing. Fra Angelico painted some of the earliest examples – rather than flat representations of people who simply pray to the deity, he painted life and animation into his figures. And look at the way they're standing – the artist has used masterful linear perspective, just as Fra Angelico did.'

'Does that mean this is genuine?' demands Dubrovski, frowning at me.

'It certainly points to it being of the right period and by someone of the school of Fra Angelico, if not Fra Angelico himself.' I suddenly feel as though I'm being too sure of myself. I have a degree in History of Art and I've just done my research on the period, but that doesn't make me an expert. 'Isn't that right, Mark?'

Mark nods. 'Exactly right. I'll need a little time to examine the painting, but first impressions are very favourable.' He turns to the monk. 'Can that be arranged?'

'Of course, take as long as you require,' replies the monk.

Dubrovski turns to me. 'You. Come with me. We'll leave Mark in peace.' He turns on his heel and stalks out of the chapel, evidently expecting me to follow. I glance at Mark, who nods. Then I hurry down the aisle after the vanishing Russian. He's already almost out of the chapel.

In the corridor outside, he stops and turns to me. 'So. You are Mark's apprentice.' He seems to be seeing me properly almost for the first time, his gaze raking my face, taking me in. Then his eyes travel down my body to my feet and back up again. I can almost feel their laser beam against my skin. He nods. 'Good. Now. Come with me.' He turns and walks briskly on, leaving me to follow in his wake.

Honestly, I've never met anyone so rude. Is it asking so much to be a little bit polite? All these orders! Where are we going? I have to walk very fast to keep up with his strides. He seems to know exactly where he is going, which is odd. As he powers ahead of me, I hear the chirrup of his phone and then he is pressing it to his ear again. 'Yes?' he says. 'It's looking promising. Very promising. Where are you? Excellent. Give me thirty seconds.'

Now what's going on?

We reach a staircase and Dubrovski descends it quickly. The heels of my shoes clatter on the stones as I hurry down after him. I wouldn't have worn heels if I'd known how much walking I was going to do, and on stone flags at that. I'm breathless as we race along another corridor, then he stops outside a large, iron-studded wooden door. As I catch up, he flings it open and goes in, and I follow.

Inside are two people, a man and a woman. They are sitting close to one another, their heads nearly touching as they both gaze down at a laptop screen. As we come in, they look up. The woman is extremely beautiful with glossy dark hair pulled back into a tight ponytail, emphasising the fine contours of her face. As she sees Dubrovski, her expression melts into

51

a smile and she says, 'Hello, darling,' in a rich, accented voice.

I'm utterly unaware of anything Dubrovski says in return: the world disappears. All sight and sound vanishes except for one thing. The man next to her, staring back me with a stunned expression, is Dominic.

CHAPTER FIVE

Oh my God.

I'm staring at him, open-mouthed, my heart racing.

He's here! I feast my eyes on his handsome face, his olive skin a little lighter than it was when I last saw him – his summer tan has faded. His hair is the same, dark and cut short, and of course his beautiful brown eyes, almost black, are as wonderful as I remembered. He's wearing a suit that shows off his perfect physique. I have an instant vision of his chest, broad and sprinkled with dark hair, that sends a charge of excitement coursing through me. Pleasure erupts within me and I'm seized by a violent desire to rush to him, press myself to him and kiss him, to taste his mouth, breathe his scent and feel his skin. But despite the wild urges possessing me, I can't move.

Dominic is staring back bewildered as he tries to take in that I am really there, then I see a dawning of realisation and happiness. A smile curves his lips and he looks as though he's going to speak. Abruptly his expression changes, he stifles the smile and darts a quick look at his boss. As he looks back at me meaningfully, I understand. He doesn't want his boss to know about us. I drag my gaze away from him and over to the woman next to him, who is still talking.

'And so, as you see, things are progressing well,' she is saying to Dubrovski, with a smile. I take in how very beautiful she is: tall and slender with perfect skin, slanting green eyes and bee-stung lips. As I look at her, her gaze moves to me. 'And who is this?' she asks in her unusually rich-sounding voice, made more mellifluous by her Russian accent.

'This is Beth,' Dubrovski says. His voice sounds particularly harsh after her mellow tones. 'She is assistant to Mark Palliser, helping him assess the painting. Beth, these are two of my employees – Anna Poliakov and Dominic Stone.'

My gaze is fixed on Dominic again; I can't help it. Where else can I look, but at the man who's meant so much to me? The man I was in love with . . . and, despite my attempts to break free and turn my love into anger, I still am.

'It's nice to meet you, Beth,' Dominic says.

'Yes.' Anna smiles. 'It's good to have another woman in this place. It's rather male dominated, don't you think? Apparently, even the cats are male.'

'Yes.' I glance at Dubrovski. He's staring at Dominic, his blue eyes narrowed.

'Dominic, why don't you take our young friend here to get some coffee? Ask one of the brothers to help you. I need to talk to Anna about the deal.'

'Yes, certainly.' Dominic gets up, his face impassive. I can tell he's making himself move slowly and with complete control. I'm tingling all over as he walks towards me. 'Does that sound all right to you, Beth?'

I nod. I can't speak. As he gets closer to me, it's as though the breath is being sucked from my body.

'Look after her, won't you?' says Dubrovski. 'I'll see you in the guest sitting room in thirty minutes.'

Out in the corridor, Dominic doesn't look at me, simply mutters 'Wait' under his breath. There are monks walking along the corridor, he obviously doesn't want us observed. We go along the passage-way, and now I feel like I'm floating, the joy of being beside him is so great. With every moment that passes, I realise more fully that I'm actually with Dominic, and that my world has transformed in the space of a few moments.

I have dozens of questions I want to ask him, but I'm speechless. Then he stops abruptly outside another door, knocks and opens it. The small sitting room within is completely empty.

He turns to me, his eyes burning, and takes my hand. He pulls me through the doorway, slamming the door shut behind us, and the next instant his mouth is on mine and we are devouring one another. He kisses me with a kind of desperate hunger, as though he can't get enough of me, his strong arms wrapping around me and pulling me to him. Oh God, the touch and smell and taste of him. It's miraculous, divine ... I'm dizzy but enjoying the extraordinary flourish of fireworks going off inside me. This kiss might be the best of my life – the reliving of something I feared I would never have again. I put my hands to his head, burying my fingers in his thick dark hair, revelling in the sensation of touching him again. He is running his hands over my back, along my arms, as if he cannot really believe I'm really here, wrapped in his embrace.

We kiss endlessly, the passion between us growing almost unbearable with every moment our mouths are locked together as we taste one another. Then he pulls away, and looks down at me. I can see the desire glowing in his eyes as he says breathlessly, 'Beth, what are you doing here? What the hell are you doing with Dubrovski?'

'It's lovely to see you too,' I retort, but smiling.

'Of course, of course, it's wonderful to see you – but . . .' he looks at me, astonished, as though he's still trying to believe the evidence of his own eyes. '. . . I just can't get over that you're here!'

'It's just as Dubrovski said,' I reply, unable to take my gaze away from his mouth, which I already miss desperately. 'I'm working for Mark Palliser. He brought me along with him to evaluate the painting the monks have found.'

Dominic looks troubled.

'What is it? Aren't you happy to see me?'

'Beth, I told you, it's wonderful. I'm overjoyed to see you,' he says in a hoarse voice. 'Can't you tell?'

I can feel his desire pressing against me and I'm overcome with longing to release him and feel him inside me again. The yearning is so strong, I gasp, my lips parting.

'Don't look at me like that,' he says. 'You'll make me lose control.'

'So lose it,' I whisper.

'I can't,' he says, his voice strained. 'God, what you're doing to me . . .'

'I've missed you so much.'

'I've missed you too.'

I stare at him accusingly, remembering how much I've suffered because of him. 'Then why, Dominic? Why did you leave me for so long? Have you any idea of how awful it's been, not knowing where you are or what's happening? Not a word, in six weeks!'

He drops his gaze from me for the first time. 'It's complicated,' he murmurs, then looks back at me with sincerity radiating from his face. 'But you've got to believe that I've been thinking about you all the time. I promise. I've missed you so much.'

'That's kind of hard to believe,' I say, my voice full of barely contained anger, 'when you haven't been in touch even once.'

He holds my hands tightly. 'I've been working. Andrei's had me in the back of beyond, working on this deal. I've been shut away from the world in various places since I left London.'

'With no email? No phone?' I can't help sounding sceptical.

'Like I said . . . it's complicated.' He drops his eyes again.

'You're lucky I'm even talking to you!'

'I know I am. Believe me, Beth, I've suffered too. And I really have been sorting my head out. That takes time.'

I teeter on the brink of real anger with him and then relent. I can't pretend it isn't wonderful to see him, and I don't want to spoil it. 'We'll talk about it later,' I say, reluctant to lose the beauty of our reunion. I want to enjoy the purity of our pleasure in seeing each other again, and the giddy torrent of desire. 'We don't know how long we've got together.'

He pulls me to him again and says huskily, 'My God, it's going to be torment to have to let you go.'

'We're staying here tonight,' I say quickly.

'Really?' His eyes brighten. 'Anna and I are here too.'

'Will we be able to meet?'

'I don't know. I don't think it's a good idea if anyone realises we're involved. It will only create difficulties and I don't want you put in an awkward position with Mark, or Andrei. So we should be extremely discreet.' He bends his neck and presses his cheek against mine, nuzzling against me and I can feel the soft roughness of his stubble against my skin. My heart starts to race again as his scent fills my nostrils. His mouth begins to move to mine, showering tiny, burning kisses over my cheek. 'But . . . I'll see what I can do.'

I draw in a trembling breath as his arms wrap round me, his hands stroking my back and my hair. His mouth falls on mine again and I open my lips to his probing tongue. Our ravenous passion is a little slower and more tender now, as we begin to kiss more deeply, taking our time, enjoying the deep burn of desire that's kindling between us. I slide my hands under his jacket, feeling the warmth of his skin through the cotton of his shirt. He presses his body tight against me, and I feel again the hardness at his groin. Heat spins in my belly and radiates down to where my sex is swelling with excitement at his nearness. I haven't felt anything like this for so long, my body responds with rapture and desperate need, as though it's been asleep for the weeks that Dominic has been away from me and has now sprung into vibrant, shivering life. I feel as though I can't get enough of him, exploring his mouth, relishing his taste, wanting him to be a part of me.

Our desire is growing uncontrollable. What are we going to do? How will we stop? We're both breathless. Dominic's hands are all over me, becoming more questing, stronger. He is about to start pulling my shirt from my waistband, I can sense it, and I don't want to stop him. I'm desperate to feel his hands on my skin, on my breasts . . .

We both hear it and simultaneously pull apart, gazing at each other, panicked. The door is opening. We have a second or two before whoever it is comes in, and it is just enough time to put space between us although we both look dazed, rumpled and guilty. I turn to see who it is and, to my relief, it is Mark who is walking through the door. He is reading a printout, frowning as he concentrates on what is written there. When he looks up, Dominic and I have had enough time to recover some of our equilibrium.

'Ah, Beth,' Mark says. 'I wondered where you'd got to. Oh, hello, Dominic, how nice to see you again, I didn't know you were here.' He looks from me to Dominic. 'Have you two been introduced?'

I nod and Dominic says breezily, 'Yes, we're just getting to know each other a little better. How are you, Mark?'

'Oh, very well, very well.' He frowns again and looks over at me. 'I've had a good look at the painting, and done some quick research. I'll need to do more, of course. I'd like to take some photos of the painting and complete my work back at home.'

'I thought it looks very promising,' I venture.

'Oh yes, it's certainly a very good candidate to be a Fra Angelico. But I need to consider when it could have been painted and why it's remained hidden for so long. I certainly need to talk to the abbot about exactly how it was found.'

Dominic, looking completely cool and collected – and still sending hot waves of lust through me, despite Mark's presence – says, 'But Andrei will want a decision more quickly than that.'

'It's my professional reputation,' Mark replies soberly. 'I can't risk that. He'll understand.' He looks about. 'Wasn't there a rumour of some coffee around here? Or did I dream it?'

*   *   *

The rest of the day is a kind of sweet agony. It's both wonderful and torturous to be in Dominic's presence again. I can't take my eyes off him unless I remember that we are supposed to be virtual strangers. I know that Dominic doesn't want anyone to guess that we're involved, so I do my best to remember that we have to act our parts but I'm not very good at it. All I can hope is that no one is really paying much attention to me.

We drink coffee in the sitting room. Anna joins us after a few minutes, talking easily to Mark. I should be paying attention but I can't concentrate on anything but Dominic, and obsessing over how or when we might be together. When a brother arrives to show Mark and me to the rooms where we will sleep, Dominic manages to get close enough to murmur 'Trust me' and give me a heart-breaking smile.

I have to force myself to walk out of the room, leaving him behind me.

My room is a bare, white-painted cell with a small barred window high up in the wall. There is a bed, a chair and a desk and a washbasin, and a shared bathroom is next door. It is simple and just as monastic as might be expected. I'm left alone to rest and dress for dinner. As soon as I'm by myself, I throw myself on the bed, my fists clenched, almost shaking with the pent-up excitement and happiness I've experienced this afternoon.

Thank God we came to Croatia! I hadn't wanted to come all that much – imagine if I'd stayed behind and

61

then found out afterwards that Dominic was here. It would have killed me.

But . . . what is he doing here? It's odd that he and Anna should be here, isn't it? What do they have to do with the painting? But then again, who knows how Dubrovski's mind works? I can imagine he's perfectly capable of making people fly across the world because he wants to see them for twenty minutes.

I think of how on earth Dominic and I are going to meet later. I won't be able to stand it if we can't, I won't be able to sleep knowing that he is so close to me. But there's nothing I can do about it now – and I want to concentrate on looking my best at dinner. Thank goodness I brought a dress, something silky and easy to pack, just in case of a formal occasion.

I spend the hour before dinner getting ready. When I look in the mirror, I can see that my old sparkle is most definitely back. My eyes are glittering with expectation and there's a flush on my cheeks. In fact, I'm glowing.

I can't wait for dinner to be over, so Dominic and I can be alone.

We are entertained in the private room, with the abbot our host once again. Dubrovski is not quite as impatient as he was earlier. Now he waits for the long grace to finish before beginning to eat. The one disconcerting thing is that all the way through the prayer, he is staring at me. The others have politely bowed their heads or closed their eyes – Anna, glamorous in a black sleeveless shift dress that shows off flawless brown arms, appears deep in prayer herself – but Dubrovski's blue gaze is fixed on me.

What is it? Do I look wrong? Have I put on too much make-up? I dab discreetly at my lips in case I've gone overboard with the lipstick, but that doesn't stop him looking at me.

When the meal begins, the conversation starts to flow. Anna seems so sophisticated as she talks effort-lessly to the abbot and then to Mark, fluent, amusing and knowledgeable. I wonder what her relationship is to Dubrovski. She seems very intimate with him, smil-ing at him flirtatiously, calling him darling and occa-sionally reaching out to put a perfectly manicured hand on his sleeve when she is making a point, but he barely responds to her. I don't understand how he can be so little affected by such a beautiful woman flirting with him. Perhaps he's used to it. I'm just glad her attention is on Dubrovski and not on Dominic who is sitting on the other side of her. I have the abbot and Mark next to me, so I'm definitely not on the sexy side of the table, but at least I get to look at Dominic, although I have to be careful not to focus exclusively on him, as Dubrovski is still landing his piercing gaze on me from time to time.

'So, Mark – this painting,' Dubrovski says suddenly, cutting through Anna's words. 'What are your thoughts?'

'I'll need to do some more research, Andrei,' Mark says, 'but I'm in high hopes about it. From my examinations, the brushwork, the paint, and everything else is as it should be if it were going to prove a genuine find. But I'll need to know more about it before I can say for sure.'

Dubrovski frowns and sighs impatiently. 'How long?'

'I can't say. I'll make it my top priority, obviously.'

Everyone is quiet as Dubrovski drops his fork to his plate and sits back, his expression stony. He stares at Mark and then says in an ominously quiet voice: 'I'm going to buy it.'

'Andrei, is that wise—' Mark begins.

'Yes. That is my final word. I believe it is genuine, and I want it.'

The abbot begins to smile. 'That is wonderful news, sir, wonderful—'

Dubrovski interrupts again. 'Mark, see to the negotiations and the details, will you? Now, if you'll excuse me –' he gets up, flinging his napkin onto his plate '– I still have work to do. We'll be returning early, as soon as this is settled.' He fixes his gaze on me again, letting it linger for a moment that seems to stretch on. I have the unsettling feeling that he knows precisely what I am thinking and the roller coaster of arousal and tantalising waiting I've been on today. *Perhaps he even knows that right now I'm tingling all over with anticipation of what might happen later.*

Then he turns and heads for the door. As soon as he is gone, the atmosphere lightens, except where Mark is concerned. He looks worried.

'I don't like this,' he mutters, almost to himself, 'I don't like it at all.'

He doesn't linger long after dinner, but also excuses himself, telling the abbot that he will make his offer for the painting in the morning. That leaves Dominic, Anna and me remaining at the table with the abbot. I'm impatient for Anna to depart as the others have, so that Dominic and I can go somewhere together, but she shows no sign of wanting to make herself scarce. I can't bear sitting there, so close to Dominic but unable to touch him, and after a while I get to my feet.

'I think I'll turn in too,' I say lightly, looking as meaningfully as I can at Dominic. 'I'm tired. Goodnight.'

'Goodnight,' Anna says cheerfully, almost as though she's glad I'm going. 'Sleep well.'

'Goodnight,' Dominic says a little too loudly. 'See you in the morning.'

I walk back to my little cell, wondering how long it will be before Dominic arrives. I try to read but I can't keep my mind on my book. I don't undress but lie on my bed, observing the hands on my watch moving round. Time moves excruciatingly slowly. What can be keeping him so long? Surely he must have made his excuses by now!

But he doesn't come. When two hours have passed and it is almost one o'clock in the morning, I realise with bitter disappointment that he isn't coming at all.

Hot tears of anger and disappointment sting my eyes, but I brush them away. I'm not shedding more tears over Dominic letting me down. I change into a nightdress, clean my face and teeth, and climb into bed. Despite my agitation, I'm exhausted and fall into a sleep within minutes.

I'm roused by the sound of a gentle tapping on my door. Instantly I snap wide awake. *Is it him?*

I scramble out of bed and go to my door. There is a small sliding panel in it, and I push it back so that I can look out into the corridor. Outside there is a hooded figure, the face shrouded in shadow.

'Dominic?'

The whisper comes back: 'Open the door.'

Who else can it be? I pull back the iron bolt and open the door. Immediately I know it isn't Dominic – this person is far too short. I gasp and go to close the door again, but the figure slides a foot between it and the jamb.

'Don't be afraid,' it whispers. 'I've come to take you to Dominic.'

I pause, wondering if I trust this stranger.

'Come.'

I take a deep breath and step out into the corridor.

'Follow me.' The man beckons me onwards and sets off at a swift pace down the corridor. The lights have all been dimmed and we walk along in an eerie shadowy twilight, our footsteps quieter than I would have expected, as though everything has been muffled by the darkness. We seem to walk for a long time, turning now and then until I have no sense of where we have come from. This is like a labyrinth. I wish suddenly that I had left a little trail of stones or unfurled some thread, so that I could find my way back if I'm left alone.

Then, we stop. The hooded figure puts his hand on the door handle and says in a strong accent, 'I will be back later to collect you.' Then he pushes the door open and I step inside. The room beyond is in total darkness and I'm unable to see anything at all after the murky light of the corridor.

'Dominic? Are you there?' A shot of fear rushes through me at the sudden thought that perhaps this is some of awful trap. I'm in utter darkness in a strange place in a foreign country – isn't that the stuff of horror films and nightmares? I'm overcome by a nasty sensation of panic, and immediately put out my hands and begin flailing in the darkness, desperate to feel something, anything, to anchor myself in the real world. The terror grows larger, it seems to loom out of the blackness to possess me and I gasp.

Then warm hands hold mine and a voice says, 'Beth.'

Relief washes over me. *Dominic.* I grasp his hands.

'It's okay. I'm here. Did Brother Giovanni freak you out?'

'What, you mean the hooded monk with the hidden face who ordered me to follow him through a pitch-black monastery? Er – yes, just a bit.' I'm able to laugh weakly as the terror recedes. I'm still completely blind though. I reach up and feel Dominic's face. 'Is it really you?' I say wonderingly.

I sense rather than see his smile. 'It's really me. And you are really with me.' His whisper becomes husky. 'It's so wonderful to be with you again . . .' His warm sweet lips fall on mine again and we kiss as we did earlier in the day, with the kind of depth I have only known with him and I think I only ever will. How could two mouths be so perfect for one another? When we meet, lips to lips, tongue touching tongue, probing and exploring, it's as though we're set free to roam within each other. The darkness is velvety and all encompassing, and the feeling of surrender to everything my body yearns for is delicious. All we want to do is offer one another the pleasure of our body and receive pleasure in return: I want to feel that hard muscle, the rough hair on his chest, lick his fingers and the tiny bullets of his nipples, while he is hungry to feel my soft breasts and suck on my nipples, smoothing his hands over my waist and hips and back. For this reunion, so sweet because it has been so long in coming, we don't need anything at all except each other.

My nightdress is pulled over my head and I stand before him naked, but he can only see me with his hands, and he groans as he takes my breasts in his palms, rubbing his thumbs over nipples that are already stiff and sensitive. He bends down to take first one in his mouth and then the other, sucking and nibbling, bringing each one to a peak of hardness. But I can't bear to be away from his mouth for too long, and I bring his face to mine so we can kiss. He presses against me and I gasp again. He's naked, and his huge erection, hot and iron-hard, juts out from his body and into the softness of mine. I put one hand down to it, and caress its velvety top.

He breaks our kiss. 'I can't wait long for you,' he says softly, and kisses at my ear, sucking on my lobe and sending hot rivers of desire gushing through me. I feel his hand at my belly, and a moment later, he is cupping my sex in his hand, pushing one finger into the depths that are already wet and waiting. He presses the ball of his thumb against my mound, creating a delicious pressure on my clitoris, and he pushes a second finger inside me, making me moan and tighten my grip on his shaft.

Unable to bear it much longer, we release one another and move without words. Within a moment, he has pressed me down onto a narrow single bed and I open my arms to him, desperate to feel his weight on me, the sublime pressure of his body against mine. His mouth finds mine again, but our kisses can't be restricted only there; now we're hungry for every part of each other. He is kissing my shoulders, pausing to tug deliciously on my nipples again, and then he is burning a trail down my body.

I gasp as he reaches my sex, and nuzzles into the patch of downy hair there. I'm worried that one touch of his tongue will send me over the edge and I don't want to come yet. But already my excitement and my body's desperate need have taken me almost to the peak. I fight for control, breathing deeply, trying to close the door to the whirling climax I know awaits me. Dominic's tongue has already begun to explore my depths, tantalising me as it circles my bud, taking its time over the approach, kissing and tasting me until I'm almost in a frenzy. I bury my fingers in his thick dark hair, coaxing him towards the sweet spot. I can't see a thing and yet I can envisage him clearly, his dark head between my legs, paying such a delicious homage to my womanhood. Then he touches it and I cry out, arching my back as the sensations crackle through. I want it and yet it's almost too much. I revel in the feelings, twisting and turning when they threaten to overpower me, eager for them and yet keen not to come too soon and bring all this to an end. I pull him up towards me and he comes to me, panting, smiling, his lips wet with my juices.

'You taste like nectar,' he murmurs. 'I've missed you so much.'

'I need you, now,' I whisper. 'Please . . .'

I have to feel him inside me, and the next moment, he's between my thighs, the hard head of his erection probing at my entrance, then he's pushing inside, filling me up. After all these weeks, I'm tight and he has to press on against the resistance, giving us both exquisite pleasure as he buries himself in me. When he's entirely inside me, we pause, panting, surrendering ourselves to the sensations, then he kisses me wildly and deeply as he begins to move. I know I cannot last long, and I don't know whether to fight it or surrender to the desire to come but soon I have no choice anyway. He is fucking away with all his might, forcing home his hard cock and at the same time pressing hard on my clitoris. I open my thighs to him as wide as I can, so that he can get as deeply inside as possible, and I grasp his firm buttocks in my hands, squeezing them and forcing him further and harder in his thrusting. Then I feel the climax building in me. My sex seems to be melting into liquid heat as the waves of pleasure grow stronger and stronger.

'That's it,' Dominic says to me urgently, 'oh God, that's it, I'm going to come, I have to, squeeze me hard.'

I dig my nails into his skin and thrust up to meet him. 'Yes,' I cry out. 'That's it, oh, Dominic . . .!' I release myself to the boiling torrent and cry out again as the feelings become too much to stand in silence. The orgasm picks me up and whirls me round, releasing me breathless and spent. Dominic's climax comes at the same time and he stiffens as it grips him and then, with two more slow, hard thrusts, he falls forward onto my chest, all his strength gone in the force of his orgasm.

We lie together, getting our breath back, stroking one another gently, kissing warm soft kisses that are all the more tender now we've gone through such an intense experience together.

'I need to ask you something,' I say, after a while and he murmurs drowsily. 'Why have you been away so long? Why didn't you get in touch with me?'

There is a long pause and then he says, 'At first, I felt that I had to sort my head out. The way we left things . . . well, you remember.'

There is silence as we both recall the seismic events between us. When, despite the heady attraction between us, Dominic told me that his sexual desires meant we weren't destined to be lovers, I fought against it and persuaded him that I was eager and ready for a taste of what he enjoyed so much. We agreed that he would initiate me, carefully and with control, into the role of his submissive and that I would allow him to play out his desires. I gave him my faith, trusting that he would know when to stop. But he hadn't. He had taken me beyond my limits to a place I didn't want to go, and his own urges had overcome his role as my guide and protector.

Even now, the memory of the flogging I endured in the dungeon of The Asylum comes back and makes me shake with the remembered fear and pain.

But I thought that my forgiveness and the love I had for Dominic would make everything better, take us to a new place of trust and understanding where we could enjoy the delicious aspects of Dominic's preferences and discard whatever was left. I thought we could experiment with our role-play, and take turns at being in control. But Dominic's crisis of faith in himself didn't allow it, and that was when he vanished from my life.

'Yes, I do remember. As I recall, you said we would stay in touch and that you would call me soon,' I say in a tight voice. I don't want to spoil our beautiful reunion but I can't help asking for the answers to questions that have tormented me for weeks.

'I had my phone changed,' Dominic says. 'It happened very suddenly – it's the kind of thing Andrei does every now and then, to guard against hacking and bugging. All communications are refreshed. Your number didn't make it to my new phone, so I couldn't call or text you.'

'What about email?'

'Same. If I ever had your email address, which I don't think I did.'

I absorb this for a moment and then say, 'But you could have reached me if you'd wanted to. What about Celia? Or James? Or even Vanessa?'

'I don't want them involved,' he says a little impatiently.

'So you'd rather we never spoke again?' I burst out, hurt.

Dominic hesitates, stroking my hair gently. 'Listen, I know it seems like it's been a long time, but I've been very busy. Dubrovski has a lot going on and I'm deeply involved in it. I've been travelling non-stop. Time has moved very fast, probably faster than it has for you. And besides, I wanted to be sure that I was ready to come back to you. I've had a lot to think about, you know.'

I nuzzle into him, finding comfort in the heat of his body and the touch of his skin on mine. I want to believe that he's just been too busy to be in touch with me, even if, somewhere deep inside me, a voice is telling me that he could have reached me if he'd wanted to. So why didn't he? I ignore it. I don't want to hear it. 'And are you ready now?' I ask in a soft voice.

'I don't have a choice,' he replies huskily, his arms around me. 'The reality of you is so overwhelming, I can never walk away again.'

I breathe out long and slowly, holding on to him tightly. 'So what happens now? Are you coming back to London?'

There is a long pause and I listen to Dominic's soft breathing. At last he says, 'I don't know. Not quite yet. Perhaps soon.'

'What is it you're doing for Dubrovski?'

'Deals. In commodities. There's a very big one on the horizon that's going to make a large amount of money – we're talking billions. Everything is focused on it.'

I frown into the darkness. 'So why he is so interested in a painting, with all of this going on?'

'I have no idea,' Dominic says slowly. 'Listen, Beth, I will be returning to London eventually. Can you wait a little longer?'

'Of course. It's the not knowing that was killing me. I can wait as long as it takes. And now we're in touch, we can work out ways to meet again.'

'Of course we can.' He places a gentle kiss on my cheek, then yawns. 'God, I'm tired.'

'Go to sleep.' I hug him. 'We have to be up in a couple of hours.'

'Brother Giovanni will be here any minute,' he says, his voice drowsy. 'I'll stay awake till then.' But within a few moments, I can tell from his breathing that he has fallen asleep. I'm filled with a rush of tenderness for him: my beautiful Dominic, sleeping in my arms. This is real joy, lying with him, our bodies pressed close, our arms intertwined, breathing together, both satisfied.

I run my hand over his arm. He shifts in his sleep, turning on to his side. I smooth my hand over his back. Then I feel it again, for certain this time. On his back are raised marks, like the welts I remember there after he made me whip him in punishment for his loss of control. I move my fingertips over them. Yes, there's no mistake. A pattern of weals, almost healed, criss crosses his back.

I am holding my breath, my eyes are wide in the darkness.

How can Dominic have flogging marks on his back? Only if someone has whipped him recently. Oh my God. But who? And . . . why? His instincts are dominant, not submissive . . . or at least, they used to be.

A cold chill is prickling over me. What can it mean?

There is a knock on the cell door and a low voice murmurs, 'Are you awake? You must come with me now.'

I'm frozen, thoughts and suggestions whirling through my mind. The knock comes again. 'I'm coming,' I say out loud, and begin to slide away from

Dominic. He stays deeply asleep, breathing softly in the darkness

It's no use. I have to go. I have no choice.

I begin to pull on my nightdress so that I can return to my room alone.

CHAPTER SIX

Mark flings the newspaper onto his desk with an expression of annoyance. 'Precisely what I didn't want!' he growls.

I lean forward to look. There is a picture of the newly discovered Fra Angelico under the headline 'Lost Masterpiece Found in Croatian Monastery'. I scan the article quickly and see Mark's name. He is cited as the expert who verified the authenticity of the work while another expert from Christie's expresses delight at a possible find but also reservations until others have had the chance to examine the piece. At the very end of the article, it is revealed that the work has been purchased privately for a sum in excess of two million pounds by a buyer believed to be Andrei Dubrovski, the wealthy Russian businessman.

Mark has gone over to the window and is staring out crossly. Since our return, the weather has become distinctly autumnal, and the branches outside shed a confetti of leaves with every gust of wind. A grey sky lowers overhead; evening is coming earlier every day. He takes off his glasses and polishes them on his sleeve. 'I don't understand,' he mutters. 'Why would Dubrovski place me in this position? Why not wait until I had got the proof? Now it's my reputation on the line. I just hope the bloody thing is real, that's all.'

'He's obviously very impulsive.'

Mark nods. 'A man who acts on his instinct and who satisfies every desire he has immediately. That much is certain.'

'Will you say anything to him?'

Mark turns back to me, sighing. He looks truly worried. 'There's nothing I could say. Besides, it's done now. I shall carry on behind the scenes, hoping I find something to guarantee this painting is what we say it is. But when he comes to dinner tonight, we must be our usual selves. Upbeat and professional.'

I nod. I still don't understand why I'm going to be at this dinner, but Mark said that Andrei Dubrovski particularly requested my presence. Besides, he explained, it is a little custom that Andrei dines with him whenever he comes to London and then takes the time to peruse Mark's collection to see if anything takes his fancy.

'Is he going to be staying in London for a while?' I asked, when Mark told me this.

'Apparently. If it's a flying visit, he usually stays at the Dorchester and he mentioned he'll be in his London apartment. That means he intends a stay of a week or two, I should think. He's a non-dom here, so he can't stay longer than three months in a year.'

The news makes a tingle of excitement spread over me. If Andrei's coming back for a few weeks, perhaps that means Dominic will be here too . . . Suddenly

Dubrovski's return takes on a new character. I'm positively looking forward to it.

I didn't have another moment alone with Dominic after I left him that dawn morning. Dubrovski was eager to be off, chivvying Mark along to get the picture negotiations finished.

'Give them whatever it takes, just hurry up!' he commanded.

Forty minutes later, the deal agreed, we were in the cherry red helicopter again, rising from the top of the tower into the sky before the nose of the aircraft dipped and we soared off back to France. I had seen Dominic at breakfast but we were not even able to talk privately, let alone kiss goodbye. I hated leaving him, but as we flew over the Italian coast, my phone shuddered in my pocket and I pulled it out to find a text from him.

That was incredible. Thank you. Take care and I will see you soon, I promise. Dx

I smiled and sent one back to him.

You made me happy. Please do it again very soon. Bx

The reply arrived at once:

Try and keep me away. Dx

When we landed at the villa, our luggage was already packed and waiting for us in the big black car.

Dubrovski didn't wait around but said a swift goodbye to us on the lawn, with the rotary blades on the helicopter still turning.

'Thank you, Mark,' he said, his dark-blond hair ruffling in little waves as the eddies of air moved it. He shook Mark's hand. 'I appreciate it.' Then he turned to me, his eyes intense, his mouth still unsmiling. 'We'll meet again, I'm sure,' he said in a tone that was more like an order than a polite remark. Then, inexplicably, 'I'm glad you enjoyed yourself in Croatia.' Without waiting for a reply from me, he turned and walked away towards the house.

'Come on,' Mark said. 'Let's go home. It's been a most peculiar couple of days.'

On the plane home, I was silent, thinking back over the delicious hours Dominic and I had spent together. Mark read while I gazed out of the window into the blackness beyond, and tried not to show that I was thinking of Dominic's smooth and beautiful cock plunging into me, driving me to that dizzy peak of intense sensation. If Mark had been aware, perhaps he would have seen my lips parted, my chest rising and falling a little too fast, my eyes unseeing because of the riot of pictures in my mind, the memory of Dominic's dark head between my legs and the soft nibbling touch of his tongue and teeth on the tip of my most sensitive part. But Mark never looked up from his book and never saw me close my eyes and lean back in my seat, eaten up by need and tormented by remembered joy.

* * *

'What's happened?' Laura demanded as soon as she saw me. 'Have you met someone? Come on, something's happened, I can see it in your face.'

I hadn't meant to tell her. I was going to keep it entirely to myself but it was impossible once she asked. I shook my head. 'No – not someone new.' A huge smile spread over my face.

'Dominic?' she asked, incredulous.

I nodded, beaming, then we both squealed and jumped up and down, and Laura hugged me.

'So everything is right between you guys?' she said, when I'd told her what had happened. 'You're back together? Oh, Beth, I'm so happy for you!'

'It's not completely straightforward,' I replied. 'Dominic doesn't want his boss to know we're in a relationship.'

'Why not?'

'I suppose it's a bit unprofessional – you know, his mind is supposed to be on his work, not on me.'

'I don't see why it matters if he still does his job. And after all, you were a couple before you started working for Mark.'

'Well . . . maybe.' I had a sudden vision of Dubrovski's face: the serious unsmiling visage, the broad mouth with his stubborn lower lip, and the piercing icy eyes. He doesn't look like the kind of man to be touched by romance. I can understand why Dominic doesn't want that side of his life revealed. 'Anyway, he's still working on some huge deal so he'll be away travelling for I don't know how long.'

'He'll be back before you know it,' Laura said, squeezing my hand. 'It won't be so hard now you're in touch. I'm so pleased, Beth. It looks like fate took a hand in getting you two back where you're supposed to be.'

I nodded, happy. But something whispered through my mind, something I didn't want to confide in Laura. I remembered the gentle ridges along the smooth skin of Dominic's back. Then I tried to forget them.

I am staying in the spare room at Mark's house this evening, so that I can get ready for the dinner with Dubrovski and not have to worry about going home late tonight when it's over. 'We won't be dressing up – not in black tie at least – but it will be smart,' Mark had said, so I went shopping along the King's Road in my lunch hour and bought a knee-length dress in red crêpe de Chine with a flattering neckline just low enough to be sexy and capped sleeves. The colour is a little bolder than I would usually choose but the elegant shape makes it stylish rather than attention seeking. In front of the mirror in Mark's spare room I carefully pin my fair hair up into a tousled style that reveals my neck and the pearls in my ears, and paint my lips scarlet to match my dress. *There,* I think, looking at myself appraisingly. *That looks sophisticated. I hope.* My blue-grey eyes look as catlike as I can make them with swoops of dark kohl and plenty of mascara but not quite as alluring as Anna Poliakov's slanted green ones. And, I reflect, looking at my heartshaped face, I'll never have cheekbones like hers. But I would love to be able to capture some of her style, so sexy and stylish and completely grown up. Maybe I've come a little close to it tonight.

Mark's guest bedroom is beautiful, as I might have imagined. The walls are papered in a pretty faded floral, and the curtains and lavish pelmets are in the same pattern, as is a fat little button-backed sofa sitting under the window. A four-poster bed is upholstered in the same floral fabric, but its white embroidered linen stops the effect from being too much. The room just looks perfectly put together and very cosy, with its antique fireplace, thick pile carpet, old prints on the walls and delicate polished furniture.

I could get used to living like this. Sometimes it's hard to remember, in this new life of mine, that Belgravia houses and private planes to France are far outside most people's experience. *I'm just lucky to have the chance to know it a little. One day it will all be over and I'll go back to normal. Or . . .* a picture floats into my mind. It is Dominic and me, living in a beautiful little flat somewhere glamorous, enjoying our lives together, pleasing ourselves, with all the hours we could want to make love without stopping.

I laugh at myself. Girlish, romantic dreams. I'll be writing out my first name with his surname soon, just to see what it looks like. But still . . . perhaps we will have a future together. I want to hug myself at the thought.

I catch sight of the time. *I've got to hurry. Dubrovski is due in fifteen minutes.* I give myself a last look in the mirror and go downstairs to join Mark.

We are in the drawing room, Mark pointing out his newest acquisitions and explaining their provenance, when the doorbell rings precisely on time and a moment later, Dubrovski is shown in.

'Andrei, good evening, how are you?' Mark approaches him with a beaming smile and his hand held out. You'd never know he'd been furious with his boss earlier in the day.

'Fine.' Dubrovski shakes his hand but he is already staring at me. 'Here is your friend. Your . . .'

'Beth,' puts in Mark.

'Beth,' echoes Dubrovski, as I step forward to shake his hand. He looks me up and down with one swift glance. 'Of course. As if I could forget.'

'I'm very pleased to see you again, sir,' I say, smiling and hoping I seem professional.

He raises one eyebrow. 'Please. Call me Andrei.'

'Oh. Yes . . . very well . . . Andrei.' I flush slightly. I'd decided to make sure it was all very proper and work-like tonight and already he has scuppered that by telling me to call him by his first name. But I can hardly ignore such a firm request. Since returning from France, I've forgotten how powerful a presence he is. As soon as he is in the same room, a core of energy and determination, I know I can't resist his will. If it's Andrei he wants, then Andrei he will be.

Mark offers him a drink and then the two of them chat easily as they examine the art on the walls. At least, Mark chats; Dubrovski listens with the occasional grunt or barked question. I follow behind them, lingering discreetly nearby, listening and appearing fascinated, sipping on my gin and tonic. To my surprise, whenever Mark shows him a new picture, Dubrovski turns to me and says, 'And you? What do you think of it?' Then, as I say a few words that I hope are well chosen and accurate, he listens, nodding. 'Yes, yes,' he says when I've finished, and then lets Mark move him along to the next painting or print or piece of sculpture.

Mark's maid Gianna announces that dinner is served, and we go through into the dining room, another stunning room painted a delicate grey and hung with eighteenth-century portraits in carved gilded frames: beautiful aristocratic women in flowing gowns of scarlet velvet or gold satin gaze down at us, their flawless skins glowing, ringlets falling over shoulders, almond-shaped eyes impassive. Silver and ivory damask curtains hang at the windows, and the round mahogany dining table is set with stiff ivory linen, silver cutlery and etched antique glasses. Candles burn gently in silver candelabra, endowing everything with gauzy softness.

Over the first course of seared scallops, Mark and Andrei talk about the painting. I listen, hearing the almost imperceptible anxiety in Mark's voice as he speaks. He's in a difficult position: the painting is bought now, and if it turns out to be a fake, Andrei could well forget that it was he who overrode Mark's objections and made him buy it. But if he tells a straight untruth, he is compromising himself and his professional integrity. I can tell he is playing for time, refusing to give a categorical yes but sounding comforting and reassuring.

Let's just hope that it turns out to be the real deal. I can't help wishing that they could change the subject and talk about when this huge business project is going to be completed and when Dominic will be returning to London, but there's no way of asking without it sounding suspicious.

The starter has been cleared away and the main course of Dover sole in lemon butter served, when Andrei suddenly looks directly at me.

'So,' he says, 'did you enjoy your trip to the monastery?'

I'm a little disconcerted to be drawn so abruptly into the conversation. 'Yes,' I say brightly. 'It was fascinating.'

'You certainly seemed to come alive there,' he says, staring hard at me. All through the meal I've looked up to find those blue eyes fixed on me but now I feel almost pinned to the spot by his arresting gaze. 'Did something happen to you?'

I flush. My cheeks grow hot. I only hope they're not as red as my dress. 'No . . . no, of course not.'

'It must have been the mountain air then,' he says in that harsh voice of his. 'Because you seemed quite transformed after our night there.'

'It was a very inspiring place,' I reply, and anger flares up in me. What right does he have to question me? What does my private life have to do with him anyway? 'The painting was magnificent. It moved me.'

'I'm glad you thought so.' He toys with a piece of fish and then puts down his fork. 'Because I would like you – and you, Mark,' he looks over at my employer, 'to do me a favour. I liked the way you responded to the painting and what you said about it, and I have it in mind for you to take on a very particular task for me – if Mark can spare you. My London apartment has recently been redesigned and I want my current collection of artwork sorted through to see if it matches the look, for suitable new works to be acquired that will enhance the décor, and to come up with a layout for them all to be hung in the apartment.' He looks over at Mark. 'Normally I would ask you, Mark, but I'm sure you have plenty of other calls on your time, and I want this done quickly and thoroughly. I don't envisage it would take more than a few weeks. Mark, I'm sure you can spare Beth for that long.' He looks idly at Mark, as though his agreement is pretty much a given. His gaze flicks back to me. 'I'll pay you well of course, certainly as well as Mark does. It will be an interesting experience for you.'

I'm speechless. I look over at Mark. It sounds like an interesting opportunity – but Mark is my boss so it's up to him. Besides, do I want to work exclusively for Andrei Dubrovski, even for a few weeks? I don't know.

'Oh, Andrei, I'm not sure,' Mark says. 'I'm sure there are plenty of people who can help you out, but I've only got one Beth.'

'You can do without her for a short while, can't you? She won't be away for long. Besides, she'll probably need your help and advice as she goes along – think of it as an extension of what you both do for me already.'

'I suppose I could,' Mark says slowly, then looks over at me. 'Beth, it's up to you. I'm sure it would be an excellent experience.'

A sudden thought floats into my mind. *I'll be closer to Dominic. I'll know where he is and when. I might even see him more often.* And I like the idea of spreading my wings a little and trying out my own taste. It will be a challenge.

I look back at Mark. 'If you're sure that you don't mind, Mark . . .'

He smiles at me. 'I don't mind at all. I'd love to do it myself, but Andrei's right, I'd find the time needed a little difficult to spare at the moment.'

Dubrovski's blue gaze is glittering at me from across the table as I think it over. He's waiting for me to decide – and I know he doesn't like waiting.

'Andrei, I'd be very happy to take on the job,' I say. The voice in my head is getting louder and firmer: *this is the way to reconnect with Dominic.* Another small voice says: *but why does Dubrovski want you so badly? You're playing with fire, aren't you?* I resolutely ignore it. 'And it's just for a few weeks, isn't it?'

'Absolutely.' For only the second time since I've known him, a smile spreads over Dubrovski's face. The change in it is astonishing. *He should smile more often.* 'You can trust me. And if you want to leave for any reason . . .' he spreads his hands out on the table, palms up, '. . . all you have to do is ask.'

Then he sits back in his chair, his face half lost in shadow, and seems satisfied. 'Good,' he says. 'That is decided. You can start in the morning.'

CHAPTER SEVEN

The next morning, Mark and I talk about it over breakfast, and he seems to think it is, overall, a good thing.

'Andrei might seem a rather daunting character at times,' he says, 'but I'm sure he'll look after you well. And opportunities like this don't come along that often. Don't forget you can always call on me if you feel out of your depth. I can help you – that's what Andrei pays me for, after all.'

I like the idea that Mark is there as a back-up if I have any queries. I've learned a lot from working with him and seeing how he uses his taste and eye to show art off to its best advantage, enhancing a room in every way, but I'm not quite the expert he is yet. 'This way I get to test out the high wire with a safety net,' I say, smiling. 'But I won't call on you until I absolutely have to.'

'At least you're starting towards the end of the week,' Mark says. 'You'll have the weekend to recover and decide if you're really enjoying it or not.'

When breakfast is finished, Mark wishes me luck and reminds me to let him know how I get on. Outside his house, I hail a taxi and tell the driver the address that Mark has given me. 'Albany, Piccadilly, please.'

It sounds strange to me but the driver appears to understand it, and we set off. As we go, I check my phone for a message from Dominic. The previous evening, before I went to sleep, I texted him:

Guess what? I'm going to be working for your boss! Just for a few weeks. Tell me when you're coming back or call me and I'll give you the lowdown. B x

I've been getting a sweet nightly message from Dominic in the week since we returned from Croatia but two nights ago, he said he was going off on another trip that would keep him busy and not to expect any contact for a few days. There's been nothing since, and there's no response now to my little announcement.

You'd better not go AWOL again, Dominic. The thought makes me feel icy with fear but I banish it. *It'll be fine. He'll be back soon.*

Within a quarter of an hour we are turning off the busy stretch of Piccadilly by the Royal Academy and into a courtyard in front of a large eighteenth-century house.

'Here we are,' says the driver, pulling to a halt. 'Albany.'

I look up at the large Georgian dark-brick building with huge sash windows. It is at least four storeys high and enormous. Is this Andrei's house? It's certainly grand enough but all this for one man? How

91

much art will there be in a house this size? A time-scale of a couple of weeks suddenly seems ambitious. I get out, pay the driver, and go up the stone steps to the front door, which stands open. At once I see it can't possibly be one house, as beyond the door a wide entrance hall leads out the back of the building and into a walkway. As I come in, a man in a dark grey coat trimmed with gold braid steps out of a small room to my right.

'Can I help you, miss?' he asks in a friendly manner.

'I'm here to see Mr Dubrovski,' I say.

'Your name, please?'

'Beth Villiers.'

He goes back into his office to consult a piece of paper and then says, 'Ah yes. He's expecting you. This way, please.'

We walk through the tiled hallway, passing polished wooden panels, large mirrors and marble busts, one engraved 'Lord Byron'. A marble plaque proclaims the titles of famous men who have lived here.

'Is this a block of flats?' I ask, curious, as we emerge into a pretty covered walkway with a small garden on either side, one with a pond and tinkling fountain, and little paths leading off at regular intervals. In front of us, along each side of the walk, stretch two long wings of pale-painted buildings.

'In a manner of speaking,' replies the porter. 'This is Albany House. It was turned into gentlemen's apartments a few hundred years ago.'

'Gentlemen's?' I echo. 'No women allowed?'

What is it with Dubrovski and men only? First the monastery and now this . . .

'Ladies are now permitted to live here,' the porter says with a smile. 'There are seventy-four apartments altogether, from tiny studios up to very large sets. You'll soon see one of the finest. It's where Mr Dubrovski lives – when he's here.'

Halfway along, we turn off the walkway and approach a stairwell with a flight of steps that leads down to the basement and up to the higher storeys. We make our way to a large front door behind the staircase.

The porter says, 'Here we are, this is Mr Dubrovski's set. Do you think you'll find your way out again all right?'

'Oh yes.'

'Then I'll leave you here. Good morning, miss.' With a slight bow of the head, he turns and heads back towards the main building.

I gaze at the door. It's imposing, with wooden panels and a classical pediment above. A huge brass fish forms a knocker, but there is also a bell to press. My finger hovers over the button for moment and I have the sudden urge to turn on my heel and go back to Mark.

Be brave, be confident, I tell myself. *You're going to be fine.* I know I can look after myself. I press down on the bell and hear a chime from within. That's it. The die is cast. I have to go through with it now.

An instant later I hear footsteps approaching and the door is opened. A burly man stands there, his

93

shaven head and black suit giving him the unmistake-able look of a bodyguard.

'I'm Beth Villiers. Mr Dubrovski is expecting me.'

The hulk nods and stands back so that I can enter and I step inside. The apartment is decorated in highly polished tawny wood, the floors, walls and ceilings shimmering with light reflected in their surfaces. Everywhere the wood is inlaid with marque-try in colours of black, dark brown and light brown – around the doorways, along the skirting, in symmet-rical patterns on the floor. It is all very classical and masculine, and evidently extremely expensive. I can tell that the whole look has been masterminded by an interior designer who has made sure of every last detail. It has a lot more character than the villa in France, which was the kind of thing I was expecting.

The hulk leads me through the hallway and into a drawing room done in the same magnificent if slightly overwhelming style. Over a grand mirror set in the polished wood panels, a golden eagle spreads its wings, an olive wreath in its beak. The chimneypiece holds black marble busts of gods and classical urns carved in alabaster. On one wall hangs a vast oil portrait of Napoleon on his horse, surveying a battlefield in triumph. It seems appropriate somehow. I glance about; no other pictures have been hung and the polished wooden panels are bare. They almost seem to be looking at me expectantly. This is going to be a challenge.

'Sit,' grunts the bodyguard, and I obediently take my place on a long black leather Chesterfield sofa that faces the marble fireplace. Large windows overlooking the walk outside are partially obscured by trimmed yew hedges, but light floods in anyway, illuminating the perfect Regency proportions of the room. The guard exits and a moment later, Dubrovski strides in, casual today in jeans and a blue cashmere jumper. I get up at once.

'Good, you've arrived.' He manages the slightest smile as he sees me and comes over. I go to put out my hand but to my surprise he leans down and brushes his lips against my cheek. 'Welcome.'

The unexpected greeting makes me falter just a little, then I regain my poise. 'Thank you. What a wonderful apartment.'

Dubrovski glances about and shrugs. 'They did what I asked. I like it.'

'This seems like a very special place to live.'

'Albany? Yes. It is very English, very soaked in history. Prime ministers and poets have lived here, the very cream of your high society. That amuses me. And it's very quiet and private. I like that too. There are all types of people here – academics, actors, businessmen, aristocrats – but we all keep to ourselves, as I prefer it.'

'I had no idea it existed,' I say politely. Then, after a brief pause: 'So. Do you have a contract you'd like me to sign?'

'A contract?' He looks surprised.

'Well, the terms of employment. What you expect from me, how long I'm employed by you. What you intend to pay me. That sort of thing.'

'I imagined a handshake would suffice in this instance. That is how Mark and I decide many things.'

'I would prefer a contract,' I say firmly. 'Just a letter of agreement, if you don't mind.'

He purses his lips thoughtfully. 'You're quite right, of course. You must feel that things are done properly. I will get one sorted out immediately.'

'Thank you.' I feel a little burst of triumph, as though I've scored a victory over this powerful man. 'In the meantime, would you like me to get started?'

He stares at me and then laughs. 'Yes, I would. Come.' He turns and I follow him across the hall into another room. 'The office. You are free to use this.' He opens the door, stands back, and reveals a room, panelled in wood like the rest, but with a pair of facing desks in it, each one well equipped with computers and telephones. At one sits a middle-aged lady with a friendly face, her dark hair streaked with grey and pulled into a haphazard style with some clips. She looks up at me and smiles, and I notice that everything about her looks a little off centre, from her coral lipstick to her green suit. Dubrovski waves in her direction. 'This is my assistant, Marcia. She looks after the London side of my life, don't you, Marcia?'

'I certainly do, sir,' she says playfully, 'and what a lot of nonsense there is to sort out!' She laughs merrily.

She's certainly at her ease with him. I don't know if I'd ever feel like giggling if I worked for this guy full-time.

'Marcia, this is Beth. She's working on my art collection and she'll be here for a few weeks. Get her whatever she needs, won't you? And I'd like you to type up a letter of agreement containing the terms of Beth's employment. I'll run you through them later.'

Marcia turns her light brown eyes to me, all the wrinkles in her face creasing as she smiles even more broadly. 'Certainly I will, sir! Welcome, Beth. We're a very happy family here.'

Dubrovski shoots her a bemused look.

What an odd match they are, I think. *She doesn't seem his type at all.*

'Beth, let me show you over the apartment,' Dubrovski says, as Marcia carries on grinning away, her hands folded in her lap. 'Come with me.'

He leads me from room to room, pointing everything out in his terse way. In a small study there is a great mass of pictures on the floor, arranged in neat piles. 'Here is what you should be looking through.'

This is going to take a while. I've already seen the drawing room, the dining room, a guest bedroom, this study and the office, as well as the hallways. There is certainly plenty to keep me busy.

In the kitchen, which I can see is exquisitely handmade in the same glowing wood as the rest of the house, a Filipina lady is loading a dishwasher with breakfast things. She is tiny, like a little delicate sparrow, with glossy dark hair.

'This is Sri,' Dubrovksi says. 'She'll get you anything you'd like. Do you want some tea or coffee?'

Sri waits impassively for me to decide, but I feel too embarrassed to have a maid make me anything, let alone one that looks so fragile, so I say, 'Oh, no thanks. I've had breakfast.'

'Fine. There's just one room left. My bedroom.' We leave the kitchen and he walks ahead of me down another hallway.

Okay – this feels a bit weird now. I'm not sure I want to see his bedroom. A bedroom is such an intimate space. I feel as though he is inviting me a step closer into his personal life than I want to go. But, I suppose, it's all part of the remit. I can't tell him that I'll do every room but not his bedroom. Ridiculous. *It's just another room*, I tell myself as he opens the door and goes in.

I needn't have worried. The room is strangely impersonal, beautiful but without much sign of what makes the person who sleeps there tick. No photographs, almost no books and of course . . . *No pictures. Because that's my job.* I gaze around. *Perhaps because he lives all over the world, he doesn't bother expressing himself so much in places that aren't really his home.* It's different to the rest of the apartment in that here, the wood panelling stops. I realise I'm quite glad to see the back of it. It's impressive but so much of it everywhere is overpowering. It's a relief to be in a room where the walls are painted a calm dark green. A large four-poster bed without hangings dominates the room, with barrel-shaped tables to either side. There is a small desk and a nearly empty bookcase, and over the fireplace a huge flat-screen television hangs like a big black painting.

'You'll know what to do in here. And I want something particular for the bathroom,' he says, pointing to a grey marble en suite that leads off his bedroom. 'Something that will make me happy when I see it every morning when I step out of the shower. Just one, perfect picture.'

Like Francis I and the Mona Lisa, I think, remembering what Mark said. 'I'll do what I can,' I say, trying to sound capable and upbeat.

He fixes me with one of his impassive looks. 'I'm sure you will succeed,' he says in tones of finality, as though it will certainly happen now that he has decreed it.

He opens another door that leads into a large walk-in closet, with suits, shirts and shoes lined in perfect order, and rows of drawers and shelves for everything else. 'No need to worry about in here,' he says, and then smiles very slightly. 'Now, let's get back. I need to get on and I'm sure you want to make a start.'

It's only an hour or so later and I'm in the study, absorbed in my work sorting through pictures, when the phone buzzes. I look at it, startled, wondering what to do, then it suddenly occurs to me that perhaps I'm supposed to answer it so I pick it up.

'Beth?' It's Marcia. 'Can you come along to the office, please?'

'Of course.'

I replace the phone and stride back along the corridor to the office. Marcia has my letter of agreement waiting for me and gives it to me to read. I sit down and go through it. It's fairly straightforward and I'm glad to see that Dubrovski has limited the employment to a maximum of four weeks, to be renegotiated after that point if the job is not complete.

But it will be. I'm determined.

There are no holidays of course and the hours are left flexible. Then I see the clause dealing with remuneration. I gasp.

'Everything all right, dear?' Marcia says, her eyes wide with concern. 'A problem?'

'It's . . . well . . .' I hardly know what to say. I can hardly protest that I think I'm being paid too much, can I? But the amount in the letter practically matches what Mark pays me in a year. For four weeks' work, or even less if I finish before that time.

'It's the money, isn't it?' Marcia says kindly. 'That's the way Mr Dubrovski is. He makes sure all his employees are very well looked after. That way we'll never want to work for anyone else.'

It sounds simple enough but still . . .

'Just sign it, dear,' Marcia says in a half whisper. 'You won't regret it. And sign this copy too. Then I'll get Mr Dubrovski to counter-sign, and one copy will be yours. Oh, and you'll need to give me your bank details and national insurance number as well.'

I don't see Dubrovski for the rest of the day, or the next, and I don't much think about him as I'm quickly absorbed in my task. Marcia is very friendly and keen to chat, talking away without stopping as she sets me up on the computer system and makes sure I've got all the back-up I need. But I'm glad that I can escape her when I go to the study and start working my way through the piles of art. First, I'm cataloguing everything and making sure it tallies with the records Mark has given me, noting any discrepancies to be investigated. When that's done, I'll start organising the works and making a plan for how they should best be grouped and displayed. I wonder idly if there is an app I can use to allow me to try out my ideas before putting the pictures up. If not, I'll have to work it out another way.

At lunchtime, Marcia and I eat together at a small table in the kitchen: soup, salad and sandwiches prepared by Sri. There's no sign of the bodyguard but I assume that he goes wherever Dubrovski goes. Marcia is friendly enough company but she chatters on and on, hardly waiting for a reply and often contradicting herself, and I can't get quite over how her lipstick is always over the edges of her mouth and her hair is swept about in all directions and pinned into place without any symmetry. Does she get ready without looking in a mirror? She doesn't seem to be like the kind of person Andrei Dubrovski would like to have around him, with his obvious penchant for tidiness and order, but I soon learn that although Marcia might look a bit all over the place, her mind is a steel trap. She knows exactly what's going on, and organises Andrei's London diary with ease, coordinating with his assistants in other parts of the world and clearly boss of all of them.

What she doesn't do is say anything about Dominic, or, in fact, much about Andrei's work at all. She's happy to talk about her cat all day but she barely mentions her job. At first I'm on the edge of my seat whenever she answers the phone, hoping I might hear Dominic's name or get some clue about when he's coming back, but Marcia gives nothing away, and she often talks in Russian or French, which of course I can't follow. There's still been no news from Dominic himself.

Be patient, I tell myself. *He's busy. Just wait.*

'What on earth is going on with you, I've hardly seen you!' Laura says when I get home that Friday night, exhausted from my first two days. 'Tell me everything.'

I tell her about how easily I can lose myself as I work through Andrei Dubrovski's beautiful art collection. I've already stumbled across a few treasures, including a lovely collection of framed Hogarth prints that I think will look wonderful as a group, perhaps in the hall.

'And what's he like?' Laura asks, clutching her knees to her chest as she sits on the sofa, her eyes wide.

'Imagine working for someone like him! I Googled him during my lunch hour and pulled up some very sexy shots. Quite the tough guy, isn't he? And I've always liked blonds. Is he very hot close up?'

'Hot?' I echo, surprised. Of course I've noticed how he looks but I haven't thought of him that way. Ever since I met Dominic, I haven't found anyone else worth a candle compared to him. But as I picture Andrei, I remember the molten energy that exudes from him and the charisma that draws every eye in the room. Even though he isn't exactly handsome, the power and experience in his face endow him with some peculiar quality that makes you want to look at him. And while the angular nose and square jutting chin ought to look too much, those large features somehow enhance him, making him look more wilful and determined.

Laura rolls her eyes. 'Come on! I saw those pictures and thought . . . imagine him in bed, I bet he's a complete powerhouse!'

'I didn't know you liked them like that,' I tease. 'Big, muscly, scary types. You've always gone for the nerdy ones, haven't you?'

Laura makes a face at me. 'So I prefer brains over brawn,' she retorts, then says dreamily, 'but even so, I wouldn't mind a man like that taking me to bed.'

I'm quiet for a moment, remembering Andrei's piercing looks, the way his laser-beam glare moved up and down my body so that I could almost feel it on my skin. It was curiously unsettling, as though we were being intimate without even doing anything.

'Hey, you're not feeling a little unfaithful to Dominic, I hope!' Laura laughs, her eyes bright as she watches my expression.

'Of course not!' I say quickly. I envisage Dominic's dark eyes, liquid with desire, and at once my stomach twists in a delightful knot of lust. *That's good.* Just for a second, I was worried that Laura might have awakened me to something about Andrei that I hadn't been aware of – but I know for sure that Dominic is everything I want in a man. It isn't just that he's beautiful and intensely desirable, it's everything else too: his intelligence, charm and wit. The way he drinks his coffee or casually flings one arm along the sofa when he reads the paper, or the way he laughs. I love the way he grew up all over the world and knows about people and places I've never visited. And I love that he loves me too, that he's fired by the same intense longing for me as I am for him. It's a miracle that someone so amazing would feel as enraptured by me as I do by him, but I've seen the emotion in his eyes, felt it in the way he holds me and makes love to me.

But there is his darker side, of course. Do I love that too?

The truth is, I can't imagine Dominic without that darker side, even though I know that it's something in him that he's been trying to resist, especially after what happened between us. Would he be the same if he were tamed? Would sex be as deeply, dangerously exciting if I knew that he would never try to push me to my limits? It was amazing that night in the monastery fuelled by nothing more than intense desire, but I know that if we were together again, we would soon have to confront the realities of Dominic's sexual needs.

And mine? What do I want?

I can't imagine a life with Dominic that doesn't include the powerful force of his instincts. As I think about it, I'm gripped with desperate longing for him.

I just want him back. Soon.

CHAPTER EIGHT

Laura and I have a relaxing weekend together, mostly watching television on the sofa and making endless cups of tea as we both recover from our working weeks. I try not to spend time obsessing over my stubbornly silent phone. The only time it rings, it's my mother wanting to hear my news. I tell her about my new job and she is impressed but glad it's temporary. I think she prefers the sound of Mark to this new Russian stranger that's come into my life.

I decide on Sunday night that if I haven't heard from Dominic by the end of the week, I'm going to have to do something drastic, though I don't quite know what. Then I try to put him out of my mind and concentrate on my new job.

I'm in the study that Monday morning, lost in my work, when Andrei comes in. Instantly I stop what I'm doing and get up.

'No, please, carry on,' Andrei says. 'I want to watch you.'

Feeling a little awkward, I pick up the print I was appraising and take another look at it.

'What do you think about that one?' he asks.

'It's a very fine example,' I reply enthusiastically. I've been thinking about prints all morning. 'And made by a very famous nineteenth-century printmaker, around about 1870. The frame dates from the same time, I think, and it's part of a set of four, all showing views of Derbyshire.'

'Mark got me those,' he says, scrutinising it.

'I'm not surprised, they're splendid.'

He nods as though satisfied. 'And have you found anything for my bathroom yet?'

'Not yet. I'm not quite at that stage. But I will.'

Andrei smiles. 'I'm looking forward to whatever you discover. But in the meantime, I'd like you to do a little job for me. Something that is rather beyond Marcia's capabilities.'

'Oh?'

'I'd like you to get a gift for a friend of mine. A close friend. I'd like her to have a piece of jewellery, something beautiful, and I'd like you to choose it for me.' He shrugs lightly. 'I do not have time for such things. Sometimes they choose for me, sometimes I have things sent to me. But as you're here, I'd like to make use of your expertise.'

I blink at him, astonished. I've never seen evidence of a wife or girlfriend, and this place is very much a bachelor pad, so I've just assumed that Andrei is one of those men obsessed by his work and with no time for a relationship. But of course a billionaire businessman is going to have a lover. Why wouldn't he? But how am I supposed to go about choosing whoever it is a present?

'Will you do this?' he asks, looking closely at me. 'I would be very grateful.'

'Well, yes, if you'd like me to.' Something in me is telling me I ought to have an objection, but I can't think what it is. After all, he's asked me to work for him on the basis of my artistic taste. This seems to be an extension of that, in a way.

He smiles at me. 'Good. I wish you to select two things; don't worry about the price. Whatever appeals to you.'

'You ought to tell me a little about who it's for, so I have an idea of what she might like.'

He looks surprised, and then says, 'I suppose you're right. Very well. She is beautiful, naturally. And with an aristocratic heritage, from a cultured background. Her family managed to survive the Revolution but, of course, without their grand estate or the money from their glory days. She is rather sentimental about what they once had, though it was long before she was born.' He laughs lightly. 'I like that. A century ago, she would have been a countess or a duchess, and I would probably have been her footman or a groom. Now her family lives in a shabby Moscow apartment, while I fuck her in my French villa or my dacha or wherever I feel like it. She opens her legs for me, the poor boy from the slums who started with nothing. Besides the fact that she is a very fine lover, knowing that I'm enjoying a daughter of privilege adds a certain sense of victory to the proceedings.'

I stare at him, shocked. I've always been careful to keep a professional distance with Andrei but here he is, using this language, putting pictures in my mind. I see them now, on a bed, naked, his broad back and strong legs moving as he thrusts into his high-bred Russian beauty. She is open to him, surrendering, unable to resist his power. His expression is impassive but his blue eyes burn with intensity as he takes possession of her, satisfying his furious desires, overwhelming her as he takes his pleasure and drives her to her peak.

He's watching my face closely. 'Does that help?'

I nod, trying to blank the pictures from my mind. With those few words, a line has been crossed between us. I feel as though he has pulled me into an intimacy with him that I cannot retreat from.

'Good. Show me later what you have bought. Ask Marcia for a credit card.'

Thirty minutes later, armed with a matt-black credit card, I'm walking under the covered walkway towards the back entrance of Albany.

This is too weird. I shake my head disbelievingly. *How have I ended up doing this?*

I let myself out with the card key Marcia gave me and emerge by Savile Row with its ranks of gentlemen's tailors. Bond Street stretches away to my left and I head that way. I already know that window fronts along there glitter with astonishing gems. I've often wondered if there are enough wealthy people in the world to keep so many jewellers in business but there must be, as the emeralds, diamonds and rubies keep sparkling away in their multi-thousand-pound settings.

I walk past a few, looking at the red satin cushions with their treasures displayed behind the reinforced glass. They twinkle alluringly but somehow I'm not attracted to them. Then, further along, I see a different kind of place, its windows packed with antique jewels of all descriptions, from fat ropes of creamy pearls to diamond tiaras, as well as signet rings, cufflinks, ornate silver frames and more. It's like a proverbial Aladdin's cave, or the haul from a Spanish treasure ship. I go to the window and look more closely. Here the jewels nestle on dark blue velvet or in vintage cream-satin-lined cases. This is more the kind of thing I like.

And Andrei sent me because he likes my taste, after all . . .

A uniformed guard stands at the door. He opens it politely as I approach, perhaps wondering if I'm really the sort of person who will be buying much in this shop, though he doesn't show it on his face. I go up to the nearest counter where a slightly bored-looking young man in a black tailcoat is rearranging a display of diamond rings.

'Yes, madam?' he says, a touch of dismissal in his voice. 'Can I help you?'

'Perhaps you can. I'm looking for something on behalf of Andrei Dubrovski—'

The change is rapid and remarkable. The assistant becomes instantly alert and full of eagerness to help me. 'Oh, madam, please, this way. Let me show you to a table, I'm sure I can bring you some pieces you'll be interested in . . .'

Within moments, I'm in a position of honour, assistants scurrying everywhere to bring me trays of jewels to examine, and I'm having a ball. I'm surrounded by a fortune, but the prettiest fortune I will ever see: necklaces, earrings, brooches, cameos, vintage Tiffany, Cartier, Victorian parures, delicate Regency tiaras. It's all gorgeous.

I survey everything, holding some of the sparkling items up to the light, or against my skin to see the effect. *What on earth does Andrei want me to get?*

I'm deliberating over rings and earrings when one of the older assistants brings out a battered red velvet case. He places it in front of me, saying reverently, 'Perhaps Mr Dubrovski might find this to his taste.'

The case is opened and inside is a beautiful enamelled bracelet, edged with tiny diamonds that glitter icily under the electric lights. The inside glows with burnished gold. The bracelet is clearly old but the enamel – cream and turquoise, rosy pink and dark blue – is still bright. It's a splendid thing, and I'm instantly enraptured. 'This is wonderful!'

'It's particularly valuable,' says the older assistant gravely, 'because it was the property of Grand Duchess Olga, the sister of Tsar Nicholas II. She managed to take it with her when she and her mother escaped the Revolution for a safe haven in Denmark. As we know, her brother and his family were not so lucky.'

I draw in a breath. This was the property of the Russian royal family, the doomed Romanovs who ruled for a thousand years before their bloody slaughter put an end to their dynasty. I have a flashback to that image of Andrei, the Moscow ruffian from the back streets, taking possession of his Russian countess. She's gasping in pleasure. The bracelet he's given her is now on her wrist. She's wrapping her arms around him, pulling him deeper inside her, and the bracelet is pressed against his broad back, its diamonds leaving little imprints on his back . . .

'Yes. This is it. I'll take this.' Something occurs to me. 'How much is it?'

The assistant names the sum. I try not to gasp but it's significantly more than my annual salary. I don't think, though, that Dubrovski would blink at it. Then I remember – he wanted me to get two things. My eyes are drawn to a pair of dark ruby earrings set in white gold. There's something about their depth and lustre than keeps me coming back to them. They're evidently old, perhaps Victorian, and very beautiful. 'I'll take these too.' I hand over the black credit card and ask them to deliver. I don't particularly want to walk the streets of London carrying quite so much of value on me.

Mission accomplished.

Later, when I'm back in the study, Andrei comes in. I look up, surprised.

'I've just seen the package that arrived from the jeweller.' He stares at me and for a moment I think he's going to bawl me out for choosing badly or spending too much. Then he says, 'Well done. It's what I expected from you.'

'The bracelet has a Romanov connection,' I say, ridiculously pleased that he approves. 'I thought it was . . . appropriate.'

His eyes glitter with amusement, reminding me of some of the aquamarines I saw earlier. 'It is exactly right.' He turns to go. 'By the way, there is something for you on your desk in the office.'

He's gone before I have time to ask him what it is or who it's from. Curious, I get up and walk through to the office. Marcia's desk is empty. In fact, it's tidied and arranged as though she's gone for the day. On the opposite desk is a packet wrapped in dark green paper and tied with a green silk bow. A tiny card, mono-grammed with an A, is tucked under the silk, and I take it out. It reads *Thank you.*

Puzzled, I pull the bow and it slips lightly apart, then lift the lid of the box. Inside is a small box and my heart beats faster as I take it out and press the tiny clasp that opens the lid. I already know what will be inside.

The ruby earrings glint up at me, dark and rich as vintage port.

Oh my goodness . . . I feel dizzy. I know exactly how much these cost. There's no way I can accept them. *But they're beautiful,* whispers a little voice inside my head. *You love them.*

I swiftly knock down the wicked little voice. *Just because things are beautiful doesn't mean you can have them. Everything Andrei owns is expensive, and lots of it is gorgeous. That doesn't make any of it mine.*

I'm glad that Marcia isn't there to see this extremely expensive gift. I head out, looking for Andrei, the box in my hand to return to him, but there is no sign of him.

'The boss has gone out,' Sri tells me when I find her in the drawing room. 'Not back till tonight.'

'Where's Marcia?' I ask. Everyone seems to have vanished. It's just Sri and me.

Sri shrugs and goes back to the dusting.

I slip the earrings into my pocket and go back to the study.

Laura's eyes are like saucers when I show her the contents of the little box that evening.

'He gave these to you?' she says, incredulous.

I nod.

'Uh oh.' She looks worried. 'No one gives a gift like this without expecting something in return, surely.'

I sigh, not knowing what to say. If it were anyone other than Andrei, I would agree. A gift of expensive jewellery is usually an unmistakeable signal. But in Andrei's world . . . well, I can't be sure. By his standards, these earrings might not seem so expensive. But I can't really take the risk. 'I know. I'm going to return them.'

'Is he coming on to you?' Laura looks less worried and more angry now. 'Because if he's being a scumbag boss who thinks he can take advantage of you, buy you with a few trinkets, well . . .'

'That's the thing.' I sit back on the sofa, confused. 'I don't think it's like that. Besides, he got me to buy his mistress or girlfriend or whoever a gift at the same time. So he's clearly in a relationship. It's a mystery.' I look over at my friend, who is visibly fired up and protective. 'Listen, don't worry. I can look after myself, really. I'm going to give them back.'

Laura nods and says, 'I think that's the best idea. And keep your distance. If you think you're being harassed, for goodness' sake, you must tell Mark or someone. What does Dominic think about all this? He must be furious.'

'He's gone AWOL again. I've no idea where he is or when I'm going to see him.'

'You should let him know that he needs to get back here right away. And you need to make sure Dubrovski knows you're a taken woman, so he can't get the wrong idea.'

I nod again. Laura is right, of course. The rubies glow at me from their box.

Tomorrow they go back.

In the morning, I'm all ready to make my speech to Andrei. I've been planning it in my head on my way to work. I've got the box in my pocket.

The bodyguard opens the door to me, so I know Andrei is there and sure enough he comes barrelling out of the dining room. 'Ah, Beth, you've arrived.'

'Andrei,' I begin, 'I need to talk to you about the gift you left for me. Of course I'm very touched that you—'

I stop because he is paying not a blind bit of notice but has walked off towards the office, leaving me talking to thin air. I go after him, the box in my hand.

'Andrei, I must talk to you about the—'

'Marcia isn't here.' He cuts across me as though I'm not speaking at all. 'Her mother is ill, she's gone to be with her. I need you to do me a favour. Can you do some research in here today and answer the phones? Of course, I wouldn't normally ask such a thing of you, but I've got important calls coming through that I mustn't miss. Someone is coming to fill Marcia's shoes but they won't be here till tomorrow. Can you do that for me?'

He barely waits for a reply, and I give up trying to deliver my speech, and put the jewel box back in my pocket. I'll have to wait till later. Andrei is bending over a notepad on the desk and scribbling some names. 'Now, here are the people I must talk to. Come and interrupt me at all costs if they call.' He rips off the piece of paper and hands it to me. 'Thank you, Beth, I appreciate it. Now, I've got some calls to make myself. I'll be in the study, so you won't be able to work there today anyway.'

With that, he walks out of the office, leaving me open-mouthed in his wake. It's only when Sri comes in to ask me if I want some coffee that I glance down at the list. My hands start to tremble. The first name on it is Dominic's.

*   *   *

116

After that, I'm a mess. I can't concentrate at all. All I can do is wait for Marcia's phone to ring, while I pretend that I'm doing research into some of the artworks. When it finally does, I jump violently, then move like lightning and scoop it up before the first ring is over.

'Yes, hello?' I gasp.

'Marcia? Is that you?' It's a very posh woman's voice on the other end of the line.

Disappointment floods through me. I've keyed myself up so much, I've begun to believe that when the phone rang it would definitely be Dominic. I hate the woman on the end of the line for not being him. 'No, Marcia's not here. I'm standing in. Who's calling please?' I scrabble for the piece of paper with the names on it.

'It's Kitty Gould. Can I speak to Andrei?'

I scan the paper. Kitty Gould's name is not on it. 'I'm afraid he's tied up right now. Can I give him a message?'

'Just tell him that I've emailed through all the details for the party. He'll have them as we speak. I'm looking forward to seeing him there.'

'The party. I understand.'

'Thank you.' Kitty Gould rings off.

I stare at the phone, my heart rate returning to normal.

At this rate, it's going to be a very adrenalin-filled morning . . .

*   *   *

During the morning the phone has rung several times, and I've had to go into the study to alert Andrei that people he wants to speak to have called, but none of them is Dominic.

I feel frustrated suddenly. Why does he think he can treat me like this? Coming back into my life and then vanishing again? I thought he wanted to be with me, to be close to me, and yet he hasn't contacted me for days. What is his game? Can he really be too busy to send a text?

At lunchtime, Andrei and I eat together in the dining room, though he spends a good deal of it on the phone, shovelling in mouthfuls between sentences or some-times in the middle of one. When he is finally off his cell phone, I remember the call from that morning.

'Did you get an email from a woman called Kitty Gould?' I ask. 'It's about a party apparently. She says the details you need are in it.'

Andrei goes still for a moment, then his gaze fixes on me. 'The party.'

'That's right. Do you know what she means?'

'Oh yes. The party is tonight.'

'Tonight?' I raise my eyebrows. That seems very short notice for giving the details of an event.

He stares at me again and then says, 'Perhaps you would like to come with me.'

'Oh.' He's taken me by surprise again. Is he ever going to stop doing that? 'Well . . .'

'Let me rephrase that. I would like you to come with me. I think you would enjoy it. It will be very lavish, a sight worth seeing.' He gives me that impassive expression. 'You can wear the earrings.'

I blush violently. I've forgotten all about the rubies and now I look rude for not mentioning them. 'I . . . I . . . thank you, Andrei, it's amazingly generous but I can't accept them.'

'Why not?' he shoots back, frowning.

'Because they're too much . . . too expensive . . . and, well, I hardly know you . . .'

He waves a dismissive hand. 'Of course you can accept them, don't be a fool. If you think I want them back, you're quite wrong.'

'You have to take them,' I say more strongly. 'You can give them to your mistress, I'm sure she'll like them.' That treacherous picture of him fucking her comes back into my mind but this time Andrei's Russian girl has dark red jewels glinting in her ears as she throws her head back in ecstasy.

'My mistress?' His eyes sparkle a little dangerously. 'How very old-fashioned you sound. I don't want to hear another word about those earrings. Give them away yourself if you don't want them.' He sits back in his chair, as if to indicate that discussion about the rubies is finished. 'Now, are you going to come to this party with me? I don't think it's the kind of party Mark would take you to – and you should seize the opportunities when you get them.'

I'm still reeling at the idea that he doesn't mind if I give away thousands of pounds worth of rubies. *I'll leave them here when I go. That's how I'll get round it.*

His phone goes and he picks it up. 'Yes? Ah, Dominic, at last.'

My stomach does a violent somersault and the blood drains from my face – at least, I think it does. I don't know if I've turned pale but that's what it feels like. Hidden under the table, my fists clench into tight balls. *Dominic is on the other end of the line!* I also feel wounded – he can obviously get access to a phone when he needs it.

Andrei is listening intently to whatever Dominic is saying, and I'm tormented that I cannot make out anything or even hear the buzz of his voice. 'I see. Yes. Will you be at the party later? Uh huh. Well, Harvey is on call with the car if you need it. And Anna?' There's a pause while he listens and then he laughs. I've never heard him laugh before: it's a harsh, grating sound in that rough voice of his, and it sounds as though it's not a thing he uses often. 'Yes, she is. I expect she'll be feeling wild tonight. She always does when we make a lot of money.' He's smiling down the phone. It's always odd to see that broad mouth with the jutting lower lip stretch into a smile. 'Good. Then I'll see you later.' He rings off and looks back at me, still smiling. When he sees my expression, he says, 'What's wrong?'

'Nothing,' I say quickly. 'Nothing at all.' There's a small pause and then I say as naturally as possible, 'That was Dominic Stone? The man I met at the monastery?'

Andrei nods. 'Ringing with some excellent news about an iron ore mine I own in Siberia. The Chinese have bought all the ore we can produce for the next two years. I'm very pleased. Dominic has been freezing his arse off there in the middle of nowhere.' He laughs again. 'But he'll be well rewarded. So. Are you coming to this party?'

The idea that Dominic will be there fills me with excitement, but I try to look nonchalant. 'You know, Andrei, you're right, it sounds like it might be fun. I'd like to come.'

He gives another of those inscrutable looks. 'Good. We'll need something for you to wear. Call Harrods and ask them to send a selection of evening dresses in your size. Ask for black, I think that will suit you best. Nothing too huge, it's not a ball. But sophisticated.'

With that, he gets up from the table and strides out of the room, leaving me staring after him. Life around Andrei Dubrovski is certainly unpredictable. But it is also exciting, and tonight is the first possible chance I've had to see Dominic again since Croatia.

I can't turn that down. I have to go.

CHAPTER NINE

Four hours later, to my astonishment, I am sitting beside Andrei in a beautiful grey Bentley convertible, admiring its polished wood dashboard and feeling the great engine purr beneath me. I'm wearing a stunning evening gown, one of many sent in tissue-lined boxes in a green Harrods van, along with shoes and bags. I spent a happy hour in the guest bedroom, unpacking the treasures within and trying them on: gorgeous creations in silk, tulle, organza, satin and any manner of luxurious fabrics, some sparkling with glitter, sequins and jewels, others adorned with frills or ruffles, some kept elegantly plain. I've never seen designer dresses up close and they are amazing. They look gossamer light but within they are carefully constructed to shape and flatter the body; the materials are sumptuous, the embroidery exquisite, and the workmanship magnificent. No wonder they cost thousands, with their hand-sewn embellishments and attention to every tiny detail. I love them all, even if I feel that some of them, with huge sweeping skirts or great frills at the shoulder, are a little much for me to carry off.

As soon as I put this one on, though, I fell in love with it. It's black silk, as decreed by Andrei, and deliciously proper and yet sexy at the same time, with a very tight, short inner shell and a gauzy overdress that floats over my arms and around my thighs. It came with a pair of dangerously high black silk heels that perfectly complemented its quality of subtle seduction. Surrounded by stiff satins with netting, boned bodices and sequins, I stood gazing at my reflection and knew that this was the one.

Now, as we glide through the London streets listening to Rachmaninov, heading out west, rich red rubies are glinting at my ears.

This is exactly what he wanted, I think to myself, glancing over at Andrei. *Did he plan this from the very start?* I had the illusion of choice – choice about accepting the earrings and whether or not to come tonight – but perhaps he knew what my decision would be. He looks incredible in black dinner suit, a silk bow-tie at his neck, controlling the car with practised ease. But then, I remind myself, all men look good in a well-cut formal suit and if they happen to have a powerful frame and a magnetic charisma, they'll look even better.

Once we are out of the London traffic and on the motorway, Andrei puts his foot down and soon we're flying past all other cars. Around us, night is falling, velvety and dark blue, and a golden autumn moon is rising.

If only this were Dominic, it would be incredibly romantic. But I remember with a delicious shiver of anticipation that he might be at this party – and that's why I'm here after all.

Andrei says nothing until, after about an hour of fast but incredibly smooth travel, we turn off the motorway and a few minutes later pull to a halt in front of a beautiful old Cotswold stone mansion, glowing golden in floodlights.

'Is this where the party is?' I ask.

'No,' he says abruptly, turning off the car and getting out. 'This is where we dine.'

He comes round to my side of the Bentley, opens the door and helps me out. When I'm standing on the gravel, he tucks my arm under his, tosses the keys to a waiting valet, and we walk inside.

It is evidently a very expensive restaurant and we're shown to a table set with crisp linen and gleaming silverware. Andrei orders for us without my even seeing a menu, and a few minutes later I'm sipping at a glass of cold Pouilly-Fumé, facing him across the table and wondering exactly how I ended up here.

'I want to tell you something,' Andrei says, leaning towards me. His eyes are intense and serious. 'You look beautiful tonight.'

'Thank you,' I say, feeling a little awkward. I realise that I'm not sure what the terms of this dinner are. I haven't been asked on a date, and if I had, I would have most certainly said no. And yet, we look for all the world like a romantic couple celebrating some intimate anniversary or embarking on a love affair. *But he's just being polite, isn't he?*

'You looked beautiful that night at Mark's house, too.' He takes a sip of wine while he seems to be remembering. 'I liked that red dress particularly. But then . . . you look beautiful when you're sitting on the floor of my study, lost in my pictures, frowning in that funny way you have, running your fingers through your hair when you're especially thoughtful. I like looking at you then, when you don't know I'm watching you.' He leans closer to me. 'But you've never looked as ravishing as that morning at the monastery, when you almost vibrated with life and sensuality. That's when I knew I wanted to get to know you, much, much better.'

I'm staring at him, in a kind of vortex of horror mixed with something painfully like pleasure. *I'm beautiful? He thinks I'm beautiful?* But then: *Oh no, he wants something from me. He wants . . . oh God, what have I got myself into? I'm sitting here, in the dress he paid for, with jewels he gave me . . . like some kind of courtesan! Of course it looks like I'm prepared to think about him in that way. Oh shit – how am I going to get out of this?*

I try to stay calm and keep my nerve. *So I'm going to have to do battle with a Russian tough guy. He doesn't scare me. Much.*

'Andrei,' I say firmly, 'I'm very flattered that you think I'm beautiful, but you know our relationship is strictly professional. Besides, you have a girlfriend or a . . . a friend, and I have a boyfriend.'

He raises his eyebrows, that piercing gaze appearing almost to read my mind. 'A boyfriend? I don't believe you.'

'It's true.'

'What's his name?'

I pause and falter, realising I can't give Dominic's name but not having another ready at hand. 'He's . . . er . . . he's called . . . John.'

'Ha!' The laugh comes out like a shout. 'You're lying, it's obvious. You don't have a boyfriend. Besides, what does that matter? I don't see why two people who are attracted to one another shouldn't act on their impulses. You are not married, neither am I.'

'But,' I say, sounding a little prim, 'I'm not attracted to you.'

A grin, mischievous and boyish, spreads across his face, and he leans in towards me almost conspiratorially. 'Oh, yes you are. You might not think so – but you are. And believe me . . .' his eyes lock on mine and his voice drops to a whisper '. . . when we do make love together, it will be explosive.'

My mouth has gone dry and I feel slightly dizzy. That picture of Andrei naked flashes back into my mind, but now the woman on the bed, throwing back her head ecstatically, rubies glinting in her ears, is me. Horrified, I dismiss it instantly and recover myself. 'I'm sorry, Andrei, but that's not going to happen. If you don't accept that, then I'm afraid I won't be able to stay here or come to this party with you. Those are my terms.'

'You like your terms, don't you? Your contracts and letters of agreement, everything set out just so. You are trying to control me, build little walls to keep me contained. I warn you, it won't work. No one can do that.' He laughs again as he picks up a piece of bread from the basket on the table and rips it up. 'What will you do, Beth? Walk back up the motorway? In those shoes? It's quite a long way back to London.'

'I could call a taxi. Or . . .' I look about. I noticed a reception area when we came in. 'I'll stay here. Isn't this a hotel as well?'

'Well observed. Yes, a very good hotel.' He seems to relent. 'Well, if you honestly don't want to come to the party with me, I will put you up here and go alone. I can get a room for myself for later and drive you home in the morning.'

I'm flummoxed. I don't know what to say. I do want to go to the party, in order to see Dominic, but I can't tell him that so after a moment, I say, 'I . . . I'll come if you accept that nothing will happen between us.'

His lips twitch again, as if he's secretly amused. 'All right. I accept it. Nothing will happen between us. Not at the party. Perhaps not even tonight. But it will one day. Not just because I want it, but because you do too.'

'I don't think so, Mr Dubrovski,' I say in my most spirited voice. 'I'm afraid you'll be waiting for that day a very long time.'

He looks pained as he says, 'Andrei, please. Let's not go backwards. We're friends after all, aren't we?'

Before I can answer, the waiter arrives with our starters and the moment passes.

*   *   *

Against all my expectations, I enjoy the dinner very much. Andrei's charm, which turns out to be considerable when he chooses to use it, soon makes me forget the awkward start, but even with our friendly conversation, mostly about art, the memory of the compliment he paid me lingers in my mind. I remind myself that he doesn't interest me in the slightest.

'Aren't we going to be late for the party?' I ask, as I notice that it's after eleven o'clock and we are still finishing our coffee.

'No, no. It will just be beginning,' Andrei says. Nonetheless, he calls for the bill and while he's settling it up, I go to the ladies' room. I freshen up and take a few moments to examine my reflection. I'm looking my best tonight, my blue eyes are sparkling with the effect of a wonderful meal and a few glasses of wine, and the dress is even more gorgeous than I remembered. The beautiful shoes lengthen my legs and make me look taller and more willowy than I am in real life. My fair hair falls around my shoulders and my cheeks are pink with anticipation. 'Not long,' I whisper to myself, 'and I'll be with Dominic again.'

I go back to join Andrei who is waiting in the lobby. A few minutes later we're on our way again, this time driving into the blackness of the countryside. Andrei seems to know exactly where we are going and I relax into the leather seats, enraptured by the dark shadowy hedges flying past outside the window.

It seems like no time at all when the car pulls to a halt again. This time we're in absolute blackness in what looks like a forest, the car headlights illuminating only trees and dense undergrowth.

'This is where the party is?' I say, peering into the darkness outside. I'm suddenly on edge. There's no obvious party at all. What if he's brought me here for some terrible reason, out in the middle of nowhere, where we're completely alone? No one knows where I am, I realise, with a chill.

Andrei leans across me, almost making me gasp, and opens the glove compartment. He pulls out two masks, one plain black to cover half the face from the forehead to just above the mouth, and the other embellished with sequins and airy black feathers, designed to obscure the eyes and cover the cheeks, the feathers providing a further veil to the features. He hands the feathery one to me. 'Put this on. I will wear the other one.'

'Why do we have to wear this?'

'It is a masked party, of course. Very glamorous.'

At least there's definitely a party. Though God alone knows where it is. I take the delicate confection and pull it on over my face.

'Very good,' Andrei says softly, and puts on his own mask. Instantly he becomes almost entirely anonymous. It's only the bright blue of his eyes against the velvety blackness and his jutting lower lip below the mask that distinguishes him. 'Come on,' he says, and his voice sounds harsher than ever. 'Let's go.'

129

He comes again to help me out of the car and we stand together for a moment in the light from the car's interior, gazing at one another, suddenly strangers with the masks over our faces. Then he slams the car door shut and we're sunk in darkness. Just as I'm wondering how we will find our way to this mysterious party, a light comes on. Andrei is using a torch to illuminate our way. I need his arm now as I negotiate the shadowy path in my heels, utterly unaware of the way. We seem to be walking on stones or gravel and I guess that we're crossing a car park or a driveway. Within a short time, though, I see a golden light and we are clearly going towards it. It soon resolves into a doorway, but beyond there doesn't appear to be a house or building, just a glowing passageway disappearing into nowhere.

We reach the doorway where masked attendants are waiting outside to guide us in. They murmur something to Andrei and his reply is evidently satisfactory, as we're led into the passageway with low ceilings and walls that appeared to be carved from rock.

'Where are we?' I say, peering ahead as we keep moving. The ground is definitely sloping downwards. We're descending.

'Caves,' Andrei replies, putting his other hand over mine where it rests on his arm. 'We're going into catacombs.'

Almost at once I begin to hear noise: music, a booming beat, the roar of a large crowd. We begin to move by other people, glamorous and strange in their masks as they stand in the passageway, holding glasses. As the passageway slopes away, I see other passages leading off towards small caves that are illuminated by candles glowing in sconces. I can't quite see what's happening in them, but I can make out movement.

Are they dancing? I wonder, but we move on before I grasp what's happening. Suddenly the passageway opens out and we reach a large chamber with a huge curved ceiling that makes me think of being inside a beehive or a wasp's nest, as it rises in gentle stages to a soft dome. Men in black tie and women in gorgeous gowns, all masked in various ways, are drinking, talking and dancing. I can't stop looking about: some wear gorgeous embellished Venetian masks, others simple eye-coverings in lace or silk. Others wear leather, embellished with studs and chains. A few men have animal heads on: wolf or lion masks. A woman in a stunning white silk dress has a white furry rabbit face with soft ears pointing perkily upwards.

Andrei leans in and murmurs in my ear, 'When no one knows who you are, you can do precisely what you please. Now, let me get you a drink.' He leads me towards an alcove where barmen stand behind a polished zinc counter, shaking cocktails for the people at the bar. Despite the crowds, a barman is instantly at Andrei's disposal, and a moment later he's passing me a vodka martini with a twist of lemon peel floating in it. He takes one himself and leads me away. I'm almost too busy looking about at the fascinating sights to

131

notice that I'm holding a drink and that my arm is still over Andrei's. But, I realise, I do need him. The floor is uneven and I'm wary of tripping in these extraordinary high shoes.

Then a thought strikes me. *How on earth am I going to recognise Dominic? Everyone is masked. All the men look the same in their dinner suits.* I feel a great wash of disappointment. The chances of meeting him in this strange place, with its many caves and passages, its throng of people, seem remote. I don't have my phone with me, even if he knew I was here. My only hope is that somehow Andrei will know where we're going to find the others. And he has his phone after all. We leave the main room and go up one of the passages to a cave that is roped off, a woman standing outside. She's wearing a long red evening dress and her mask is plain black and very simple, just covering her eyes. She has bright blond, almost white, hair that ripples down her back and around her shoulders, and brightly painted full lips.

As we approach, she regards us curiously and Andrei mutters 'Dubrovski' to her.

She squeals and says, 'Andrei! I didn't recognise you at all. But you look marvellous.' She leans forward and makes a kissing noise as her cheeks brush his. 'How wonderful to see you.'

'Thank you. How are you, Kitty?'

'I'm very well, thank you. Doesn't the party look gorgeous? We're going to have a riotous time. Let me know if you want someone to show you around, but there's plenty to amuse. And very private places if you find you need one. Just say the word. There'll be a cabaret a little later as well.'

Cabaret . . . A picture floats into my mind. I'm sitting in The Asylum, the private club that came to play such a role in my life. James is with me, and we're watching a cabaret but it's no ordinary show. It's an erotic burlesque that ends with a display of flogging, and watching it are people quietly indulging themselves in all manner of activities. Afterwards, customers take private rooms to work out any lusts that have become inflamed after what they saw.

I realise suddenly and with great clarity that this is a party where anything goes. With the surfeit of beautiful people, the strange anonymity of the masks, the drink and the music – this is a place where no one wants to stop when their desires are sparked into life.

Oh my goodness, what have I done? What have I let myself in for? Is this going to become an orgy? Is that why Andrei wants me here with him?

These thoughts fly through my mind as Kitty unfastens the velvet rope and allows us inside the cave beyond. It is furnished with velvet banquettes, wide enough almost to be day beds, and small tables, and lit by Moroccan lanterns. No one else is there. We go in and sit down. I take a shaky sip of my drink. Everything has changed.

'What's wrong?' Andrei says, watching me carefully.

I don't say anything. Anger is roiling in the pit of my stomach. How dare he bring me to a place like this without any warning, any preparation?

As though he can read my mind, he says, 'You will not see or do anything you do not want to see or do. While these parties are very free, they are also done with immaculate taste. Kitty makes sure of that. Only those who desire to cross boundaries do so.'

'And is that what you do?' I say, my voice tight.

'I do whatever I wish. You should do the same.' He leans a little closer to me. 'You English girls can find it a little difficult to please yourselves and follow your deepest desires. You can be very repressed. You should let go.'

'You know nothing about me.' I'm almost spitting the words out. I'm furious that he should speak to me like this, about a side of my life that belongs to me. *Just because he's got money doesn't mean he can buy people or see into their souls.* 'Nothing at all. How dare you assume anything about me or my life?'

Andrei looks surprised, then his eyes flash with temper. But a second later, his expression softens and he looks almost repentant. 'You're right. I'm sorry. That was rude. Unforgiveable. I've made a mistake. I shouldn't have brought you here. Finish your drink and we will leave.'

'Perhaps that's best,' I reply icily. I don't want to meet Dominic here, like this. It's not what I want at all. I take another sip of my drink. It's strong, citrusy and burns a little as it slips down my throat.

'You think this is sordid,' he says. 'But I would hate such a thing myself. I would not tolerate it. I love beauty, you know that. We're here because it is a wonderful, liberating experience to be anonymous, free to enjoy yourself, to dance and drink and forget everything for a few hours. I was wrong to imply anything about you personally. I've been thinking only of myself and my desire to relax in safety.'

My anger diminishes as I see it from his point of view: he's a famous man, a rich man, who can trust nobody. Here, masked, he's unknown, like everyone else, not having to judge motives, watch his back, or worry that he's being furtively filmed or whispered about. I realise suddenly how attractive that must be. *This is ridiculous – now I'm feeling sorry for him! He shouldn't have spoken to me in that way but . . .*

I gaze into my drink thoughtfully, and look up to find his blue eyes on me. 'We can stay a little longer,' I say. 'You don't have to hurry away on my account. I don't want to spoil your evening. We have only just arrived, after all.'

Before he can reply, there is a movement outside and two people enter the cave, a man and a woman, both masked. As soon as they are inside, the woman says, 'Andrei' in a deep purr, and I recognise Anna Poliakov. A burning breath opens up my lungs as I look at the man beside her. His dark eyes are almost impossible to make out behind his black mask, but they glitter in a way I know very well, and instantly I recognise the graceful shape of his nose, the full lips with their faintly pirate look, and the beautiful broadness of his shoulders. I look at his hands. There is no mistaking him. It's Dominic.

My heart begins to beat wildly, my breath coming short and hot. I'm staring at him but he's barely glancing at me. Why would he? He has no idea I'm here. Anna is taking his attention as she sits down and leans over to brush her scarlet lips across Andrei's cheek. She looks ripe and voluptuous in a strapless black gown that pushes her breasts up high into ivory mounds and clings to her every curve. Dominic is watching her as she presses close to Andrei, who is returning her kiss.

She's so beautiful. Doesn't Andrei see it or feel it? I'm surprised any man can resist her.

An awful thought comes into my head. The last two times I've seen Dominic, he's been in Anna's company. They are obviously spending a great deal of time together, and now he's observing her as she sits close to Andrei, his mouth set and his eyes glittering. It looks as though he can't take his eyes off her, and as though he's eaten up to see her so close to Andrei.

A fiery jealousy suddenly burns in my stomach. She is so gorgeous and Dominic is as red-blooded as they come. Can he really resist her? Or has she managed to dazzle him with those exotic looks and her obvious sensuality? I'm horrified at the idea but I can't shut it out once it's taken root in my imagination.

Andrei looks up at Dominic. 'Hello, you made it.'

'Good evening, Andrei,' he returns, polite but emotionless. 'I'm very glad to be back. Siberia is not my favourite place in the world.'

'You need a drink,' Andrei says with a grin, and he lifts a small golden bell from the table and rings it. A girl in a black cat-suit and black eye mask appears at once. 'Champagne,' he says. 'Very cold.' As she disappears to obey, his gaze falls on me. 'I nearly forgot. I've brought a companion for the evening, the newest member of my team. You remember Beth Villiers, the little art expert who joined us in Croatia?'

Anna says, 'Of course. How charming, you look wonderful, Beth. I would never have recognised you in that magnificent mask – and what a pretty dress.'

But I'm watching Dominic. At Andrei's words, he's stiffened and is staring down at me, his lips slightly parted in astonishment. I can tell he's fighting for control.

Why is it, Dominic? I feel as though my insides are curdling. *Because you don't want me here, spoiling your chances with Anna? Or are you two already together, and it's torturing you to watch her cosying up to Andrei?*

Don't let your imagination run away with you, cautions a voice in my head, but I'm already past caring as scenarios zoom past my mind's eye, of Dominic and Anna together.

'Yes, of course, I remember Beth,' Dominic says slowly. I can see that his fists are clenched, the knuckles white. 'Nice to meet you again.'

137

So here we are. I don't think this is what you want, is it, Dominic? You'd prefer to keep me well away from Andrei and Anna. Your little secret. I say softly, 'You too.'

'Where is that champagne?' demands Andrei, just as the cat-suited girl returns with a tray holding an ice bucket with a champagne bottle and four glasses. In a moment, she has put down the glasses and opened the bottle. The pause gives me time to get back a little control, and Dominic looks infinitesimally more relaxed.

'Darling, such a time we've had!' cries Anna, tossing back her long dark hair. 'The negotiations were the most strung out I've ever experienced. But in the end, we got everything you wanted. Are you pleased?'

'Very pleased,' Andrei says, handing out the glasses of fizzing liquid. 'We'll toast your success.' He lifts his glass and we all follow suit. 'To iron ore and the Dubrovski mines – long may they flourish.'

We all lift our glasses and then sip the champagne. It prickles over my tongue. I feel a little light-headed – not surprising considering I've just drunk a martini – but I also feel brave and powerful in the middle of my pain. This wasn't what I wanted but this is how it is. I will wait for Dominic to make the next move.

Anna is chattering away to Andrei, telling him about the talks with the Chinese. Dominic comes and sits down beside me. We seem to be listening to Anna but actually he is so close that his firm thigh is pressing against mine and I can feel the heat of his body.

'What the hell are you doing here?' he murmurs into my ear, making everything in me buzz in response.

'Am I spoiling the party?' I whisper lightly. 'I'm so sorry if I'm getting in the way.'

'What are you talking about?' he mutters. 'Why has Andrei brought you here?'

I don't say anything, worried that we can be heard.

'Talk to me, dammit. Why are you here with him?' he hisses, and Anna stops talking and looks over enquiringly. Andrei turns as well.

Dominic keeps perfect control. 'I'm afraid that Beth is finding our business talk a little dull. I'll take her out and show her around the party while you two catch up. I'll bring her back safely, don't worry.' His hand closes round my arm, tight as a vice, and he pulls me to my feet. Only I can feel how hard he's doing it but I manage to bite back an exclamation of pain.

Before the others can say anything, he has manoeuvred me across the room and out in to the passageway. Once we're outside, he drops all pretence and properly yanks me along the path. People are milling about and he bumps us both past them without apology, and onwards to a quieter part of the caves.

'You're hurting me,' I protest. His hand is still gripping my arm hard, his fingers digging into my skin. 'Let go!'

'You're coming with me,' he says through clenched teeth. The next moment we have stopped in front of an area curtained off from the main passageway. A girl in a cat-suit and mask, like our waitress, is standing outside. 'We're going in,' he snaps at her. 'I want privacy. No one else to come in, do you understand?'

The girl nods and draws back the curtain. Dominic pulls me inside with him. We're in a large cave furnished with an enormous bed, big enough for at least half a dozen people. There are mirrors everywhere reflecting its broad expanse, and surrounding it are smaller places for sitting and reclining, covered in cushions. I take it all in, slightly horrified. So there are orgies here, obviously – for those who like to take part and those who like to watch. But we do not stop. Dominic takes me through the room and to a door on the opposite side. He opens it and we go in. Now we are in a smaller cave, hung with blue silk and twinkling with electric stars in the ceiling. Here are toys of a kind I've seen before: whips and ticklers, floggers and paddles, all laid out on shelves or hanging from racks. Here is a different kind of apparatus: not a cosy soft bed, but hard leather seats with stirrups and cuffs; there are bars against one wall, and a cabinet full of more instruments of pain and pleasure. I can't help the thrill that rolls through me at the sight. It reminds me vividly of my nights of exploration with Dominic.

I whirl round to face him. 'Why are we here?'

'We have to be alone,' he says. He whips off his mask, then leans forward and pulls mine from my face, discarding them both on the floor. His eyes are burning fury at me and I think my own are sparking in return as we face one another with hostility crackling between us. 'Now, tell me what the hell you're doing here with him.'

'What the hell are *you* doing here with *her*?'

'What?'

'I saw the way you were looking at her! Are you already lovers or are you just hoping it will happen?' I know I sound a little crazy, but I don't care. I'm so full of conflicting feelings: anger, and the disappointment of a shattered fantasy, sadness at being cheated of the romance I long for with Dominic, joy at seeing him, the bitterness of jealousy and fear that I've lost him. It's all boiling up inside me, ready to be released. 'You obviously want her!'

'What are you talking about?' Dominic says, his eyes flaming. 'Do you mean Anna?'

'Of course I mean Anna. Who else? Or are there others I should be worried about?'

'I should spank you for that,' Dominic says through gritted teeth. 'I might be many things, but I'm not a liar or a cheat.'

'So you say,' I retort. 'But as you couldn't take your eyes off her, forgive me if I don't believe you.' I feel on the edge of hysteria. It's too weird to be in this place, now in some kind of play dungeon that takes me right back to the nights we spent in the boudoir when Dominic did such delicious things to me. I know I'm not thinking straight, but I can't help it.

He glares at me, his hands clenching.

Perhaps I'm a little drunker than I realise, but I feel compelled to taunt him, to push him to the kind of emotional place I am in right now. I turn my back on him and slide my hands under the gauzy overskirt of my dress, and raise the short inner shell, pulling it up so that it reveals my bottom. I'm not wearing any underwear because I had nothing suitable to put on when I got changed at Andrei's earlier. I let the overskirt fall back so that the globes of my buttocks are slightly obscured. 'Come on then,' I say, glancing back at him over my shoulder. He is staring at my behind, his lips slightly open. 'Isn't this what you want? To spank me? Is that what she lets you do? Is it only other women you can bring yourself to do that to now?'

He grabs me suddenly, whirling me around and pulling me to him. One of his hands grasps my bottom hard, squeezing it with the vice-like grip he used on my arm. With the other hand, he tips my face upwards so that it's close to his. I'm staring up at him defiantly, breathing hard.

'I don't know what you're playing at, but you're pushing me too far,' he says throatily, and he suddenly lifts my overskirt with one hand, pulls back the other and brings the palm down swiftly on my bare bottom, making me jerk against him and gasp as the sting flares out across my skin. Before I have time to think, he's administered another stinging blow and then another. My bottom is burning, and the sensation startles me out of my slightly hysterical state. Instead it awakens an extraordinary and desperate desire for him. I can feel hot lust flood out within me and the knowledge that he is relishing the feel of my bottom under his palm excites me even more.

I open my mouth, willing him to kiss me. I'm desperate for his tongue and lips, but he holds back, even though I can see the desire glowing in his eyes.

'Oh, not yet, my rebellious little miss. What's put this idea into your head? Huh? What makes you think I'm involved with Anna?'

'You haven't been in touch with me,' I say, breathless, hardly able to hold my stream of thought with his tantalising nearness. To my surprise, my bottom is itching for another of the hot spankings he's been administering. They hurt, but in a way that gives me a delicious rush. 'I didn't know what to think. And then, when I saw you together twice, and the way you were looking at her . . .'

'You're being ridiculous. You have to learn to trust me a little more,' he murmurs. 'Anna is a beautiful woman, but I believe we have a rather solid little arrangement of our own, don't we? You're the woman for me, and I intend to show you that properly at my leisure very soon.' His eyes search my face. 'And besides, what about you?'

'Me?' Before I have time to anticipate it, his palm comes down hard on my bottom, the pressure forcing me against his body. I can feel his arousal through the dark wool of his dinner suit. *Oh God.* My belly is full of hot, delicious knots of lust. The harsh prickle across my backside makes me swell with need between my legs. 'Oh!' I cry softly, as I cling on to his arms. My legs are going weak.

Dominic is steady as a rock, and persistent with it. 'You'd better answer me. What are you doing here with Andrei? It looks far from innocent from where I'm standing. I got the shock of my life when I realised you were with him, dressed like that.'

He's not going to give me what I want quite yet, I can tell. I try to gather my scattered thoughts but the sensations rushing through me are almost overpowering. 'He asked me to come – I said yes because I thought you might be here.'

'Has he tried anything?' Dominic snaps.

I shake my head. The stupid conversation over dinner was just talk, inappropriate flirtatiousness that I knocked on the head. There's no need to upset Dominic over it. 'He hasn't laid a finger on me, and he won't either. I wouldn't let him.' I let myself fall against him. 'Oh God, Dominic, I need you so much.'

'I need you more,' he says, and I can hear the longing in his voice. 'But we haven't got much time. He'll look for us if we're gone too long.'

'I don't think I can wait,' I say, my voice almost a whimper. As if to judge the truth of what I'm saying, Dominic moves his hand from my bottom and rubs it across my damp pubic hair and downwards. His fingers slide across my clitoris and into the wet heat below, making me gasp.

'You're very ready for me,' he says, smiling. 'I don't think I've ever felt you so ready.' He moves his fingers around as if exploring how aroused I am, and it feels like my whole being is suddenly at the mercy of his teasing fingertips. 'I don't know though . . .' He rubs his fingers hard over my clitoris and I shudder with the sensations firing off inside me. 'I can remember some other times when you've been this luscious . . .'

Suddenly I put my hand over his, stopping him from toying with me. 'No, stop,' I pant, hardly able to believe what I'm saying. 'Not here. Not yet.'

'Don't you want to?' he breathes.

'Of course I do,' I say longingly. 'But not in here, where anyone might walk in, even though that girl is at the door. It doesn't feel right.'

'We might not get another chance.' He smiles. 'But I know what you mean.' He finds my lips with his and we share a lingering kiss as he takes his hand away. I moan, regretting my decision, wondering if we should ignore our reservations and satisfy ourselves as we both yearn to, but he's already pulling my skirt down over my bottom. He picks up our masks and the next moment we're heading out of the play dungeon and back through the bedroom.

'When do you think we can be together?' I say breathlessly as we walk quickly out of the private area, passing the girl in the cat-suit who's been standing guard.

'Later. Let's get back to Andrei. One of the reasons I haven't been in touch is that I have a feeling my calls and emails may be monitored. Once I knew you were working for him, I didn't want to take the risk. Believe me, it's best if he doesn't know we're involved.' We stop in a passageway, oblivious to masked partygoers pressing past us. Dominic looks deep into my eyes. 'There's a very big deal on the horizon. The Siberian one is small fry compared to it. I'm managing it, and my completion bonus will buy me independence from Andrei. I'm setting up on my own after that, and we'll both be free of him.'

'But why would he care that we're together? Or that you're leaving? Surely people leave his employment all the time.' I remember Marcia's words about Andrei paying so well, so that people will never want to leave.

Dominic takes one of my hands in his. 'You've seen a charming side of Andrei. There's another side, believe me. Territorial. Reckless. Irrational. He'll take a rejection, *any* rejection, even someone not falling in love with him or deciding to move to another job, as a sign of betrayal. He could even be jealous of our relationship, if he knew about it. He likes to be centre of the universe and he just can't help himself.' He brings my hand to his lips and kisses the knuckles gently. 'I couldn't bear to put you in harm's way.'

'Harm's way?' I echo. 'He wouldn't hurt me.'

'He might, subtly. He might make life difficult for you. I've seen it, I know. You must trust me on this. It's why I want us to play it safe, only for another few weeks, I promise.'

'And us?' I ask quietly. 'Are we all right?'

He leans towards me and says huskily, 'If you mean, am I faithful to you, then the answer is *yes*.'

'But the other things, the issues about wanting to hurt me, about feeling like you betrayed my trust . . .

146

have you worked through it?' I search his face, wanting reassurance.

'Beth . . .' He releases my hand and strokes his own across my face. 'I want that more than anything. We need some time and space to discuss things properly, not here in this madhouse. The good news is that I'm back in London while this deal is settled.'

'Really?' Joy surges through me. 'You're back?'

He nods, smiling. 'I was going to surprise you, but you managed to turn the tables on that one, rather more effectively than I could have guessed.'

I wrap my arms around him and hug him tightly. 'Oh Dominic, that's amazing. How wonderful. I'm so happy.'

'So am I. All I've wanted for weeks is to be back in London with you. It's the first time I've ever been miserable travelling. You're doing something very strange to me, Beth Villiers. You're turning me into a homebody.' He laughs, the happiest, most delightful sound I've heard for ages, and then we're kissing, deep, hard, passionate and yet so tender. *Oh, these kisses are amazing*, I think, as my insides spin lazily, sending out pleasurable tingles across my body. *They're so full of promise and so loving* . . . I adore the frenzy of our sexual passion too, but these sweet kisses are like a balm for a wound, full of delicious healing that restores the two of us and all we mean to one another.

He pulls away suddenly, his eyes worried. 'We're not wearing our masks. Anyone could see us.' He hands mine to me and I slip it on. The next moment, we are as anonymous as anyone else at the party, but Dominic holds my hand as we head back to the private room. When we arrive, the room has plenty of people in it but none of them are Andrei and Anna. We head back out and down into the main party chamber, standing at the edge of what has now become a giant dance floor, as music thuds all around us.

'Look,' Dominic says, and indicates where a couple are dancing together. I recognise Anna from the lush dark hair snaking down her back and the strapless dress. She's dancing close to a man and I'm sure it's Andrei. Her arms are twining around him, pulling him close and his hands rest on her small waist as he gazes down into her masked face.

'You see,' Dominic says, speaking loudly to be sure of being heard above the music. 'Anna has a completely different fish to fry.'

'She's after Andrei?' I ask. 'She has been very flirtatious with him. I wondered if they were in a relationship.'

'They are. One of those fluid, unacknowledged relationships. A beautiful woman and a powerful man, working together, both single . . . they sleep together from time to time. I'm not sure if Anna wants more, or if that's enough for her.'

'And Andrei?' I think about what he said to me over dinner. That seems so long ago now. 'What does he want?'

Dominic shrugs. 'No one knows. But I wonder if there's room for anyone in that heart of his. I've not yet seen any woman manage to make him love her more than he loves himself.'

'Poor man.'

Dominic squeezes my hand and smiles. 'That's what I love about you, Beth. Only you could look at billionaire tough guy Andrei Dubrovski, maybe the most selfish man on the planet, and feel sorry for him.'

'We all need love,' I declare, 'no matter how rich or poor or whatever.'

'Of course we do. But some people are their own worst enemies.'

Just then, Andrei turns and his blue eyes land exactly on us, as though he knew where we were all the time. He lifts a hand and beckons us over.

'Come on,' Dominic says, 'and remember – no touching, no looks. We don't know each other.'

'Right.' I mentally set my shoulders, and prepare for the challenge.

I can't wait for all this to be over so that Dominic and I can be together, as we're supposed to.

'Dominic, come and dance with Anna for a while, she's tiring me out,' commands Andrei.

Dominic gives my arm an imperceptible squeeze as he says, 'My pleasure. Anna, shall we try out some moves?'

'Sure,' Anna says. She seems a little drunk, or at least lost in the vibe of the party. The music is changing from exuberant dance tracks to something a little more trancey. The beat is more thudding and repetitious and it's no longer about upbeat party songs, but the experience of writhing bodies getting close to one another. Coloured lights flash around the walls and ceilings, some in psychedelic patterns, others randomly. I notice an old black-and-white movie playing across one wall – *La Dolce Vita,* I think – the action silent and played out against the rhythmic beat. In other parts of the great circular dome, I realise that other films are playing, or rather appearing and disappearing in random patterns, and I see flashes of thigh, the mound of a buttock, arms wrapped around a naked back, faces with lips parted and wet. The flashing nature makes it strangely more beautiful and erotic than if it were a steamy film played straight. The party is obviously developing from the gorgeous masked ball to something more liberated and licentious.

I look over enviously as Anna starts dancing with Dominic, and think crossly, *To hell with this secrecy! I know what I want – I don't see why we have to dance to Dubrovski's tune.*

At that moment, the man himself come up close and speaks loudly in my ear so that I can hear him over the noise. 'Come on, Beth, let's get another drink.'

I don't really need another drink but I don't feel as light-headed as I did a while ago – in fact, I feel quite sober – so I suppose it can't hurt. We make our way through the dancers, and I glimpse couples who are already embracing with a passion I wouldn't usually expect to see on the dance floor. I see the white rabbit woman from before, her body pressed against a masked man who is kissing her chest just above the low neck-line of her dress. As I watch, he gently pulls the white silk down an inch, and runs his tongue over her breast and nipple.

'Perhaps we should go soon,' I say as we approach the bar, although I can hardly bear the idea of leaving Dominic here in this place that's heaving with sexual possibility.

'Yes,' Andrei replies. He signals to the barman. 'The house special, please.' He turns to me. 'After this drink, we will go. We will stay at the hotel tonight. I've arranged a driver to return us there.'

The barman puts two drinks in front of us, pale pink liquid over ice cubes. I have no idea what they are. Andrei hands one to me and clinks his glass against mine.

'To your very good health,' he says.

'And yours.' I take a sip of the drink. It's fruity and sweet, almost like a glass of cordial, but I'm sure that it must be more potent than it seems. *I won't drink much. We'll be leaving soon.*

Anna appears through the crowd, her cheeks hectic and her eyes sparkling. 'I'm thirsty!' she declares. 'Barman, a glass of water please.'

I look behind her, straining to see if Dominic is following but there's no sign of him. The barman serves Anna quickly, and she gulps her water. Then she puts her arm around my shoulder. 'Are you enjoying yourself, Beth? Are you having fun?'

'Yes,' I say, 'it's certainly interesting.'

She throws back her head and laughs, showing her perfect teeth, her hair rippling down her back. 'Interesting? Perhaps. You should dance. But I warn you, the dance floor is turning to mud. Look at my shoes!' She lifts her skirt and raises one of her slender calves to show Andrei and me that her satin shoe is coated in a yellowish mud. With her foot lifted, she overbalances and falls against me so that I have to put my arms out and hold her up. She clutches me, giggling. 'Whoops! I'm sorry, Beth, I nearly made you spill your drink. It looks good – let me taste it.' She takes my glass and sips at it.

'I'll get your own drink if you want one,' Andrei says. He is watching her impassively, neither amused nor irritated by her evident tipsiness.

'Don't bother. Where's Dominic?' she cries. 'I want to dance! Can you see him?'

We look over at the dance floor but it's a sea of bodies and masked faces. I can't see him anywhere. *What's he doing? Dancing with someone else?* I imagine him in the arms of another woman, perhaps the rabbit girl with her slinky white dress. It's a horrible but irresistible picture. *I've got to keep on top of this jealousy . . . it's ridiculous.*

Anna gives my drink back and grabs her skirts and lifts them up around her thighs, shaking them like a Spanish dancer as she returns to the dance floor.

'She's enjoying herself,' remarks Andrei. 'Perhaps a little too much.'

I watch as she disappears into the crowd, wishing I could be as free and unrestrained as Anna. I'd love to be dancing in there with Dominic, our bodies pressed close, our mouths meeting . . . it's frustrating to know he's so near and yet I can't be with him.

The effect of the lights and music is hypnotic. The volume has been turned up until it's almost too loud to talk, and we stand at the bar, sipping our drinks and watching the crowd. My eyes are drawn to the flashing lights, the snippets of film, the black-and-white movie playing on the wall, and when I try to see Dominic in the mass of dancers I can't make him out at all. Some people have discarded their masks but most are still wearing theirs, and I become entranced by the sight of so many anonymous figures moving in time to the music. They look strange now, their masks bizarre, everything seems weird. I turn to Andrei and he's not there. I'm surrounded by people and all the men look like him, in dinner suits and masks, but none of them are him, I'm certain. I would recognise those blue eyes and the jutting lower lip and I can't see them. I begin to push my way through the throng at the bar, looking for him. *He was right here, he was just beside me a moment ago. He must have moved a few steps away, I'll soon find him.*

I skirt the bar, craning to see over the broad backs of the men or the slim shoulders of the women, but he's nowhere to be found. It's hot now. I realise that the walls are shiny with moisture and that great drips, like giant tears, are sliding down them. The floors are getting muddy and slippery. The heat generated by all the dancers and their bodies is condensing inside the

153

old catacombs. Suddenly I long to get away from the damp heat and breathe some fresh air, to shake out the dizziness in my head. *But I must find Andrei, where is he?* I decide to go back to the room we first went to. Perhaps he's gone back there to sit down quietly for a while. I head back in the direction I remember we came from, but after a moment it dawns on me that I must have taken the wrong pass. I'm stumbling along a dimly lit, low-roofed passage, past people who are locked in embraces, some pressed against the walls regardless of the wet or the white lime coming off on their clothes and skin. I pass nooks and crannies where there is more activity: shadowy forms joined together, moving in rhythm, some standing, some lying entwined on a floor of cushions. Skin glows white or gleams darkly where dim light catches it, hands reach for bodies, fingers are caressing, tongues sucking, licking and lapping. I keep on, not knowing where I'm going but feeling I mustn't stop in case I'm absorbed into one of those dark places to become a body like the others, pulled in by the anonymous hands and made one of them even if it's almost tempting to surrender myself to it all, to become simply a body devoted to bodily pleasure. I could close my eyes and let my hands and tongue go where they wanted . . .

No. Don't do it. I have the horrible feeling I'll be lost for ever if I step inside one of those caves.

My heart is pounding and panic is beginning to take over. I'm lost. I must find . . . I don't care about Andrei any more, I must find Dominic. If I find him, I'll be

154

safe. *But he's behind me, in the big cavern, dancing . . .
I must go back there.* I spin around in the gloom and
start stumbling back the way I came, feeling the fetid
heat rising from below as though I'm approaching an
oven. I come to a fork in the passage and can't remember which way I came from, or even seeing a fork
before. I choose the most likely and press on, past the
couples kissing and caressing in the passageway.

Oh no, I must have chosen the wrong path!

I'm heading off in the wrong direction now, turning
away from the centre of the catacombs and towards
somewhere quieter and cooler. A sob of panic catches
in my throat. I can't think clearly, I can't decide what
to do. What if I never find my way out of here? What
if I'm doomed to wander lost among these caves until,
at last, I fade away down here in the darkness, alone?
My breathing comes faster. I can't keep going on like
this. I must stop. Turn back. Try to find my way back
to the cavern.

I start to retrace my steps. If only the booming didn't
resound from the walls and deceive my ears, cheating
me into taking the wrong way. Suddenly I'm in a
passage that's very quiet and dark. I press forwards
and put out my hands. I touch a wet, cold, hard wall.
I've reached a dead end. I'm completely alone.

I gasp out loud. How did I arrive here? I can't understand – I seem to be losing small patches of time. I hear
a rustle behind me and whirl round. Against the dim
light from the way I've come, there is a tall dark solid
shadow. A man.

I stare at him, my eyes wide, unable to make a sound. I'm trapped in a weird nightmare over which I have no control. Only moments ago, or so it seems, I was at the heart of the party. *How did I get here?*

'Beth?' The word is hardly more than a whisper, but it is the greatest thing I've ever heard.

Dominic!

'You found me!' I say, my voice catching. 'Thank God, you've found me.' I throw myself into his arms and reach up for his head, pulling his face to mine. 'I've been so stupid, I got lost, I thought you'd never find me! I'm so glad you're here.' I kiss him fiercely with all the passion of my relief and joy at seeing him. He pulls off my mask and discards it on the floor.

His arms wrap around me tightly and he begins to kiss me back with great intensity. I close my eyes, yielding myself to his tongue, and feel as though I've lifted off my feet and am floating in the air, as though we are both spinning magically through space, or as if the whole universe is revolving around us and we are the only still point in it. It's a wonderful feeling but very strange, and the kiss is beautiful but not like any kiss we've ever had before, with its fantastical power to make me feel like this.

I'm hungry for him in a way I cannot resist and I press my hand against him, feeling his erection strong and hard inside his clothes.

'Do you want this?' he whispers.

'Yes, oh yes, please . . .'

'You didn't want to before. Are you sure this is right?'

'I want it now, right now.'

He murmurs to me: 'No more games' and clasps me around my waist. It feels as though I'm flying as he lifts me up and turns me round, setting me down so that my back is to him. He takes my arms and lifts them, putting my hands out and against the wall. The rock beneath my palms is chilly and hard but I barely notice. I'm too focused on what is happening elsewhere as Dominic pushes down the top of my dress with one hand, and pulls up the skirt with the other. My breasts are released, fully exposed as the dress had built-in cups and I'm not wearing a bra. One of his palms cups me roughly and I hear a harsh growl of pleasure from him as his hand rubs around my naked bottom and then round to the front, where he brushes his fingers lightly across me.

It's electric, and with every touch he seems to be setting off a riot of coloured stars around me. My body responds enthusiastically, almost slavishly. There's nothing I can do to stop the fevered longing for him to possess me. The way he touched me in the play dungeon was just a preparation for this, and it's as though I'm an engine already warm, waiting to roar into life and speed to its limits. Everything in me thrums under his hands and to the rough, needy fingers flicking over me, rubbing my nipples into stiff peaks, burning a trail over my belly at the sensitive point where it meets the soft thatch of hair below, and tantalising me as he nears my most secret places.

I know that he's ready too. He's squeezing and caressing my breasts, kissing my back at the base of my neck, but I know we won't be playing for long, our desires are too urgent. He pulls my bottom into his groin and moans, relishing the feel of me pressing against him. Then with one arm around my waist, he's pushing my legs apart with the other hand. Another instant and I feel the heat and hardness of his shaft pressed between my buttocks, and I let out a low sound of neediness. He's so close, so tormentingly close. All I can think is that I want his iron hardness inside me now, this instant. 'Please,' I say, a begging note in my voice. 'Please, I've waited so long . . .'

'It's all yours,' he says, his voice low and whispered. 'Just for you.'

He presses my legs further apart and I lean forward. My breasts touch the old stone of the wall and my nipples rasp against the rough surface. They are so sensitive with arousal that the rock scratches and burns them with a delicious kind of pain. I put my head back, knowing that I'm open and ready now, just waiting for the touch I'm desperate for.

He pulls away just a little and then I feel it: he's pressing against me, nudging at my entrance, teasing me with the hot, velvety head of his erection. When I think I can't stand it any longer, he pushes forward and his shaft enters, sliding easily inward with my readiness, giving me the most delectable sense of completion. My hands tense on the rocky wall, my head goes back with the desire to have him entirely inside me. I want to surrender everything, take him as far as he will go. He's deep within me now and his chest is pressed to my back, one hand below my belly, tickling at my wetness, the other on my hips. He drops his head and bites at my neck and shoulders until I'm whimpering with the need for him to start fucking, *now*. Then he pulls back just a little and thrusts forward hard. I cry out as he seems to reach right up into my belly. *Oh God yes – as far, and as hard as you can.*

It's as though he's read my mind. He thrusts again and then again, pulling back on my hips so that I'm brought deeper on to his hard penis. My breasts hit the hard rock with the force of his inward drive, but I relish the heat and pressure of his body at my back and the cold stone at my front. He's getting a rhythm now, driving in and out, every thrust making me cry out involuntarily. My eyes close, and I'm all sensation now, greedily taking him in again and again, and wanting more. The pleasure is beginning to possess me, I'm starting to know nothing but the rise of ecstasy climbing inside me and then lifting me up into that place where I totter on the brink of coming.

He's panting hard in my ear, a throaty noise that buzzes against me, setting off more tiny, crackling fireworks. Then he puts two fingers to my bud and starts to stroke me hard and fast, rubbing back and around, exciting it beyond endurance. It's all it takes to push me over the edge. I hear a high-pitched sound, a keening 'oh', and I know it's my own voice, as I suddenly rush into the torrent of my orgasm. It's all it takes to

159

make him come as well and he thrusts harder still but more slowly, his grip at my waist tightening even more tightly and his weight pressing me forward as he's possessed by the force of his climax. At least it subsides, and we are both left panting. His penis is still hard and thick within me and my muscles hold him there tightly as though unwilling to let go of their beautiful plaything.

'Sweet girl, did you enjoy that?' he whispers, his arm now tight around my waist, supporting us both. His mouth moves in my hair, kissing me lightly.

I nod, speechless.

'Did you want it?'

I nod again.

'Did you need it?'

'Yes . . .' I whisper, my voice light with post-orgasmic weakness.

He withdraws gently, and I sigh as he pulls out, wishing we could stay joined together for ever. A moment later I feel a soft cloth beneath me. He's taken a handkerchief and is wiping me tenderly, making sure that his spending isn't pouring down my thigh. 'There,' he says.

The next moment, I'm overcome with tiredness. It isn't simply fatigue, but a black, all-encompassing exhaustion that utterly saps me. As Dominic is pulling my skirt back into place and I'm trying to put my neckline straight again, I am suddenly overwhelmed by it. My knees begin to buckle and I go weak.

He catches me as I start to fall.

'Tired out, sweetheart?' he says, but his voice sounds distant and slightly warped.

Thank God he's here, I think, and it's my last conscious thought before I switch off like a light and everything goes into blackness.

CHAPTER TEN

I wake in the morning and have no idea where I am, only that my head is pounding and I'm dying of thirst. My eyes hurt as the morning sunlight burns my lids and it is a while before I can open them and look around at my surroundings. I'm naked in a bed in a hotel room, a luxurious one judging by the look of it and by the fact that my bed is a vast double with a toile de Jouy canopy over it. But I'm alone.

I groan at the throbbing in my head, and manage to get myself out of the bed and into the nearby bathroom to get a glass of water. My reflection is truly shocking: my hair is all over the place, my eyes are bloodshot and my skin pale and dry where it isn't red and blotchy.

'Oh my goodness,' I say, appalled. 'What the hell happened?'

I try to recall the previous evening. It is all clear enough until the time when Dominic started dancing with Anna. After that, I have to put everything back piece by piece, searching for flashes of memory until it gradually comes back. I remember how odd I felt, how spacy and disconnected. I remember the horrible panic of being alone in those tunnels, and the strange writhing on the floors of the caves I passed, as if they were

162

covered with snakes slithering over one another. *Then ... of course ...* In the mirror I see my face respond to the memory as my eyes widen and I draw in a sharp breath. I met Dominic in the tunnel. He found me. He rescued me. So where is he now? And who the hell put me to bed?

It takes several glasses of water, a bath and a cup of sweet tea to revive me even a little. The pain in my head subsides to a low thud. *This is so weird. I don't have any clothes except last night's dress. I don't even have a hairbrush or my phone. I hope Laura isn't worried about me, I told her I'd be home even if it was late. And I have no idea where I am, or where anyone else is.*

I assume I'm in the hotel where Andrei and I dined last night. I'm staring at the phone and considering calling Reception to ask for Mr Dubrovski's room, when there's a knock at the door. I pull the hotel bathrobe I'm wearing a little tighter around me and go to answer it.

A bellboy stands outside, holding a large breakfast tray. 'Room service,' he says, and I stand back to let him in. He sets up the tray on a folding table by a white armchair, lifting the silver cloche on the tray to reveal soft scrambled eggs falling over toasted muffins with folds of dark-pink smoked salmon on the side. A cafetière of coffee, a glass of juice and a small basket of French pastries completes the meal. As I smell the coffee's rich aroma, I realise that I'm starving.

The waiter prepares to leave and says, 'Mr Dubrovski sends his compliments, miss. He says someone will be here to collect you in one hour.'

'Thank you,' I reply. So that's part of the mystery solved. *The rest will have to wait until after I've had my breakfast.*

Restored by the delicious food, I put on my evening dress, which has been carefully draped over a chair – *who did that? I don't think it was me* – and dry my hair with the hopeless hotel dryer and only my fingers as a comb, so that I'm ready when the knock comes an hour later.

It's strange that last night this dress was the most gorgeous thing in the world. It feels all wrong this morning. Like a badge of shame. Like I've had a one-night stand and everyone's going to know.

I open the door expecting to see Dubrovski standing there, but instead it is Anna, laughing, her slanted green eyes dancing.

'Oh wow,' she says through her laughter. 'You look pretty bad.'

'You don't,' I say honestly. She is bright and fresh in a white shirt, black pencil skirt and a bright blue cardigan belted at the waist. Her make-up is perfect and her dark hair ripples glossily over her shoulders.

'The fact I have luggage might have something to do with it,' she says, with a touch of sympathy. 'Here.' She holds out a black trench-coat and I take it gratefully.

'I wasn't expecting to come to a party last night,' I say as I put the coat on. It's a little too big as Anna is taller than I am, but it'll do very well. 'Let alone stay the night somewhere. I didn't even bring a wrap.'

'Don't worry, we're only going from here to the car. You'll be home again in no time,' Anna says cheerfully, and we start walking together down the hotel corridor.

I feel a little awkward as I say tentatively, 'Anna, I know this sounds awful, but I'm a bit hazy about what happened at the end of last night . . .'

'I know,' she replies as we near the lift. She presses the button to call it. 'I could tell you were out of it when Andrei brought you up out of the cave.'

'Andrei brought me up?' I frown. That doesn't sound right.

Anna nods, watching the lift indicator that shows it's approaching. 'Yes. Dominic and I were waiting for you at the entrance to the catacombs, and Andrei brought you out. Well . . . he carried you, really. You were sound asleep, or passed out, or whatever. Then the driver he organised drove us all back here in the Bentley. It was a little cramped but we managed.' Her green eyes slide to me as the lift pings and the doors open. As we step inside, she says, 'It was me who put you to bed, in case you're wondering. All very proper, no men allowed.'

This is a relief, though I can't help flushing slightly as I imagine the beautiful Anna tussling with my unconscious body, somehow getting the evening dress

off me and discovering my lack of underwear underneath. It's not exactly a charming picture.

'You must have had a lot to drink,' she says as the
lift descends. 'Or maybe you're not used to it, huh?
Andrei forgets that not everyone was brought up with
vodka in their milk.'

'That's the funny thing,' I say, frowning. 'I had some
wine with dinner, a martini and a glass of champagne,
but all of that was stretched over hours and I felt fine
until we were—'

Just then, the lift doors open and we step out into
the lobby. I recognise it from the night before. Standing
by the front door are Andrei, still in his evening clothes
but without a bow-tie, and Dominic, in a dark pinstripe
suit and holding a suit bag over one arm. They turn to
see us. Anna's heels click loudly on the floor tiles as we
approach.

'Good morning,' cries Andrei effusively. 'How are
you? All right? Recovered?' He walks a few steps
towards me and takes my hand. 'I must apologise to
you. It's all my fault. I kept you up far too late, and
made you mix your drinks. No wonder you felt so
sleepy. Please forgive me.'

'Of course I forgive you,' I say, a little stiffly from
my embarrassment. 'I hope I didn't make a fool of
myself.' My gaze slides involuntarily to Dominic. He's
looking at me intently, his expression impassive except
for a faint light of tenderness and encouragement
mixed with concern that I'm sure only I can see. 'Good
morning,' I say. I wish that we were able to hug one

another, kiss hello. I want to draw comfort from the softness of his freshly shaven skin, the warm lemony scent of his cologne. Dammit, I wish we'd been able to sleep together, wrapped up in one another the whole night. *This situation is crazy.*

'Good morning,' he returns. 'Did you sleep all right?' His voice is perfectly normal but I think there is an undertone of intimacy that I hope no one else will detect.

'Yes, thank you.'

Andrei pats my shoulder. 'Are you ready to go? Let's head home. The car is waiting in front.'

The four of us go out onto the gravelled forecourt. The hotel looks quite different from last night, when it was floodlit by golden beams. In the grey autumn morning, it's a chillier sight but still beautiful. The Bentley waits, its front wheels turned expectantly towards the gate. We climb in, Andrei and Dominic in the front, Anna and me in the back. As Andrei turns on the engine and drives out of the front gate in a spray of gravel, I sit back in my leather seat, the sense of puzzlement I felt earlier coming back to me like the memory of a bad dream.

What is it that's bothering me?

Apart from having to pretend that I barely know my boyfriend?

Apart from the fact that I passed out and had to be carried by my boss?

That's it, I realise, with a clammy chill. Anna told me that she and Dominic were waiting for me and that

167

Andrei brought me up to the surface. But my last memory is of being with Dominic, and having lost Andrei completely.

I stare unseeing out of the window.

What's going on? How could I have such a big blank in my memory? I wonder if Dominic left me alone at some point and then subtly sent Dubrovski to find me.

Left me passed out, alone, in a passageway? Surely he wouldn't do that. Maybe I wasn't out cold. Maybe I was conscious but just can't recall anything.

I remember looking into Dominic's face the previous night and hearing him say that I had to learn to trust him a little bit more. He must have handled everything the right way, he would definitely have known the best thing to do. What other explanation is there? I can hardly trust my vivid imagination, which is always eager to spring into life and paint me pictures so real I sometimes have trouble remembering that they only happened in my mind.

We're on the motorway now, gathering pace, swiftly overtaking all the other traffic. We're going back to London.

But this time, I remember with relief, *Dominic will be there. At last we'll be together.*

I smile for the first time and try to turn my thoughts towards that.

Andrei decrees that I take the rest of the day off.

Back at Albany, Dominic and Anna do not come in, but head off together with their luggage. I watch him

168

go. It feels strange and wrong that he is going with Anna, leaving me behind with Andrei. In the guest bedroom, I put on my clothes from yesterday, leaving my beautiful new dress on the bed – after all, it doesn't belong to me – and the earrings in their box on the dressing table. All the borrowed finery, left where it belongs. My phone has died overnight, its screen black and unresponsive, refusing to awaken until I give it some power.

When I'm dressed, I let myself out of the set very quietly, hoping not to meet anyone. I hear an unfamiliar voice in the office as I go past. That must be Marcia's stand-in. No one sees me as I go out the front door and through the stairwell into the covered walk. I'm glad to be free. I couldn't concentrate on art today.

I'm not as tired as I expected, though, and I certainly don't feel like going back to my empty flat to sleep during the day. Besides, I feel ill at ease in a way I don't understand. Then it occurs to me. I'll go and find James. I haven't seen him for a while and I miss him.

It is a short walk to James's gallery, up Savile Row, through Hanover Square, over Oxford Street and along Regent Street, then off through smaller, windier back ways to the Riding House Gallery. It's just as it was the first day I stumbled across it earlier in the summer. That feels like a lifetime ago. The notice in the window advertising for a temporary gallery assist-ant changed my life, because James decided to take a punt on a girl who walked in off the street and offered herself for the position. The only difference now is that the window is displaying a different artist and new works adorn the plain white walls within. Through the glass, I can see James's assistant Salim at the desk, looking at something on the computer, but no sign of James himself.

'Hi, Salim,' I say as I enter. 'How are you?'

'Beth, hi.' Salim grins. We've met a couple of times since he took his old job back. 'Good to see you. Have you come to catch James?'

I nod. 'Is he about?'

'Downstairs, getting irate with his own filing system. I've tried to show him a better way, but he won't listen.'

'Thanks.' I head down the poky stairs and the sound of swearing and muttering leads me to where James is knee-deep in cardboard boxes, looking through piles of yellowing paper. 'Don't worry, it will be in the last place you look!' I announce, smiling, as I go into the tiny storeroom.

James looks up startled, then his face breaks into a smile. 'Very helpful.' He puts his hands on his hips and sighs. His glasses are dusty and he has a grey smear over one cheek. 'Bloody paperwork, how I hate it. Invented by utter shits.'

'Something important?'

'Oh, I've got to prove the provenance of something or other, and I know I've got the documents some-where. God alone knows exactly where though.'

'You should stop chucking everything in boxes with the vague idea that you'll come back later to sort it out. You never do.'

James shoots me a look. 'Yes, thank you for that. When I need a statement of the bleeding obvious, I'll know where to come next time. You're as bad as Salim. But . . .' his expression brightens '. . . now you're here, I can stop and forget about it for five minutes. Has Mark let you off the leash?'

'Not Mark,' I say slowly. 'Actually, I'm currently working for Andrei Dubrovski.'

I enjoy watching the surprise cross his face. He rubs his dusty hands on his trousers as he says, 'I think this requires coffee. Pronto. Let's go out.'

Ten minutes later we are in a nearby café, each with a foamy cappuccino in front of us, while I give James a quick rundown of everything that's happened so far. He blinks at me from behind his little round glasses. His face is thin, with high cheekbones and little hollows beneath, and he looks like a professor or an old-fashioned English literary gent. But I know there is much more to him than appears on the surface – he's seen a lot and knows a lot and is very hard to shock. Even so, he is amazed by my revelations.

'You do get yourself in some nice tangles, Beth,' he says, stirring his coffee. 'This is a good one, even by your standards. Secret liaisons in Croatian monasteries? A love that dare not speak its name in case your boss takes against either you, or Dominic, or both?' He shakes his head. 'I can't wait for the next instalment.'

'There's more, if you must know,' I say, and try not

171

to look guilty. 'The thing is, I didn't go home last night.'

James's eyebrows shoot up. 'A dirty stop-out? What *have* you been up to? And now I look at you, you do look a bit crumpled and yesterday's knickers.' He's being jocular and silly but suddenly his expression changes. 'Hold on, Beth. Not . . . not *Dubrovski*.' He looks deadly serious now, worry in his gentle grey eyes. 'Surely not.'

'Of course not!' I say, offended.

James breathes out in a low whistle. 'Thank goodness. I would caution very strongly about getting any nearer to that man than you have to. As you know, I wasn't all that cheerful about you meeting him at all. Now you're bloody well working for him! But as long as it's only for a short while and you keep your distance, you should be all right.'

The colour on my face heightens and I drop my gaze. *I never can keep anything from James. But then, I don't want to. I need his advice, after all.*

He stops stirring his coffee and goes still. 'Beth,' he says in a warning tone. 'What is it? Tell me at once. What's happened?'

'It's all so complicated!' I burst out. 'And I don't know why, I don't want it to be! Andrei asked me to this party and I only said yes because I thought Dominic was going to be there. I didn't know it was going to turn into what seemed like a date with Andrei, he'd never spoken to me in that way or treated me like that. But suddenly, there I am, dressed in Dior and rubies, having dinner with him in a hotel and he's telling me . . .' I falter.

'Yes?'

'Telling me I'm beautiful—'

James groans. 'Oh no.' He puts his hands to his face as if in despair.

'And that I looked most beautiful of all in Croatia – and I could hardly explain to him that my radiance was down to the fact that I'd been getting well and truly laid by Dominic!'

James takes his glasses off and rubs a hand across his brow. 'Is there more?'

'He said . . . he said . . .' I almost can't bring myself to say it so it all comes out in a rush. 'He said that he thought we would make love together one day and that I would want it.'

'Oh, Beth.' James is looking at me with concern all over his face. 'This is bad. What did you say to that?'

'I said no, of course!' I reply, indignant that he could think I'd have said anything else. 'I told him our relationship could only be strictly professional. And that I have a boyfriend.'

'Oh, I expect he'll abide by that then,' James says with airy sarcasm. 'Yes, that should deal with him all right. That's what got Dubrovski where he is today you know, backing down at the first obstacle, not pursuing what he wants with dogged single-mindedness. So how come you ended up staying out?'

I tell him about the party and my descriptions of the orgy make him groan even more, but when I tell him,

173

without too much detail, about my liaisons with Dominic and the revelation that Andrei and Anna are sleeping together, he looks a little happier.

'That's something, I suppose.' He frowns. 'But you remember nothing between meeting Dominic in that passageway and waking up the next morning?'

I shake my head. 'It's a complete blank. Anna says Andrei carried me up out of the catacombs, unconscious.'

'Run me through what you had to drink again . . .'

When I do, he looks even more puzzled. 'That might make you drunk. It might even make you ill or extremely sleepy. But it won't make you comatose – at least, I don't think so. What was that last drink you had?'

'I don't know. Andrei ordered it. The house special. It was a cocktail, pale pink and fruity and very sweet.'

'Oh, dear.' James looks more serious than I've ever seen him. In fact, he's gone a little pale. 'And you felt strange immediately afterwards?'

I think back and remember sipping the pink liquid and how I soon began to feel different. I remember Andrei and me standing together, then Anna, her arm around me, her head thrown back in laughter, and her muddy shoes; and then, a while later, everything changing. I'd thought it was the lights and the music that were making me feel so spacy and strange, and causing time to speed up, slow down and sometimes vanish altogether. That was when Andrei simply disappeared and when I began to wander vaguely, unable to find my way properly. 'Yes,' I say slowly. 'Well, quite soon afterwards.'

James puts his glasses on and thinks hard for a moment, staring down at his coffee. Then he looks up at me, staring me straight in the eye, and says, 'Beth, I think your drink was spiked.'

I stare back, speechless.

'Drugged. God knows what with. Speed? Something that like, I expect.'

I try to process this. 'You think Andrei drugged me?' I ask, appalled.

'I wouldn't leap to that conclusion. It was the house special, you said. I have a feeling that most party-goers would know that the house special contains a halluci-nogenic, or they would be given the nod by the barman if they appeared not to.'

'So . . . Andrei must have known that he was giving me a spiked drink?' A cold horror is draining through me, feeling as though it is taking all my blood with it.

'Let's be charitable and say he didn't but he looked such a sophisticate that the barman assumed he must know the routine. But it's a possibility that he did.'

'Why would he do such a thing?' I feel awful, know-ing that I took drugs like that without realising. I've never touched them and never wanted to. There was a small gang at school who boasted about taking drugs, and some spaced-out boys who smoked a lot of weed, just as there was a racy, party-loving crowd at uni who knew how to get cocaine, ecstasy and all the rest, and didn't consider it a night out unless they'd snorted,

175

smoked or swallowed something contraband. But I never wanted to. I liked the high that came from drinking too many beers and dancing the night away, but not that often and never to excess. Hangovers were too miserable as far as I was concerned. And I never considered drugs anything other than a dead end: if they made you happier than you could be without them, why would you ever want to give them up? Better never to start.

'Perhaps he thought you'd be more in the party mood if you had something to liven you up,' James says. He gazes at me and neither of us say what is going through our heads – that he thought I'd surrender to him more easily if I were high.

'But it didn't happen,' I say. 'I didn't see him again that night – not as far as I remember anyway.'

'Yes. Thank goodness for that.' There's another pause and then James says, 'It definitely was Dominic in the cave with you, wasn't it?'

I have a vivid flashback of the dark outline of him against the dim light of the passageway. I remember his touch, and what he said to me. His voice – well, it was a whisper, hard to identify, but what he said all made sense. It was Dominic. 'Yes,' I say firmly. 'It definitely was.'

'Good.' James's relief is obvious. 'But it would appear that Andrei is not quite the harmless little lamb you believed. Let's just be glad that nothing worse happened than a bit of confusion and a headache in the morning. And thank goodness Dominic was there too, or I dread to think . . . So now will you listen to me and keep your distance?'

I nod. I feel a deep cold anger towards Andrei. And to think that last night I almost felt sorry for him. He'd convinced me to stay at the party with his sob story of how he never gets the chance to relax, just so he could slip me a spiked drink and try his luck. Thank goodness it hadn't worked. 'Yes. You're completely right and I've been all wrong about him. But I'm clued up now and you know what they say – knowledge is power. I'll be on my guard from now on.'

'I think you should walk away from this job right now,' declares James fervently. 'Just get out of there, as soon as you can.'

'No,' I say slowly, 'I can't do that. From what Dominic's said, that's the wrong way to handle Dubrovski. You have to be cunning or he'll decide to crush you. I'm not afraid for myself but I would hate for Mark or Dominic to suffer because he suddenly takes against me. I'll be all right – it's not for much longer and then I'll be done with this private commission, and his deal will be over and he'll probably leave London and forget about me. And Dominic won't be working for him any more either so we'll both be free and able to be honest about our relationship.'

'Just promise me you'll be careful,' James says.

'Of course I will,' I say with a bright smile, though inside I'm feeling less confident than I look. *This is*

177

going to be like trying to get out of the lion's den without him noticing you're even there. Tricky.

I have to wait to charge up my phone until I get home that afternoon, but when I do, there's a backlog of messages and texts from Dominic, asking where I am and what I'm doing. I didn't receive them and perhaps our phones wouldn't have worked underground even if I had. The messages seem to end around 2 a.m., which must have been when he came looking for me and found me, but I don't trust the time stamps on messages anyway, not when they haven't been received in real time.

There is a message from Dominic sent today from his work account. It says simply:

Hello Beth
It was very nice to see you last night, I hope you enjoyed the party and you're feeling better today. It's great to have you on the Dubrovski team!
See you soon,
Dominic.

I read it a few times, wondering if there is some kind of message hidden within the blandness, but I can't see one. I'm just beginning to feel frustrated when another message pops up, this one sent from an email account I don't recognise.

Hi gorgeous
Now I'm back here, I've been able to get on to a laptop that isn't monitored by work. God, I can't wait

178

until we're both free of Dubrovski, I feel like we're being watched all the time. It was marvellous to see you at the party last night even if circumstances were less than ideal. We could have had a much more enjoyable time if it'd been just the two of us ... I can't wait to see you again. How about tonight? In the boudoir?

Love

Dx

I smile as I read it. At last, this is what I've been longing for. Communication – real and loving, like any girl might expect from her boyfriend. My fears and jealousies melt away. I quickly type back a reply.

Thank you for your lovely message, sweetie, and I can't think of anything better than us being in the boudoir again. But the truth is, I'm totally wiped out from last night and I need an early night if I'm going to be any use at all tomorrow. I have to get back to work, all the sooner to get this job done. Can I see you tomorrow night instead? The boudoir sounds amazing. Yes please.

B x x x

The answer comes back almost at once.

Understood. I'm tired myself after that late night. Are you okay, though? I was worried about you last night. When I left you with Andrei, you seemed all right but you were obviously out cold later on. Tell me all about it when I see you tomorrow. Sweet dreams and sleep well tonight, gorgeous. Let's arrange our rendezvous in the morning.

 Dx

I stare at it for a while, a nasty feeling swirling in the pit of my stomach, reading it over and over again. I was fine when he left me with Andrei. When is he talking about? Because I don't remember him leaving me with Andrei after our passionate encounter in the cave. By then, I was oblivious to everything, no doubt lost in my drug-induced haze. So does he mean when Andrei and I left him dancing with Anna? A horrible nausea engulfs me and my hands clench around my phone. Because that would mean he thinks he didn't see me again until after the party.

I stand up, my heart pounding, feeling sicker than ever. My thoughts are racing wildly.

That would mean that it wasn't him in the tunnel. *Oh God. If it wasn't Dominic, then it must have been . . .*

I turn around and catch a glimpse of myself in our sitting-room mirror. I look grey and terrified. The obvious, the only conclusion, is that if the man in the tunnel wasn't Dominic, he must have been Andrei. He greeted me by name. Only Dominic or Andrei would do that. *No. I won't believe it. I can't! I've got things confused, that's all. I'll sort it out with Dominic when I see him.*

But then the nature of my own, personal trap becomes clear. If I ask him whether he made wild love to me in the cave and he says no, he'll know that someone else did. The very thought makes my head spin with horror. Even if he believes that I honestly thought it was him, will it change everything between us?

I was so jealous when I thought even for a moment he was attracted to Anna. What would he think if he knew I'd had sex with someone else?

I shudder. What about me? Have I really been seduced without knowing who it was? I remember the way I welcomed every touch and kiss and caress, how much I yearned for that hard, satisfying fucking. He asked did I want it, was I sure . . . and I said yes. He said 'No more games' and I thought it was Dominic referring to our meeting in the dungeon earlier. I opened myself willingly. I begged for it.

But did he know that I thought it was Dominic? Did I call him by name?

I can't remember if I spoke Dominic's name out loud or not. The thought makes me feel doubly ill. Because if it were Andrei with me in the tunnel last night and I did say it, he can be under no illusion now about how I feel about Dominic.

I sink down to the floor moaning. *Please, let it not be true. Please. Did I have sex with Andrei? And did I really love it as much as I remember?*

CHAPTER ELEVEN

Dominic is furious with me. His eyes are black with rage, his face pale.

'You did *what*?' he says in an ominous voice that quivers with suppressed rage.

I am lying on my front on the bed in the boudoir, wearing only a leather harness that criss-crosses over my breasts and is collared at my neck, and cinched in hard and tight round my waist, leaving my upper back and buttocks bare. My hands are bound to the bed, pulled up over my head and cuffed to the railing that runs along the head. My legs are spread-eagled and each ankle is tethered to an opposite bedpost, leaving me entirely exposed. I want to curl up into a ball, but it's impossible.

'You fucked him?' His voice gets louder until he's almost shouting. 'You fucked Dubrovski? When you know how I feel about you – and about him? How could you, Beth?' His voice changes again, quiet but sharp as a knife. 'Did you enjoy it? His cock shoving away inside you? I bet you did.'

I'm sobbing. 'No, please believe me . . . I thought it was you, I thought you were in the cave with me! Not him. I had no idea, I promise.'

'Likely fucking story, Beth. Give me some credit.'

'I was drugged, tripping, and it was pitch black!'

'You fucked him. And you loved it.' His voice is icy.

'No, no . . .' I can't believe this is happening; I can't make him believe me. My voice deserts me as sobs grip my chest and throat. My power to explain is gone.

I hear Dominic moving about the room, then he is standing behind me.

'You betrayed me, Beth,' he says in a low voice. 'After everything we've been through, and everything I've done for you. You cheated on me. Now you can do something for me.'

'What?' I managed to gasp between sobs. 'I'll do anything for you, you know that.'

'Really? Then you'd better show me by taking what's coming to you.'

I'm waiting for him to tell me what I can do to convince him when the blow comes. The cat o' nine tails, that stinging creature with its hundreds of sharp little teeth, comes down hard on my back. I'm braced for pain, the crackling of my skin underneath its bite. I know that the cat is usually brought out when the skin is already warmed by softer, gentler instruments – Dominic is obviously determined to make me suffer the most extreme of punishments. But I don't feel the bitter pain I'm expecting. Instead the whip's touch is more like a hot caress, sending out tiny cracks of lightning over my back. I gasp.

It comes down again and I can hear from the thwack that it's coming down harder and faster. Dominic's putting his strength into it. But again, rather than cutting me with agony, the blow is deliciously invigorating to my senses. I feel myself begin to come alive underneath it, the smarting whack making my sex hot with need.

'I can see you,' Dominic says. 'I can see you getting wet with your punishment. Are you thinking about Dubrovski?'

'No,' I whimper, but not loudly enough for Dominic to hear and he's preparing another blow for me anyway. They begin to pelt down on me, falling on me like burning rain, making me melt and burn in my groin and feel a desperate need for him to take me to the edge of this pleasurable pain.

'This is your punishment,' he says. 'Are you sorry?'

'I'm sorry, yes, I'm sorry . . .' I manage to say as the cat flicks maddeningly all over my fevered back, sometimes over the tops of my thighs and the soft globes of my buttocks.

'Sorry what?'

'Sorry, sir. I'm sorry!'

'Beg for forgiveness and perhaps I won't cut you to shreds.'

The whip cuts me again, a couple of its strands coming down over my tender exposed sex, licking inside like sharp leather tongues. I scream out. *Are there any limits here? What did we agree?* I can't remember.

'Beg me,' he hisses.

'I beg you for forgiveness, sir.'

'Aren't you enjoying your thrashing, my little slave?'

'No, sir, no . . . I mean, yes . . . oh God.' I cry out again as the cat takes a sudden stinging journey over my buttocks. My sex throbs with need.

The blows suddenly stop and I moan. I'm not there yet but I'm in a maddened place where my body is yearning for it so much, I can hardly stand it. I feel a pressure on the bed. He's behind me, kneeling between my spread thighs. He's gripping me by the hips, lifting up my backside and then he's plunging his hot hard cock into my slippery depths, not pausing to savour me but thrusting on with fierce intensity, fucking with no thought for me but for his own pleasure and it's unbearably exciting. I want to be his vessel, to let him take his pleasure. My back is alive with the sizzling after-effects of the whipping, my bottom tender but thrilling to the thwack of his groin and balls against it. He's fucking me so hard, concentrating only on driving his shaft in and out.

He leans down over my back. 'Do you like this?' he whispers.

I'm shuddering and stiffening. My body is working independently of my mind, its quivering and ready to release my climax on to the hot cock that's slamming in and out of me.

The voice in my ear says, 'Come on, come for me, Beth, I know you love it, just like you loved it in the cave,' and as I gasp and shriek with the intensity of my orgasm and as I whirl into the intoxicating sensations,

I realise that it is not Dominic who is fucking me, but Andrei Dubrovski.

I wake up hot and confused. I'm in my bed at home, and not in the boudoir at all. But it was so horribly real, so intensely physical ... I feel drained and yet agitated and unfulfilled at the same time.

Did I come in my sleep? And who did I imagine was fucking me? I feel ashamed at the thought that I might have been unconsciously fantasising about Andrei. *You love Dominic*, I tell myself harshly. And I know that I definitely, most certainly, do not want to have sex with Andrei.

Dreams are tricks, not revelations. They don't tell a straightforward story.

I lie back on my pillows, pulling my duvet up around me, remembering the whip in my dream. Ever since I felt the marks on Dominic's bare back, I've been dreaming of whips in one form or another, but never like this. Never with this kind of intensity. *Or pleasure.*

I shiver as I recall it. But whips don't simply sting deliciously, I know that. They hurt and cut, and make tender skin bleed, weal and scar. I've felt the power of an extreme flogging and I hated it. So why, in my dreams, do I love it so much?

Perhaps my imagination is working overtime because I'm seeing Dominic tonight, and in the boudoir, where he first initiated me into the more adventurous ways of making love.

And perhaps I'm also worried about what I'll find out. I'm relieved that Dominic, as yet, has no idea of my fears about what happened in the cave. I feel sure, in my heart, that it was Dominic who made love to me. But perhaps that's just wishful thinking.

I arrive at work nervously.

Laura noticed the change in me over breakfast when I was reluctant to talk about everything that had happened since she'd last seen me.

'You mean Dominic's back?' she demanded, stirring milk into her muesli, a towel wrapped around her damp hair. 'And your pet billionaire took you to a masked ball and a night in a plush hotel? No wonder you're depressed.'

I smile. 'Of course I'm not. I'm very happy Dominic's home again. I'm sure it will lift my spirits. It's just . . .'

'What?'

'I don't know.' I shrug. 'Feeling low.'

Laura tsked. 'No pleasing some people. Well, send your sexy Russian my way if you're tired of him, that's all I can say.'

If only she knew, I think as I pass the lodge at the entrance of Albany and nod my hello to the porter. *But I can't tell anyone. Not even James. This has to be my secret and mine alone.*

Sri answers the door to me, rather than the body-guard, so Andrei must be out.

'Gone to work,' Sri confirms in a small voice when I ask.

187

I can hear the clack-clack of a keyboard from the office, and when I go in there is a young man I've never seen before, dressed in a cream suit, his fair hair neatly combed. He looks up enquiringly as I come in and says, 'Can I help you?'

'I'm Beth, I'm working on Andrei's art for the flat.'

He nods. 'Oh yes. I've heard. I'm Edward, and I'm filling in for Marcia while she's away.'

'Any news about her mother?' I ask.

'Recovering, apparently. She's got something in her chest. Polaris.'

'Polaris?' I echo. 'Isn't that a kind of missile?'

Edward frowns. 'You're right, it's not polaris.'

'Pneumonia?' I suggest.

He looks a little affronted. 'I think I would remember if it was pneumonia. That's very easy to remember, isn't it?'

'Well then . . . um . . .'

'I'm sure it begins with P,' he murmurs, gazing down at his keyboard.

'Polio?' I suggest.

He gives me a slightly withering look. 'If you're going to be silly . . .'

'Psoriasis?' I hazard, teasing him.

'That doesn't even begin with P,' he retorts. 'It doesn't matter anyway. She's getting better. I shan't be here for long, just a day or two, so I won't get in your way.' He leans towards me, suddenly cosy and conspiratorial. 'He's quite a one, your boss, isn't he? Very He-Man. And by the looks of things, he's dragged

She-Ra back to his den for a bit of one-to-one combat, if you know what I mean.'

I frown, remembering my brothers watching cartoons during the summer holidays when I was very little. 'He-Man and She-Ra were brother and sister, weren't they?'

'Were they?' He shrugs. 'It's all a bit before my time. Anyway, he's obviously quite the lady-killer from the sounds of it.' He gestures over his shoulder with his thumb in the direction of the hall. 'You'll see, I expect. Now, I'd better press on, this man's diary is more complicated than *The Times* cryptic crossword.'

I think he's stopped talking about fantasy figures now, so I head to the study. So much has happened since I was here only two days before. I realise that the pile of work still to do has diminished and that I'll soon be able to start considering how to hang the pictures. There is more than enough to create a stunning collection here. But there is nothing that is quite suitable as the stand-out piece Andrei wants for his bathroom.

I feel grateful that Andrei isn't here. I don't know how I could face him now. Perhaps James was right and I should tell him to stuff his stupid job . . . But . . . *what if it wasn't him, but Dominic? Then everything's all right* . . . And if it wasn't, and it *was* Andrei . . . *then did he know I thought he was Dominic? Or did he think I wanted him?* 'No more games.' That was what I heard. Could it have referred to our conversation at dinner, when he flirted with me and I rebuffed him?

And then there's my worry that, if it was him, Andrei heard me call him the wrong name and has guessed my feelings for Dominic.

It's an awful mess but I remind myself that I'm seeing Dominic later. Surely then I'll find out one way or another, even if I can't ask him directly what happened.

I feel the need for coffee before I start, so I wander out in the direction of the kitchen, hoping to find Sri there. She can show me how to make it. I'm lost in thought and almost bump into a tall figure in a red silk robe.

'Dreaming again?' says a teasing voice and I look up into Anna's bright green eyes. She's standing in the hallway, glamorous despite her lack of make-up and her tousled hair.

'Hello, Anna,' I say, flushing. It's obvious she's just come out of Andrei's bedroom.

'Hello to *you*.' Her rich voice always sounds as though it has a laugh rolling somewhere inside it. 'Have you recovered from your little adventure the other night?'

'Yes, thank you,' I say, a little stiffly. I don't want to discuss it with her and I hope she gets the hint.

She stretches a little and yawns. 'Good. Now, I need some coffee. Shall we get some together?'

Without waiting for an answer, she turns and heads for the kitchen, her dark-red silk robe fluttering around her long legs as she goes. She doesn't seem to find it at all awkward that she has just emerged from Andrei's bedroom after having clearly spent the night there.

'Sri, your finest Columbian blend, please, strong as you can make it without dissolving the spoon,' she cries as she breezes into the kitchen. 'You always make such excellent coffee, the best anywhere.' Sri obeys, bustling about as we sit down at the kitchen table.

Anna fixes me with her direct look. 'I expect you're wondering what I'm doing in Andrei's bedroom.'

'Not at all,' I say politely.

She laughs. 'You're so English! So funny.' Then, adopting an exaggerated English accent, she says in a funny voice, 'Nort et awl.'

'Well,' I say, relaxing a little, 'it's obvious, isn't it? I think you and Andrei were playing a very long drawn-out game of Battleships.'

She throws back her head and laughs properly, showing her elegant white throat. 'Yes, that's right! Battleships. That's an excellent name for it. One day you will tell me what Battleships is. It sounds good fun.'

Sri brings over a pot of steaming coffee, a milk jug and some cups, and puts them on the table for us.

'Thank you, Sri,' says Anna. She takes the pot and starts to pour out our coffee. 'You have guessed no doubt that although Battleships sounds like a marvellous way to spend a night, that is not what Andrei and I were doing. We are lovers. Occasional, but no less passionate for that.'

I take the cup she proffers and tip in some milk. *Why is she telling me this?* I say nothing and she continues.

191

'I expect you've already noticed that Andrei has a passionate nature, very passionate indeed. He's quite the romantic hero, in some ways: strong, powerful . . . dominant.' She fixes me with her liquid gaze and lets it rest on my face for a while as if reading my reaction carefully. I stay silent so she goes on. 'I thought that when I saw you both come up out of the catacombs after the party. He was carrying you as easily as if you weighed nothing, his arms wrapped around you. You looked rather dramatic, as though you'd fainted, with your head on his shoulder, your arms around his neck, that pretty dress floating all around you. I was glad to learn that you were all right. Dominic and I were quite worried about you.'

My stomach twists nervously. 'You were?' *Can she tell me more about that night, something that might give me a clue? Does she know something?*

She nods. Before answering, she takes a sip of her black coffee, then says, 'We were afraid you'd managed to get lost. We all went off to look for you, each one of us took a different route to the surface, hoping to find you on the way, and it was Andrei who did.'

I can't stop myself asking, 'Not Dominic?' There's almost a pleading note in my voice. I hope she hasn't noticed.

'Oh no. He met me at the surface not long after we all separated.' She laughs again. 'If I were a jealous woman, Beth, I might be jealous of you.' She shakes her finger at me as though scolding me. 'To see you in my lover's arms, as helpless as a rescued kitten . . .

well, I might be afraid that you'd stirred something in him, something protective, perhaps even . . . loving.'

'Don't be afraid of that,' I say. My voice is strong simply because I feel numb and almost horrified. *Is it really true? It was Andrei who found me – not Dominic?* 'There's nothing going on between Andrei and me. And besides, that was two nights ago, and he was with you last night. So you've got nothing to fear.'

She sighs happily, almost contentedly, as though recalling a delightful, voluptuous experience. 'You're right. He was.' She puts her hands up to her face, propping her chin on her fists, and her silken sleeves slide down her arms, revealing her wrists. My eye is drawn immediately to the bright circlet of colour around her right wrist. A beautiful enamel bangle edged in tiny diamonds sits there prettily, the stones glinting in the overhead lights. She sees where I'm looking and says casually, 'Oh – I see you've noticed this. Do you like it?' Her other hand goes to it and circles it gently around her wrist, showing me the enamelled pattern. 'Lovely, isn't it? Andrei gave it to me. It belonged to a Russian princess, an ancestor of mine, in fact. He bought it for me especially, knowing the connection. Isn't that sweet of him? He's so busy and yet he found this for me.' She smiles. 'I'll always treasure it.'

'It's beautiful,' I respond, not knowing whether to call her on the exact Russian princess she's talking about, or just be pleased that the gift I bought has so obviously been a success. I can't help glancing at her earlobes in case Andrei has taken the earrings I left in

193

their box in the guestroom and given them to Anna after all. But her lobes are bare. 'Your relationship with Andrei must be serious.'

'Mmm.' She smiles again. 'I think so. But time will tell, I'm in no hurry to tie myself down just yet. What about you, Beth? A pretty girl like you, there must be someone important in your life . . .?'

'Yes,' I say. 'I've got a boyfriend. He's wonderful. It's going well.'

She leans towards me and I catch her perfume in my nostrils: a rich and dark scent. 'What's he like? Tell me about him.'

'I . . . I don't like to talk about him. I prefer to keep it private.'

'Does Andrei know?'

I wonder why she's asking but I say, 'Yes. I told him.' *Just in case you two indulge in some pillow talk. Your stories will tally.* I take a gulp of my coffee and say, 'Thank you for the charming chat, Anna. I must get back to work now. Perhaps I'll see you later.'

'Perhaps,' she replies, lounging back in her chair, playing with her bracelet again. 'Or some time. Take care, Beth.'

I get up, thank Sri for the delicious coffee, and head back to the study. In the safety of my own space, I shut the door, lean against it and let out a deep breath. This place is getting stranger, with the odd Marcia replaced by the even odder Edward, and now with Anna wafting about in a cloud of sexual satisfaction and very much marking her territory, while her lover has been coming on to me . . .

And perhaps even going further.

I close my eyes, trying to keep calm. If Anna's telling the truth about what happened after the party, it seems more and more likely that I made a terrible mistake that night in the catacombs. The thought of it makes me feel sick with regret and fear of what the consequences might be.

I go back to my work, trying to push it out of my mind. I need to get this job done so I can get out of here, and one step closer to a normal life with the man I love.

If I haven't wrecked it already, that is . . .

CHAPTER TWELVE

The thoughts rolling around my head in a ceaseless loop are almost driving me crazy. The only way I can cope is to put them out of my mind altogether, and think solely about the job in hand. That afternoon, I finish going through the collection in the study, an achievement that raises my mood just a little.

I go to the office to finish typing up my work, and try not to listen to Edward gossiping on the telephone to his friends. I suppose he doesn't much care about this job, as he'll only be here till Marcia gets back.

An email pings into my inbox and I click on it. It's from Dominic, sent via his private account.

Hi gorgeous
 I can't wait to see you tonight. Shall we say the boudoir at 8? I think we'll eat in tonight, don't you? Let me know if you can't make it, otherwise I'll see you then.
 Dx

Just a few days ago, an email like this would have sent me into the stratosphere with delight and anticipation. Now I read it over, feeling guilty and miserable. No matter that I'm innocent in my heart, if I'm technically in the wrong, then how can I possibly explain it in a way that Dominic will understand?

How will I live with myself? And if it was Andrei, surely he'll speak to me about it – and what on earth will I say?

I leave Albany at five o'clock and wander along Piccadilly, and then down to Jermyn Street, trying to take my mind off my worries by window-shopping. I turn off into another street where there is a series of art galleries, their windows displaying magnificent works, showing them off to their best advantage with the soft glow of spotlights. My eye is caught by a painting of a girl reading. She is in profile, sitting on a settle or in a window seat against a plump silk cushion, her head bent to read the volume she holds in one hand, while her other arm is draped comfortably over the arm of her seat. She is young, with fresh pink cheeks and a smooth forehead, her eyes downcast to the page she's reading, her hair pulled up into a simple high bun around which a ribbon has been tied. She looks modern, and yet she's wearing the costume of the eighteenth century with a distinctly French air: a pale yellow dress with a tight bodice, long sleeves with lacy white cuffs, a pink ribbon tied in a flouncy bow at the low breast. A white ruff – what they called a fichu, I think – is around her neck, fastened at the back with more of the pink ribbon she evidently likes so much. It's serene and beautiful, and captures the girl so well I almost expect to see her chest move, or her fingers flutter forward to turn the page.

I can see that the gallery owner is about to shut up; he's preparing to pull thickly latticed iron shutters across the windows. With a work like this inside, I can understand why.

On impulse, I hurry in. The owner is balding with a frill of white hair hanging wispily around his neck, and he's red-faced and rather jowly. 'We're closing, I'm afraid,' he says in curt tones.

'The girl in the window, the beautiful painting of the girl reading. How much is she?'

The man blinks at me, open-mouthed, then says, 'That, my dear child, is far more than I think you have to spend.'

I raise my eyebrows at him. 'Try me. Who is the artist?'

'The artist is Jean-Honoré Fragonard.'

Now it's my turn to be surprised. 'Fragonard . . . *the* Fragonard?'

'Well, there are several *the* Fragonards, not least Jean-Honoré's wife, Marie-Anne, not to mention his son and grandson. But yes, if you mean the chocolate box, rococo Fragonard . . . well, that painting is by him.'

I can hardly believe it. Fragonard's most famous works are highly theatrical: costume dramas of frills and flounces, unbelievably slender waists and limbs, and porcelain cheeks with spots of pink. It's Italianate romance done French-style: aristocratic high-jinks in grottos, all silken gowns and picture hats, as kisses are stolen from society ladies by sighing swains. I remember my trip to the Wallace Collection earlier in the summer where I saw his famous painting *The Swing*: a Baroque lovely sits aloft in her swing, flinging her anatomically impossible legs in the air as one tiny pink slipper flies off a minute, white-stockinged foot, and giving her smiling beau a good look under her skirts as she sails over his head. Her pink flounces and ribbons probably inspired hundreds of portraits of fairy-tale princesses and made young girls hunger for dresses just like her rosy confection. The work is beautiful and masterful – but nothing like the painting in the window, with its bold, wide strokes, and its use of colour to show the effect of the light upon the skin and fabric. The girl's face and hair are naturalistic, with tones of blue and lavender, and her proportions are true, which is why she looks more like a late-nineteenth-century, or even early twentieth-century, portrait. The only hint that she might be a Fragonard is her little finger with its jointless curl. Apart from that, I never would have guessed.

The gallery owner has been watching me absorb it all, and now says, 'Yes, it is not the style he is renowned for. You're thinking, no doubt, of his highly constructed works. You may not know his portraiture quite so well, but he was very influential on the Impressionists, including Renoir. Yes, this is his work.' The gallery owner has warmed a little towards me as he enjoys my frank astonishment. 'There is something similar in the gallery in Washington DC. Look it up if you don't believe me.'

'And how much is it?'

He looks at me almost pityingly before he says, 'More than you can afford, my dear. And now, if you don't mind, I must close.'

I let him chivvy me out of the gallery, my mind racing. It's so beautiful. Could this be the *Mona Lisa* for Andrei's bathroom? How gorgeous this girl would look there, her yellow and pink silk and her warm rosy skin against that grey marble! But wouldn't it be wrong to put her in there, where no one but Andrei would ever see her? She should be in his drawing room, perhaps directly across from Napoleon, her quiet peacefulness contrasting with his vainglorious quest for power, her tranquil reading facing down the roar and clamour of the battlefield.

I take one last look at her before I head off. I'll ask Mark. He'll know best. I resolve to go and see him very soon.

At a quarter to eight, I arrive at Randolph Gardens. It's been so long since I've been back to the boudoir, and I want to go and absorb the atmosphere before Dominic and I meet there again. In the lobby of the old apartment building I remember to turn left, rather than right, which was the way I used to go when I was living in Celia's apartment. The little lift takes me up to the seventh floor and as it ascends I remember the times I approached this floor, nervous of what awaited me in the boudoir but also deeply excited and certain that it would be an unforgettable experience. It always was. I've missed it.

And here I am again, I think to myself, a burst of happiness exploding inside me. *I'm going to be with Dominic. I feel as though this is our real reunion.*

I let myself in. The little flat feels deserted and unloved, and I walk through its rooms, now dusty and a little chilly. It's crazy to leave this place empty, but I don't want to live here on my own, it would be too lonely. I thought Dominic and I would use it as our hideaway, but then he left and it's been empty ever since, waiting for him to come back. *Just like me.*

I go to the bedroom last of all. After Dominic left, I cleaned the room and made it all neat and ready again, just in case he should come back unexpectedly. If I'd known then how long I would have to wait, I would have wept. But that's all over now.

The bed is the same, with its rigid posts and iron rail, so useful for tethering cuffs and silken ties. Opposite is the cabinet that contains some of the implements Dominic enjoyed using on me so much, along with ropes and blindfolds. I shiver lightly as I remember some of the erotic journeys he took me on. Over in the corner of the bedroom is the white leather seat, long and narrow and sloping upwards, with places to fasten hands or feet so that the body is exposed for the kiss of the cane or the whip. In the cupboard across the room is a variety of underwear, in both slippery silk and leather, and the collars I wore

201

to signify my obedience. I go over to the cupboard and open it. There, on the shelf, is the collar I wore on the first night: an innocuous-looking bit of PVC with a pattern of holes punched into it and a bow at the front. I touch it, feeling the urge to pick it up and put it on. Dominic used to give me instructions on how to be dressed – or rather, undressed – and how to wait for him. My longing for him now makes me want to do the same again, to show him my love and need. I want him to see me ready and waiting, eager to do what he desires.

I can take anything if it means we can be together.

I remember the flogging in the dungeon of The Asylum. That was too much for me, I admit that. But I took almost as much in this room and even though some of what Dominic desired to do to me went further along the road than I really wanted, I never regretted how he made me feel. I know I want to feel that way again.

The sound of a key in the front door startles me and I quickly shut the cupboard. As I move, I realise I'm already aroused by the memory of what happened between us and the anticipation of pleasure yet to come. 'Dominic, is that you?'

'Of course,' he says with a smile as I come out into the hall to meet him. 'I hope you weren't expecting anyone else.'

I laugh, but inside there's a sudden pang of guilt. I push it away for now. I want to enjoy this moment without worrying. *After all, if he wasn't in the passageway with me, there's no way he can know what happened there.*

Dominic stands before me, handsome in a dark suit, a lime-green silk tie providing a note of colour, and he opens his arms to me. His eyes are meltingly brown and his beautiful mouth is curved in a tender smile. 'Come here, Beth. I've waited so long for this moment. The two of us, alone, in our old place.'

I'm overcome with joy and throw myself into his arms, pressing my face against his reassuring chest and relishing the feeling of his arms wrapping tightly around me. 'I've waited so long!' Emotion rushes up inside me. Dominic has been so far away and hard to reach, my texts and emails seemed to fall into a black hole. No matter how hard I tried, I couldn't summon him back. But now, at last, he's returned to me. My lip is trembling as I pull myself close against him, my arms around his broad back. The smell of him, warm and male and delicious, so beautifully familiar, makes my chest contract and I realise that tears are welling up. One immediately overflows and trickles down my cheek. I sniff.

'Beth?' He pulls back and gazes down at me. With one thumb, he wipes away the errant tear. 'Beth, honey, what's wrong?'

'Nothing.' I smile up at him, even though tears are flowing fast now. 'I'm just so glad to see you, that's all.'

His eyes soften. They're unbelievably beautiful, framed with dark lashes, a deep brown that turns darker at moments of great emotion: I've seen them black with anger and black with lust. 'I'm happy to see you too.' He runs his thumb down my cheek as if scooping up tears with it. 'But don't cry. Tonight is happy, isn't it?'

I nod, blinking away the last of my tears. 'I think seeing you like this was just a bit much for me. I'm happy, really, I promise!'

'Good.' He bends his head down to mine and I feel the soft warmth of his lips as they brush my mouth. Oh, that kiss . . . I close my eyes and tip my head back to receive it properly, but instead I feel his thumb brushing over my lips. 'Not yet,' he murmurs. 'Let's eat first. You can be my dessert . . . and I'll be yours.'

'That sounds delicious,' I whisper. Then I'm suddenly crestfallen. 'But I didn't bring any food! I forgot completely.' My appetite was entirely lost in the excitement of seeing Dominic.

'Don't worry,' he replies, and smiles. 'I did.'

It's a simple supper but perfect for us: Dominic has brought lamb steaks, already marinated in rosemary and garlic, some vegetables and a bottle of good red wine. 'Quick and very easy,' he says as he heats the grill. 'See what you can find in the cupboards.'

The apartment hasn't been properly lived in but I manage to assemble plates and cutlery and some mugs to drink the wine out of. An old screw bottle opener, located at the back of a drawer, gets the cork out, and I pour the wine. A delicious aroma of grilling lamb fills the kitchen and I realise I'm starving. When Dominic puts the plate in front of me ten minutes later, I'm very ready to eat.

'How was your day?' I ask as I fall on the food.

'Not too bad considering how long I've been out of town. Just a few glitches and headaches but mostly good progress on the big deal. Another week or so and we'll be completing, if all goes according to plan. And then . . .' He looks up at me and smiles. 'Watch out, Dubrovski!'

'What do you mean?'

'I'll be resigning and setting up my own company to manage my money and start investing. I know exactly what I want to do and how to do it. So far Andrei's been profiting from my expertise while I've learned all I need to know from him, but now I'm going to take control and do it my way.'

'What a surprise,' I say teasingly. 'Taking control? Doing it your way? That doesn't sound like the Dominic I know and love.'

He looks a little bashful, then says, 'I'm no good as an employee. It takes all my willpower not to tell Dubrovski to go and jump in a lake when I don't agree with what he wants to do. I'll be better as my own boss, that's for sure.'

I observe him as we eat. I know he's right. It's obvious that Dominic wants and needs to run his own ship. It must have been a huge test of his character to submit to Andrei's wishes and do his job someone else's way. But how will Andrei feel about his one-time employee becoming a rival? He's a man used to being top dog.

Surely he won't ever see his protégé as a serious contender. I think suddenly of an old wolf being taken on by a fitter, younger male in the pack, one who was once a trusted lieutenant but who has now sensed weakness in the leader and is prepared to risk a battle to the death. *But Andrei's not there yet. He's not old and he's far from weak. And I'll bet he's prepared to crush anyone who wants to take what he considers his.*

'How about you?' Dominic says, oblivious to my thoughts. 'Good day?'

'Strange day.' I glance up at him as I say, 'Anna was in the apartment today. She obviously spent the night.' I watch him carefully for any change in his expression – *even though I'm sure he's not involved with her, I can't help worrying just a little* – but he doesn't react. 'It looks as though she and Andrei are together again.'

'For now,' he says with a shrug. 'I don't know how they really feel about each other, but they enjoy sleeping together, so best of luck to them.'

'It's not right though, is it? An employer sleeping with someone who works for him?'

'If it were anyone else but Anna, I might be concerned. She definitely knows how to look after herself. In fact, if anyone ought to look out, it's Andrei.' Dominic gives me a broad smile. 'Believe me, Anna's tough.'

Tough . . . clever . . . successful . . . beautiful . . . sexy . . . what more could a man want?

Don't think like that, I tell myself strictly. After all, I know it only leads to jealousy and misunderstandings.

I think of my own possible misunderstanding. I've been replaying the events in the catacombs all day but my memory is always the same: a passionate encounter with Dominic, followed by a complete blank. It's only the details I've learned since that have bred this awful suspicion into me, and Anna's words this morning made me doubt even more the version I believe in. *I have to ask him. I don't know if I'll be able to give myself properly to him if I'm afraid that I've been unfaithful.* Once again, I see the trap I'm in: I can't ask him without also letting him know what I've done. *I'll have to ask him subtly.*

'Did you enjoy dancing with Anna at the party?' I ask casually.

At once he fixes me with a stare and his smile fades just a little. 'Don't start that again, Beth. I think I made myself perfectly clear on that point. You've got nothing to worry about.'

'I know, I know,' I say hastily. 'I didn't mean that. I just meant – we had more fun when we were together, didn't we?'

'Of course we did.' His expression relaxes again. 'You know that. Just being near you was great, and all the more because it was so unexpected. You looked so beautiful – you were the most stunning woman at the party.'

I smile, touched and happy at his compliment. 'I wanted to look my best for you – you were the whole reason I was there. That's why being alone together meant so much.'

'I know,' he says softly, his eyes liquid. 'It was amazing to touch you like that . . . to feel you again. I've been so hungry for you. Honestly, Beth, sometimes when I've been in some tin shack in the depths of Siberia with only a handful of miners for company and a stove for warmth, I've imagined you with me, your beautiful ripe body, your gorgeous curves, and it's what's kept me going. Knowing you were waiting for me, just like you promised, and knowing I would one get day get to hold you again, like I did at that party.'

'I've longed for you too,' I say huskily. 'I wanted us to make love again . . . that's why it was so, so sweet when we did. I couldn't resist you, it didn't matter where we were.'

'It was incredible for me too,' he replies.

Relief floods over me. *That's what I needed to know. It was Dominic in the tunnel, not Andrei. Oh thank God! I'm free of that awful, horrible guilt.*

'What's so funny?' he says, amused. 'You're smiling fit to burst!'

'Nothing, nothing – I'm just so happy!' I leap up and go around the table to throw my arms about him. I give him an enormous hug. 'I can't believe we're together again, and everything's all right.'

'Hmmm – how about we come back to this dinner later?' Dominic takes one of my hands and presses it to his lips, biting it lightly with his teeth, and adds, 'Only, I've just thought of something I'd enjoy far, far more . . .'

We start to kiss properly, exploring deep into one another's mouths. It's so addictively pleasurable that we can hardly pull apart long enough to stumble out into the hall and from there into the boudoir but somehow we manage it, discarding our clothes along the way until we're in the bedroom. I'm wearing only my underwear now, and Dominic kisses me hard as he unclasps my bra and releases my breasts, giving a low murmur of appreciation as the rosy pink nipples, already protruding, are revealed. He runs a hand over the soft mounds, cupping them. 'You're so gorgeous ... I've dreamed about these beauties, about tasting them and sucking them ...' He drops his head and pulls one of my nipples into his mouth, tugging gently. Then he releases it, smiling a lazy smile. 'And tasting you here too ...' He hooks a finger under my silk knickers and brushes it light across me. I shiver as he leaves a burning trail over my skin. Within a moment, the knickers lie in a shiny black puddle on the floor and I'm completely revealed to him. What he sees evidently pleases him, from the sight of his boxer shorts. I slip my hand into the opening and wrap my fingers around his erection, and he moans softly.

Suddenly he picks me up and lifts me onto the bed, lying me on my back. I watch as he slides his boxers down and takes them off. I can't take my eyes off his enormous erection. I haven't seen it for so long – our encounters since he left have been in darkness so I've only felt it. Now the sight of it makes me throb and ache with need, but I try to control it. We have all the time we want tonight.

He lies next to me and pulls me round so that our bodies are pressed against one another, and rubs his hands over my hips, back and bottom, while I savour the sensation of his hardness rammed against my belly and the firmness of his muscled arms. We kiss again, slow, tender kisses growing by the second in passion, until I can't stand it any longer and I have to touch him. I break the kiss and push him away so that I can take his hot shaft in my hand; it's so smooth and soft under my touch, it's hard to believe how very demanding it can be.

'Remember when I used to be your slave?' I say throatily. 'You liked me serving you.'

'Mmm,' he says. 'I still do.'

I feel a pleasurable thrill

'Do you want me still? To dominate me?'

'Yes . . . but this time, rules. And limits. Last time you trusted me.' He smiles a little sadly. 'And I let you down. A master owes his slave protection. The slave puts her faith in the master, that he will demand her obedience and take his pleasure, but that in return she will be allowed to taste the same delights. Her pain, of whatever kind, can only be what she is willing and able to bear.'

'You want to have limits?' I say, holding his stiff shaft in my hand, gently rubbing the skin back and forth. I hear his breath hitch in his throat as I draw my hand up to the smooth velvety tip, over it, and back again. 'We don't need that. I trust you. I know you

don't want to do things to me that I'm not ready for –
such as . . .'

'Such as what?' he says. I run my hand downwards
to the soft balls and behind, to the sensitive place
beyond. I let my finger run lightly over the spot.

'Like . . . here.'

'You mean anal sex?'

I nod.

He stares at me and then says, 'All right. If we ever
went on that journey together, it would only be with
your total consent. But even if you don't want me to
penetrate you fully, then you might find other things
acceptable. Smaller tools can create an amazing feeling
– a finger, a slender dildo, a specially designed plug just
made to fit your sweet little ass. It will make you feel
even fuller when I'm fucking you.'

I gasp at his words. Even if I'm not sure how I feel
about anything anal, the idea is titillating, and the way
he's talking is sending darts of excitement all over me.
He runs a hand over my bottom and takes his finger
between the cheeks, not deeply but enough to make me
tingle oddly in a place I don't expect to. I can't imagine
wanting to having anything pressed into my behind
when it could just as well go where I feel a need and a
hunger to be filled.

'I don't know,' I say. 'I can't agree to it explicitly but
I trust you to know when I'm ready to go there.'

'Uh uh.' To my surprise, Dominic shakes his head,
although he's still smiling at me. 'You have to say it
out loud. Anything you don't ask for, you don't get.'

'Is that really the ethos of a master?' I say, gripping his cock again. I'm longing to taste him. In fact, I don't think I can wait any longer.

'I can't control others if I can't control myself,' responds Dominic. 'That's something I learned from what happened between us.' He looks serious for a moment and puts his hand down to stop me massaging him. 'I'm serious, Beth. Things have changed since we were last together. Of course I'll always want to be your master, and have you yield to me and everything I want to do to that gorgeous body of yours. But the effects of what I did when I lost my head . . . they've stayed with me in ways I can't explain. Not just yet, anyhow. And that means, we have limits now. Some are yours – and some are mine. If you want me to follow my desires and use your ass when I feel it's right, you're going to have to tell me now. Or it won't happen, honey. I mean it.'

His hand lets go of mine and I grip his shaft with even more force. 'Hmm,' I say. 'Let me think about that . . . I'll need just a little time, if that's okay . . . sir.'

He gives me a half smile and his voice takes on the commanding tone of my sexual master. 'You may have some time to do whatever you like. I'll tell you when that time is over.'

'Thank you, sir.' I slide my way down his body, running my hands over his belly, letting my fingers play in the trail of dark hair that circles his navel and heads down to his groin. I kiss his smooth olive skin, marvelling at his firm stomach and the ripple of muscles

212

I can feel there. He rests one hand on the top of my head, caressing my hair gently, and his breathing deepens. I roll over onto my front so that I'm between his legs and use my knees to nudge his thighs apart and make room for me to crouch in the hollow that's created, as though I'm about to worship him – which in a way, I am. I intend to pay full homage to the part of Dominic that brings me so much pleasure. I grip the hot length of his erection in my hand, and it seems to stiffen even more in anticipation of what I intend to do. But I'm not going to give him that satisfaction quite yet. First I blow lightly upon his shaft and put out my tongue to touch it very softly, giving him a tiny taste of what is to come. Then I move to the soft package of his balls with its covering of dark hair and blow lightly on it, taking the whole thing in my hands and squeezing softly, before I starting kissing and licking them.

He moans as I work away with my hands and tongue. Both of his hands are now in my hair, and his fingers tighten over my scalp as he responds to the delicious feelings I'm giving him. I run a finger behind his balls, then slide my open mouth from the root of his cock slowly up its thickness. He throbs under my wet lips and the darting movements of my tongue as I approach the top of his manhood. I play around the top of his shaft with my tongue, rubbing at the skin around its head and tickling softly down it with my fingernails until I can feel that he's impatient for more.

'Suck me,' he says roughly. 'Put me in your mouth. All of me.'

I am only too eager to obey. I'm hungry for him now and I want to engulf him fully in the soft warm wetness of my mouth, even though I know it will be difficult. I lean forward on my knees and bring my head into a position that means I can take him deep inside. I close my eyes and let him slide into my mouth, welcoming him with the lapping movements of my tongue. He's huge and I'm not sure if I can accommodate him entirely, but he pushes in and I concentrate on relaxing so that he can reach as far as he likes. Just when I think that I can't take him another millimetre, he pulls back so that his tip grazes against my teeth, giving me a second to recover, before he pushes forward again, his hands hard on the back of my head.

'I'm fucking your mouth,' he says in a low voice. 'I want to fuck you like this till I come, do you understand?'

I nod as I go on letting him slide in and out of my mouth, following his retreat with my darting tongue and then welcoming him back with my open throat. He starts to fuck me a little harder. Now I begin to move my head back and forth just a little, so that when he pushes in, I'm pulling back just enough to stop him ramming down my throat altogether, but not so that it interferes with his pleasure or the sensation he has that he's getting his entire cock into me.

'Stop,' he commands suddenly, and I let his shaft slide from my mouth, releasing him. His cock stands before me, glossy with my saliva. I'm hungry at the sight of it, my appetite growing. But if Dominic has decided not to come quite yet, then I'm sure he has something interesting planned for me. 'I'd like to see you play with yourself for me. But,' he warns, 'don't come.'

Oh boy. That's going to be hard. I'm hot now, aroused and ready to do whatever he wants. I've never felt like this before. When I was last in the boudoir, I had boundaries to deal with, as well as my own fear and trepidation of what might happen to me. But now I've learned that my body has limits far beyond what I suspected. I know that pleasure comes from abandonment, not from repression or playing it safe. Out of the bedroom, I may not want to be a slave or a possession, but in it I know I can find delicious satisfaction from being dominated by my masterful, my voluptuous, licentious, demanding lover. My body is his to use, because I know he'll use it to bring me to a state of ecstasy as well as for his own pleasure.

I want to obey his orders. I roll on to my back and drop my fingers between my legs. I'm soaking wet with juices.

'Not like that. I can't see. Kneel up and hold yourself so that I can watch.'

I do as he says, turning to face him on my knees, raising myself up so that my crotch is almost level with his face as he reclines on the pillows. One of his hands rests lazily on his erection as he gazes with dark, lustful eyes at my mound.

'Go on,' he says. 'Do it.'

I run my forefinger slowly down my stomach to my patch of downy hair, then let it tickle gently around my lips and the clitoris I can feel emerging stiffly from the top of my slit. Dominic licks his lips swiftly and I can tell that he is imagining what it would be like to lean over and suck on it, pulling it into his mouth and nipping it with his teeth. The thought makes me even wetter and my clitoris twitches for attention. With his burning gaze on me, I put my middle finger on the very sweetest place and give a rapid stroke that makes my thighs shudder as the electric sensations shoot out. Once I would have found this impossible to do in front of someone. Now I'm worried that I'll come too soon. But I have to obey, so I circle my bud with my finger and then begin to tease it, moaning softly as my body obeys and ripples sweet electricity outwards. Almost without being aware of it, I cup my breast with the other hand, pinching and rubbing the nipple which increases my excitement even more.

Dominic is watching intently, his hand still on his erection, though he isn't moving it. 'Push your fingers inside,' he orders.

I run my fingertips down into my wet groove and then push them up into the slippery warmth within. I can feel my fingers inside, and I start to rise and fall on them, fucking myself with them. Dominic pulls in a deep breath and his hand twitches over his length. I know that I'm tantalising him almost to his limits.

'Good,' he says, his voice low and thick with lust. 'Very good. I like that. I want to fuck you before you give yourself the orgasm you want. But first . . .'

He gets off the bed and goes to the cabinet. I watch, taking my fingers back to my engorged clitoris, as he opens the cupboard and removes a length of rope. He brings it over to the bed and says, 'Get off and put your arms together above your head.'

I do as he says, pressing my hands together. He takes the rope and lashes it quickly from just up above my elbows up to my wrists, leaving a long end by my hands. 'Get on the bed with your back to the railings. Kneel with your legs apart.'

I obey again. He pulls the rope back and tethers it to the bedrail, forcing me to lean backwards. Now my arms are held tightly to the rail, while my thighs are stretched and my body is open and exposed, my sex pouting forward. I realise quickly that if I try to lean forwards, my arms begin to hurt, but if I relieve the pain in my arms by leaning back, my thighs immediately protest. There's only one position somewhere between the two where I find relief, so I settle there as best I can while Dominic gets on the bed and watches me for a while, evidently enjoying my writhings and twistings to get comfortable.

'I want to lick all the honey from you,' he says in a dark voice. 'But keep your pleasure back for later – understand?'

I nod, running my tongue over my lips.

'Close your eyes. Don't open them.'

I shut them, and all at once it's as if everything is concentrated in my sex. All I know is that at some moment soon, I'll be gifted with the delightful touch of my master's tongue and I want it so much I'm almost whimpering with it. As I wait, I shift to relieve the tension in first my arms and then my legs. *This is unbearable.*

I want to open my eyes but I fear that if I do, Dominic will punish me further by tying me tighter or holding back even longer from licking me, and I crave that tongue in me, it's the only thing that can answer the need that's burning there.

I wait and then, at last, I feel his breath ripple over my hair, tickling it delightfully, the rapture of it making me jerk and twist in my bonds. I open my thighs wider to tempt him in, but it's long moments before I feel another tantalising breath shiver over my mound. I let out a noise like a squeak and say, 'Dominic, please . . .'

A light slap on my bottom is the only answer I get. I squeeze my eyes shut, fearful I will forget and open them in my breathless anticipation.

I try to be patient. *Be humble and submissive and your master will give you what you want.* But as I wait for what seems like hours, I can hardly control my need, which is intensified by the way I have to keep moving to relieve the pressure in my limbs from the tension of the rope. If I could be still, I could be patient, but my moving keeps my sex hot and ready.

Then I feel the lightest touch, the very tip of his tongue on the apex of my bud, then pressing down a little harder and I let out a long 'Ahh' of fervent pleasure and gladness that my wait is over. The tongue probes at me for a moment, finding its way to the hard little seed at the centre of my clitoris and gives it a devilish flutter, before leaving my bud and sliding downwards, lapping slowly all the way as if feasting on my nectar. When he reaches my entrance, he lets his tongue play ticklishly there, sucking and biting gently at my lips before pushing his tongue hard inside and probing me with it. I twist back and forth under the racking sensations that come not just from the delightful activities of Dominic's tongue but also from the tension of my bonds and the lines of pain that flare out along my arms and thighs when I forget myself and relax. It's no pressure to keep my eyes shut now though, as I welcome the darkness that lets me focus everything on the feelings that Dominic's slippery velvet tongue is creating inside me.

Then, suddenly, his tongue is gone and his fingers are thrusting hard into my longing depths, while he is sucking my clitoris into his mouth, his teeth grazing it as he pulls at it long and hard as if it's delivering ambrosia to him. It begins to throb and vibrate with the pressure, and I can feel my hips jerking in time to the fucking of his fingers deep within me. I'm getting so close, and the effect of the rope and the strain in my muscles is making me long for the release even more.

'Let me come,' I beg. 'I've got to!'

'Come?' His voice is masterful and almost taunting. 'You're just another of those greedy girls who wants to be tickled, aren't you? Tickled till you spend your juices all over the place. Not yet. You're going to be fucked first.'

I draw in a shuddering breath. I don't know how much more I can take of the pain in my muscles or the erotic torment. I keep my eyes shut tight, hoping I'll be able to endure a little more before I beg for release – in both senses. Now he's between my thighs, his body huge, strong and hot, nudging my legs even further apart. He's leaning over my stretched-out torso and I guess that he's seizing the bedrail on either side of my bound hands. His rock-hard erection is pressed against me, his balls tickling my out-thrust sex. Taking my left earlobe in his mouth, he pulls it into his mouth and bites it just enough to nip me, then whispers, 'Don't give in to it. The best is yet to come.'

His penis is now pushing at my entrance but he doesn't intend to help it enter. His hands are firmly gripping the rail and my own are bound. He is torment-ing me just a little further as his tip noses for my hole, sliding in my juices and unable to get in me.

'Please,' I beg, 'please.' I'm moving my hips to help guide him inside me but he's always slipping away, until I'm on the brink of screaming with need and frus-tration. Then he hits the sweet spot and my muscles open easily to admit him. I sigh as he fills me up, taking his shaft into the very hilt, his root rubbing against my mound. I have a burst of renewed vigour, my blood reheats and I begin thrusting up to meet his deep pushes. Now my bounds provide a kind of resistance that allows me to lift myself higher and let him in even further, and his pubic bone grinds against my clitoris, strumming it into a frenzy. He fucks on, gripping the bedrail for support, letting me rise up on my straining muscles to meet him. I start to cry out with every thrust, and I can feel my climax approaching at last.

'May I come?' I say in a broken pant.

'What?'

'May I come . . . *please*?'

'*What*?'

I scream it now. 'May I come, please, *sir*!'

'Open your eyes.'

I obey. He's staring down at me, taking in my helpless state, my excitement, the arousal that's making my eyes unfocused and desperate.

He leans forward and kisses me, pushing his tongue as deep in my mouth as his cock is reaching inside. Then he pulls away and says, 'Come for me. Do it for me now.'

As if in perfect obedience, my climax erupts like a molten, golden volcano, engulfing in hot, almost excruciating pleasure. All the pain I've felt in my limbs vanishes, transformed into the most intense delight that makes me shudder all over. As the sensations leave me, I feel Dominic gathering pace, seizing me under the bottom with one hand so that he can force me further onto his shaft, before he pours out a boiling orgasm within me.

I fall limp and now I feel the full effect of the rope. My muscles are strained and hurting. Now that the pleasure is over, they ache, and I moan softly.

'I'd better let you down,' Dominic says with a smile. His expression is replete with satisfaction.

'Yes please,' I say, and as he releases me, I fall to the bed in blissful relief.

He lies down beside me and wraps me in his arms. Nuzzling into my neck, he kisses me gently. 'That was wonderful,' he says.

'Yes,' I whisper back, hugging back. 'Worth waiting for.' I luxuriate for a moment in the closeness of our bodies and the afterglow of our climax. Then I say, 'You haven't used ropes on me quite like that before.'

'Haven't I?'

'No.'

'Oh. Didn't you like it?'

'I did. It's weird how being restrained like that can intensify everything I'm feeling.'

'That's the idea. And I got the impression it was remarkably effective if your wailing had anything to do with it.'

I nudge him swiftly. 'I did not wail! I ... I ... emoted.'

'You emoted from here to Timbuktu,' he replies and laughs.

'You still want to control me, don't you? I mean, you still want to be the dominant partner in our lovemaking?'

He runs a hand along my arm as if savouring the soft touch of my skin. 'I suppose so. I don't know if I'll ever change, Beth. Can you bear it if I don't?'

'Oh yes,' I reply quickly, 'I can bear it, that's fine. I just wondered ... how we'll explore that, I suppose.'

His voice becomes serious. 'You don't have to worry, Beth. I've done a lot of thinking while we were apart and I know one thing – I'm not going to use any of those other things on you again. Not whips, or paddles, or floggers. I can't bring myself to do it ever again.' He drops a kiss on my shoulder. 'I know you'll be glad to hear it.'

'Yes . . . yes, of course,' I say. 'I want what makes you happy, you know that.'

'Thank you, my darling, that means so much to me – everything, in fact. After what happened before, I can never risk it again. Like I said, we have limits now. And that's one.'

I know that the effects of what Dominic did to me with that whip almost drove us apart for ever. I know it sent Dominic into a tailspin when he realised what he'd done. And yet . . .

I should be pleased that he doesn't intend to whip or flog me ever again. But I thought that I was the one who set the limits.

As we drift in a comfortable doze, I wonder why on earth I feel so uneasy.

CHAPTER THIRTEEN

When I arrive at Albany the next morning, the body-guard lets me in with a totally blank expression, as if the sound of loud screaming isn't echoing through the flat. As he's never said a word to me in the past, I suppose there's no reason why he would start now, but even so, it's rather odd that we both pretend we can't hear the feminine shriek, and then 'Andrei! Oh, Andrei!' delivered in a rich Russian accent.

I feel quite light-hearted as I listen to it, as though all is right with the world now that I'm sure that it was Dominic, not Andrei, in the passage that night. And Andrei is obviously very taken with his Russian princess or whatever Anna is – and that's as it should be. They are very much welcome to one another as far as I'm concerned – I'm just relieved that my conscience is clear. As for whether or not he went so far as to spike my drink . . . well, I'd rather not think about that right now. Not while I still have this job to complete. At the moment, I'm prepared to get it finished and then get out.

I walk along behind the guard as though I'm also oblivious to the shrill stream of Russian that's now pouring out from within Andrei's bedroom despite the thick wooden doors.

It doesn't take a genius to work out what's going on in there.

Yeah, an inner voice shoots back at me. *Battleships.*

I go into the office and Edward is there, an iPod plugged into his ears, rocking away gently as his fingers pitter-patter over the keyboard of his computer. When he sees me putting my bag on the chair opposite him, he suddenly yells very loudly:

'Pleurisy!'

I jump, shocked at the unexpected volume. 'What?'

'Sorry,' he says at a more normal level, as he tugs the headphone out of his ears. 'I'm listening to something cheerful and uplifting in keeping with the general atmosphere – Mozart's *Requiem*. And what I said was pleurisy. That's what Marcia's mother has. It's a lung problem. But she's getting better apparently and Marcia will be back on Monday. So . . .' Edward turns his eyes heavenward and cocks his head back towards the door ' . . . no more of that racket for me, thank goodness. They've been at it since I got here.' He makes a face at me. 'That girl's got a set of lungs on her. Definitely no pleurisy there.'

Marcia's back on Monday. It's Friday. The weekend is coming. I've lost track of time with the party in the middle of the week. And I've made such good headway on the collection that I'm ready to start considering how to hang it. That means I might get this whole job over with quicker than I thought. The image of the reading girl comes back to me, floating in front of my mind in her purity and serenity. *I must ask Mark about her. Perhaps I'll go and see him today.*

'Doesn't it bother you?' asks Edward, and I look at him blankly. 'Mrs Banshee in there, wailing away like she's practising for the annual convention!'

'Um . . . no.' I'm not getting into a discussion about Andrei and Anna with this guy.

'Oh well,' Edwards says, picking up his earphones and inserting them back into place. 'Back to the riotous knees-up that is the *Requiem*. And let's hope those two have reached the end of their own Gloria by the time I've finished.'

I leave Edward to his Mozart and concentrate on accessing my email, so that I can send a message to Mark asking if I can drop by to talk to him. He pings back an email almost at once saying I'm welcome any time, he's at home, why not come for lunch; in fact, he was going to ask me to come round soon if I wasn't being kept too busy by Andrei.

I'm ridiculously pleased that I'm going to see Mark. I've missed him. As I send back an email confirming I'll be there, I notice that the noisy lovemaking appears to have stopped. A picture pops into my mind: Andrei is prone in Anna's arms, they're both breathing deeply with post-coital languor. She's running a hand over his head, ruffling his dark-blond hair, and his blue eyes have softened to dark corn-flower. It makes me think of someone stroking a lion.

A wild beast is never truly tame. It just decides not to attack you. For now.

An email arrives from Dominic:

Last night was everything I hoped it would be. You're so gorgeous, I can't think about you or I'll get no work done at all. But we've got the entire weekend to play with . . . if you're not too tied up . . .

I don't want to rope you into anything, but keep it free for me

Dx

His jokes awaken the memory of being bound to the bed and send a delicious tremor through my body. A sudden ache of need startles me. I send back a reply.

I'm in knots just thinking about it. My time is yours, my everything is yours . . . Bx

I try to put aside the distracting memories of what Dominic did to me last night and do some research into Fragonard, but it's hard to concentrate. After a few minutes, I decide to head to the kitchen for some coffee, offering to get Edward some as well. I hope Sri isn't around. I pretty much know where all the coffee stuff is now and I don't like her making it for me when I'm sure she has plenty of other things to do. I'm pleased to see that the kitchen is empty, and I get on with setting up the coffee machine as

I've seen Sri do it. I've got my back to the door, so I only know that someone is behind me when I hear a voice.

'Is there enough for two more?'

I turn to see Andrei in the doorway wearing a dark-blue cashmere robe that makes his eyes look almost turquoise. 'Of course,' I reply politely. 'I've made a whole pot in case anyone else wanted some. It'll be ready in a moment.'

He advances towards me, his bare feet silent on the wooden floor. I realise I haven't seen him since we returned to Albany the morning after the party – not since I discovered that he might possibly have drugged me and I might have had high-induced sex with him. *No wonder I feel a little awkward.* Even though I'm now sure that I didn't have sex with him, I still feel highly suspicious and resentful about the drink he gave me.

'How are you getting on with the job?' he asks, smiling. 'I'm looking forward to hearing all about it. I haven't seen you lately, I've missed that.'

'It's all fine,' I reply, stiff and unsmiling in return. 'Nothing to report.'

'Ah.' He clearly senses my attitude as his eyes cool and the smile fades. 'All the same, I'd like a report. First thing on Monday.'

'Fine.' I turn back to the coffee pot, which is now full, and reach for two coffee cups from the cupboard.

'There's no need, you know,' he says in a low voice.

'What do you mean?'

'No need to be jealous. Of Anna. She's a good friend and she helps me to release some tension from time to time but it's not serious.'

I draw in a sharp breath. *He really thinks I'm jealous! How on earth has he made that connection?*

Andrei goes on: 'Anna has a passionate nature . . . as you've probably heard. She doesn't bottle anything up. I'm sorry if it's made you uncomfortable. I won't have her here again.' He reaches out a hand and puts it on the counter, close to mine and adds in a low voice, 'If you and I were ever to . . . be together . . . well, she would be history. Anna understands, she wouldn't be upset. I want you to know that.'

His words light a fuse of anger in me. I whirl round. 'Andrei, I know people are usually too frightened to tell you what they really think, but I have to say that if you're thinking that I'm in here dying of love for you and weeping because I can hear you and Anna in bed, you're in for a big rethink. I don't love you, or want you, and I never will, so there's no point in kicking Anna out of your bed quite yet!'

His eyes flash as he absorbs my words. 'I see,' he says in a quiet, cold voice. 'Perhaps I've misunderstood. I was under the impression that we'd become . . . close . . . after the party. Obviously that was wrong.'

'Of course it was. I told you, I have a boyfriend – and besides, a friendly dinner and a flirtatious atmosphere do not make us a couple!'

'Come on, you don't expect me to believe in this boyfriend whose name you couldn't remember. And it was a little more than that, our connection—'

I continue without listening to him, getting angry now. I've suffered over the last two days because of what he did, and the guilt and fear it created. It's all coming out. 'But that's the end of it, Andrei, because –' fury flares up in me and I can feel myself losing control '– trying to drug me does not exactly endear me to you either! Do you have any idea how dangerous that was? Not to mention against the law!'

His eyes glitter and he goes very still. 'What?'

'You heard me! I know what you did at the party – you gave me that drink, the cocktail. The one spiked with drugs for anyone who wants a really spacy trip, with some hallucinations and memory loss thrown in for free.'

Andrei stares at me, his face impassive. 'You better think hard before throwing around an accusation like that.' His voice is low and hard as steel.

'Are you trying to deny it?' I retort, feeling reckless. I've taken him on – there's no going back now. The idea that my employer, someone in a position of trust, has done such a terrible thing spurs on my sense of betrayal and hurt. It was just lucky for Andrei that the consequences were no worse, but they could have been. 'Let's say you didn't slip anything in my drink yourself – are you honestly expecting me to believe you don't know that the house cocktail is a rather spectacular homemade punch? You and Kitty Gould are obviously old friends, and you're a regular at her little gatherings. You must know how it works.'

'I don't know what the hell you're talking about,' he says. He looks angry now, his mouth hard and his eyes freezing. 'The house cocktail is not spiked. In fact, it's not even alcoholic. It's a virgin Sea Breeze. That's why I gave it to you. I could see you'd had enough to drink that night.'

I'm stopped in my tracks and for a moment I can only gape at him until I manage to stutter out, 'What did you say?'

'You heard. You can ring Kitty Gould herself if you like, and ask her. She'll tell you that it's non-alcoholic and certainly drug free.'

My mind is a whirl of confusion. I remember the sweet, innocuous taste of the drink. Perhaps he's right and it was just fruit juice. Have I got it horribly, appallingly wrong? *Oh God, what have I done and said?* I feel afraid. I've misjudged him . . . haven't I? *But I was drugged; I know I was. I've never felt that way before, never. And if the drink is served clean, then that means that Andrei must be lying to me. He must have spiked it himself.*

He's taken a few steps nearer and I can smell the musky scent of his cologne mixed with the warmth of a body after sex. It has a strangely heady effect on me, but I try to ignore it. His gaze is raking my face. 'I can see you don't believe me. I don't know what makes you assume you were drugged – I think you have confused it with the effects of champagne mixed with a strong vodka martini after quite a lot of wine at dinner. You were drunk, Beth. I would never hurt you and I'm deeply wounded that you think I would abuse your trust like that.' He's looking deep into my eyes, that piercing sea-blue gaze almost hypnotic in its intensity. 'Well?'

He's so persuasive and compelling. One part of me is telling me not to trust him, and another is totally convinced by his words. *No wonder this man has succeeded in life. His power is incredibly potent.*

'I can see you don't truly believe I would hurt you,' he murmurs, getting closer to me. The knowledge that only a thin layer of cashmere lies between me and Andrei's naked body is making me a little dizzy. He's so tall and broad, and so close. His scent fills my nostrils, and the warmth of his skin almost seems to caress mine. 'Trust your judgement,' he says quietly. 'You know that whatever happens is of your own free will and nothing more . . . don't deny it. Don't resist what you know in your heart. I feel it. I know you do too . . .'

He's so close to me now. My heart is racing and I can feel my chest rising and falling more quickly. I'm responding to his proximity without wanting to, it's almost automatic. He's intoxicating me with the strength of his masculinity and his powerful will. He begins to bend his head down so that his face is almost touching mine and I know that he's only a moment away from kissing me. My breathing is rapid now. I want to resist but I'm frozen. At least I think I want to resist . . . There's nothing in my mind but his nearness and the way my body can't help tingling in response.

'Andrei, where's that coffee? You've been an age!'

The rich Russian voice breaks in and I shake my head as if waking up from a daydream. As I try to figure out what was just happening, Andrei turns towards the door, where Anna is standing in her red silk robe, eyebrows raised imperiously and a suspicious look on her face.

Andrei speaks to her in a voice of quiet authority. 'I'm bringing it now, Anna. Go back to the bedroom.'

She lingers for a moment, looking first at me and then at Andrei, obviously reluctant to leave us together, but she daren't disobey. With a flounce, she turns on her heel and leaves.

I'm grateful to her. The interruption has given me the chance to come back to my senses. I'm horrified at myself for almost giving in, but also at Andrei. *What is it with this man? There's no end to his arrogance. Even though I've just accused him of spiking my drink, he still thinks I'll come running whenever he likes.* But it almost worked. If his lips had met mine, I don't quite know what I would have done, and that makes me ashamed of myself. Where's my self-control?

I never want to betray Dominic and what we've got! Never. Just as he would never betray me.

My anger at myself makes me blush hard and move away quickly.

'I don't care what she thinks,' Andrei says, an urgent tone in his voice. 'And neither should you.'

I turn on him, my voice hard. 'You don't get it, do you? I'm not interested. Sleep with Anna, marry her for all I care! Just leave me alone. Our relationship is strictly professional, do you understand? And once this job is complete, I'll be out of here for good. I, for one, can't wait.' I turn and pour the coffee into my cup so forcefully that it splashes all over the counter-top. 'I'm sorry if I've accused you unjustly but the fact I thought it might be true speaks volumes. Now, if you'll excuse me, I'm going to get back to work.'

I push past him, ignoring his angry expression and stride out, feeling his gaze burning into me as I leave.

I'm trembling with the adrenalin rush when I get back to the study. I'm elated to have spoken my mind but also scared. I just talked to Andrei Dubrovski in a way that no one does. At least, no one who values the luxuries of life, like unbroken arms and legs, not to mention their job.

Let him sack me. I don't care. I'm not going to be treated like that.

A voice whispers to me: *Treated like what? You were the one who almost let him kiss you.*

I don't like that voice at all. Not a bit. I refuse to listen. Andrei is the villain here, a liar and an exploiter and a man who is sleeping with one woman while coming on to another – one who happens to be completely uninterested and his employee to boot. It's all very unedifying stuff as far as I can see.

It's a relief to escape at lunchtime and leave Albany. Outside the air is crisp and the day bright. The sun is shining in a mellow autumnal way, bathing everything in light, but a sharp breeze is cooling and invigorating. As I walk down Piccadilly, I notice that the trees in Green Park are beginning to turn bronze and piles of leaves are already appearing. On the top of the tour buses, tourists are well wrapped up in puffy coats and scarves. I walk past Park Lane and then around Hyde Park Corner and down towards Belgrave Square. Here the houses are great white palaces with pillars and balconies and grand front doors. Many have flags to show that they've become embassies now, and the cars parked around look like diplomatic issue. I breathe deeply as I walk, trying to find some calm amid all the emotional confusion. Just when my relationship with Dominic looked back on track, this extra drama starts unfolding around me. I'm sure that as soon as I'm free of Dubrovski, everything will be fine.

But . . . I know that despite the mind-blowing sex yesterday, I'm feeling worried about what is happening with Dominic. I try not to dwell on it, telling myself that the weekend will iron out all the kinks. We've been apart for a long time, after a crisis in our relationship. No wonder it's going to take a little while to get everything running smoothly. The main thing is that we love one another and we're committed.

I resolutely shut out the memory of my body's treacherous response to Andrei. As far as I'm concerned, it didn't happen. Perhaps I'll never know the truth about whether I was drugged or not, but it doesn't matter now. It was Dominic in that passageway. I cling on to that fact like it's a life raft.

Lunch with Mark is like returning to civilisation from the battlefield. His house is a haven of peace and taste and he is the serene heart of it.

We eat a simple lunch of salad Niçoise with glasses of very cold Sancerre, and I tell him about my work. I don't enlighten him as to the more intimate events going on in Albany, and I don't mention the party, or Anna's presence, but talk about the works I've discovered and my ideas for them. Mark listens and comments. He has a magnificent memory and he can recall just about everything he's ever bought for Andrei.

As we eat lemon sorbet served with tiny *langues du chat*, I tell him about the Fragonard I've fallen in love with. Occasionally, as I glance at some beautiful object or savour the delicious food, I think how radically my life has changed in the last four months. Earlier this year, I was a waitress in a café in my hometown, without a clue what I wanted to do with my life. I spent my spare time hanging out with the boyfriend I thought I loved but who, in reality, was a bit of slob who took me for granted. I was devastated when Adam cheated but I'm grateful to him now. Without his bad behaviour, would I be sitting today in a beautiful Belgravia house discussing Fragonard with a leading art expert? Would I have my dream job and a man in life I truly love? Very unlikely. I'd probably still be serving prawn sandwiches and mugs of tea, and cooking fry-ups for Adam. *What a near miss that was!* My life has taken some lucky turns, and I'm grateful for it.

When I've finished relating my find and sharing my enthusiasm for the reading girl, Mark nods.

'Yes,' he says. 'I know the piece. I think it's an excellent choice and something that will appeal very much to Andrei. He has a particular affinity with France, no doubt because of his country's history. The Russian aristocracy prided themselves on their French style and ways, much as these days the oligarchs' wives display their wealth and taste by wearing Chanel and Givenchy.'

'I almost wish we could keep the painting ourselves,' I say. 'She'd look marvellous in your drawing room.'

'There are enough beautiful works of art to go around, thank goodness, but I know how hard it is to part with something you love. However, we dealers must learn to let go. I think Andrei will like what you've chosen.' Mark smiles at me again. Is it my imagination, or is he looking thinner? Perhaps a little, in the face. Otherwise he looks normal, if tired. 'I'm longing to have you back, Beth.'

'I can't wait to return,' I say honestly.

'Aren't you having fun?'

'The work is great, but being there is a bit like living in a big game park. I'm never quite sure if I'm about to become someone's lunch.

He laughs. 'You'll be fine. You can handle yourself very well. You're strong enough to take them all on, even if you don't yet know it.'

I laugh too as I think: *I hope he's right. Something tells me I'm going to need all the strength I can get.*

CHAPTER FOURTEEN

I'm so pleased that it's Friday night that I almost don't mind when Dominic sends a message to say he's going to be busy that evening. After all, we'll have most of the weekend together and I'm exhausted by everything that's happened in the week. When Laura suggests a quiet night in together with a Thai takeaway and a film, it sounds pretty irresistible.

It's a relief to close my mind to the possible repercussions of what happened with Andrei and everything else that's bothering me. I enjoy chilling with Laura; just two girls in pyjama bottoms and cosy jumpers, eating noodles and laughing uproariously at the movie we've downloaded. When she asks how things are going, I don't go into details, just reassure her that I'm happy now that Dominic is back, and warn her that I'll be away for most of the weekend.

'And this little art gig of yours comes to an end next week?' she asks.

I nod. 'Yup. And it can't come soon enough. I've seen enough of the millionaire lifestyle to last me into the next decade.'

'Come on,' she teases, 'when Dominic asks you to

elope, you're going to end up dripping in diamonds and bathing in asses' milk.'

'No, thank you!' I retort and toss a cushion at her, which she dodges. 'That's really not me. A country cottage, a garden and normal happiness, that's all I want.'

'I don't believe that,' Laura returns. 'You're ambitious and you want to make your mark. You might think you want a cosy life and domestic bliss, but you'd hate it soon enough. You're made for adventure, Beth. Remember when you got back from Croatia? You were so excited and keen to do more travelling. Excuse me if I find the whole retirement dream a bit unconvincing.'

'Maybe,' I say. 'But we all need a fantasy to retreat to, so I'll keep my thatched roof and picket fence for now.' I think for a second. 'Actually, as it's a fantasy, I'll have the pretty cottage, and a flat in London, one in Paris and one in New York as well.'

'New York!' sighs Laura. 'It's my total dream to go there. The Empire State, Central Park, Fifth Avenue, subways, yellow taxis . . .'

'The Met, the Frick, MOMA,' I say longingly. 'There's some amazing art to look at. And I want to have a cocktail at one of those chic hotels you read about in magazines.'

Laura lifts her chopsticks, struck with sudden inspiration. 'Hey – we should do it. Let's go to New York together!' Her eyes sparkle with excitement. 'I might meet some gorgeous guy with a loft in the village, or wherever it's really cool, and go and live with him.

We'll start a magazine, something cutting edge and influential, and I'll leave management consultancy behind for a glamorous life as part of New York's literary scene.'

I beam back at her. 'That sounds fantastic. I never understood why you didn't become a journalist like you always wanted to.'

Laura is lost in her fantasy for a moment, then pulls herself back the present, shrugging as she digs into a tray of pad thai. 'My careers adviser told me that print was dead and I'd only be joining thousands of other out-of-work journalists. My dad told me that management consultancy would pay off my student loans quickly and get me on the property ladder. So that's what I did.' She gives me a congratulatory look with the faintest trace of envy in it. 'Now you're the one with the glamorous job.'

I feel sad suddenly that, without encouragement, dreams can fade away. I lean towards her. 'Let's do it. Let's go to New York together. Maybe just before Christmas so we can see the decorations up in Bloomingdale's. A girls' weekend away. What do you think?'

Laura lights up again. 'Do you mean it?'

'Of course I do! Andrei's paid me well for my work – let's splash out on a trip and a really good hotel right in the heart of everything.'

'I would *love* that!' She smiles broadly at me. 'Miss Villiers, you have a deal.'

'Great. Now – do you want some more noodles?'

*   *   *

The day is cold and grey. The warm sunshine and blue skies have vanished for the moment. It's time to dig out some warmer clothes, and I settle on a soft grey Fair Isle jumper over a cami vest, a dark grey miniskirt, tights and boots. I give it a little colour with a green scarf and a plum-coloured felt trilby, and then set out to meet Dominic.

It's not far to walk from our flat in East London to Borough. As I cross Tower Bridge, I can see up and down the Thames. There's the Tower of London, nearly a thousand years old, white, square and a little Legoish; the huge dome of St Paul's topped by the cross of glittering gold, the chimney of Tate Modern, the London Eye and Blackfriars Bridge – which makes me think of the monastery in Croatia and how long ago it all seems.

From Tower Bridge I walk along the riverbank past City Hall and then up at London Bridge, where Dominic is waiting for me by Southwark Cathedral. He looks more gorgeous than ever in a dark-green striped jumper, jeans, boots and a navy cashmere scarf knotted at his neck. The colours bring out the hazel lights in his eyes, usually lost in the dark brown, and the chestnut glints in his dark hair.

Standing across the road, I get a few moments to admire him as he waits for me, unconscious of my presence. Then, as the lights change and I approach him, he sees me. At once a big smile illuminates his face, and he opens his arms for me to run into.

'Hi, beautiful,' he says, hugging me tight. 'You

look good enough to eat.' He stands back and looks at me appraisingly. 'Hmm, autumn suits you even better than summer. I'm a bit of a pushover for a miniskirt and boots. I should have been young in the sixties.'

'Then we'd have missed each other by about . . . oooh, fifty years or so?' I kiss him happily. He tastes of coffee and toothpaste. 'What's our plan today?'

'I thought we could go and take a look at this place.' He gestures behind him to the cathedral. 'And after that, we'll pick up some food in the market behind here.' I can already see some stalls and smell some delicious aromas. 'It's a famous foodie haunt,' Dominic goes on. 'So we'll get some goodies for later. Then we can take a walk and see where our fancies lead us, before we head for home.'

'Sounds perfect.' I smile and take his hand. *This is real happiness. Being a couple like any other, spending a lovely Saturday together, just the two of us. Except, of course, no one else is quite as happy as we are.*

Holding hands, we descend from the bridge to the cathedral garden, where people sit drinking coffee and children play, jumping up and down over the low walls and racing about. Inside the cathedral, we wander about, looking and absorbing. There are famous graves within – John Gower, the English poet is buried here – and a stained-glass window adorned with characters from Shakespeare, whose plays were performed not far from here and who almost certainly came to services in this very place. The thought fills me with awe as I try to imagine the great dramatist sitting here, looking at the same stones and the same arches and windows. After Dominic and I have tried to identify all the characters but not quite succeeded, we head back outside, out of the cathedral grounds and into the bustling food market just across the way. This place is a feast for the senses. Everywhere I look I see something to delight me: piles of white and yellow cheeses, barrels of olives, meats, fruits, vegetables, bread and cakes, sweets, nuts, delicacies from all over the world. There are chocolate stalls, stalls piled high with fish and crustaceans, or hung with poultry and offering choice cuts of beef or lamb, or the new season's game. Other stalls sell wine, in bottles and casks, or else hot to drink now from a paper cup, unless you prefer mulled cider, spicy with cinnamon and cloves and sweet with honey. There are coffee stalls, doughnut stalls and crêpe stalls; some are dedicated to gluten-free pastries, others to organic eggs. And then there's the street food: burgers and bacon sizzle on hot plates, ready to be put in a roll and smothered with ketchup. There's paella, the yellow rice studded with goodies and unbelievably aromatic, and falafel in pita breads; meatballs in a rich sauce served with spaghetti, or soup, thick and wholesome. There's fish and chips; venison steaks to eat in an envelope of brown bread with a tangy relish; or wraps of soft tortillas filled with grilled chicken, rocket and mayonnaise; there's pancakes and ice cream and churros, those delicious pastry twirls to dip into chocolate sauce. It's all to eat now, with a plastic fork, or a spoon or with greasy, sticky, salty fingers.

We browse to our hearts' content, stopping to taste cheeses or breads or olive oils, or anything that's offered to us, until we almost don't want anything else, except that we can't resist a hog roast, and buy soft buns full of meltingly soft pork and apple sauce. Loaded with shopping bags of delicious food we've bought to cook tonight, we return to the cathedral gardens to eat.

'This is so lovely,' I say to Dominic as we eat sitting on the low wall in the autumn sunshine, the shopping around our feet. The pork is sweet and delicious.

'I know,' he says, his expression happy as the wind ruffles his dark hair. 'It's days like these that I love London better than anywhere else. I'm so happy to be back here – with you.' He looks at me a little closer. 'And by the way, you've got apple sauce on your chin. Here . . . let me.' He wipes it away with a finger and follows up with a kiss.

'I can't imagine being more happy,' I say. 'Let's always be like this.'

He looks serious for a moment. 'You know what, Beth, I truly never have been more happy. I know that now. It was a shock to me, almost too much to handle, when I realised how you made me feel, because no one else ever has. I think that's been my trouble – I haven't loved properly before. That's why I got everything so confused in my mind, about how sex works and what it means. It hasn't always been about loving the other person, not in the way I feel about you.'

'Wow,' I say, feeling humbled and thrilled at the same time. 'I . . . I'm so glad I make you feel like that.' The words sound inadequate but Dominic seems to understand that they are completely sincere and that I feel almost overwhelmed by what he's saying to me.

'You truly do.' He takes my hand. 'I don't want to lose this. Ever.'

We gaze into one another's eyes, reading there the promise of what is to come tonight and then, all being well, night after night. It seems to occur to us both at the same moment that we have the rest of our lives to feel this happy – and, despite our rolls and greasy fingers and drips of sauce, neither of us can resist the impulse to hug each other hard and laugh with joy.

This is love. This is normality. I think we're through the worst. It will only get better now.

I am kneeling on the floor of the boudoir. My hands are bound tightly behind me, and when I tug lightly to test the strength of the bond, it is firm. I cannot move my wrists even a centimetre. This feels different from being tied to the bedrail. Even though I'm less exposed, I feel more vulnerable. A flutter of fear goes through me and I try to subdue it by breathing calmly and thinking, *he will not cause me real harm. He wants me to prove my obedience to him.*

That thought comforts me, because I love Dominic, my master, and I want to offer him my body to do as he pleases with it. This way, I will prove my love to him, and he will reward me with delicious pleasure.

I can see nothing – a silk mask has been tied over my eyes. I'm also wearing a kind of harness made of rope that is wrapped around my chest under and around my breasts, pushing them upwards. Dominic has done all this with speed and skill, taking me almost by surprise. Now I sit here, waiting, not sure what he has in mind for me, or when he's going to do it. All I know is that he took great pleasure in preparing me for this moment, stroking me gently, running the rope over my skin, coaxing me to touch it, lick it, kiss it. As he began to bind me, he flicked my nipples lightly and ran the rope over them to stimulate their delicate nerve endings with its pleasing roughness. And, almost as if by accident, he brushed against my sex, taking the rope between my legs occasionally so that I could feel it sliding over me like a relentless slender snake. Its slithering made me begin to swell with desire as my hot blood responded to its movements, while Dominic nipped at my neck and shoulders with tiny little bites that made me shake a little with excitement. Then, when my harness was complete, he bound my hands, saying, 'You look a little different. A bit more toned and athletic.'

'I've been kick-boxing.'

'Good. That will make you stronger for some of the things I'd like you to experience.'

Now I kneel waiting, anxious but with tingles flashing up and down my vagina whenever I think of him watching me, planning what he's going to do me, and enjoying seeing the rope biting just a little into my flesh.

I feel something new. It is more rope being threaded through my chest harness, and now there is another sensation of tightening, although not around me. Then I'm pulled to my feet.

'We're going on a little journey,' Dominic says, his voice stern but loving. 'Not far.'

I'm walking behind him, relying on him for guidance, taking tentative steps but not lingering in case it looks like disobedience. The carpet beneath my feet disappears and is replaced by something smooth and cool. We are in the hallway. He moves me into position and says, 'Something to keep your mind occupied.' I feel a hard clamp squeeze down on my nipple and gasp. It is immediately followed by a clamp on the other nipple. It hurts, but not too badly, it's bearable; but he's right, it makes it hard for me to think about anything but the burning pressure on my delicate buds and the way that it's causing me to get wetter and more ready.

I'm in the position that he wants and he grunts, satisfied. Then he guides me downwards so that I'm kneeling on the floor again. Now I feel his penis at my lips, its soft head hot and insistent, rubbing at the rim of my mouth. I open obediently and he slides his shaft in. I lick and suck as he presses in, hoping that's what I'm supposed to do. He gives three quick thrusts and withdraws, very slowly. His length is wet with my saliva now, I can feel it as he pulls out between my lips.

I'm being raised up again now and pushed back onto a long narrow leather seat that slopes upwards. I know this chair. It is one I've taken rides on in the past, and I sigh and shiver with anticipation as I feel its cool smooth leather at my back. Another rope tightens somewhere and I can tell that I'm bound to the chair. I wonder how I must look to him and the picture I see in my mind is exciting: a naked girl with a corset of ropes that thrust her breasts out, her arms bound behind her, is lying on the white leather. He moves my legs so that one is either side of the seat. I know I am a glistening ruby jewel of arousal, open and ready. I wonder how long he wants to wait before he plays there and it's only a matter of a few seconds before I feel him at my entrance, eager to thrust into me. He pushes his erection forward and it slides in, easing my tightness in a delicious movement, filling me up with his girth. He's not touching any other part of my body, I can only feel that column of hot flesh deep inside. Then he starts moving, withdrawing almost to my entrance so that he pauses just for a second, his penis held inside me by the circle of muscle there, and then pushing back hard, making me gasp with the impact. But it's so delicious, that sensation of expanding around him, that I only want it again. I don't have to wait for long as he thrusts forward into me, and back again, like the waves receding up a beach only to break again with even more power. As he moves in and out, still touching no other part of my body, I am aware of how open I am to him, how vulnerable. My body, tied up and lashed to a

249

leather seat, is powerless and I can only accept what my master decides to give me. I find the idea thrilling in a way I never have before, even though I still feel the fear and nervous anticipation of what Dominic will choose to do to me. I understand now that this fear is an essential part of the process and that, for Dominic, seeing my courage in giving myself to him and putting my trust in him, is highly exciting. He adores the sight of my body accepting him and everything he chooses to do to it, and he loves me all the more when I take what he gives me without complaint.

Now he's fucking, on and on, thrusting into me harder and harder. He must be holding something to give some resistance, so that he can power forward so much. The clamps around my nipples are suddenly removed and the sensation of relief from their bite is wonderful. It sends a strong gush of renewed pleasure to my belly, where Dominic's penis has entire possession of me. Every now and then he hits my clitoris with his groin and my buttocks tense and squeeze upwards to help him touch my most sensitive place, where every pressure is rippling delicious charges outwards through my limbs, but I can tell that he's not paying particular attention to my bud. He's just fucking on, harder and harder, until I feel drenched with juices and an orgasm growing within me, one that's sending messages of bliss from my scalp to my toes. Then, abruptly, his cock is pulled, and he's gone.

I'm left in the vermilion darkness behind my lids, panting and empty. Where . . .? Why . . .? I can barely think straight. I feel myself being moved, pulled down the seat until I'm almost on the edge, my legs still splayed. A rope somewhere is loosened, then my chest harness is pulled so that I am sitting up, a little dizzy from the disorientating effects of the vigorous fucking and its sudden cessation. Then he's there again, at my mouth, but this time wet and pungent from my juices. I open obediently and he pushes in, slowly so that I can taste every inch of it. It's a sweet, tangy flavour, rich and alive, and I lick and suck it off, knowing how exciting he will find the movement of my tongue. My nipples are buzzing and alive from their clamping and they must be partly responsible for the way my sex is still throbbing and swelling, still twitching for Dominic's cock, even though he's no longer there. No . . . he's deep in my mouth, his hands suddenly on the back of my head, holding me still so that I have to accept the movement of his shaft. I concentrate on relaxing my mouth and throat so that I won't be betrayed by my gag reflex, but even so my jaw aches almost at once from accepting his huge girth, no doubt swelled by the hard fucking he's been doing. He pushes in and out, but I sense that he's not going to give me more than I can handle, and I relax into savouring him and giving him all the pleasure I can, tickling his tip with my tongue when he retreats, circling the velvety head and lapping his length as he returns. His thrusts become fiercer but he's keeping away from the back of my throat. He goes on and on, sometimes letting me shift my head a little so that I can move my jaw and sometimes making me hold there despite the discomfort. And the strange thing is that the excitement of knowing he is getting such enjoyment from my mouth is equal to the desire to close my mouth and relieve my muscles. It feels like an age before he gathers speed, pressing down more firmly on my head, thrusting hard and fast and swelling to an even great size.

'I'm coming,' he cries throatily. 'Take it all in, suck it down . . .'

There is a burst of salty, tangy wetness in my mouth. It comes in several long eruptions and his whole cock jerks in my mouth as he groans with the force of his orgasm. I let it fill my mouth, surprised by the sudden hotness, gulp hard and swallow. The come leaves a burning trail down my throat.

He's panting hard as he finally pulls out. I'm breathless too, still blind but feeling as though I can see his face, blissed out with the satisfaction of his climax. I'm so happy to have given him that shuddering release.

'You've done very well,' he says and everything in me thrills to the caressing tone in his voice. 'I'm very pleased with you. You've given me a delicious experience and now I want you to have a reward.'

He leans forward, his body radiating heat. I'm desperate for the touch of his skin on mine and my sex is eager for its own satisfaction now. His nearness is so tantalising but he doesn't allow me more than little brushing of skin on skin. He is untying my arms and they fall free, aching from their long imprisonment.

But I can sense that he doesn't intend to release me, and sure enough he lies me down on the leather seat and ties me again, this time tethering my wrists lightly together beneath the seat.

'Beautiful,' he breathes admiringly, as he retreats a little. I can sense that he is standing, staring at me, and my sex throbs with the knowledge he can see me wet with need. 'Your breasts are delectable in that harness, my darling. I can't resist them.' I feel his mouth drop onto my left breast and he begins to suck and bite the nipple, still tender from its clamp, while he squeezes and tweaks the other between his fingers. He leaves the nipples to kiss and cup my breasts, saying, 'These beauties look even more amazing with their rope ties. I can see the pink tracks they're leaving on your skin and that excites me . . .'

I'm moaning lightly, wondering if it's possible to come just through having my breasts caressed like this. The growing sensations within tell me that it is.

'And now, for being so obedient . . .'

He gets up and leaves me alone for a while, and I hear sounds: the cabinet door opening, objects moved, and then he returns. Now I feel a probing at my entrance again, but it's not the hot head of his erection, rather the smooth warmth of silicone, oiled with lubricant. The tip of the toy is small and slides in easily but its girth increases very quickly and soon it is engulfed within me, filling me up completely.

'Now you may have your reward,' Dominic says, a smile in his voice.

I feel it deep within me curving upwards inside, but also on the outside it reaches from my entrance up to my clitoris, where a long, soft latex finger ends right on the top of it. I'm so eager for my climax that I start to writhe, moving my hips, thrusting lightly to make the thing inside me shift a little, rubbing against my clitoris.

'Stop!' His voice is firm, commanding. 'No movement. Nothing. Wait.'

I freeze and lie there, trying to control my breathing and the frenzy that threatens to erupt inside me if I don't get what my body is crying out for, and soon.

I don't know where Dominic is, or what he is doing, but after what feels like an age, I hear a low humming noise and the thing within me begins to vibrate. It's a sweet feeling as the plump body inside and the finger outside thrum away, stimulating the depths of my vagina and my sensitive place at the same time. Then, without any apparent interference, the vibrator picks up speed, humming away more quickly, pulsing faster, driving me a little wilder with its relentless movement. *Oh, the way it's pressing on my clit and throbbing inside me . . . it's gorgeous, it's unbearable.* The knowledge that Dominic is watching it all, controlling the sensations that the device is giving me, is even more exciting. I'm panting now, lost in darkness, my eyes screwed shut even under my mask, as my body responds to the ceaseless stimulation. The device changes up a gear, humming faster now, and I feel my back arching, my head going back, my shoulders moving. It's stirring up a whirlpool of sensation, calling it up from my secret depths. My thighs spread even wider apart as I give myself up to the voluptuous pleasure of this new friend. Then I gasp, my limbs kicking out involuntarily. The motion of the thing has changed. It no longer simply vibrates within me. Now the little engine is working a wickeder, more delightful trick as it whirs inside me, and then a wave of motion pulses along the finger on my clitoris and presses down. *Oh, that's amazing, oh . . . I can't take it.* I'm moaning as the machine continues in its delicious rhythm, rolling over my clit and giving it that divine pressure. Now it feels as though my pleasure zone is expanding, hot and liquid, and I can sense the orgasm growing exquisitely inside me. *Oh my God, it won't be long now . . . I can't resist it . . .*

The gear changes again and now the silicone fingers takes on a different motion, harder, more insistent, more rhythmic, and inside me its body throbs and purrs in time. *Ah, ah, ah . . .* With each delicious push, I'm losing control. The thing won't stop, Dominic won't let it stop, he'll only make it work harder and harder, revving up its engine until it's driving me insane with pleasure, watching with lascivious enjoyment as it draws a climax of deep power from my depths.

I know it's here now. *Pulse, pulse, push, push,* it kneads my sex into a frenzy and then it comes, rolling up, a deep shuddering orgasm that stiffens my limbs and convulses me with delectable sensations. They ripple through me in huge waves and I cry out with the wonder of it, before they leave me, panting and spent. The little engine is still working away in me as my orgasm subsides. Then the motor slows and it stops. It is no longer my pulsing, vibrating friend, but a smooth column of silicone shiny with my juices. I feel it sliding out of me and then it's gone.

As I recover from the incredible power of my orgasm, I realise that I'm being untied and lifted up. Now my chest harness is unknotted and the ropes fall easily from my body. Then, Dominic's hands are at the back of my head, and the mask comes away. I blink. It takes a while to readjust but I can see again. We're in the boudoir bedroom, and the lamp is glowing softly. I gaze into Dominic's face. He's looking at me with such tenderness.

'You've done wonderfully well,' he murmurs, and takes my hand. He guides to where his erection stands, rearing out from his body, huge and swollen. 'Look what you've done to me.'

'It was . . . amazing,' I say weakly, but unable to prevent a thrill spinning inside me at the sight of his desire.

'You loved it, didn't you?'

I nod.

He leads me to the bed, and lies me down on my back, spreading my thighs so that he can look into my honeyed centre, red from the ministrations of the relentless vibrator. 'Oh, you're so beautiful. Delicious. I want to make love to you.'

My heart swells to hear it. In the past, Dominic has not allowed me or him to be loving here in the boudoir.

It was the thing that wounded me, the deprivation of his love. I adore the way he drives me to peaks of ecstasy in so many ways, but my greatest moments are when he shows me the love he has for me.

He's between my thighs now, kissing my skin, sucking my fingertips, nuzzling my breasts. Now, as his tongue enters my mouth, his penis takes me as well, going in so gently but all the more exquisitely for that. My hot, fevered parts accept him like a soothing balm. I'd anticipated pain, considering what a fucking I've already had from him and from the vibrator, but it is the most beautiful sensation, as though the best fucking only comes after those fierce bouts. I sigh and wrap my arms around him. It's a delight to touch him, all the more as I've barely been able to feel him since we began. His skin is warm and smooth, unutterably delicious. I smell the sweet warmth of his underarms, the place at the base of his neck, his hair and moan again with delight. My hands run down to his firm, muscular bottom and squeeze, relishing his hardness, my thighs spread wide to accept him and I love the way his broad chest presses down against my breasts. We kiss long and deep as he moves inside me. My clitoris is well used now, and the vibrations it gives out now are less electric and more profound, as though it's become one with my vagina, and is slowly working to give me not the sizzling thrill of the first orgasm but the deep contractions of the final and best.

My heart opens to him as we make love, without toys or ropes or anything else this time, but in a position as old as the world, following the ancient rhythm as he moves his hips to thrust inside me and I rise to meet him. I don't know how long we run our course, only that everything outside the two of us has utterly vanished, we are hot, sweating, lost in our growing passion as our bodies finally take us up and out on that glorious roller-coaster ride, and we come together, both crying out as the long-awaited climax grips us with incredible intensity.

'I love you, Beth,' he says as we lie close together afterwards, his arm across my chest.

'I love you too,' I reply.

This, I'm certain, is happiness.

CHAPTER FIFTEEN

The following day we sleep late and make gentle, luxurious love before showering and going out for breakfast. Dominic takes me to a diner-style café, where we eat scrambled eggs on thick slices of whole-meal toast and pancakes with maple syrup, accompanied by lots of strong milky coffee. We relax over the Sunday papers and then take a long walk around the park, enjoying the last remnants of warmth in the autumn sunshine, chatting and laughing as we go. Eventually we stop at a van to buy cups of tea and sit on a bench, huddled together against the wind that's sprung up and watching the light already beginning to fade away.

'I can't believe the day is almost over,' I say, pressing my cheek against his olive cord jacket. 'It feels like we just woke up.'

'I know. That's one of the things I found strangest when I came to live in Britain. How you could live with the darkness coming down so early in the winter.'

Dominic was brought up mostly in South-East Asia where his father was a diplomat, so I can imagine the seasonal patterns of northern Europe were quite a shock. I sip at my hot tea, and watch families putting on coats and getting ready to head home before it gets too dark.

'Work tomorrow,' Dominic says, 'is going to be phenomenal. I may not be able to see you too much this week. This deal is coming to a close. But afterwards, all going well –' he gazes down at me, and I admire the chocolaty richness of his eyes '– I'm going to be on the road to freedom and success in my own right.' He laughs. 'I can't wait to see Andrei's face. First we'll toast the deal, and then, with my cash in the bag, I'm going to tell him that I'm stepping out on my own.' He looks so pleased and excited that I don't want to tell him that my first instinct is to worry. *Don't rub Andrei's nose in it, that's not the way to deal with him!* But I say nothing for now. I'll try and advise him when the time is right. I'll tell him that acting humble to Andrei, telling him he's the greatest and will never be matched, is the way to go.

But I'm hardly one to talk. I remember the things I said to my boss on Friday and a cold shiver that has nothing to do with the autumn wind goes down my back.

'And how about you? Are you nearly done with Andrei's project?' he asks.

I nod. *Although I might not have a job on Monday. I'll have to see.* 'Yes, it should be over by the end of the week.'

'Don't let him persuade you to carry on,' he says, a small frown creasing the area between his brows. 'I know Andrei, he likes to collect people and keep them, and he's obviously taken a shine to you. Watch out, okay?'

'Believe me, there's nothing he could say that would make me stay,' I say feelingly.

'Why?' Suddenly Dominic is searching my face. 'Has something happened? Has he made you feel threatened?'

'No, no,' I reply hastily. 'Of course not. He's fine, really. I just don't like the atmosphere, or the way that Anna is always around. She's determined to let me know just how much she and Andrei enjoy having sex – as if I care.' I know I'm shifting the subject away from Andrei but I don't know how I can begin to explain to Dominic about the tensions between Andrei and me. Would it help him to know that his boss has come on to me? Or that I had the crazy idea that I might have had sex with him, *by mistake*? And that there is still a question over whether or not he drugged me in the catacombs? Of course it wouldn't. Dominic needs to keep a cool head this week, and any of this stuff might make him furious and unable to deal rationally with Andrei. 'What do you make of her?'

'Anna?' Dominic shrugs. His gaze slides away from mine for a moment and then returns, dark and candid. 'She's an interesting woman, full of talent and very clever at her job. She loves to immerse herself in life, you know? Show her a challenge and she's there. Tell her she can't ski down that slope and she'll be at the top before you can say Jack Robinson. Dare her anything, and she'll take it on. She does everything at full tilt, so it doesn't surprise me that she makes her presence felt at Andrei's place.'

'If you told me she has a good secondary career as an opera singer, I wouldn't be surprised, not with her lung power,' I remark drily, and Dominic laughs.

'She'll do anything,' he says, and then more thoughtfully, 'I sometimes wonder if that's what draws Andrei to her. Not just her beauty – there are hundreds of beautiful women who'll sleep with him – but because she's so unafraid. Whatever he wanted, she would do – and she would love it.'

His words fill me with a kind of dread. Is he telling me this because he wants me to be the same? Does he wish that I didn't have my limits, places I will not go? Perhaps Anna is the perfect woman because she has no limits. But is she submissive? Could she lie down and take whatever someone else longed to give her – and truly want it? She doesn't seem that type at all to me. I picture her in spiked heels and a corset, brandishing the instruments rather than letting them be played on her. But who knows? No one knows what goes on in the bedroom unless they're in there too.

'Are you happy ... with us?' I venture in a small voice.

He looks at me, puzzled. 'Of course I am. Don't I seem that way?'

'Yes ... but I mean, with our sex life.'

He lifts my free hand to his lips and kisses it. 'Yes,' he replies firmly. 'Very happy.'

'I like where we are,' I say, feeling a little braver. 'I like what you do to me.'

He leans in and whispers in my ear, 'I know. I've seen you coming, remember?'

I laugh. 'I just wondered if . . . well . . .' I hardly know how to say it, but openness and trust are going to be our watchwords from now on, so there's no point in being shy. 'Are we only going to use rope from now on?'

He looks straight into my eyes. I can't stop gazing at his face: he's so handsome, I can hardly believe he's really mine. 'Would that be a problem?'

'No . . . no. I like it but I wonder if . . . all the time. I remember we used to enjoy other things too.'

'Do you have anything in mind?'

'Well . . .' I want to squirm. I'm embarrassed to say, considering how everything ended before, but I need to be able to talk about my own needs and desires. 'You know, sometimes I liked it when you used things on my bottom. I never liked anything too harsh, but a little stimulation sometimes got me very hot. You know that little flogger, the one with the soft suede tails . . . I remember how you used that so that it was as gentle as feathers to start with, and then gradually gave it more bite, and I found that kind of nice.'

Dominic looks away, and his fingers start knitting through mine, as though he's thinking hard. When he returns his gaze to me, he looks serious. 'Beth, I told you. I took a vow not to use those things on you again.'

'Never?'

'That's right. Because of what happened.'

'So – you don't trust yourself.'

He doesn't answer for a while but sighs heavily and then says, 'There's a part of me that's like a bad limb I want to get rid of, because it's gangrenous and could infect the rest of me. So I'm cutting off the blood supply and waiting until it falls off and I'm not bothered by it any more. Does that make sense?'

'Kind of. Yes, I suppose so,' I say, and it's true, it does, in a way. But I still feel there is something unanswered. 'And you – you're still the same?'

'Er . . . I think so.' He sounds amused. 'Do I seem different?'

'Well – I mean, you're still a dominant lover, aren't you?'

'I'm afraid so,' he murmurs. 'I'll never stop being turned on from seeing you yielding to my desires and letting me take you to extremes of pleasure . . .'

My stomach tightens delightfully as his words buzz in my ears. But I have the sense that there's something I've forgotten, something I ought to remember and ask him about. But it stays on the edges of my mind and won't let me seize it and pull it to the centre where I can see it.

I push it out of my mind and snuggle into him.

'Finish that tea,' he commands. 'I want to get you home and ravish you, if that's all right by you.'

'Yes, sir,' I whisper back.

All the way back through the park, we play a silly but exciting game in which I am already his slave, doing his bidding, obeying his commands. When I fail in something or mess up an order, he punishes me in small ways.

I'm ordered to let my master cross the road but when the traffic signals don't immediately change so that we can cross, I'm at fault for not arranging things better. My punishment is Dominic's hand, cold from the wind, pushed up my jumper and pressed against my warm flesh, making me squeal, though I try to stifle it.

It's jokey but also provocative, and by the time we're walking through the Mayfair streets, it has taken a more serious tone. I walk obediently ahead of him, letting him watch me, waiting in case he issues another order. Darkness has fallen and the city is illuminated by the sodium orange of street lighting. As we get closer to Randolph Gardens, he suddenly orders me to change direction and walk towards Grosvenor Square. I obey, wondering what he has in mind. In the square, one side is dominated by the huge modern building that houses the American Embassy, with the concrete fortifications and armed guards patrolling in front. The guns and guards have always given me the shivers when I pass, making me think of bombs and terrorists and attacks, the kind of dreadful things I hope will never disturb the peace of the beautiful city again, even if they are an undeniable reality.

'Stop.' It's Dominic issuing a command.

I halt immediately. We are on the edge of the square, near the gardens. Around them, just shadows in the darkness, are benches facing into the garden, where people might stop in the daytime but which are now deserted, except one on the other side of the square that has a tramp fast asleep on it.

Dominic walks past me, goes to the nearest bench and sits down. 'Now come over here,' he commands. 'But look only into the garden. Don't look at me. Come and stand directly in front of me with your back to me.'

I do as he says, looking only into the dark shadows of the garden, with the odd patch of orangey grey where the light of a street lamp has fallen. When I'm standing immediately in front of him, he says, 'Lift your skirt at the back, higher than your bottom.'

I'm wearing a short pleated woollen black skirt with thick tights and black brogues. What does he have in mind? Does he want to spank me? Have I erred in some way that I don't yet understand? I do as he says, lifting the skirt up high. My bottom feels the cold air despite the tights. I hope no one can see me.

'Good. Now pull down your knickers and tights. Just at the back, if that's possible. Show me your bare bottom.'

I pull in a quick breath at this, but I have to obey. It's tricky but I manage to slide down my tights and knickers, exposing my bare bottom and the tops of my thighs, while keeping them up in the front. I hope to goodness the guards over the way can't see my white bottom in the darkness.

'Excellent. Now sit in my lap. As far back as you can. Lower yourself slowly, pushing out your backside.'

I think of the squats we used to do in gym lessons, and push out my behind. The chilly air is biting it now, and the skin goosebumps with cold. Then I begin to lower myself towards him. I have a feeling what is coming next but it's still shock to feel the hard top of his penis pressing against my bottom, right at its centre.

'Mmm, delicious,' he murmurs, 'but I don't intend to deflower that part of you here. It requires a little more finesse than I can manage at the moment. Press out your bottom a little more.' He puts one hand on my hip to guide me. Now the head of his cock is hard against my entrance. 'That's it. Just right. Now. Lower yourself. Sit on me.'

It's a curious sensation to impale myself on his shaft. I'm damp with arousal from our games and the turn it has taken, but not so wet that he can go in easily. He seems to like this, though, and I can hear his breathing quicken as I have to force myself downwards, coming up a little in order to go further down on the next push. It's exquisite, pressing down and swallowing him up, each centimetre giving me a greater feeling of repleteness, and once I'm sitting back in his lap and he's entirely engulfed within me, he pushes my skirt into place at the front so that I look quite normal.

'Good,' he says again, approval in his husky voice. 'Now. Stay very still, do you understand? Listen, someone's coming.'

I can think of little else than the gorgeous feeling of him filling me up, hot and throbbing inside me.

There is the rapid tapping of footsteps and a man in a dark overcoat comes quickly towards us. He glances at us and then away without interest. We must look like a young couple enjoying the evening air, a girl sitting on her boyfriend's knee. There's nothing to show that he's buried in me to the root. The man disappears, his footsteps fading away. Dominic slips his hand down the front of my skirt, pulling my jacket round so his arm can't be seen, and his fingers creep under the band of my knickers and downwards. They quickly find the plump clitoris and he begins to play with me.

'Don't move,' he whispers. 'If you move, I'll stop.'

I don't want it to stop, that delightful tickling that is exciting me as the penis within me stretches me round it with such delicious sensations. I stay still, despite my instinct to move up and down and make the hard shaft pleasure me. That finger though, rubbing harder and harder on my clit . . . my heart is racing, my breath coming in short, sharp pants. I know I'm not going to last long if he carries on like this. The whole scene is exciting – the night air, the people walking about the square, the armed guards, unaware of the congress taking place so near. Two more people stroll past us.

'Evening,' Dominic says, so that they look directly at us.

'Good evening,' replies one politely, nodding at us, just as Dominic rubs me right on my sweet spot and I gasp loudly.

'Yes,' I say quickly, my voice curiously high and breathless, 'it's a . . . a . . . lovely evening.'

And they move on, apparently noticing nothing.

'Oh God, Dominic,' I say between sharp pants of rising excitement. 'You're making me come . . . oh, it's lovely . . .'

'I don't think we should linger too long over the starter,' Dominic says in a low voice. 'We'll spoil our appetites for the main course.' With that, he begins a strong thrumming on my clit, thrusting his hips so that his huge erection starts to move and massage inside me. The dual effect is exhilarating and I know that I won't stand it much longer without giving in to the rolling pleasure that's building inside me.

'Yes,' I say, longingly, 'just there . . . that's right, Dominic . . . oh yes . . . oh *please,* yes . . . don't stop . . .' His fingers make delicious circling motions on my bud, just hard enough to work the sweet spot up into a frenzy and suddenly my orgasm overflows, and I throw my head back and cry out as my limbs stiffen and I feel a gush of liquid inside me. I'm contracting and squeezing on Dominic's cock and I hear his panting as he feels me nip and tighten on him with the power of my orgasm. Then I go limp, my head drooping, as I recover from the climax, feeling the last ripples of pleasure ebbing outwards.

'Everything all right, miss?' comes a deep voice.

I look up to see a policeman standing nearby in the light of a street lamp and looking at us suspiciously.

'Oh . . .' I gather my senses and smile. 'Oh yes, absolutely fine, nothing to worry about.'

'I'm looking after her, officer,' Dominic adds solemnly. His hand has slipped out of my skirts and is now innocently on the bench.

He regards us for another moment. 'As long as you're sure, miss . . .'

'Quite sure. Thank you.'

After a pause, he nods a good evening to us and walks slowly away.

'Come on,' I say, laughing. Dominic's erection is still hard inside me. 'Let's go home before we lose all control and get done for indecent exposure.'

In the boudoir, we are barely through the door before Dominic's passion overwhelms him. He begins to kiss me fiercely, his tongue deep in my mouth as he pulls my clothes off me, stripping the layers away as I do the same for him. Within moments, we're only in our underwear, and I can see the strength of his desire in the erection that threatens to break free of his boxer shorts. He's kissing my neck and shoulders now, getting closer to my breasts that rise in two soft mounds from the cups of my bra.

'You drive me crazy,' he whispers between kisses. 'I don't think I could ever get enough of you, Beth.'

'I feel the same,' I say, my breathing deepening with the growing desire inflamed by his kisses. 'I'm hungry for you, for your gorgeous body and . . .' I slip my hand in the opening of his shorts and touch the hard girth of his penis '. . . this.' It twitches at my touch, responding to me. I stroke it and watch the lust fire up in Dominic's eyes.

'Beth, do you want to play today?' he asks throatily. 'Do you?'

'When I see you like this, your beautiful body wanting me, I feel the need to take you to those places, to control your pleasure.'

'Does it give you joy?' I ask, one hand wrapped around his swollen shaft, my thumb playing over its top, and the other running across his chest, savouring its feel. He's so powerfully masculine and everything in me responds to it. He makes me feel deliciously desirable.

He suddenly takes my wrists in his hands, and grips them tight, gazing into my eyes. 'It gives me great joy. It excites me to watch you give yourself to me, you know that. When you relinquish control and let me do what I want to do, that's when I find my fulfilment.'

'I know.' I've accepted this about Dominic. I've come to love it too. I understand that living out our fantasies does not make them reality. It doesn't mean that, in our real lives, I'm his slave. I could never be that, or accept that situation. I control my own life – and I control my own submission. My faith in Dominic has been restored since that awful episode in the dungeon. Now I trust him again to take me only as far as I can go. I know that there are many more deeply exciting places he wants to go with me, and the idea makes me shiver with delight.

'I want you to go into the bedroom and get dressed in whatever you think will please me,' he says, his voice husky with desire. 'Then come back here.'

'Yes . . .' I breathe in and whisper, '. . . sir.'

The word that signals I'm entering the game, the fantasy of my enslavement to him. His breath catches a little and when he speaks, he has that tone of command that enters his voice when he's my master. 'Go. You have exactly five minutes. If what you choose pleases me, I will let you come when you want to.'

I go obediently to the bedroom and look quickly through the closet for what I'm going to wear. I select a brown leather collar that buckles around my neck, and a leather harness that makes a pleasing pattern against my skin when I put it on, leaving my breasts and my sex poutingly accessible. I pull my fair hair back into a ponytail and bind it up. There. It's a simple outfit but I feel sure that my master will be pleased with it. Then, guessing my time is almost up, I return to the hall, keeping my eyes downcast. My master is there, delectably handsome in a long cotton robe. He's keeping his battering ram of a penis hidden from me for now but I know it's in there, ready to give me pleasure when the time is right.

I stand before him, my head bowed. He walks around me slowly, examining my body and what I've chosen to wear for him.

'Very nice,' he says at last, and my heart rejoices that I've pleased him. 'I thought I wanted something a little more elaborate but now I see what you've chosen, I admire the simplicity. You could be a slave girl to an emperor or a consul, perhaps. Yes . . . that's a pleasant thought. A naughty slave who has run away and then been caught. Now she is back, and her master must punish her for her misdemeanour, to show her humility and make her learn that her place is here, serving him. Don't you agree, slave?'

'Yes, sir,' I say humbly. 'I should not have run away. I apologise. It won't happen again.'

'It certainly won't. But first, a lesson must be learnt. Look up.'

I look where I'm directed and my eyes land on something I've not seen before: it is a wooden frame with metal loops at regular intervals. It looks like something that is used in a flogging and I feel a shiver of both excitement and apprehension.

Is Dominic going to flog me? After what he said about his decision?

I half hope this will be the case, even though I dread the punishment. It will mean that he has come to terms with what happened, and that we really are starting again. It will mean he trusts himself, and me. But the sight of the frame reminds me of the vicious pain of the flogging I endured, and my fingertips tremble. *I could take a little. But not too much.*

'What do you think of it?' he asks in a soft but steely voice.

'I think . . . it frightens me, sir.'

'Does it?' He is pleased, I can tell. 'In what way?'

'I think you're going to hurt me, sir, to punish me.'

He runs the back of his hand down my face. 'I am, my poor little slave girl, and I expect the punishment will hurt you, but you will be able to bear it, I promise.

273

Now. Look at this.' He's gesturing at a long coil of scarlet rope. 'What do you think I'm going to do with that?'

'Tie me up, sir.'

'That's right. I'm going to lash you up so you can't escape again. Pick up the rope and bring it to me.'

I obey, picking up the heavy coil and handing it to him. He takes it and smiles at me. His eyes are black with the anticipation of what he's going to do to me, and I feel an answering thrill bubbling through my core.

'Bend over,' he orders. 'Grasp your ankles.'

I do as he says, feeling exposed as my backside sticks up in the air. He takes the rope and works quickly with it and a few moments later, my wrists and ankles are bound together, connected by a line of scarlet rope.

Dominic steps back to admire his handiwork. 'Yes,' he says with satisfaction. 'That will do for now. You look so beautiful.' He stands behind me, his hands on my buttocks and then stroking my back or grasping my hips. I feel so vulnerable to him and a prickle of fear goes through me that I might look disgusting with my bottom on show to him, but his sigh of pleasure at the sight of my sex turned upwards and pressed out, the lips pouting and eager, quickly reassures me. He begins to rub and massage my buttocks, pinching them lightly. My breathing quickens and I wonder how long I can stay in this position, bent over like this, but the sensations he's creating help distract me from my anxiety. Now his fingers are playing underneath me at the entrance to my slit, rubbing back and forth in the juices there, and I can feel how primed I already am.

'You're excited, slave,' he says almost disapprovingly. 'Look at this naughty slipperiness. Do you think I'm going to fuck you and give you pleasure?' He laughs throatily. 'Maybe I am.'

I feel something nudging at my parts and I know it's his hot penis, released from the robe. His hands are hard on my buttocks again, pinching at my soft skin and setting tiny places alight all over my bottom, while his velvety head rubs all over my sex, revelling in the wetness there. I long for him to push it into me and fill me up, and the sudden lust that possesses me inflames my senses, making my sex swell even more. I'm panting hard, my heart racing.

'Oh, my headstrong girl,' he says gently. 'I know you want me to fuck you hard.'

'Yes, sir,' I say. 'Please fuck me hard.'

'Tell me what you want.'

'I want your huge cock, sir, inside me. I want you to push it in and out and I want you to suck and lick my parts, sir.'

'What a greedy slave you are!' He slaps my bottom with a stinging blow of his palm. 'I give the orders around here, not you! Suck and lick your parts?' He's relishing the words and the excitement they inspire in both of us. 'I'm not sure I want to do that. Perhaps you should be the one doing the sucking. Yes, later I might make you open your greedy mouth and let me fuck you there as well.'

'It would give me great pleasure to serve you, sir.'

'I'm sure it would.'

'Please, sir,' I sigh, 'don't wait too long before you start fucking me.'

'You'll wait as long as I want.'

I've lifted my head to reduce the pressure on my neck and stop the blood rushing there. My back is almost flat and he rests his hands on it as his tip explores my hot wet regions. Then I feel it hard against my bottom hole, nudging there, as though wanting to go in. A rush of apprehension goes through me. I don't know if I'm ready for that, not yet. I've never felt any desire to be penetrated there . . . *But lots of people do. And Dominic wouldn't hurt me . . . he would only give me what would pleasure me . . .*

I wonder if this is the moment when he will want to initiate me there. Certainly the probing top of his cock seems to be stating an intention but perhaps he senses through the stretch in my back and the gasping squeak I can't help emitting that I'm not into this enough. His penis slips further down and he finds my vagina. With a hard thrust he's inside and I make a loud moan as he hits home. It's sudden and unexpected, and the angle of our bodies makes his movement in me feel particularly deep and strong. He pulls out. His hands are round my hips, gripping me hard. I can feel the cotton of his open robe against my legs as he rams his way into me again.

Oh God, Dominic, that's beautiful . . .

His movements walk a fine line between pleasuring me and hurting me, but there is more pleasure than anything else in feeling his huge girth pushing me open around it, filling me and hitting my very depths. With each forward thrust, I cry out, the sound pushed from me almost against my will. His iron grip is supporting me, holding up against his onslaught, making sure I can sustain his force without being toppled. He's gathering speed, and with each hard push, he grunts loudly with an animal pleasure, and he fucks on hard for some minutes.

Then, when I'm wondering if he might be going to come, he stops and pulls out of me, leaving me dripping with my own hot arousal.

'Not yet,' he says commandingly. 'Although, as I am a kind and good master, I can't leave you entirely unsatisfied while I arrange your next punishment.' I feel something cool, hard and large enter me. My muscles grip around it, holding it in. 'There,' he says. 'Now wait.'

He walks into the bedroom and is gone. I'm left in the hall still lashed into position with something hard and large inside me. *A dildo of some sort.*

I feel a rush of panic. *How long is he going to leave me like this?* But I calm myself down. I know this is part of the punishment; the mind games are just as powerful as the physical ones. He's stoking fear, controlling me. *I must trust.*

After a few minutes, he returns. 'You've done well,' he said. 'I can tell you haven't moved. Very good. My slave shall have all the fucking she wants.'

He pulls the dildo from me and unties my wrists and ankles. I stand up gratefully, rubbing my wrists where the ropes have bitten, and see that he's standing by the wooden frame. 'Come over here.'

I obey. Now he takes the rope and binds my wrists together, lifts my arms above my head and threads the rope through a hoop at the top of the frame. He fastens it into place, and I'm well and truly tethered, hanging by my arms. He runs his hands over my back and bottom and sighs. I think I can hear something like regret or sadness in its sound. *Is he wishing he could bring out the floggers like he used to? Is he imagining what it would be like to brush my skin with the whip and bring the blood rushing to the surface? He always loved to see my skin turn rosy with the blows.*

He's not going to do that, I know. He's channelling that desire into this rope work, getting his thrill from my restraints and my helplessness once I'm lashed up.

'Beautiful,' he breathes. 'Oh, Beth . . .'

I love him saying my name. I'm not the slave for a moment, but myself. Now he moves around to my front and begins to kiss me. I wish I could embrace him but, restrained as I am, it's not possible. Instead, I kiss him back with passion, missing his mouth horribly when he takes it down to my breasts to kiss and lick my nipples. His fingers go down to my clitoris, rubbing and tickling with delicious intensity. I want to hold him and caress him in return but I'm helpless. I can only allow him to do whatever he wishes to me.

He is becoming more excited, I can tell that from his deeper breathing and from the glassy look in his eyes.

I've seen that look before but I can't recall exactly when. Something is niggling for attention in the back of my mind, but the activity of his hands is keeping me from being able to focus. I want to relax into the delightful sensations he's stimulating in me, but the need to stay upright and keep the pressure off my arms prevents me. As it is, I have to shift every few moments to relieve the ache that's growing in my muscles.

I can tell that Dominic is finding this scenario exciting. The slave girl scene has stimulated him, and his toying with my clitoris gets rougher as his breathing comes faster. He plunges his fingers into me, first two, then three, then he's knitted all four together and is thrusting them into me while his thumb rubs over my clit. I let my senses accept what he is doing, feeling waves of excitement, but every now and then, I lose my connection with my desire and feel pain instead, the scraping of his fingers within me, the sting on my clit of too fierce attentions before the bud is properly ready for such treatment.

He stops his work on me and unties me. I let my arms drop down, relieved that the pressure on my muscles is gone. My hands sting and tingle as the blood flow returns, but I have little time to think about that.

'Lie on your stomach on the floor,' he orders. I drop obediently to the cold marble floor and lie on my front. The marble cools my swollen sex and I rest my cheek on it. Dominic takes something from his pocket and places it in the centre of my back. It feels like a small leather cross with the coldness of metal at its centre. *What is it?*

Now he has picked up the rope again. I can see him from the corner of my eye as he takes its length and prepares it with expert speed. He takes one of my arms and folds it so that my elbow is above my head and my hand downwards, almost on the back of my neck. He pulls my other arm down in the same way and wraps the rope firmly around my wrists before tethering it to the leather cross on my back. He winds the rope around the cross so that it's now hanging free below the cross. Then he grasps my ankle and bends my leg at the knee so that my heel is against my thigh, then he lashes it in place. He does the same with the other leg and then takes the rope that links both legs and threads it through the central cross again. He pulls the rope and I feel it tighten, pulling my arms and legs and stretching my spine so that my head rears back.

I'm hog-tied, I realise. The sensation is of painful, muscle-wrenching helplessness. I feel a choking sensation in my neck, even though nothing is tied there; the collar I'm wearing presses down on my windpipe when the rope is pulled and my head is forced back.

Panic shoots through me. *I don't like this.* I'm struggling to assess how this makes me feel and whether my initial dislike for the position will pass. I know that sometimes I have to relax and trust in order to control discomfort and fear . . . but that's not happening now. I feel Dominic kneeling between my legs. He puts his hands under my hips, forcing my bottom higher, and the next moment, without any preparation, I feel his penis at my entrance and he slams into me, as though he's put all his force into it.

He begins to fuck hard and fast, giving me his full length with the whole strength of his body behind it, in and out, over and over.

I'm panting but it's hard to breathe with the collar around my neck pressing down like this. My back is hurting and my arms and legs ache in a powerful way as though the muscles are wrenched out of position. I won't be able to stand this for long, not from pleasure, but from pain and dizziness, but it's difficult to focus on what I need to do to get out of this situation. The fierce onslaught is shaking my entire body and I don't have time to recover from one huge slam before another follows. I'm utterly helpless in my bonds, reduced almost to a torso for Dominic to fuck. Then, to my horror, I realise that when he thrusts, he's pulling on the rope, stretching my spine even further, pulling the muscles in my limbs into agony and cutting off my oxygen.

For a moment I wonder if this is what it feels like to be on the rack, then I'm flooded with fear. All my sexual desire has died and with it, any pleasure I might have felt with this rough treatment.

He has to stop, is all I can think. My head feels pressured and swollen, my eyes are blurred. I'm worried that I will pass out in a moment if I can't stop Dominic. I have no idea if he intends to stop of his own accord or if he's near his climax.

Use the safe word.

Of course. Relief floods my body. I'll use it. It's . . .

'Scarlet!' I cry. It comes out like a stupid little croak. He doesn't hear it. I gather all my strength and use it again. 'Scarlet, Dominic, scarlet!'

This time he hears. The effect is immediate. He lets go of my rope and pulls out of me. 'Beth?' His voice is high with anxiety. 'Are you all right?'

'Stop, please, it's not working for me, it's all wrong.' My throat is sore, I'm still breathless. Dominic works swiftly and a moment later, I'm sitting upright, coughing slightly as I rub my wrists and ankles and flex my shoulders. Dominic is beside me, his expression concerned, trying to help.

'What went wrong?' he asks. 'I thought you were really into it.'

I shake my head. 'Not this time. It was too much. Too extreme.'

'Really? Was it the ropes? Were they too tight?'

'They were tight and I found the hog-tying just too much. I didn't like being reduced in that way. It felt like I'd become a nothing. And . . .' I frown and cough again. 'I didn't like being restricted in my breathing. Not at all. That's a definite no-no.' I look him straight in the eye. 'Thank you for responding to the safe word.'

'Don't be silly,' he says brusquely. 'Of course I would respond to it. It would be unforgiveable not to.' His eyes suddenly darken and he says grimly, 'I just wish that it hadn't come to using it, that's all. I'm a fool.'

'No you're not,' I say softly. 'You were trying out new things. You're not to know what's too much for me unless I tell you. I like some of the things you do with rope, but I don't want to be tied up all the time, and I don't want to be trussed like an animal. That much we now know.'

He's staring at the floor as though some terrible battle is raging within him. 'I should have known,' he says stubbornly. 'I know you, Beth. I know what you like and respond to and what you don't. I got carried away and began to flex my power on you, beyond what I knew you could take.'

'The master-and-slave scenario is always going to create the possibility of going too far,' I say gently. 'We have to be prepared. We'll just learn from our mistakes, that's all. And the safe word worked, didn't it?'

It seems a little strange that I'm comforting him after the physical experience I've just had, but I can tell that it's shaken him up. *And last time this happened, he vanished. I don't want to risk that happening again.* 'It's okay, Dominic, really.' I wrap my arms around him and kiss him tenderly but I can feel that he's distant. 'Why don't we go back to bed and just do what comes naturally to us? We don't need a scene tonight, do we?'

He kisses me back and smiles a little ruefully. 'Bed sounds good,' he says. 'But I think I'm all done as far as sex is concerned.' He puts a hand over mine. 'I'm sorry.'

I kiss his neck, inhaling his sweet scent. 'That's okay,' I say softly. 'And please, don't make it an issue. It's fine, really.'

Dominic grunts a little but says nothing else. I can tell that behind his silence, his mind is racing and I wonder what on earth he is thinking.

CHAPTER SIXTEEN

On Monday morning I approach Albany in a whirl of emotions. Dominic and I parted first thing this morning with kisses and tenderness, but the events of last night lay between us.

I'm lost in thought as I walk along Piccadilly, part of the stream of people heading to work. I'm oblivious to them, though, I can only think of Dominic.

Why does it all have to be so difficult? Why can't we just love each other like normal couples?

It seems so unfair that a man I adore and who is perfect for me in every way should have this kink, and even though I've accepted it, and even welcomed the excitement and adventure it's brought to my life, it's still causing problems.

I can do without using any whipping or flogging instruments if that's what Dominic wants, even if my imagination persists in tantalising me with fantasies of the feathery tails of the suede flogger kissing and warming my bottom. But will his desire to take things to extremes just come out in different ways? And is he going to be tortured with doubt about himself every time I use the safe word?

Everything is churning inside me as I walk through

the Albany courtyard and approach the main house. The grey Bentley convertible is parked outside so I know Andrei is there. Great. That's all I need. He wants a full report from me today as well.

I can't wait for this job to be over. I don't know how many times I've thought that in the past week, but more than ever I long to be back working for Mark, as I was before Andrei Dubrovski became so involved in my life. It was so much easier when he was just Dominic's boss, a faceless no one who meant nothing to me.

Marcia is sitting in the office, back at her desk after her vigil by her mother's bedside. She's ecstatic to see me, as though I'm her oldest friend and we've been separated for years. She's practically weeping in my arms at seeing me again. Once I've managed to prise myself free, she tells me that her mother is much better and on the road to full recovery.

'That's great, Marcia. I'm so pleased for you both.'

'She's a dear old bat,' Marcia says fondly. 'I'd miss her terribly if she went, so let's hope she's around for a little longer yet.'

She chats on for a while and I'm grateful when she finally returns to her screen to start work, muttering under her breath about the mess Edward has made of her systems. I spend the morning writing a report for Andrei but there's no sign of him.

'Is Andrei about?' I ask Marcia at lunch.

She shakes her head. 'He went out early today, on foot. I'm not sure what he's up to. Things always get a bit confused when a big deal is about to close.'

I'm relieved. I want as little to do with him as possible and the thought of seeing him again after the way our last interview ended fills me with dread. I spend the afternoon taking photographs of the works of art I want to hang in the flat and making sketches of the various rooms so that I can play about with the images and see how things will look where. It's absorbing and rather entertaining – I feel like a child with a sticker book that can be rearranged at will.

When the end of the day comes there's still no sign of Andrei, but when I return to my inbox, I find an email from Dominic:

> Thanks for a lovely weekend, gorgeous. I'm sorry it didn't end in the way it started, but please be sure that I'm taking steps to resolve my issues. I've already gone far along the road but it's clear I'm not there yet. Just hang in there for me, and we'll be fine, I promise. I won't see you much this week but why don't we go away when all this stuff is over? Just the two of us. Then I can show just how much you mean to me.
>
> I'll thinking of you and all the delicious things we do until we can be together again . . .
>
> Dx

The idea of going away with Dominic is thrilling. I imagine a hot beach, a beautiful hotel room and hours to do exactly as we please. But what does he mean by resolving his issues? I hope it doesn't mean he is going to disappear for weeks like he did last time, but his email implies we'll be together in a matter of days, so I put the anxiety to the back of my mind.

Just as I'm packing up my things to escape home to meet Laura for our kick-boxing class and have an early night, another email appears in my inbox, this time from Andrei.

> Beth
>
>   Apologies that I haven't been around for our promised meeting. If you have an hour to spare now, can you meet me at my club? Marcia will arrange a taxi for you.

I read the terse message a couple of times, exasperated. *He doesn't even bother to sign off.* He expects me to drop everything and come running, whenever he wants me to. I'm really looking forward to getting away and if I meet him now, there's a chance I won't be back in time for class. I sigh. *Better to get it over with. After all, soon he won't have any call on me.*

I fire back an email to say I'll be there right away, and ask Marcia to sort out a taxi. It's in the courtyard practically before I've finished talking, so I head out, my report in my bag. The taxi is waiting, engine running, and I climb in. As we pull out of the courtyard into the busy Piccadilly traffic, the city is already glittering with lights in the early evening darkness. The streets are busy with shoppers and the store windows glow golden and enticing. There is the hint of Christmas already in the air. The taxi turns left towards Piccadilly Circus, and we crawl around it, hampered by traffic lights, buses and unwary pedestrians. When at last we've got free, it's still slow progress down Haymarket and into Pall Mall. The driver takes me all the way along almost to St James's Palace before coming to a halt in front of a vast stone building that looks like some Regency mansion. Through the open front doors I can see a red carpet and a huge brass chandelier with dozens of lights glittering from its curved arms.

This is ridiculous. I could have walked here in about five minutes.

'Fare's taken care of, ma'am,' says the driver.

'Thank you.' I climb out of the taxi and stand in front of the huge imposing building. London is so full of places like this: grand and rather forbidding, with the sense of an exclusive life of privilege going on behind those doors. *Well, today the doors are open to me – even if I'd rather they weren't.* My flat and a night in with Laura hold infinitely more allure than this. Sighing, I set my shoulders and march up the steps.

Inside a man in a dark tailcoat is standing behind an old-fashioned desk. 'How can I help you, madam?' he asks in a very posh voice.

'I'm here to see Andrei Dubrovski. He's expecting me.'

His face changes and he becomes instantly more obsequious. *I don't know why I'm not used to this by now.* 'Yes, madam. Of course. He's in the Blue Room. I'll show you there at once.'

We walk up a vast sweeping staircase, carpeted in crimson and dominated by an enormous oil portrait of some grim-faced nineteenth-century nabob staring down disapprovingly. At the top of the stairs we walk along a wide corridor, passing drawing rooms and reading rooms, all lavishly furnished and decorated with crystal chandeliers, oil paintings and gilt cornicing, where elderly gentlemen sit in leather armchairs reading newspapers. The man stops outside a door and knocks. It is opened a moment later by the familiar figure of Andrei's bodyguard.

'A young lady to see Mr Dubrovski,' explains my guide.

The guard looks at me as if he's never seen me before, although I smile in a friendly way, then gives a nod and stands back to let me in.

The Blue Room lives up to its name: its walls are lined with patterned blue silk, it's carpeted with a huge blue-and-gold Persian rug, and furnished with chairs upholstered in blue damask. The effect is relieved by a large wooden desk, and portraits of old, important-looking men from the last two hundred years break up the blue walls. Andrei is dressed in a well-cut black suit, standing behind the desk at the window with his back to me, looking down on Pall Mall below while talking rapidly in Russian. I wait quietly, gazing around at the room and taking it in, until he's finished. After about five minutes of waiting, I'm relieved to see him put his phone down and turn to face me.

'Beth. Good. You're here.' He doesn't smile. His craggy face is as impassive as it was when I first met him. With a jolt, I realise that the Andrei I know now is very different to the one I met back in France in what seems like an age ago. He's more human, for one thing. I've seen him laughing, eating, partying and even fresh from his bed after romping with Anna. But all that's gone. He's back to the domineering tyrant I first encountered. I feel a sudden pang of regret that it's going to end like this. I realise that for a while we were almost friends. *I suppose that's why I felt able to talk to him the way I did. Barriers were down. Well, they're back up now, that's for sure.*

'I've got your report,' I say, taking it out of my bag and putting in on the desk. 'Just as you wanted. It catalogues your Albany collection and gives descriptions and current market values. I'll provide the hanging plan separately, if that's all right.'

'Fine.' He glances without interest at the report. 'I'll read it later. I'm sure it's all in order. I trust you to do a good job.'

'Thank you.' My voice is cold. In fact, the whole atmosphere is so icy I want to put a scarf and mittens on.

Andrei speaks in Russian to the bodyguard standing at the door, who immediately exits, leaving us alone together.

'Sit.' Andrei gestures to the chair in front of the desk. I'm irritated by the peremptory tone. *I wish he'd stop giving me orders like this. I'm not his slave.*

I smile inwardly. *There are times when I don't mind being a slave, and taking orders. But not from Dubrovski. No way.*

But there's no point arguing with him. I sit down. Everything in me is expecting him to say that no one talks to him the way I did and that I'm fired this minute. I half hope that this is going to happen. Then I could walk away from all this and back to Mark, and Dominic and I could go public about our relationship.

He sits down himself in the chair behind the desk and stares at me, pressing his fingertips together. At last he says, 'Beth, I've been thinking about what you said to me. I'm very hurt by the suggestion that you think I would drug you, presumably to take advantage of you.'

'I'm sorry. I withdraw it,' I say. As soon as he speaks, I can't help believing him. 'Perhaps you're right and I was drunk. It certainly seems to be the most likely explanation.'

'I hope so. You didn't seem to be so drunk that you didn't know what you were doing, but you're not a great drinker, are you?' He smiles at me. 'Not like us Russians. You certainly were tipsy, though, and enough to go out like a light very quickly.'

'When you found me in the cave,' I say.

'Yes. When I found you in the cave.'

There is a long, pregnant pause as we stare at each other. I can't read his expression but his blue eyes bore into me as though we share some kind of connection, something deep and profound. I'm seized by a desire to blurt out the question – so did we have sex or not? But I push it out of my mind. *Dominic. It was Dominic. It had to be.*

Then I realise that I've never asked Dominic why he left me alone, presumably passed out, in a passageway in the catacombs for Andrei to discover. Why would he do that?

I'm suddenly terrified that Andrei's going to say something that will shake up my world and turn everything upside down, and I start to talk very quickly.

'I've prepared the plan for hanging in the apartment, would you like to approve it before I go ahead and arrange it? I think you'll be happy with it, but if you're not, it will be very easy to change it—'

Andrei shakes his head. 'I don't think so. Just go ahead and do what you think is right. Like I said, I trust you.' He stands up and walks slowly around behind the desk, his hands linked behind his back. He's frowning, making his rugged features even more stern and imposing. 'I can tell that for some reason you have taken against me. I hoped that when I'd put your silly ideas about being drugged from your mind, you would soften a little. But it seems not. I'm sorry for that. Your work for me is almost done and no doubt you'll be pleased to return to Mark.' He turns and looks directly at me. 'I have to take a trip to Russia at the end of this week. Mark is going to come with me, to have the Fra Angelico checked by an expert at the Hermitage. I wonder if you would like to accompany us – I can arrange for you to have a private tour of the museum with an expert guide. I'm sure you'd like that. Perhaps it would help convince you that my motives are good ones.'

I gape at him. *The Hermitage museum? That would be amazing . . .* I've always longed to visit that stunning treasure trove. Most of the great art museums of the world are still on my list to visit and the Hermitage is at the top . . . *but I can't. By the end of the week, the deal will be done, Dominic will have resigned and I'll be at his side. Andrei won't want me then. He probably won't even want to see me again . . .*

'Well?' he says. 'Will you come?'

'You're very kind, Andrei, but—'

An expression of astonishment crosses his face. 'You're going to say no?'

'I can't accept. I just can't. I can't explain why, and I have to ask you not to press me on it. It's a wonderful offer, but . . . no, thank you.' I stand up as well, and we face each other across the desk. He leans forward, putting his hands on the polished surface and glowering at me over it.

'You puzzle me,' he says in a kind of low growl. 'Why don't you want what I can offer you?'

'I told you, I can't explain my reasons. But one thing is for sure: the moment I took anything you want to give me, you wouldn't be puzzled any longer. You'd see me for what I am – an ordinary girl, who doesn't fit into your world. The thing that you can't understand is that I don't want to.' I smile at him. 'I want us to be friends, Andrei, I truly do. And I want you to be happy with my work. If there's nothing else, then I'll go. And your pictures will be up within a day or two. Goodbye, Andrei.'

He says nothing but watches me as I turn, walk across the room to the door. My hand on the handle, I turn back for a moment.

'Thank you for the offer,' I say softly. 'I'll always appreciate it, even if I can't accept it.'

Then I leave.

On the way out of the club I call Dominic on my mobile but he doesn't answer. I don't leave a message. He's busy. It's only a few more days and then I'll be able to have him all to myself.

When I get home, I'm exhausted but there's just time to get to kick-boxing class, although I have to go alone as there's no sign of Laura. As I'm changing my phone chirrups to let me know that a text has arrived. It's Laura, telling me she won't make the class because she's been kept late. I do the class on my own, and afterwards the calm that follows a good workout descends, and I feel a lot better. But it's almost 10 p.m. by the time she finally gets in. She drops her briefcase in the hall and comes to flop on the sofa next to me.

'Hi,' I smile. 'There's some dinner for you if you want. Just some pasta and sauce in the pan, but you're welcome to it.'

'Anything as long as the minimum of work is required,' she says in a tired voice. 'I'm bushed. I'm sorry I missed the class tonight. How was Sid?'

'Don't worry about it, it happens. Sid was great, a total tyrant but great. You get out of your work things and I'll heat the food up,' I say, getting up and going through to the kitchen. She soon joins me, in her baggy check trousers and a comfy old T-shirt she likes to wear around the house.

'It smells good,' she says, smiling and looking a bit more relaxed. 'Your pasta is always yummy.'

'Thanks. You look like you need a hot meal.'

'Yeah.' She nods. 'It's tough in the office. They might pay well but they certainly make sure they get their money's worth. Old Booth had me checking and double-checking proposals and reports until my eyes were crossed. How are you? I haven't seen much of you lately. One or other of us always seems to be out somewere, whether work or play.'

'I'm fine.' I get the Parmesan out of the fridge so I can grate a good helping over Laura's pasta. 'I'm not going to see much of Dominic this week, so we'll have a chance to catch up. He's working on this big deal, but once it's over we might go away for a while, just a little break somewhere quiet and romantic. Doesn't that sound lovely?' There's a silence in response, and I look over at Laura who has a wistful expression.

'Sure. It sounds great. It's just . . .' She looks a little sad, standing there, twisting her ponytail round her fingers in that habit she has. 'I guess that you're going to be spending more and more time with Dominic, aren't you?'

'I hope so . . .' I say slowly. I know what she's getting at. The two-single-girls-in-the-big-city scenario is not working out like we'd both envisaged.

'Should I be looking for a new flatmate?' she asks in a small voice.

'Oh honey.' I put down the cheese and go over and hug her, then stand back so I can look into her big grey eyes. 'It's nowhere near that serious yet. Really! I promise. But I guess I will be seeing him when I can . . .' I feel my loyalties divided. I can't make promises I won't keep and yet I also love spending time with Laura and don't want to lose our closeness. I remember our plans for a trip together. 'But I meant it about New York! We will definitely do that, I promise, just you and me. No Dominic.'

'I'm really happy for you, Beth,' she says hastily. 'I think it's great that you and Dominic are taking your relationship so seriously and that it's moving forward so fast. And I'm really excited about a trip for the two of us to New York. But speaking very selfishly, I'm going to miss having you around just day to day.'

'I'm sorry, Laura.' I feel like a heel for making my friend feel lonely when I'm supposed to be her flatmate.

She laughs. 'Don't be sorry! Why should you be? You're madly in love and you want to be with him every minute you can. That's natural. But just one thing . . .'

'What?' I feel so guilty that I'd do anything for her. I wish I could magic another Dominic out of the air for her, so we could be happy together.

'Can I be bridesmaid?' she asks cheekily, and when I start to stammer and flush, she says, 'Only kidding. Now are you going to hand over that pasta or not? I'm starving.'

CHAPTER SEVENTEEN

I'm glad Andrei isn't here to watch as the men start banging nails into his very expensive polished wooden wall panels, and hope to God I've got it right.

Mark gave my layouts the seal of approval after I emailed them over to him, so I'm confident that it's going to work, but I won't know for sure until it's all up. Mark also asked me to drop by and see him the following day, and I'm looking forward to telling him that the hanging is complete.

'Okay, that's great,' I say to the workmen. 'Now let's hang that Stubbs over there – I want it in the middle and that group of sketches hung on either side, the way you can see it here on the layout.'

Just then my phone buzzes to let me know that a text has arrived. It's from Dominic.

Come outside.

I leave the men to it, and go to the front door. I open it and step into the hall. There's no one in the stairwell. I look up the stone staircase with its black iron handrail to the upper floors but it's all quiet. I go out on to the covered walk but it's also deserted. Even the workmen, who are sometimes about cleaning and maintaining everything so the place keeps its immaculate looks, are nowhere to be seen. My phone buzzes again.

Come downstairs.

I go back into the stairwell and to the top of the flight that leads down to the dark lower level. I can't see Dominic there either, but I go slowly down, descending into the shadows. I am in a long arched passageway beneath the building that stretches the entire length of it.

Turn to your left so you're facing the main house. Walk.

Where is he? I smile. I love the way Dominic likes to spice up our life like this. I do as directed and start walking along the passage. When I reach the end of the building, I come out of the passageway and have to go down some steps and around the bay window of an apartment in the basement of the main house. But now where?

Go through the doorway in front of you.

A black door straight in front of me leads under the main house. I push at it and it opens easily enough. I step inside, into a cold stone corridor, dusty and dirty, lit by a faded yellow light from a dusty bulb.

'Dominic? Are you there?' I'm not frightened but this place is a bit spooky. There are mousetraps every-where, placed at intervals along the passage, and black-painted wooden doors marked with numbers. An old wardrobe, one door swinging open to show tins of paint and rags, stands against a wall.

Wait.

I do as I'm told, breathing in the dank, rather dusty air, wondering what Dominic has in mind. Then suddenly a door creaks open to my side and a hand comes out. I jump violently and scream. The hand grabs me and hauls me inside and before I know what's happening, I'm in a large, dark recess, some kind of storage closet as far as I can tell, and pressed up against Dominic, who's laughing quietly in my ear.

'You rotter,' I say and pound him lightly on the chest.

'Did I scare you?' he says, still laughing.

'You know you did.' I look around. 'How did you find this horrible place?'

'I came in to drop something off for Andrei. I thought it would be fun to nose around and find somewhere to summon you so I can kiss you.' With that, he gives me a long, delicious kiss that makes my irritation at him fade away. 'Mmm. You're delicious. I needed that.'

'Me too.' My fright passed, I'm very amenable to whatever he wants now. 'So . . .' I say in a purring voice, slipping my hands under his shirt. 'Have you got time to play a little?'

He groans. 'Oh my God, I wish I did. I can't think of anything nicer and I'd like to take my mind off this blasted negotiation. It's the trickiest, knottiest deal we've ever done. We're all on a knife-edge because if it falls through, we have to pay a £300 million break fee. You can imagine how much Andrei wants to hand that kind of money over for precisely nothing. The only person enjoying it is Anna. I swear to God she gets an actual sexual thrill from difficult situations like this. I can see why Andrei keeps her on; she's a superlative person to have on side. She gets the stoniest, most stubborn businessman eating out of her hand eventually.'

I run my palms over the smooth skin of his sides and chest. 'Stay for five minutes?' I plead. 'I love seeing you.'

'Honey, I really can't. I shouldn't have stayed this long, I just couldn't resist seeing you.' He gazes down into my face, his eyes glinting in the semi-darkness. 'You know what? This deal is going to make me a lot of money. An enormous amount. When it's done we're going to celebrate. I'd like to buy you something. Maybe . . . maybe a ring.'

I draw in a breath. *A ring?* The next words spring into my mind without my wanting them to: *an engagement ring?* My heart starts to pound and my fingers tremble. *He can't mean that, not yet. We've only been together a few months – and apart for most of them . . .*

302

Dominic doesn't say anything to put me out of my agony and I can sense him smiling softly in the gloom.

'No need to decide right now,' he says, obviously enjoying the different ways his words can be interpreted. 'Just think it over for a while. We'll go shopping soon, okay? Once this business is finished.'

'Okay,' I whisper. 'That would be nice.'

'I want to spoil you a little. You don't mind, do you?'

'Of course not,' I say, embarrassed but pleased. I run my hands around to his back and over its broad, muscular surface. My fingers touch something: a patch of raised skin, running in a long line across his back. There's another and another. In fact, a criss-cross of lines covers his back. 'What are these, Dominic?' I say, suddenly anxious.

'Huh?' He reaches round and pulls my hands out of his shirt. His tone has changed to a cooler one and he's stiffened slightly. 'What are you talking about?'

'You've got marks all over your back! They weren't there on Sunday. Where did they come from?'

He says nothing, still holding my wrists and standing very still. I can't read the expression in his eyes in this murky light but I have a feeling they've darkened and become unreadable anyway.

I'm scared now. He's got the marks of a flogging on his back. Just like in Croatia. How did he get them? 'Tell me, Dominic – who did this to you?'

303

'No one.' His tone tells me he doesn't want to discuss this. The cosy, loving atmosphere between us has completely disappeared. 'Now, come on, I've got to get back.' He tucks his shirt in and pushes open the door, letting more light into our cramped hideout. 'Let's get out of here.' He steps out past me into the corridor.

'Dominic, I want to know! Who's been whipping you?' There's a note of accusation in my voice, born from fear. I can see it all now, very clearly. He's decided not to use whips and floggers on me, but that doesn't mean he won't use them at all. As I follow him out into the corridor, I remember how he first discovered he was into domination games, when he joined a secret society at Oxford and began to witness floggings. The participants didn't have sex with one another, they simply worked out their desires with their chosen implements, the tops giving out the punishment and the bottoms taking it, to their mutual satisfaction. It was how Dominic learned the craft and nurtured his controlling instincts until they became an essential part of him. Could he be doing something like that again? *But he's a master, not a slave! How can he be taking the punishment instead of giving it?* 'Who is it, Dominic?'

He turns and looks at me, his eyes hard and his face set in an obstinate expression. 'I told you. No one. I won't be questioned like this. You have to trust me.' He starts walking back the way I came.

'Is it Vanessa?' I shoot out, thinking of the woman he once loved who was his partner in those first games.

She is a professional mistress and dominatrix now, and still a close friend to Dominic. I'm flooded with anxiety and panic. Why won't he say? Is it wrong to expect an explanation? I can't stop myself going on: 'Are you two playing games together again? Does she keep her skills honed on your back, or do you take turns?'

Dominic halts and turns around. He looks heart-stoppingly gorgeous in his suit and Hermès silk tie, his dark hair curling softly round his ears. His expression is stormy and stubborn. 'Beth, stop it. Don't spout this rubbish! Vanessa is abroad. I haven't seen her in months and anyway, that part of our lives is over with. You know that. Why are you saying this?'

'What do you expect me to think? You won't tell me why you're covered in marks!'

We're standing in the open area below the covered walkway at the entrance to the passage that leads beneath the building.

'I told you to trust me,' Dominic says in an ominously low voice. 'Please do that, Beth. It will be clear in time, I promise. Whatever I do, I do for us both.'

My eyes fill with hot tears of anger and frustration. 'I want to trust you – but doesn't that mean honesty from both of us?'

'Yes.'

'I'm honest with you, but you're not being open with me. You're holding things back.'

'I told you to drop this, Beth,' he says in a warning voice. 'The time isn't right.'

'When will it be right? I can't understand why you won't tell me. You must see how it looks to me. You refuse to touch a whip or a flogger when I'm with you, but you're covered in welts! Please, put me right, explain to me . . .'

'Beth—' He takes a step towards me and then we're both startled by a cooing voice from above.

'Well, hello, you two. What are you doing down there?' Anna is standing in the garden just above at the entrance to the covered walkway. She's leaning over the low iron railings, her long dark hair dropping down towards us as though she's Rapunzel letting down her tresses for the prince to climb. She looks ravishing in a dark suit, the skirt very short and showing off her amazing legs.

'I told you to wait for me outside, Anna,' snaps Dominic.

'But you were taking such an age,' she coos down. 'I came in to find you and then I heard all this shouting. What on earth are you so angry with Beth about? And why are you hiding down there?'

I can see strong exasperation in Dominic's face, and feel a shiver of apprehension. Anna didn't know about us but she's going to have a good idea now. What does that mean for Dominic? Will she tell Andrei, in one of their pillow talks? How will he respond when he finds out?

Oh, shit. We're in trouble now. I hope that Dominic manages to come up with a convincing story, fast.

'I'm coming up now, Anna,' he says, and heads for some stone steps that lead directly up to the garden.

'I'll see you later, Beth, all right? We'll talk then.' He goes quickly up the steps, joins Anna at the railings and says something to her in a low voice that I can't quite hear.

I gaze up at them both from below, as though they are on a high stage and I'm simply in the audience, watching and admiring from a distance. They are certainly a beautiful couple, their dark colouring complementing each other, looking like a gorgeous god and goddess of business in their dark suits. I'm jealous of Anna for the first time because she looks as though she is meant to be with Dominic, and I do not. Not in the darkly glamorous way that she has.

Perhaps I'm more suited to someone like Andrei. Ugly. But he's not ugly, I know that, and neither am I. *Except that I'm not a beauty like Anna.* I try to put that thought out of my mind, knowing it's stupid and pointless. Dominic loves me as I am, I know that. He thinks I'm beautiful, and that's the main thing.

Anna looks down over the railings again. 'Goodbye, Beth, perhaps I will see you later? I'm coming to the apartment this evening. I would love to see you.'

Not if I see you first, I think. 'Goodbye, Anna. Goodbye, Dominic.' I gaze up at him, trying to hide my desperation for an explanation from him while Anna is watching. Goodness only knows how much she heard. I watch them walk off through the main house and disappear from sight.

Sighing and unhappy, I make my way back towards Andrei's set. *How on earth are we going to sort this one out? Has Dominic really betrayed me?*

I try to shake off the misery and confusion for now. I have work to do after all.

The job is nearly done by six that evening when the men doing the hanging for me finish up for the day. The groupings and arrangements look wonderful, I have to admit, and my mood lifts when I think how pleased Andrei will be with the results. The pictures transform the apartment. It looks like a home, at last, and everywhere is a feast for the eyes and imagination. We have a few pictures left to put up – and there's a still a place in Andrei's bathroom where he wants his own personal *Mona Lisa.*

Marcia has left and Sri has gone out shopping as I start packing up to go home. I've heard nothing from Dominic all day, but I try not to dwell on it. He says I have to trust him, and maybe I should. But I can't help feeling he still has secrets from me, things I need to know about him. I just wish he felt he could confide in me, and that we could face things together. I'm afraid that Dominic wants to tackle problems on his own and solve them without me, so that he doesn't worry me with them; he doesn't realise that we're stronger together and that I want to help him, and feel needed and important. I wish I could see him and explain this to him but as it is, the argument and the sense of horrible suspicion has stayed with me all day, and completely taken the shine off the mysterious question Dominic asked me about the ring.

He won't want to get me a ring now, I think miserably, *engagement or otherwise. He was so angry with me for pressing him.*

For a brief moment, I imagine being married to Dominic. I picture a romantic wedding with the handsomest groom in the world, vowing to love me for the rest of his life. I'm in a gorgeous white dress, my family and friends watching as I make my pledge to this extraordinary man. Then, a wedding night of enticing surprises and special bridal gifts that no one outside the honeymoon suite should ever lie eyes on . . . lacy lingerie, soft silk ribbons, a glittering white mask and white leather cuffs lined with white fur. And after that, a life together, of love and tenderness and mutual support . . . *It could be so beautiful . . . what if he really did mean an engagement ring?*

I catch myself up in these stupid thoughts. I need to give myself a good talking to. *It's ridiculous to imagine something like that when we've been together such a short time.*

Yes, replies another part of me, *but we both know this is special. Our connection is beyond anything I've ever known . . .*

So why the hell is he letting someone whip him? And why won't he tell me who it is?

It's driving me mad not knowing. I decide I'll leave him strictly alone while this deal is completed and then demand he tells me the truth if we're really going to move forward in this relationship.

I'm just lifting my bag on to my shoulder when I hear the front door open. I go out into the hall expecting to see Sri back with the shopping, but Anna is standing there, her dark hair glistening under the hall spots. She looks as beautiful as she did earlier, and her green eyes glitter with that secret amusement she always seems to carry with her.

'Hi, Beth,' she says, smiling. 'I'm glad you waited.'

'I was just leaving, actually,' I reply, caught in the usual trap of not wanting to sound rude but also feeling I must correct a misapprehension. The truth is that I was hoping to get away before Anna got here. Another five minutes and I would have been clean away. I make a mental pout of annoyance. At the same time, I wonder what on earth Dominic told her about what she witnessed today. I need to ask him so we can get our stories straight. 'I have to get home. Sorry, Anna.'

'Oh, come on,' she coaxes, advancing towards me. 'You can stay just a little longer. Have a glass of wine with me. Show me the pictures. I was admiring the ones here in the hallway – these old architectural prints are gorgeous and they look fantastic grouped over the console table like that.'

I'm flattered despite myself. 'You like it?'

'Yes, of course. Now, come along. We'll go to the kitchen and get some of Andrei's excellent Gavi, and then you can give me the tour.'

She walks off confidently. I teeter on the brink of telling her again firmly that I must go, and then give in. What's the harm in one glass of wine and a look at the pictures? I'd like to hear her opinion after all, she seems to have good taste. I put down my bag and follow her. In the kitchen she pours us both large glasses of cold white wine and hands one to me.

'Now,' she says, 'let's go and admire your work.'

As we go from room to room, I forget my earlier jealousy of Anna, and the fact that she's been a little cool with me lately. She's friendly now, listening with interest to my explanations of the paintings and making intelligent comments. She also praises my hanging and the general arrangements. I'm enjoying her company and, as we wander on, sipping our wine, I even forget to wonder if she's going to ask me about Dominic.

We reach Andrei's bedroom, where, for the main focus, I've hung a large Dutch floral still life with red roses and yellow tulips that looks amazing against the dark green of the walls, and opposite a large oil painting of a fox, stealthy and slinking in a grey landscape. It's gazing out of the painting, baring its teeth, its tail held out proudly and its prey dead at its feet, as though it has just been interrupted in the act of carrying it off.

'Very good,' Anna says in her rich voice, laughing. 'Yes, yes. A fox. How suitable for the wily and sometimes deadly Mr Dubrovski. He will like this here. Perhaps he will sometimes mistake it for a mirror.' She turns her green eyes on me. 'You obviously know him well.'

'Not as well as you do,' I counter, also smiling. We're friends for the moment, after all.

'Perhaps not,' she drawls languidly, and moves to the bed where she sits down on the paisley bed cover. It's a four-poster in turned oak but with no hangings, just the four bare posts. I have a flashing image of Anna spread-eagled naked on the bed, a wrist or ankle tethered to each of the posts. I brush it quickly away.

'Come and sit here,' she says in a low, purring voice, and she pats the bed beside her. 'I want to ask you something.'

I hesitate, then go slowly towards her. I have a feeling she wants to ask me about Dominic. I wish very hard that I'd managed to talk to him earlier so that we could agree on the version of our story. I'll just have to be slippery and talk my way out of awkward questions, that's all.

Her scarlet lips curve up into a smile as I approach. I have the sudden idea that perhaps I should have commissioned a portrait of her for Andrei's bathroom. *Yes. A nude. How wonderful – the king's mistress kept in his private room where only he can admire her perfect body.* I make a mental note to ask Mark if he knows of a good portraitist who might like a commission. I can imagine that any artist would enjoy the opportunity to paint a naked Anna.

'Come, come, sit here, that's right,' she says, as I perch next to her on the end of the bed. 'Be comfortable, sit further back. Like that. Good. Now.' She takes a sip of her wine, gazing at me over the rim as she does. 'This is nice. This is friendly.'

I take a sip of my own wine, realising I've drunk quite a lot of it.

Anna goes on, her voice soft and gentle. 'Now, Beth, you know the nature of my relationship with Andrei, don't you? It's very intimate. We're lovers. The reason why we're lovers is that we are a perfect physical match. Do you know what I mean by that?'

'You have the right chemistry.' *Oh good, she's talking about Andrei, not Dominic. She wants to show off again. Fine. Let her.*

She nods. 'Yes, yes. The right chemistry. We love the taste and smell of each other, but we are also a very good fit. He loves the feel of me and what I can do for him, and he in return provides me with great pleasure. I'm sure you know what I mean, how a man and woman can feel exactly right when they are joined into one, as if they were born to be slotted together, two halves of a whole. That is how it feels to me when Andrei enters me.' Her eyes glitter at me, as if she's trying to draw me into her world. 'Do you know what I mean, Beth? Have you felt that with a man?'

I find I can't look into her bright green eyes. This conversation is not going where I expected at all, and the personal turn it's taken makes me feel awkward. I don't reply.

'However,' she goes on, her voice low and honeyed again, 'from time to time Andrei likes something new, a little variety. I know this and accept it. I keep myself for him, but that is my choice and not for any other reason. He is free to do as he likes.' She leans towards me very slightly, her head tipped to one side, her eyes wide. 'Perhaps he has even asked you to consider him as a lover . . .?'

Oh I see. You want to know if there's something going on between me and Andrei. That's what all this soothing talk and the tongue-loosening white wine is all in aid of. Well, you're not going to get me that easily, Miss Poliakov.

'No,' I say quickly. I don't intend to give anything away to Anna. 'He hasn't.' My tongue feels a little fuzzy in my mouth, as though it's swollen slightly, and I feel a rush of light-headedness. I must stop drinking; the wine has gone to my head too fast. I ought to eat something.

'Don't worry,' she replies lightly, smiling again. 'I only ask because he's mentioned you to me. He's says he's interested in you and wants to know more about your nature. I said I would ask you.'

'My nature?' I echo.

'Yes.' She's closer to me than ever. I can smell that perfume of hers, so dark and rich. It reminds me of a scent called Poison that a friend of mine used to wear. 'You look so prim and proper in your trim little suits and with your neat British ways. But I suspect that under the surface you're really a little volcano, bubbling with passion and desires. I've been watching you, Beth, and I can see the signs of it in the way you move, in your sensual mouth and your eyes. I think you relish your sexuality, am I right? Yes, I can see I am. You're a girl who loves to make love, and you do plenty of things that would surprise the people who think they know you best, don't you, Beth? You like some kinky things, don't you? Am I right?'

Her words are whirling round my head, making me dizzy. I can't answer, my mouth won't obey me when I try to talk.

'So, Beth, I have a suggestion for you. Don't answer at once. Your instinct may be to say no, but when you think about it, you will see what an enticing proposition I am making you. What I'm suggesting is that you join Andrei and me in bed, and show us both what kind of fire rages in your body.' Her voice drops to a whisper that almost seems to caress my skin. 'Andrei shows his pleasure and approval in many pleasing ways. You'd enjoy both physical rewards, and practical ones. Believe me, the three of us could find a great deal of satisfaction together. Andrei would love it . . . and so would I.'

She is moving her face towards mine, as though she's going to press her scarlet lips on my mouth. I jerk my head away and regain some control. 'No!' I say strongly. 'I don't want that. It isn't my scene at all.'

'Are you sure? You would enjoy it, I promise. And no one would want to whip you, or tie you up in ropes, I promise that too. Although, to spice it up a little, I might like to slip a mask on you so that you can't see whether it is Andrei or me who is making love to you.'

I gaze at her in horror. *Whip me? Tie me up in ropes? How can she possibly know?*

She's leaning in towards me again, and her hand lands lightly on my arm, where she strokes my skin. 'There won't be any dungeons or floggings until you can't bear it any longer. You don't like that, do you, Beth? You nearly refused him completely after that, didn't you? It nearly drove you apart. But I think you've forgiven him now.'

My stomach drops with horror and my mouth goes dry. With a racing pulse, I say through dry lips, 'How do you know about that?'

'About you and Dominic? Because he told me, of course.'

'Today? After what you saw?' I'm trying to absorb this information, work out what it means, but I can hardly grasp the implication of what she's saying. Except that she knows about things I've never told anyone. *Things that only Dominic knows.* I pull my arm away from her caressing hand.

'Not today,' she says. 'No. I've known for a long time. You know those marks on Dominic's back, the ones that made you so upset earlier? Well . . .' Anna drops her chin and gazes up at me winsomely from underneath her lashes. 'I don't want to cause trouble but I know it's something you want an answer to, and I don't think Dominic will give it, so I will. The person who put them there was me. I thrashed him soundly, just before we made love.'

A vile nausea churns in my stomach. 'No,' I manage to rasp out. 'That's not true.'

'Ask yourself, Beth. How would I know these things if Dominic hadn't told me? About your experience in the dungeon and how far beyond your desires he took you? How would I know about the rope marks if I hadn't put them there? Your heart is telling you the truth – that Dominic and I are lovers.' She laughs and spreads her hands magnanimously. 'I don't mind if he enjoys you. He is a little infatuated, it's true, but it will wear off in time, it always does. He likes taking innocent girls on these romantic journeys with him, it excites him. And while he softens their hearts, he toughens their bottoms with the whip. I expect he'll mention a ring to you at some point, he likes to get that in early and enslave them even more.'

I can't take it another moment. Every word she utters is breaking my heart. I jump to my feet, dropping my glass which falls onto the carpet, spilling what's left of my wine. 'It's a lie!' I cry out, agonised. 'I trust him, I love him! He wouldn't do these things, or treat me like that! I don't believe you. I'll ask him and he'll tell me it's all lies.'

'Of course he will,' she says, getting smoothly to her feet. 'And no doubt you'll make love to him with even more surrender when he convinces you he's innocent. But he's not. Think about it, Beth. There's no other explanation.' Her smile is suddenly malevolent, her eyes as hard as ice. 'Really, you should thank me. I've saved you from him. You could have been used for months more before he finally got tired and dropped you, like he dropped the others.'

'I won't listen!' I cry. 'You're despicable, talking like this! You're trying to ruin everything and I won't let you!' I am in a whirl of rage and panic and all I know is that I must get away from her at all costs. She is poisoning my mind, her voice creeping into my head and into my bloodstream and sending its venom all over my body. I can't listen to any more. I won't. I turn for the door and start to stride towards it.

Her voice follows me, cold and clear. 'Don't you want to know who fucked you in the caves, Beth? Huh?'

I stop dead, with a gasp. I stare at the door, then close my eyes and let out a deep breath. So this is it. Her trump card. She knows. With one word she can spoil my life. But can I believe anything she says? If only there wasn't some truth in those terrible words she's uttered to me – but there is. I turn slowly to face her. She's gazing at me, a mixture of amusement and hostility on her face. I have the sudden feeling that if I changed utterly at this moment, told her I would give in to her desires and join her and Andrei in bed, if I went over and begged her to kiss me, she become the purring kitten again in a second. *She's almost schizoid,* I think, aghast at her. *All that beauty on the outside, all that vileness within.*

'Okay, Anna,' I say, suddenly calm and measured on the outside, despite the tornado raging inside me. 'But tell me one thing. How would you know what happened in the caves that night? You weren't there.'

She looks at me for a long moment, evidently enjoying her power over me. Then she says, 'Wasn't I?'

I stare at her, horrified by the idea that she witnessed whatever happened in the catacomb tunnel.

'You are a little fool,' she says with a laugh. 'What if I wasn't only watching? What if it was me who had you?'

I turn and run, desperate only to get away from her. Her horrible laughter follows me as I go.

CHAPTER EIGHTEEN

I run down Piccadilly in a panic, hardly knowing where I am or where I'm going. It feels as though for days I've been on a knife-edge, afraid that someone is going to bring my world crashing down around me. I thought it was going to be Dominic or Andrei – I never guessed that it would be Anna. But it all makes an awful kind of sense now.

She is Dominic's lover. It must be true. She knows intimate, private things she can only have learned from Dominic. She knows about the rope marks. She even knew about the ring. *How can that be possible unless she's psychic? Dominic must have told her, it's the only way. And he would only share those things with someone close and intimate . . .*

I shiver and huge tears fill my eyes, blinding me.

And what about that terrible thing she said – hinting that she had made love to me in the cave. How could that be? It isn't possible, surely – I know a man's touch and taste and feel. It was definitely a man who had sex with me that night. But a horrible doubt gnaws away at me. Could I have made a mistake? Perhaps I did, considering the state I was in. No . . . *no*. Everything in me rebels at the idea. I don't want to have had an experience like that without my consent. It's completely and utterly wrong.

A voice in my head screams at me: *But how did she know you had sex in the catacombs at all? She must have seen you. Unless it was Dominic and he told her! Or . . . it was Andrei and he told her!*

I stop on the pavement, squeezing my eyes shut. I press my hands to my ears, wanting to block out all the internal voices chattering at me, making accusations and counter accusations, asking questions, supplying answers, making links, breaking them again. I can't stand the noise and the babble but most of all I can't stand the pain that's growing inside me like a steel balloon expanding in my chest, threatening to suffocate me from within. I'm choking back tears. I want to call Dominic and yell at him, demanding an explanation, the *truth* at last. But I can't. I can't speak. I can't think. I just want to curl in a ball and weep, and then die and leave this horrible mess behind me.

I'm losing strength in my body, my knees buckle and I think I'm going to faint. In the chilly darkness of the London street, with people rushing past me, I sob hard and manage to make my way to the side where I lean against a shop window, so despairing that I have no idea what to do next. Then a thought comes into my mind.

I pull out my phone. Somehow I manage to make it work, scrolling through my contacts until I see the one I want. I press call and a moment later, James's familiar voice sounds in my ear.

'Hello, darling, how lovely to hear from you! How's life at Dubrovski's? No more dodgy drinks, I hope!'

I try to speak but it comes out as a gasping sob. Instantly he's concerned.

'Are you all right, Beth?'

'N . . . n . . . no, I'm not,' I manage to say.

'Where are you?'

'By Green Park Station. Oh, James, it's terrible!' I can't prevent huge sobs racking me.

'Stay there. I'm on my way.' He cuts the call.

I feel better knowing he's coming, but I'm still lost in a miasma of misery, tears pouring down my face. Passers-by look curiously at the girl crying her eyes out by a car showroom window.

James is there within a quarter of an hour despite the rush-hour crowds and when I feel his arms around me, I can't help letting go and weeping into the lapels of his overcoat.

'There, there,' he says gently. 'Let's get you inside and sort this out.'

He hails a cab and bundles us both in. I sob all the way back to his flat and James just lets me get it all out, not asking me anything but passing tissues and keeping a firm arm around me when the sobs get too much to bear.

By the time we're going into his cosy flat, I've calmed down a little and am in the hiccupping and sniffing stage, with fresh falls of tears when I remember the cause of my misery. James settles me on the magenta velvet sofa among a riot of orange, teal and gold silk-and-velvet cushions, and gets me a glass of water. There's no sign of Erlend, his partner.

'All right – tea or a stiff gin?' he asks when I've had a sip and got rid of my hiccups.

'Stiff gin, please. And then tea,' I add.

He goes to the drinks tray and pours two large measures of Hendrick's into crystal glasses, adds the contents of two small cans of tonic, lemon slices and, from a miniature magenta freezer, ice cubes. He brings one to me and then folds his long thin frame into the large armchair opposite. 'Erlend is out late tonight, we've got the place to ourselves. So shoot,' he says. 'Tell me everything.'

I explain what's happened since I last saw him, culminating in my meeting with Anna today and her awful claim that she is Dominic's lover and that he is simply using me as a plaything.

'And you believe Anna over Dominic?' James asks, one eyebrow raised. 'After everything you two have been through?'

'I know that sounds ridiculous,' I reply wretchedly. My eyes are already feeling swollen and sore. I blow my nose into another of James's useful tissues. 'But I don't know what else to think. I don't want to believe it, but I don't see what else I can do, considering what she knows.'

James leans forward and peers at me over the top of his glasses. 'So the evidence is . . .?'

'She knows things she could only know if he's told her.' I huddle back into the cushions. 'The things we used to do together – the fact that the flogging was our breaking point. I didn't even tell you the exact details but she knows what happened and where. Then there are the marks on Dominic's back – how can she possibly know about them unless she's seen him naked? They only appeared after I was with him on Sunday, so she must have been with him since then. And she says that he's done this before, dated girls like me—'

James holds up his hands and closes his eyes. 'No,' he says thoughtfully. 'That's not evidence. That could be something nasty she's saying to cause even more pain. She can easily make up malicious stories to fit the facts.'

'But she knew he'd mentioned a ring to me!'

'Or it was a lucky guess,' James replies. 'After all, if he hadn't mentioned a ring, it wouldn't have made any difference to her insinuations. She'd just have assumed that if or when he did mention a ring, he'd have made her lies seem true.'

I give a huge sigh. The crying has exhausted me and I'm in a state of confusion, going round and round. All I know is that it looks very bad for the state of Dominic and my relationship. James takes a sip of his gin, his brow furrowed.

'The puzzle is the things she knows,' he remarks. 'How can she know about the dungeon? He must have told her, you're right. That's the only obvious explanation because no one else could, if you two are the only ones who know what happened. But that doesn't make them lovers. Perhaps he's been indiscreet and told her more than you'd like her to know – that is bad of him. But it might not be the tragedy you're making out.'

'But how did she know about what happened in the cave?'

'Perhaps she was spying. Not a particularly pleasant thought, but it's an obvious explanation.'

'But . . . she as good as said it was *her*.' My lips tremble again. 'Can that be possible?'

'It's possible,' James replied frankly. 'You wouldn't be the first woman to be fooled by another woman pretending to be a man.'

'No.' I shake my head emphatically. 'I just can't believe that. The height, the bulk, the dinner suit . . . it was definitely a man.'

'It is more likely,' James concedes. 'It usually takes a great deal of preparation for a woman to make a convincing man, and to make another woman accept her as one. It's almost as important to be psychologically convincing as it is to have the physical attributes. *Belief* is the main thing. Once that's established, a well-chosen dildo, perhaps with a bulb of hot water to provide a convincing orgasm, can usually do the job quite well.'

I shiver. 'No. It definitely wasn't that. I might have been pretty out of it, but I'm sure that didn't happen.'

James runs his finger around the rim of his glass. I think he's enjoying this detective work, and I'm glad he's able to think straight when I can't. 'Yes,' he says finally. 'You're right. Thinking about it, she would have to come prepared with a lot of equipment and have the time to get changed into it, find you, seduce you effectively without being interrupted, then get changed back again and make sure Andrei finds you at exactly the right moment, while meeting Dominic above just in time. And why? Naturally, you're an attractive woman, Beth, but she'd have to be extremely determined to have her way with you. No, it's not possible. I think we can put her last comment down to fucking with your mind, not your body.'

I give a big shuddering sigh. *Thank God for that.* I couldn't bear the thought that I'd been so deceived. I'd felt violated. But in my heart, I was sure it couldn't really be true. It's just a huge relief to know that, in James's considered opinion, her sexual trickery would be impossible.

'It seems to me,' James says, crossing his legs and jiggling the ice in his glass, 'that you need to talk to Dominic. He's the only one who can give you the answers. He can tell you whether or not it was him in the catacombs. Only he can tell you how those rope marks got there, and only he can tell you how Anna knows what she knows, and whether he is really being unfaithful.' He gazes at me, his grey eyes serious. 'My dear girl – it's Dominic you need to talk to.'

Later, after providing me with a restorative supper, James puts me in a taxi home. I stare out of the window at the city as we make our way eastwards and home. Pulling out my phone, I look for a message from Dominic but there's nothing. I stare at it, wondering what to do. He's close to the end of this vital deal, the most important deal of his life, the key to his entire future. *Maybe to both our futures.* Can I ring him with the awful things I've got to say to him, and put the whole thing in jeopardy? What if he's innocent and I ruin everything? I could never face him again.

I try to cling on to James's conclusion that all I need to do is talk to Dominic and clear up the mess, but with every mile that disappears under the taxi wheels and separates us, James's sound advice becomes less convincing, and the doubts come swirling back. I recall the raised welts on Dominic's skin. I didn't imagine them. Someone had to have inflicted them. And Anna knows about that deeply private fact. I try to think like James and consider other explanations: perhaps she's seen the marks in another context. Could Dominic have got changed in front of her, or told her that he's got some marks on his back? It's possible. *I mustn't judge. I mustn't leap to conclusions. I mustn't convict him without hearing his side of the story.*

James's final words of advice ring through my ears. Before I talk to Dominic, I have to calm down and prepare to accept his explanation. I can't approach it with the idea that he is guilty. 'Take your time,' James said. 'Get on top of your emotions and use your head, not your heart. Remember – who do you trust more? Dominic or Anna?'

He makes it sound very simple and yet it isn't. The horrible suspicions are ready to leap into my head and start their whispering, undermining all the joy and trust and love.

I send a text to Dominic:

Call me when you can, when the deal is done. I'd love to talk x

Nothing comes back immediately. I lean my head against the cool glass of the taxi window as we head further east, towards the ancient winding streets of London's old heart.

By the end of the week, I'll know. One way or another.

The next day I do not go back to Andrei's apartment. I won't, not while there is the slightest chance that I might bump into Anna. I never want to see her again. I only have a few things left to do and then I'm free of Anna and Andrei for good. Mark can deal with Andrei from now on, I'm going to keep well clear.

I go straight to the gallery in St James. The Fragonard is still in the window and it looks as exquisite as ever. I love that girl, rich with blood and breath beneath the surface of her beautiful skin, her eyes downcast, absorbed in her book. The gallery owner is wearing a curious outfit of tweed plus-fours and a moth-eaten jumper, his white hair hanging down in that strange thin curtain from the edge of his bald spot. He doesn't seem to recognise me at all from the other day.

Perhaps I've been changed by misery, I think grimly.

I'm tired from all the extreme emotions of the day before, and the dull pain I'm still feeling. My eyes are bloodshot and swollen after all the crying I did. And there's no word from Dominic yet. He's pulling away from me again, it seems to be a pattern after there are cross words between us. He won't give himself back to me immediately. He makes me wait. *Always in control.*

'Can I help you?' asks the gallery owner.

'Yes. I'm glad to see that the Fragonard is still here,' I say. I contemplate the back of its frame as it stands on the window-facing easel.

'Yes,' the owner replies. 'But she goes to auction in a few days.'

'Auction?'

'That's right.'

There's no time to lose. 'I want to buy her,' I declare.

He looks at me, amused. 'My dear child, she's not something to be acquired on a whim. She costs a great deal of money and I intend to get the full market rate for her.'

'I'll pay that,' I say firmly. 'I know what she's worth.'

The owner sighs with irritation. 'Now, that's enough of your silly games. Why don't you go and amuse yourself in someone else's gallery? Because I don't take Monopoly money.'

I take out Andrei's black credit card. 'I don't expect you to. Now, here's what I'm going to pay you for the painting.' I name my sum.

*   *   *

Mark laughs when I recount the story to him that afternoon over cups of fragrant Earl Grey tea.

'What did the old rogue say?' he asks, sitting back in his armchair, his eyes gleaming with amusement.

'He didn't know what to say. He was speechless.' I laugh too, remembering the utter astonishment on the gallery owner's face. 'But once I mentioned your name and Dubrovski's, he understood that I was serious. After that nothing was too much trouble. He was delighted to sell it for so much money and without having to pay commission to an auction house.'

'And you put it all on a credit card?' Mark's disbelieving.

I shook my head. 'It was a little more complicated than that. It took a little while to sort out authorisation and movement of funds and so on, but we eventually did a fast transfer. The painting belonged to me within a few hours.'

'You mean, to Andrei.'

'Of course. To Andrei.' I smile at him. We're sitting in his drawing room, close to the fire that's burning hard in the grate. It's a chilly autumn day outside, just a grey murkiness that eventually fades into night. Mark is well wrapped up in cashmere sweaters and scarves, a pair of fingerless gloves on his hands, sitting as close to the fire as he can. He must feel the cold badly. It's not surprising, there's not an inch of fat on him to keep him warm. In fact, he's thinner than ever, almost gaunt. *He needs to eat a little more. He's fading away.*

'And where's the painting now?' Mark asks, wrapping his fingers around his teacup.

'Hanging in Andrei's bathroom, just as he wanted. I hope it will be a marvellous surprise. He hasn't seen any of the work yet, so I have no idea how he feels about it, but I'm happy with it.'

'That's good.' Mark nods. 'Confidence in your own work is vital. You must trust your instincts.'

'So that's it.' I sigh happily and take a sip of my tea. 'I've finished my job now. The Fragonard is my final flourish, my sign off. Now I can come back and work for you. Won't that be nice?'

'It will be wonderful, Beth.' Mark looks thoughtfully at his highly polished chestnut leather brogues, and then back at me. 'I need you now, more than ever. I'm afraid I've got some bad news. That's why I asked you here today. You might have guessed from looking at me that I'm not exactly at my peak. I've been feeling unwell and generally off colour for months and lately it's got even worse. They sent me for various tests, and now, at last, they know for sure what it is.'

I go still, a feeling of dread crawling over me. *Of course he's not well. I should have guessed. It's obvious from the way he looks.* But somehow I haven't seen it, I've been too wrapped up in myself and my own feelings to pay much attention to him. I feel fearful for Mark. 'What is it?' I whisper.

He shrugs lightly. 'One of those awful things where the cure threatens to be worse than the disease. I shall have to go into hospital to have something nasty cut out of me, and then for radiation treatments and perhaps chemotherapy. They're hopeful I can be put right, I believe. But you know what doctors are like, they only tell you bad news when it's completely unavoidable. So, for now, my chances are good and the prognosis could be worse. We shall see.'

I feel terrible for him, and desperately sad to know he has this battle ahead. He looks so frail already. 'What can I do? How can I help? Do you need me to be here with you? I'll do anything, you know that.'

'You're very sweet,' he says with a smile. 'I do know that. But it's not necessary. My sister is coming to stay with me, to help me through the treatment. She'll be taking me to hospital and generally looking after me, you don't have to worry about that.' He pauses and says, 'But there is something you can do for me.'

'Anything,' I say eagerly, keen to help in any way. 'Just name it.'

'I'm glad that this job with Dubrovski has come to an end now, a little earlier than we anticipated. If you're willing, then I'll need you to help with the business. If you take it on, you'll have to take over a great deal of my work. You can turn to me for advice, of course, but I won't always be there from day to day. You'll have to manage on your own, although Jane will help. Do you think you can do that?'

'Of course I can.' I'm delighted that there's a way I can lighten his burden while he tackles the illness. 'I've learned a lot from you and I'll look after everything very carefully, I promise.'

Mark smiles at me. 'Thank you. Your salary will be adjusted to be commensurate with your new responsibilities. But I'm afraid there's something else that may not appeal to you quite as much.'

I look at him enquiringly. 'What is it?' Then I add, 'I don't mind, I'll do anything that will help you, you know that.'

He gazes back at me, his expression apologetic. 'I'm afraid you'll have to go St Petersburg with Dubrovski to have the Fra Angelico assessed at the Hermitage. There's no way I can make such a trip. Can you do that for me, Beth? I know it's a lot to ask.'

I can only stare back at him and stutter, 'Of course, it's no problem,' but inside my heart is sinking.

Just when I thought I was free of him.

CHAPTER NINETEEN

Laura senses my misery that evening, but I can't begin to tell her about the situation with Dominic, or that I still haven't heard from him. Instead, I explain about Mark's illness.

'Oh, Beth, that's terrible, poor Mark! No wonder you're so upset. That's just awful,' she says. Her sympathy makes everything worse, and I end up weeping it all out again on her shoulder.

'You just need to be strong for Mark,' she says, hugging me. 'I know you will be – you can let it all out when you're with me. He said his chances were good, you've got to hang on to that.'

I nod, and dry my eyes. 'He wants to me to go to St Petersburg for him at the end of this week.'

'Well, that's good, isn't it? You've never been to Russia, it sounds like an amazing opportunity.' Laura's expression is hopeful. She really wants to cheer me up.

'I'll be with Andrei, that's all,' I say dully. 'We're not getting on very well.'

'Why not?'

I gaze into her candid eyes and feel rotten at not coming completely clean. I really want to confide in her about everything that's happened but I don't know where to start. Besides, it could lead to me having to explain things I'm really not ready to share. I shrug. 'I don't know. He's busy. This deal . . .'

'Have you had a chance to talk to Dominic?'

I shake my head and feel the weight of depression falling on me again. 'He's busy too.'

Laura frowns. 'Now, come on, Beth, this isn't like you. Where's your fighting spirit? So Andrei's being off with you? Charm him when you travel with him to Russia and win him back on your side. And if Dominic's busy, well . . . tell him to make time for you, or else!'

I laugh despite myself. She makes it all sound so simple. 'I'll try,' I say.

'You can do better than that. I know Mark's illness is a blow but it's something to deal with. That's what life is, right?'

'Right.' I feel better listening to her.

'So go out and get 'em!'

Laura's pep talk is what I need. I'm still tormented by the situation with Dominic but now I feel that when I do see him, I'm going to demand answers. He's going to tell me the truth, the whole truth, once and for all. If he turns out to be a liar and a cheat, I'll handle that and walk away with my pride intact. If he isn't, he still has some explaining to do.

I hope with all my heart that he's not sleeping with Anna – not just because of the pain of betrayal but because I'm beginning to understand quite

how devious and unpleasant she is. It's a puzzle though
– why is she set on wrecking my relationship with
Dominic when she's happily loved up with Andrei? Or,
if she's sleeping with Dominic, why is he happy for her
to sleep with Andrei too? Possible answers and what-
ifs float through my mind and soon I'm envisaging so
many strange scenarios that I can't begin to grapple
with them all.

Rein in your imagination, I instruct myself. *Stick to
the facts, like James does, and be logical. That's the
only way out of this unholy mess.*

Somehow I manage to get to sleep, but I'm woken in
the night by a text message coming through to my
phone. I pick it up and click on it so that the screen
illuminates, glowing bright in the darkness. It's
Dominic, at last.

> Sorry, honey, it's been so crazy here. We're still going
> at 3 a.m.! But this thing is going to be finished in the
> next two hours, one way or the other. It looks like it's
> going our way though. I'm going to get some sleep
> afterwards but I want to see you tonight, okay? I'll
> text again later. Dx

Another text follows almost at once:

> Hey, I hope I didn't wake you! Forgot you would
> probably be asleep. Sleep tight, honey, see you
> tomorrow. x

I stare at the message for ages. He sounds completely normal, as though he has nothing to hide. And the moment I've been longing for is finally almost here, when Dominic will be free of this Gordian knot of a deal, and then free of Andrei. *And Anna . . .*

But rather than feeling happy, I'm apprehensive. So it'll be tonight, then – the moment when I find out the truth.

In the morning, my eyes are dry and I feel groggy from my broken night. It took over an hour to get back to sleep after Dominic's messages. I'd better warn him not to text me in the middle of the night again unless it's a real emergency. Another message is waiting on my phone when I get back from my shower.

Success!!! We're done!!! I'm heading home to sleep, I'll see you later. Can't wait. x

I close it. *So that's it. Dominic's a rich man, Andrei's even wealthier. He can start making his dreams come true.*

But at the moment, I have no idea if I want to be a part of those dreams, or not.

I'm on my way to Mark's house when I get a message from Andrei asking me to call in at Albany, so I change my route. I guess he's back from the all-night session and has seen the results of my work. He either loves it or hates it.

Surely he can't hate it, I think as I climb on a bus headed up Piccadilly. A cold chill makes me shiver lightly despite the dark coat I'm wearing. *Unless he hates the Fragonard. I might have got that badly wrong. Oh well, I guess I'm about to find out.*

I'd thought that the end of this hanging commission would mean the end of my relationship with Dubrovski but I see that isn't the case – at least, not yet. While Mark is ill, I'm going to be working directly for him. As long as he knows he can't push me around, I suppose we'll manage to get along for as long as we have to.

I walk back into Albany. I thought I'd left for good but here I am again, going along the covered walkway, looking at the huge lanterns suspended from the ceiling. The bodyguard, still silent and stony-faced, answers my knock on the front door and lets me in. I go through to the drawing room, struck again by the transformation that the hanging of the pictures has wrought. They bring soul and character to the apartment.

Napoleon is still there, hanging where I first found him, glamorous and warlike on his charger. I wish for a moment my little reader was opposite him as I once imagined but I'm happy with the choices I've made. A series of Impressionist oils of gardens, in tones of green, orange, gold and lavender, bring the note of serenity I'd looked for, to balance the fury and violence opposite.

I'm still considering the effect, when Andrei walks in, his hair still wet from a shower.

338

'Beth!' he says when he sees me, a huge smile on his face. He walks towards me and takes my hand, shaking it hard, and before I know what's happening, he's pressed two strong kisses on to my cheeks. 'I want to thank you. I've just taken a shower with the most beautiful girl you can imagine.'

Anna? I think, then suddenly realise what he means. 'The Fragonard—'

His blue eyes are almost warm as he smiles down at me. 'She's gorgeous. What an inspired choice. I love her.'

'I'm delighted,' I say sincerely. I really am thrilled he likes the painting. Then he adopts a solemn expression.

'Did she cost a very great deal?' he asks seriously.

'Yes,' I say simply.

'Good!' He roars with laughter. 'And as from today, we can afford plenty more. Mark can choose them, and you can hang them for me.' He gazes at me for a moment, and says, 'I know things have been difficult between us, but I hope we can continue to work together.'

'Andrei, like I said, I want to be your friend,' I say quickly, 'and that's the point – being your friend is *all* I want to be. Nothing more.'

'I understand and accept, naturally. It would be dishonourable to do anything else.' His expression is grave and I can't help believing him. Then something occurs to me.

'But Andrei, has Mark been in touch with you?'

He shakes his head.

'Let's sit down. I've got something to tell you.'

We sit together on the sofa and Andrei listens as I explain the new situation. At once he is on his feet, striding about, reaching for his phone. 'I'll find the best specialists in the world,' he says. 'We'll have Mark flown wherever he can get the best treatment. I'll take care of the bills.'

I get up too and put a hand on his arm to restrain him. 'No, Andrei. You mustn't interfere. Mark is handling it at the moment, he wouldn't like you taking over. I'll let you know if you can be of real help to him if that time comes.'

He stands still and stares at me, his blue eyes glowering slightly. Then his expression softens. '"No, Andrei",' he says in a low voice. 'Very few people say that to me without regretting it.' We stare at one another for a moment. I refuse to look away and then he relents. 'All right. I'll do as you say. As long as you promise to let me know when I can help.' His eyes soften. 'I'm sorry, Beth. I know how fond you are of Mark. I am, too. It's very sad news.'

I think of Mark, so gaunt and thin and ill, but so brave, treating his illness with such contempt he won't even name it. My eyes fill with tears and I blink hard. I don't want to cry in front of Andrei but he must see anyway, because he puts a comforting arm around my shoulder. 'There, there, Beth. It will be all right.'

'It's one thing money can't buy,' I say, still a little choked but managing to control myself. 'Good health.'

I think of something I ought to tell him. 'And it looks as though I'll be going with you to St Petersburg – if you still want the Fra Angelico assessed.'

He raises his eyebrows with surprise. 'Ah! Of course, Mark cannot go.' He smiles at me. 'Well, I hope you will get something from this trip, despite your hatred of being with me.'

'I don't hate you,' I protest, anxious that he thinks the very worst of me. 'I was rude to you when we last met, and I'm sorry for that. Can we start afresh, now that we're going to be working together?'

'I would like that very much,' he says softly, staring at me. 'And I'm very glad to hear that you don't hate me.'

There's a long moment and I feel that ripple in the air between us again, the crackle of something connecting and causing a spark. *Oh no. I don't need this.* 'How is Anna?' I say pointedly. I wonder if she is in Andrei's bed at this moment, if they've been celebrating the closing of the deal in their traditional way. I never want to see her again, but perhaps it won't be possible to avoid her now that I'm working with Andrei again. I wonder briefly what I'll say and how I'll feel when she walks into a room I'm in. *I'll handle her, don't worry about that.*

'Anna is no longer in my employment,' Andrei says in a throwaway manner. 'We have agreed that it is better if she works elsewhere.'

Because it's not ethical to be fucking your employee? Is this so that you two can be together properly? I'm

341

startled by a violent emotion that rushes up inside me. I know for sure that I don't want Andrei to marry Anna, not at all. *Why?* The question echoes through my mind but I instantly supply the answer. *Because she's one crazy bitch who cannot be trusted! She'll make his life hell. And I would hate someone like her to get the satisfaction.*

Yes, that's it. I don't want to see her devious nature rewarded with Andrei's love. It's not right. But, I remind myself, it's also not my problem.

'I hope you'll be very happy together,' I say firmly.

'What?' Andrei frowns, puzzled. 'What do you mean?'

'You and Anna. Are you making your relationship public now?'

His face clears and he laughs. 'No, Beth. She's out of my life for good. Completely. In every sphere. You don't need to worry about that.'

'I'm not worried,' I say crossly. *We're not starting this again, are we?* 'Why have you broken up with her?'

'I think I will keep that to myself but suffice it to say, I have my reasons.'

I flush, embarrassed. 'I'm sorry, it's none of my business. Please forgive me.'

'Certainly I will,' he says pleasantly. 'Perhaps one day I will explain. But not now.'

I'm still feeling awkward, though, so I reach for my bag. 'I'd better be going, Andrei. I'm so glad you're happy with the pictures.'

'Yes, I am,' he replies simply. 'I knew you would do an excellent job, and you have.'

'Let me know about the arrangements for St Petersburg.'

'I will have Marcia send you all the necessary details.' He smiles at me. 'Until then, Beth.'

'Yes,' I say. 'Until then.'

I go back to Mark's house, feeling a little lighter in my mind. Anna is out of the Dubrovski organisation. The news is very welcome. I was dreading having to see her again and now I won't have to. I wonder why Andrei has taken that step, and then it occurs to me that perhaps Anna wasn't sacked, but she did what Dominic intends to do and resigned immediately the dotted lines of the deal were signed.

Another thought floats into my mind. *What if she and Dominic are planning to go into business together? What if they are lovers, and now want to be business partners as well?*

It's a horrible, bitter idea that makes me feel sick. Then I remember that tonight, I'll know everything.

Mark is resting when I arrive at the house, so I go into the office and start making myself acquainted with the current state of affairs. I'm poring over some invoices when there's a knock on the door and Mark's maid Gianna comes in.

'A parcel has just been delivered for you, miss,' she says, bringing it over to me. It's a small cardboard box.

343

'Thank you, Gianna.' When she's gone, I open it. Within it is another box, a dark green one this time, and a small card with the monogrammed A. On the card is written in scrawled handwriting:

This time, take them, for God's sake! With my thanks, A

I open the box and there they are, the gorgeous red ruby earrings that I left in the guest bedroom at Andrei's after the party. It looks like they are going to be hard to get rid of, if Andrei has anything to do with it. I laugh softly, admiring their beautiful depth of colour. *Well, perhaps I can accept them. After all, if I made commission on the Fragonard, I would easily be able to afford them . . . I guess I can take them in that spirit.*

I write a thank-you note to Andrei, accepting the earrings, and put it on the tray for posting later. I put the earrings on, and look at their lustrous gleam in the mirror. They are proper jewels. *I'll treasure them.*

Then I try to concentrate on my work and put the upcoming conversation with Dominic out of my mind.

CHAPTER TWENTY

The expression on Dominic's face as he opens the door to his apartment makes me feel even more wretched. He's beaming, his eyes are sparkling and he's radiating energy and excitement. He looks happier than I've seen him for a long time.

This deal has obviously been weighing down on him hard. He even looks younger than he did when I last saw him.

'Beth!' He gives me a smacking kiss on the lips and grabs my hand. 'It's wonderful to see you.' He pulls me inside the apartment and as soon as we are in the hall, he gets me into a dancing hold and skips me round the apartment as if we're at a barn dance. 'It's over!' he whoops. 'We're free!' And he crows and cheers as he whirls me about, until I'm laughing and breathless, unable to resist his good mood. At last he stops and we flop down onto the sofa together. I look around the room. It's so masculine and stylish, in its tones of black and taupe. I realise that I haven't been in here since Dominic left. We've spent all our time together in the boudoir two floors above, which Dominic acquired especially to provide a private place for our adventurous play.

He takes my hand in his and smiles as he stares into my eyes. 'I can't tell you how happy I am, Beth. The deal is done, my funds are secured. Tomorrow, I'm going to resign. Then we're both free. I feel like a new man. It's fantastic.'

I try to smile but it twists somehow on my lips. This is awful. What should be a wonderful, joyous moment has been utterly poisoned for me by what Anna told me. *Lies? Or the truth?*

Dominic is frowning at me, his expression puzzled. 'What's wrong?'

I can't speak. I can only look down at his large hand wrapped around mine – his smooth, lovely hand that's brought me such pleasure – and feel a lump in my throat. I want so badly to believe that everything is all right, that he loves me and that Anna is a devious meddler who wants to wreck everything between us ... but there are questions that need answering before my faith can be restored. I hate the doubts, I want them out of my head, but they're tenacious. Only Dominic has the power to exorcise them.

'Beth?' His smile has faded and his dark brown eyes are worried. 'Come on, I can read you. What is it?'

I try to speak but somehow I can't, not immediately. Gathering all my strength, I manage to say in a strained voice, 'And Anna? How is she celebrating?'

'I've no idea,' he replies. 'We all drank champagne at dawn when the deal was signed, and then I came home to sleep. I left her with Andrei and the rest of the team and haven't seen any of them since. What is this?'

'What story did you tell her, Dominic? After she saw us arguing in Albany? How did you explain that to her?'

He goes quiet and drops his gaze. Then he says, 'Okay. I had to tell her about us. There was nothing else I could think of that would sound at all convincing.'

When I respond, my voice still has that unnatural, high, strained tone to it. 'And was she surprised?'

'That's the funny thing – she wasn't surprised. She said she'd guessed about us that night in the catacombs. She saw us kissing in the tunnel without our masks on – remember? We took them off in the private dungeon and didn't put them on again until we were almost back.'

'So she already knew.' I try to link this with all the facts and circumstances. *Was Anna spying on us all night?* A picture of her floats into my mind: she has her arm about my shoulder and is showing me her muddy evening shoe. 'What did she say?'

'She found it very amusing – or at least, she seemed to. You never can quite tell with Anna. There's a lot going on under the surface. She laughs sometimes, and I think it sounds more like a snarl. She's very intense, one of those people who feel things deeply and passion-ately. Sometimes too passionately for her own good.' Dominic is suddenly lost in thought, staring into the middle distance.

He's imagining her. She's alive right now in his mind, as we're talking together.

I'm angry. I want her out of our lives and gone. But first, we have to get to the bottom of all the secrets and mysteries that have plagued us over the last few weeks. I turn to face him. 'And what exactly did you tell her about us? Did you mention the games we like to play? Did you tell her about what happened before you left, with the whipping experiments that ended up in The Asylum?'

'Of course I didn't,' he snaps back. 'Why would I do that?'

'Then it's very strange,' I say, 'that she knows all about it.'

'She doesn't,' he replies swiftly. 'She can't.'

'Dominic, she does. She sat me down in Andrei's bedroom and told me exactly what had happened between us.' I know my eyes are accusatory, but I can't help it. James told me to stay calm when I talked to Dominic, but it's hard. He's already denied telling her when I know it must have been him. Who else could it possibly be? I go on: '*I* didn't tell her. I've never even told Laura the extent of what happened between us. Even James, who knows more than anyone else, doesn't know it all. You know, and I know . . . and Anna knows. So, are you going to carry on denying that you told her?'

His brown eyes flash. I can see anger sparking in them. Have I already pushed him too far?

But I need answers, dammit!

'Well?' I ask.

He stares straight at me. He's gone a little pale and his expression is set. 'Of course I didn't tell her.'

'Then how does she know?' I demand, my voice rising.

'I don't have any fucking idea!' he barks, and gets to his feet. He looks frustrated. 'Are you sure she didn't just make a lucky guess and you filled in the blanks and assumed she knew it all?'

'Give me some credit, of course I didn't. And I didn't admit anything when she came out with it either.'

He fixes me with a steady gaze and says, 'I didn't tell her, Beth. You have to believe me.'

I look up at him and there must be something in my expression because he says, 'What? What is it? There's something else, isn't there? You've got another reason for believing her, I can read it all over your face.'

'All right.' There's no point in keeping it back. 'She . . . she knows about the marks on your back.'

He gapes at me, stunned. He looks genuinely astonished. At once I'm certain he's not pretending, and a wave of relief washes over me. Dominic shakes his head. 'She *knows?*'

I get up too, agitated, unable to stay sitting down. 'Yes. She took great pleasure in telling me she knows.' I can't quite say the rest. Not yet.

A strange expression passes over Dominic's face and he goes very still. When he speaks, his voice sounds odd, almost distorted. 'She told you something, didn't she? She's said something awful, something that changes how you feel about me.'

My eyes fill with tears. 'How did she know all those things, Dominic? *How?*'

He looks at me like a lost boy. 'Beth, I'm telling you, I don't know! Now, what did she say to you?'

I walk to the window, lean on the sill and look out. Across, very close, is the opposite block of apartments and I can see right into the one directly over from this. It's where I stayed when I came to London during the hot summer months. It was through that window I first glimpsed Dominic and wondered who he was. The sitting room is empty but one lamp glows gently on a side table, casting a soft light that shimmers over the silver-lacquer walls. Celia isn't there. If she were, I'd be tempted to go straight to her, pour out my heart and ask for her advice. I wish for one moment I was back there, on my first night in London, broken-hearted from my split with Adam, unaware of all the delight and torment that awaited me if I just looked out of the window. Knowing what I know now, would I look?

That all depends . . .

I turn around and face Dominic, who's standing in the middle of the room watching me. A part of me bleeds for him, because his previous happy mood has completely vanished, all the joy gone. But then, if he can't explain how Anna knows those private things, what am I supposed to think?

'She says –' my voice comes out low and monotonous, as though I don't want to invest any of this with emotion '– that you and she are lovers, and that she put those stripes on your back by thrashing you herself. Before you made love.'

Dominic makes a kind of gasping noise of disbelief, his eyes wide. Then he begins to laugh, in a loud, forced way. 'Oh, come on! God give me strength, you don't believe that shit, do you?'

I just stare at him. I can see his passion rising. He stretches out his arms, palms upturned as if in supplication.

'Beth – you don't . . . you *can't* . . . believe her!'

'I don't believe her but . . .' I shake my head almost frantically. I can't stop going round in circles over this. My fists clench. 'How does she know?' I cry loudly. 'That's what I don't understand. How does she *know*?'

He strides towards me and grabs me, one hand gripped around each upper arm, and almost shakes me in his frustration. 'I'm not her lover, all right? Once, a long time ago, something almost happened between us but it was strictly physical, and once I started to get close to her, I didn't like what I saw one bit. I don't mind her at a distance; she's amusing and very good at her job. But I've never been able to connect with her, she's too weird and flaky for me. Honestly, Beth, she's unstable but people can't look past that because she's such a knockout with that gorgeous body of hers. They only see that and they don't want to see what she's really like. But she's an optical illusion. Look at her hard and that beauty disappears and you see what's underneath.'

As he speaks, I picture Anna sitting on the bed as she was the day before yesterday. That scarlet smile became infused with malevolence, the green eyes sparkled with something hostile and destructive. I know what he means when he describes the beauty disappearing, like an angel looking up and revealing a devil's face.

I say nothing. Dominic stares furiously into my face for a moment, his dark eyes glowering and pleading at the same time. Then he lets go of my arms, walks to an armchair and sits down.

'Okay,' he says in a dull, almost defeated voice. 'I'll tell you about me and Anna.'

A cold chill somersaults through my stomach. *Oh God, no. Is this it? His confession?* I don't want to hear it if it's going to make my worst fears come true, and yet I will do nothing to stop it. I have to listen. I have to know.

I sit down on a chair by the window and wait to hear what he's going to say.

He begins in a quiet, even way. 'When I first met her, I was dazzled, just as everyone is, I admit that. I was single and so was she, and we were attracted to each other. One night, after we'd done some big deal and made a lot of money, we went drinking together. Sometimes success like that can give you the most incredible high: you feel powerful, reckless . . . horny. That's how Anna and I both felt that night and we got drunk together.'

'And you slept together,' I say in a steely voice.

He silences me with a look. 'Actually we didn't. I almost wish we had, because then none of this might have happened. As we got drunker, we got more unin-hibited. We started talking about sex and she told me some pretty wild things. She loves sex, maybe more than anyone I've ever met, and she'll do anything if she thinks it will excite her. But she's never been submissive. When I told her about my . . . character, she was very turned on. She wanted me to initiate her into the master/slave relationship. She was fascinated by the whole thing.'

'You must have liked that,' I say, trying to keep my voice neutral while inside I feel like I'm dying with every word he says. So Anna wanted him to be her master? How could he resist that? I imagine that beautiful body bent over, exposing a lithe, smooth back, ready for the lash.

'I took her to The Asylum,' he goes on, almost as though he hasn't heard me. 'We were going to go to the dungeon and take it from there. But—'

He stops and stares into space, remembering.

'But?' I prompt.

'Something stopped me. Something in her eyes. I had the distinct feeling that she was unstable and that I could unleash something very dangerous in her. The dungeon is a place where we look into the dark heart of our imaginations and make our fears come true. But all the time, we keep a part of ourselves in the real world, the part we access through the safe word or through the voice that tells us that this situation isn't a true one. We might feel like we are giving ourselves entirely to our fantasy, but we're not. There are people, though, who lose the ability to distinguish between the fiction and the reality. They want to take it as far as it

353

can go. Maybe they enter a place that lies on the farthest boundaries of what human beings can stand. Maybe they go further even than that. I knew, suddenly and without a doubt, that Anna is one of those people. I couldn't do it. I couldn't risk opening her to those possibilities.'

I'm hardly breathing. I think I understand what he's saying to me. He is very calm now, and very serious. He looks at me, and I am suddenly filled with love for him. My Dominic. His darkness is not so very dark. His fantasies might be of control and domination but he is kind, loving and understanding. He's a world away from a person like Anna. 'You tried to save her from herself.'

He shrugs. 'You make it sound very noble. But I also lost my desire for her. My connection with her vanished and I couldn't go through with it. So it never happened.'

'Then why is she saying all this now?'

Dominic looks uncomfortable. 'Beth,' he says awkwardly, 'I should have said this earlier, I know that. But I honestly thought that it didn't matter and that it wouldn't impact upon you.'

'What is it?' I demand, the fear that had subsided lurching into sickening life again. 'Tell me, right now!'

Dominic sighs. 'Okay. The truth is that Anna never got over the fact that I turned her down and didn't want to sleep with her. I think she saw the lust die in my eyes that night, and I don't think she'd ever seen that before. I became a challenge for her. For months I fought off her attentions. She was completely tireless in her attempts to seduce me, you've never seen a woman try so hard. When I kept refusing, she was both incensed and excited. I almost considered sleeping with her just to give her a rest, but by then, it was impossible. I had no taste for it. I didn't desire her, and she *knew* it.' He smiles in a bewildered way. 'We were trapped in a vicious circle – the harder she tried, the less I wanted her and so the harder she tried. I thought that eventually she would give up and go away, and for a while it seemed she had, when she and Andrei started sleeping together. She loved that whole game she was playing with him, pretending to be an aristocrat so that he could get off on the idea that he was despoiling a real lady. She's from a perfectly respectable background but she's no duchess, that's for sure. Andrei only saw that sweet exterior and smoky eyes, and heard that come-to-bed-and-fuck-me-for-ever voice. And that was enough for him.'

'So she was over you?' I ask. I hardly dare speak in case I interrupt his flow, but I have to know.

Dominic gives me a wry look. 'Not exactly. She told me that she was sleeping with Andrei to make me jealous. And she said that if I didn't give her what she wanted, she'd have me sacked.'

'She threatened you . . .'

'Yeah.' Dominic shrugged. 'But it had no effect, of course. I'm not afraid of Anna, no matter how crazy she is. I knew Andrei wouldn't do anything on her say so. He doesn't take orders.'

'So that was why you didn't want anyone to know about us,' I say slowly. It's beginning to fit together at last.

He nods. 'I didn't want to make the whole situation worse. Getting away from Dubrovski also meant getting away from her. And escape was so close, why make trouble for myself? So it made sense to keep us under wraps.'

As I consider this, I feel calmer. That makes sense to me. And it fits with what I've seen of Anna's behaviour. 'But,' I say, frowning, 'you had to tell her when she saw us that day in Albany.'

He nods. 'Yes. Like I said, she claimed to have known already, after the catacombs.'

Look at my shoes! Anna is pointing to her mud-caked stiletto, she's throwing back her head and laughing, she's toppling and nearly falling on me. I shake my head to clear the memory.

'That makes sense in hindsight,' Dominic says, 'because for the last week, Anna's been saying strange things to me – about you.'

'Really?' An icy finger of fear creeps around my neck and down my back. 'Like what?'

'Stuff about you and Andrei.'

'What stuff?' I sound calm but inside I'm churning up with guilt and fear. I hear Anna's voice again. *Don't you want to know who fucked you in the caves, Beth?*

Oh my God. What has she said? I suddenly realise with a horrible swoop in my stomach that the lies can work both ways. *Lies about him. And lies about me.*

Dominic is looking straight at me, his gaze candid. 'She said that you two were getting close and that she thought Andrei was interested in you, and maybe you were interested in him. I didn't believe her, of course. I knew it was another of her little ploys to make me jealous.' He gives a short, sharp, mirthless laugh. 'She even said she walked in on you two kissing in the kitchen.'

I open my mouth but I can't speak. A violent red flush sweeps into my face. As he sees it, Dominic's face changes and his expression becomes puzzled, uncertain.

He says slowly, 'She's lying. Right?'

I can feel that my cheeks are crimson now. I know I must look beyond guilty. 'We didn't kiss,' I say, but it comes out stuttering and implausible.

'*We didn't kiss*,' he repeats. 'We.'

'We didn't!'

'I would expect you to say *I* didn't kiss him. Not *we* didn't kiss.'

'What's the difference?' I say, my fear making me sound defensive and even more guilty. 'The fact is, we didn't kiss. I didn't kiss him.'

'But you almost did. Didn't you?' He's staring at me, hurt and anger on his face.

Shit, how do I explain? How can I tell him that I was busy telling Andrei to get lost when he moved so close, froze me with his nearness, and then went to put his mouth on mine? It's so clear in my mind and yet I can't seem to get the words on to my lips, and I know that however it comes out now, I look and sound

357

guilty. 'We didn't kiss,' I repeat stubbornly. 'I'm not interested in Andrei Dubrovski, I swear on my life.'

Dominic stands up, puts his hands in his pocket and begins to pace the room, like a barrister cross-examining a witness in the courthouse. 'Maybe there's more to Anna's testimony than I gave her credit for. She said you were flirting with Andrei. And he gave you jewels – some ruby earrings worth thousands, apparently. Is that true?'

'Yes – but I tried to give them back—'

'Did you?' His gaze moves to my ears and he sees the rubies glinting there. A horrible change comes over his face and he spits out, 'Just not hard enough, I suppose.' His voice is dripping with scorn. 'I can't believe you're actually wearing them now. His gift to you. You wear them to see me.' He pulls a hand out of his pocket and he is holding a box, square, brown and edged in gold. A jewel box. *A ring box.* 'I was going to give you this tonight.' He laughs bitterly and tosses it on the sofa. 'But I guess it wouldn't have seemed much after what Andrei can give you, right?'

I leap to my feet as well. *How has everything turned like this?* Fury rushes through me. 'When did this become about me? What about *you*?' I can see the little ring box discarded on the sofa. Even though it's tiny, it seems big enough to contain all my lost dreams. I feel as though everything is slipping away in a landslide of angry words, suspicion, fear and guilt.

'I guess it became about you when I found out that you're in the habit of kissing Dubrovski and taking his presents.' Dominic's voice is cold and his expression stony.

'I didn't kiss him!' I yell. 'The earrings were a thank-you for my work and I only got them today, that's why I happen to be wearing them! They are not a secret indication of my passion for your boss, for crying out loud!'

We stand facing each other, eyes blazing, both breathing heavily with our indignant passion and wounded pride.

I can tell from the way Dominic's fists are clenched hard, his knuckles white, that he's being racked by strong emotions. We're both trying to stay anchored to common sense but it's becoming increasingly difficult as the things we've kept hidden from each other are revealed. The possibility of grim revelations and of broken trust suddenly seems closer than it ever has.

'How does Anna know about the marks on your back?' I cry. *I'm the injured party here!* 'That's all I want to know. Just tell me that.'

Dominic is breathing hard, his lips set in a straight line, his expression glowering. When he speaks, his voice is like steel. 'And I want you to swear on your life that nothing has ever happened between you and Dubrovski. Come on, Beth. Swear.'

I stare back at him. *Swear,* I command myself. *You're innocent. Tell him.*

But the memory floats into my mind. I'm up against a cold wall of rock in the catacombs. A man is fucking me hard from behind and I never see his face. He only whispers to me, so I never hear his voice, not properly. I know in my heart that Dominic never truly confirmed one hundred per cent that it was him. I just wanted it to be him so badly that I believed it. The truth is, there's a chance that it was Andrei.

Swear now! Do it!

But I can't. I can't swear on my life that nothing happened. Because there's a tiny chance that it did.

Dominic's face is changing. Real horror is crossing it, and in his eyes I can almost see love shattering and turning to dust. 'Beth,' he says, his voice broken. 'No. Please, Beth, swear to me nothing has happened between you.'

I open my mouth. I try to say it. But I can't.

He puts his face in his hands. 'Oh Christ, no. Not this. I can't stand it. Not you and him.'

I want to run to him, grab him, make him listen. I want to tell him everything, spill it all out – all my hopes and fears and worries, everything I've suffered since that night in the caves. But I don't do that. I'm frozen to the spot, stiff and cold as a traitor. Instead I say in a voice I hardly recognise as my own:

'How does she know about the marks on your back?'

'I don't know!' he yells, making me jump.

'Is it because she put them there?' I persist. I just don't want him thinking about me and Andrei. The idea of what pictures he might be seeing in his head sickens me.

'No! No! For God's sake, she didn't put them there.'

'Then who did?'

'*I did!*' It bursts out of him. 'It doesn't matter now, not any more. Shit.' He walks to the dining table, puts his hands on it and leans forward as though he hasn't got the strength to support himself any more.

I can't believe I've heard him right. '*You* did?'

He looks up at me wearily and I almost flinch at the coldness in his eyes. 'Yes. I've been punishing myself for hurting you. After what happened on Sunday, when you used the safe word, I felt tormented enough to try and beat out my desire to go too far.'

Mortification of the flesh. Where did I hear those words?

'So now you know,' he says. 'It wasn't Anna. It was me, with my knotted scourge, attempting to cleanse myself.' He closes his eyes and looks beaten. 'Laugh if you like.'

'I'm not laughing,' I say in a small voice. I'm almost humbled that he would treat himself like this, and punish himself for hurting me. 'You don't need to do that.'

'I know that now,' he says bitterly.

'I didn't mean that—'

'Beth. Please. You know the truth. I honestly don't know how Anna knows I've got marks on my back, but she does. I don't know how she knew about what happened to us before – maybe it was a lucky guess. But I can swear to you that I'm innocent and you can't make the same vow back. And that tells me what I need to know.'

'Dominic . . .' Now my voice is full of pleading. My anger is dissipating. He's been honest and now I want to be honest with him and tell him the full story.

He looks up at me, hope burning in his eyes. 'Can you swear?'

Swear, goddammit!

Slowly I shake my head.

'Fuck.' He spits out the swearword venomously, then says stonily, 'Get out. Please. Just go.'

I try to speak but he cuts me off.

'Go. I'm begging you. I can't bear to see you right now.'

I can see it's pointless to continue. I walk to the door, turn and look at him. He's leaning on the table, staring at its surface, his shoulders drooping as though he's defeated. I yearn for him so badly, and yet I feel like we're a hundred miles apart.

'Goodbye, Dominic,' I say softly. 'You know where I am when you're ready to talk.'

He says nothing. He doesn't even turn around to watch me go.

I feel like I'm closing the door on my dreams. *I think it's over. I think that really happened.*

No. As long as I believe in you and what we have, I'll fight for you, Dominic. I promise.

EPILOGUE

The take-off is so smooth, I hardly realise that we're airborne. The plane is incredibly luxurious. I guess the one that took Mark and me to France was just one of the fleet, while this is obviously the command ship, Dubroski's Air Force One. Now we're on our way to Russia.

Andrei has already shown me the two bedrooms, each decorated like a suite at one of the most expensive hotels in the world. Now he's sitting in a leather armchair in the plane's sitting room, a cup of coffee on the table in front of him, alongside a sheaf of photos.

'Beth,' he says, 'which one of these do you think is best?'

I put down the magazine I've been skimming, get up from my own chair and go over to see what he's looking at. On the table in front of him are photographs showing children in a cheerful room decorated with posters, books and toys. The youngsters are all under the age of ten or so, and they sit on big bright cushions reading books or playing with toys. Some sit on a small plastic slides or dress up in funny hats. Others are wearing aprons, holding paintbrushes and concentrating hard as they slap colour onto pieces of paper.

'I like this one,' he says, pointing to a picture of two angelic-faced children bending over a jigsaw.

'What's it for?' I ask.

'It's some publicity material for an orphanage I sponsor in Russia. We're always looking for new donors to support the work they do there. And hoping to melt a heart or two so that some of the children might find new parents to love them.'

I look over at him, and notice how much softer his face is when he looks as these pictures. He looks up at me and says, 'One day you should come and visit with me. You would love these kids. I wish I could give them all home – but this is the best I can do for now.'

'They seem very well looked after,' I say softly. I'm seeing a side of Andrei I didn't know existed. 'The orphanage looks wonderful.'

He nods. 'Yes, I insist on that. Clean, happy, well equipped.' He fixes me with those blue eyes of his. 'Because I was an orphan myself, you know. I have an idea of what it's like. Only I was in an orphanage during the Soviet years. Not fun at all. That's why I tell them to put plenty of colour around. Children need it, it helps them feel happy.'

I feel sorry for him. No wonder he grew up tough and hard. But now he's able to give something back to stop other kids being brought up that way. 'I agree with you,' I say. 'That jigsaw picture is excellent.'

'Good. Then that's the one.' He sits back, satisfied. Now he's looking at me again, those piercing eyes reading everything about me. 'Beth, are you all right? You seem very low.'

I smile but I know it's a weak one. 'I'm fine. Really.'

Of course I'm not. I'm in complete turmoil. I've heard nothing from Dominic and he's not returned the message I sent asking to meet so I could explain:

Nothing happened with Andrei. I'll explain why I didn't swear – just let's meet and we can clear this up. Please, Dominic, don't let Anna win by destroying us.

But my words have clearly left him cold. I can hardly bear the grief that's engulfed me and I'm only coping by going numb. I still haven't quite taken in that it might be over. When I do let that thought into my mind, it's so terrible I have to shut it out again. I tell myself that I won't let it be over, and refuse to contemplate the idea that it's finished.

'It's been a very strange week,' Andrei remarks pensively. 'I've both gained and lost a lot. I've gained a great deal of money with my successful deal. But I've lost Dominic, my trusted colleague.' He shakes his head. 'I should have seen that coming. I'm a fool that I didn't.'

'So – he's resigned?' I ask, my stomach fluttering at the sound of his name. It's such sweet agony to hear it.

'Yes. He thinks he can play me at my own game now,' Andrei says, and shakes his head. 'He'll learn.'

'You're not ... angry with him, are you?' I ask tentatively. Dominic was always so apprehensive of what Andrei might do when he'd left.

'Angry is not the word,' Andrei returns, and he leans back and closes his eyes for a moment. 'A little bored that I've got a new adversary, that's all.'

'Surely he's not an adversary—' I begin, but Andrei opens his eyes and cuts me off.

'The saying is, "He who is not with me, is against me." As a rule of thumb, it's worked well for me over the years. Don't worry. I'm sure I can handle Dominic.'

'But he learned all he knows from you,' I point out. 'Perhaps he's even learned how to out-think you.'

'Ha!' Andrei's laugh is loud and sharp. 'I would like to see that. I really would. But I won't.'

'You've also lost Anna,' I say. 'Has she gone to set up against you as well?'

'No,' Andrei says shortly. 'And I didn't lose her. I threw her out.'

'You said you would tell me why.'

'I don't think I did say that, but I suppose it can't hurt.' Andrei takes a sip of his coffee before replying. 'I sacked her because I discovered that she was in possession of some hallucinogenic drugs, and I suspected she may have been using them to doctor my drinks. It would certainly explain some of the more extreme experiences I had with her while we were making love. I always thought it was the effect of vodka – now I'm not so sure.'

My breath feels like it has been punched out of my body. The memory plays in my mind as vividly as film. I'm in the catacombs by the bar and here is Anna, she's toppling on to me. She's taking my drink. She's showing me her shoes and directing my attention to the dance floor. Then, she gives me back my drink.

Don't you want to know who fucked you in the caves, Beth?

She did it! She spiked my drink. I'm certain of it. A wash of horror mixed with relief floods over me.

'What is it, Beth?'

'I accused you of drugging me, don't you remember?' I say excitedly.

'Of course.'

'But it wasn't you or the barman – it was Anna. She came over and she must have slipped something in my drink then!'

Andrei frowns. 'But I never understood why you thought you were drugged.'

'Because I . . . because I felt so strange and disconnected, and then I passed out like that. And now we know that Anna has done the same to you, it makes sense, doesn't it?'

'I can see that she drugged me to increase my pleasure with her, and to keep me tied to her. What would be her motive for drugging you?'

I stare at him and he looks at me with those impassive blue eyes, his expression set, his mouth unsmiling. *Ask him. Ask him if he made love to you that night. Do it.*

I say, 'I think she was jealous of me. She wanted to cause mischief.'

'And did she? Did something happen to upset you?'

I speak slowly, feeling my way towards what will help me find out what I need to know. 'I don't know. I . . . I can't be sure. I might have hallucinated events that didn't take place.'

He raises his eyebrows. 'Talking mice? Rainbows? Pink elephants with wings?'

'No . . . something more personal than that.'

'A hallucination?' he asks in a low voice. 'Or just something you hope was a hallucination?'

'Andrei, you found me in the caves, didn't you?'

'Yes, I did.'

'Was I asleep, or awake?'

'You were both. Drifting in and out of a happy, sleepy sort of state. You were talking about Dominic, though I couldn't make out what, exactly.'

I feel a rush of joy and pain. I must have just been with Dominic! He must have left me only when he heard Andrei nearby, and I can't remember it because of the damned drug.

Oh Dominic, I could have sworn to you and been telling the truth! I should have trusted all my instincts and asked you straight out about the caves! Then we would never have got into this awful mess . . .

I want to pick up my phone and contact him at once, explain what a dreadful mistake we've both made, but I can't. Not right now. I must control myself and wait until I have the opportunity, once I'm on my own.

Andrei is watching me with quiet interest. 'Beth,' he says, 'put it behind you. Forget it, whatever it was. What does it matter? Anna is gone. What's done is done.' He smiles at me. 'I'm so happy that you're coming to Russia with me. I think we will have a very enjoyable time, now that you and Dominic are no longer involved.'

I gasp. 'How do you know about that?' I say without thinking.

'I make it my business to know everything about my employees. And believe me, you're better off without him. And certainly now he's made the mistake of leaving my employment.'

'Perhaps you've been misinformed,' I counter, knowing it sounds a little desperate. 'Anna likes her little stories, doesn't she? Assuming it was she who told you this.'

'Mmm. Come on, Beth.' He leans towards me, his eyes glittering and says in a low voice, 'No more games.'

My blood chills. I've heard that before. Those very words. In the catacombs. My lover murmured them into my ear while I begged him for sex. I can scarcely breathe, my heart is pounding and my skin is clammy. Everything I thought I knew spins round again.

Andrei leans back in his chair, his face impassive again. 'Relax, Beth. This trip will be most enjoyable if you will only let go and enjoy yourself. Forget Dominic, he's in the past. Embrace the future.'

I try to keep calm but inside my head, thoughts are clamouring and vying for attention. Only one keeps coming to the surface, louder and more persistent than all the others, as the plane heads on its way from all I know and love into a strange country with this even more mysterious man by my side.

Oh my God – what have I done?

ACKNOWLEDGEMENTS

Thanks to all those who have helped me on this journey: Harriet, for her editorial wisdom and great encouragement, Justine for her eagle eye and excellent suggestions, and Lucy for her unflagging support and wonderful ideas. Thanks to everyone at Hodder for their hard work on behalf of these books.

Thank you, too, to Lizzy, for all her advice and support, and to my husband, who helps to make my writing possible.

I also want to thank all those who've sent such wonderful messages to me via Twitter to let me know they've enjoyed the books. It means a lot. Thanks, to all of you!

The first novel in Sadie Matthews' provocative
romance series that will captivate, exhilarate and
intoxicate you like no other . . .

fire
after
dark

It started with a spark . . .

Everything changed when I met Dominic. My heart
had just been broken, split into jagged fragments that
can jigsaw together to make me look enough like a
normal, happy person.

Dominic has shown me a kind of abandonment I've
never known before. He takes me down a path of
pure pleasure, but of pain, too – his love offers me
both lightness and dark. And where he leads me, I
have no choice but to follow.

*Deeply intense and romantic, provocative and
sensual, FIRE AFTER DARK will take you to a place
where love and sex are liberated from their limits.*

HODDER

Obsessed with the *After Dark* series?

You'll be captivated by the final novel
in Sadie Matthews' provocative
romantic trilogy . . .

promises

after

dark

Intensity, sensuality, and seduction awaits . . .

HODDER

Available February 2013

The best books live on in your head long after they are finished. As you read, you are turning the pages faster and faster to find out what happens next, only to feel bereft when you reach the end.

If that is how you feel now, you might like to join us at www.hodder.co.uk, or follow us on Twitter @hodderbooks, and be part of our community of people who love the very best of books and reading.

Whether you want to find out more about this book, or a particular author, watch trailers and interviews, have the chance to win early limited editions, or simply browse our expert readers' selection of the very best books, we think you'll find what you're looking for.

And if you don't, that's the place to tell us what's missing.

We love what we do, and we'd love you to be part of it.

www.hodder.co.uk

@hodderbooks

HodderBooks

HodderBooks